Suddenly she turned and dropped her bag. Lucas's heart stopped. And then she was running toward him. Two feet from him, he saw in her face what he was feeling in his heart. Opening his arms, she ran into them.

He allowed her to show him what she wanted.

Standing on her toes, she put her mouth on his and kissed him. It wasn't a peck, it wasn't soft, and it wasn't neat. Her lips covered his and she pressed her tongue deep into his mouth.

Instinct took over. Pulling her against him, he lowered his head and dove into the kiss. She tasted like strawberries, coffee, and honey. This was not an invitation. This kiss was probably the only one she would allow, the only one she planned to ever give him. He knew that about her.

With that thought, he drew back slightly from the kiss. He didn't plan for this to be the only kiss they ever shared, but he damn well intended it to be the best one either of them had ever had. Which meant turning down the heat to a simmer instead of a full boil. Keeping his mouth on hers, he decreased the pressure and played with her lips, feathering, retreating, savoring.

Under the roar of passion and lust in his head, he heard a groan. Surrender. Arousal. Need. Though everything within him wanted to press her against the wall, strip her pants down, and love her till neither of them remembered their names, he knew that'd be the biggest mistake of all.

Finally, knowing she needed to breathe, Lucas pulled slowly away and looked down at the aroused, heated woman in his arms.

Panting slightly, she whispered against his lips, "I couldn't have lived ███████████████████████████e." Then, before he cou███████████████████████████on cue, the elevator di███████████████████████ran toward it.

LAST CHANCE

CHRISTY REECE

BALLANTINE BOOKS • NEW YORK

A Ballantine Books Mass Market Original

Copyright © 2010 by Christy Reece

Published in the United States by Ballantine Books, an imprint of The Random House Publishing Group, a division of Random House, Inc., New York.

BALLANTINE and colophon are registered trademarks of Random House, Inc.

ISBN 978-0-345-51774-6

Cover illustration: © Image DJ/agefotostock
Cover design: Jae Song

Printed in the United States of America

www.ballantinebooks.com

9 8 7 6 5 4 3 2 1

To my mom

prologue

Rio de Janeiro, Brazil

Lucas Kane knew he'd been in more critical situations, but coolheaded logic had always saved his ass. This time he was too furious to be either cool or logical. After living a once dangerous life and surviving with only a couple of insignificant scars to show for his efforts, how ironic to be held captive and beaten profusely just for having some extra money in the bank. If he weren't so infuriated with himself, he'd be laughing his ass off.

Bastards had taken him from his bed. Thankfully he'd been alone at the time. Though if he was going to die, the memory of mind-blowing sex would've been a nice send-off. Unfortunately, if he died today, it would be with the unpleasant memory of yakking his guts up. He'd thought it was food poisoning, and while the poisoning part of it was likely correct, it hadn't been the food's fault. Someone had arranged the situation. Food poisoning and an abduction on the same night? Not bloody likely.

That knowledge made him even more determined to live. Damned if the bastards would get away with it.

Shifting to try to find a comfortable spot, Lucas cursed. Hell, there was no comfortable spot. The mattress beneath him could have been used as a torture device in the Spanish Inquisition. Felt old enough.

The ropes around his wrists gnawed into his skin every time he moved; the burlap bag over his head scratched his face. And his throbbing nose felt like it was the size of Buckingham Palace. The crunching sound he'd heard when one of the bastards hit him assured him it was swollen for a damn good reason. It was broken.

He'd been lying here for at least half a day now without anyone even checking on him. Not that he had much of an ego about his fame, but if these idiots had thought he was worth kidnapping, the least they could do was check and make sure he hadn't escaped. Did he look like he couldn't or something? He had finally recovered from his bout of sickness and was ready to kick some ass. Now someone just needed to present him with the opportunity.

A noise hit his ear. Good. Somebody was coming. Hopefully someone other than that Victor asshole, who was apparently in charge. The guy got on his nerves, throwing around all sorts of dire threats like some sort of gangster from a bad movie. Lucas had kept up with him for the first few hours and then got bored. Would've been best if he hadn't told Victor. Bastard had damned near kicked him to death.

The door opened and closed. Footsteps came closer. Since he couldn't see, he relied on his other senses. The footsteps were light . . . so Victor had a woman working with him. She smelled nice, too—soap and water were powerful aphrodisiacs to a man who hadn't had a bath in days.

A soft hand touched his arm and Lucas froze. *What the . . . ?* Goose bumps ran down his spine and arousal surged. All from one small touch? Something was definitely off with him. Maybe lying in the same position for hours caused some sort of odd erotic reaction he'd never heard of.

What the hell. If he was going to get turned on by the

woman, the least he could do was get her name. "What's your name, love?"

A soft, breathless gasp was her reply and he hardened more. Damn, if he kept this up, he'd be proposing before he even saw her.

When she didn't answer, he tried a more conversational tone. "Would it be too much trouble to take the sack off my head? My nose is itching."

"Shh. Be quiet," she whispered.

A nice voice, too. Soft, husky . . . American . . . midwestern, most likely. Twentyish. Judging from the distance she spoke from, he was guessing she was about five foot four. Hard to tell weight, but the hand had felt small, delicate. Frissons of sensation raced up his skin; arousal surged harder. No doubt about it, if she weren't working for a psychotic kidnapper, they might've had something.

More footsteps, heavier. The loud clomp sounded all too familiar. *Great, psycho man is back.*

"You ready to have some fun?" Victor asked in heavily accented English.

The woman giggled. Damn, there went his arousal; he'd never cared for gigglers.

"Are you going to let me get in the first slice?" she asked.

That didn't sound good. First slice of what?

"You tell me why I should," Victor said.

A giggle again—high-pitched and a bit nervous-sounding. Or perhaps maniacal?

"Didn't you say you wanted to film it? You know I can't work the camera like you can. Cutting's the easy part."

"Yeah . . . you'd only fuck it up."

The heavy footsteps sounded as though Victor was walking away.

"Where are you going?" the woman asked.

"Oscar said he wanted to watch."

"Oh yeah. He likes stuff like this, too." Another strained-sounding laugh, then she said, "Umm, do you think it's safe? I mean, since somebody stole that woman from us . . . do you think he should stay with Jeffrey and be on the lookout and stuff?"

A heavy, disgusted sigh. "Yeah, I guess he can watch it before I mail it. That'll have to do."

The footsteps headed back toward Lucas. "Take off the bag and let's get started," Victor said.

The bag ripped away from his head. Lucas squinted as he looked up into soft, guileless gray-blue eyes. Now how the hell could someone who looked as innocent as an angel be wanting to slice something off?

McKenna Sloan swallowed a horrified moan at her first live glimpse of Lucas Kane. If the hideous bruises on his handsome face were any indication, Victor had lost his temper more than once with his hostage. Though she was no longer shallow enough to be attracted to a man because of his looks, Lucas Kane had blurred those beliefs. But Victor's wrath had taken its toll, and while he would heal, McKenna had a hard time not turning around and giving the bastard a little of his own medicine. The creep would pay for this.

"Okay, camera's ready," Victor said.

McKenna pulled the knife from the sheath at her waist. Ignoring Kane's swollen eyes and his obviously broken nose, she took a breath. This would take some careful timing.

"Open your mouth, Kane," she demanded.

He didn't react the way he should have . . . or at least the way she needed him to react. He laughed, showing off an incredibly beautiful smile, which was completely incongruent with the rest of his battered, bloody face.

"I have to admit to being a bit of idiot in some respects, but opening my mouth on your say-so goes even beyond what *I'm* willing to do for a beautiful woman."

He thinks I'm beautiful.

Oh hell, stuff like that meant nothing to her. She glared down at him with her meanest expression. "Do it, or I'll chop off your fingers."

"Actually, if you're going to chop anything off, I'd prefer that . . . and if it's not too much trouble, the right hand, please."

More than a little stunned, McKenna turned her startled gaze to Victor, who was holding the camera and smirking.

"Told you he had a smart mouth," Victor said.

Quickly regrouping, McKenna whirled back around to Kane and snarled, "Fine. But I'm taking all five fingers."

"Good, that'll make it easier to make a fist. Thanks."

Resisting the urge to stomp her foot and demand he act at least a little scared, she pulled at his shoulders to turn him slightly toward her. It would be easier to get to him this way, anyway. He just had her so off-kilter, she was having trouble staying in character.

"Are you really going to cut his fingers off?" Victor asked.

McKenna shot him a glance out of the corner of her eye. She couldn't tell if the freak was excited about it or disapproved.

"Yeah, why?"

"Because five fingers will be harder to get through the postal service than a tongue."

She dared a look at Kane's face. Though both his eyes were swollen, she could have sworn she saw amusement glinting in them. It was all she could do not to laugh herself. Just what kind of freaky life did she lead that mailing cut-off fingers and tongues was even a topic for discussion?

She shrugged. "I'll just cut off a couple."

"Fine, but I still want his tongue."

"Ah, Victor," Kane drawled. "I didn't know you wanted tongue when we kissed before."

Aw, shit.

It happened fast; she barely had time to prepare. With a roar, Victor dropped his camera, pulled his gun, and lunged toward Kane.

Knife in hand, McKenna stepped in front of Kane. Knowing she'd only get one chance, she swung upward, stabbing the blade deep into Victor's belly.

Eyes wide with shock and pain, Victor grunted and dropped his gun. Grabbing his stomach with one hand, he swung at McKenna with the other, smacking her full across the face. Pain exploded; she wobbled but managed to stay on her feet. If he came at her again, she had to be ready.

Victor stumbled backward and then dropped to his knees. His hands held his stomach as tears poured down his face. "You bitch, I'll kill you for that!"

McKenna stiffened her spine. What was done was done. Victor Lymes had abducted and tortured his last victim. However, seeing him or anyone else suffer wasn't in her plan. Sliding a smaller knife from a sheath under her pant leg, McKenna stalked over to Victor and grabbed hold of his hair. She pulled his head up and, ignoring the horror in his eyes, neatly sliced his throat. He was dead before he hit the floor.

"I must say, that was quite impressive."

Whirling around, she glared at the man she'd come to rescue. He hadn't exactly made it easy for her. "I have a couple more I need to take care of. I'll be back in a minute to get you."

"Okay, but would you mind cutting my ropes before you go finish your bad-girl stuff?"

McKenna glanced down at her bloodied knife and

swayed. Hell, this was not good. Passing out before she finished a rescue would pretty much ensure a failed mission. Straightening her shoulders, she stalked over to Kane and sliced the bonds on his wrists and his ankles. The instant he was free, he grabbed her and pulled her down beside him.

She jerked away. "Let me go. I've got to—"

"You're going to pass out if you don't give yourself a moment. Close your eyes, take deep, even breaths, and . . . think about daisies."

She had closed her eyes and was breathing in when she heard the last part. She opened one eye. "Daisies?"

"What's wrong with daisies? Don't you like them?"

This was the most bizarre rescue she'd ever experienced. She closed her eyes again, took another breath. A noise in the other room had her eyes shooting open. They were coming.

She got to her feet. "Lay back on the bed. Don't say a word," she whispered. "I'll be back as soon as I can."

Somehow his hand was at her neck; McKenna shivered as she felt his fingers caressing her skin with soft, tender strokes. In the gentlest of voices, he said, "Shh, love. Just relax."

How odd. She didn't like it when men touched her. So why did his touch make her want . . . Darkness blanked her mind.

With utmost care, Lucas placed his little rescuer on the bed. What an intriguing young woman. Unable to resist, he fingered silky strands of her white-blond hair. Bleached, no doubt. Beneath her heavily made-up face, he saw soft, young skin. She couldn't be older than her early twenties. Who was she and why had she saved his life? That was a puzzle he had every intention of solving. She'd succumbed with the lightest of touches and wouldn't be out more than a few minutes. He had some necessary business to take care of and then he had some questions for her.

Stretching, he loosened stiff joints and muscles that'd been cramped too long as he looked around for what he could use. The room was bare with the exception of the bed he'd been tied to and a wooden chair. Voices outside the room told him he had little time to prepare.

Lucas took the knife the woman had dropped on the floor and the gun that lay next to Victor's bloodied corpse. His footsteps cat-silent, he went to the door and listened. Two men, one middle-aged, the other one late twenties . . . both Brazilian.

He stood to the left side of the door; waited for it to open. The older man appeared first. Lucas jumped on his back, took him to the floor. His hands cupping the man's head, Lucas gave a hard, quick twist, heard the snap of his neck . . . guy barely made a sound.

Out of the corner of his eye, he saw the younger man come toward him. With a quick roll, Lucas moved off the dead man's body and sprang to his feet. The man lunged toward him; Lucas twisted, dodging him. The guy stumbled past him and fell on top of his dead partner.

Since making too much noise might attract the wrong kind of attention, Lucas chose the knife over the gun to take out the man. Gripping the knife, Lucas took a step. The man jumped to his feet and fired his gun.

Pain bloomed in his right shoulder. "Shit. Should've seen that coming." Lucas threw the knife, feeling a brief triumph when he heard a yelp. Unfortunately, it hit the man's upper arm and only managed to piss him off. Planting his feet on the floor, Lucas raised his gun; his vision wavered.

A slender blond blur appeared before Lucas could fire. His pretty rescuer had regained consciousness and was back on her feet. With a high kick she would've found erotic if he hadn't been in so much pain, she knocked the gun from the man's hand and followed with a solid kick to his chin. With a loud grunt, the man took the slug, then slammed his fist toward her, catching her a glancing blow across her jaw. She fell backward.

Lunging, Lucas took the man to the floor. Using his left hand, he applied massive pressure to the man's larynx. The body beneath him stiffened and then relaxed into death.

"Are you okay?" his rescuer asked.

Lucas rolled off the body beneath him. Landing with a thud on the floor, he looked up at the lovely creature. "What's your name?"

A slight smile curving her lips, she said softly, "You can call me Ghost."

He lost consciousness with her smile in his mind.

one

He was tired of chasing a ghost. More than once he'd
told himself she was a figment of his overactive imagination or a hallucination caused by too many blows to his
head. That some three-hundred-pound bruiser by the
name of Rudolph or Hans had rescued him, not a deli-
cate-as-air blond angel named Ghost.

But she wasn't a figment; he'd felt her, touched her,
smelled her. And he couldn't get her out of his head.

On his return from Brazil, he'd launched two investi-
gations. One was to determine who else had been involved in his abduction other than Victor Lymes. The
other was to find his mysterious rescuer.

The investigation into his abduction had taken less
than a week. Lymes, working with two of the hotel employees where Lucas had been staying, had seen an opportunity and taken it. The plan had been to ransom
him and split the earnings. The two conspirators had
confessed immediately when confronted by the authorities. The two men Lucas had killed in Brazil had apparently been locals Victor had hired there. The case was
wrapped up quickly, neatly. Quietly.

The second investigation hadn't gone as well. It was as
if the young woman who'd aided in his rescue didn't
even exist.

"Kane, do you agree?"

Lucas jerked his head around. Staring out the window like a daydreaming bored employee didn't exactly inspire confidence. The twenty executive members of Kane Industries stared at him as if he had a third eye.

"Yes, the takeover should go through without a hitch. Just make sure we have jobs for everyone." He made a pointed stare at Stanley Humphries. "If I hear that even one worker was displaced, heads will not be the only body parts rolling."

The stiff nod of agreement was belied by the mutinous expression on Humphries's face. Lucas noted it, adding to his growing list of concerns. The man had become increasingly belligerent and uncooperative over the last few months. Lucas knew he was going to have to do something about him soon.

Though Humphries wasn't a member of the executive board, he'd been with Kane Industries for well over thirty years and had earned his spot in making decisions. However, Lucas had become aware of recent shortcuts and mismanagements that the man was directly responsible for.

When Lucas had taken over his family's empire, he'd been determined to do a few things differently. That included making sure no one was adversely impacted as Kane Enterprises thrived. Humphries apparently didn't like that concept.

Lucas needed to make a decision about the man's involvement in future projects. Times like this, he wished for his father's tough-minded decision making. Lucas could kick ass and kill with the best of them, but when it came to dealing with wayward employees, he was at somewhat of a loss.

Harbin Nickels, CFO of Kane Industries, stood. "I think that about wraps up everything we needed to review with you, Lucas. Anything else that comes up, we can go through your assistants. When do you leave for your trip?"

His mind occupied between finding a ghost and disciplining an employee, Lucas answered with a careless "A few hours" and then was silent.

He knew they stared at him for several seconds before they made their way out of the room. Being distracted wasn't good for morale. A distracted leader led to uncertainty in his employees. He'd worry about that when he returned. Now he needed to get on his flight to Paris and talk with the one man he believed could help him.

Paris, France
Last Chance Rescue headquarters

"Noah, did you give Micah another piece of chocolate?"

Before moving his gaze from the computer screen in front of him, Noah swallowed the remaining evidence. Turning to her, he gave his most innocent look. "Mara, why would you say that?"

Hands on her hips, amazing eyes flashing, Samara advanced toward him. "Because he's as hyper as a wildcat. Angela's with him in the conference room, chasing him around the table."

Before he could proclaim his innocence of giving their two-year-old son chocolate, Samara added, "And because you have chocolate on your chin."

He sighed. Nothing got past his Mara. "So come over here and lick it off for me."

Her eyes darkened and she got that look on her face that could heat his blood in an instant. She came toward him and then stopped. "Wait. What time is Lucas Kane supposed to be here?"

Noah groaned and looked at the clock. "Fifteen minutes. Not near enough time."

"Here." She handed him a tissue from a box on his desk. "Get the chocolate off for now. We'll stop at the store on the way home and get some more for later."

He grinned, already anticipating the night ahead. "Deal."

Settling into a chair across from him, she returned to the topic of their upcoming meeting. "So you really just want my observation on the man? Nothing more?"

"Right."

"Are you planning on telling him you know McKenna?"

"No. Her association with LCR must remain private. But I want to meet with him before I mention his search to her. When she relayed the details of his rescue, it got me interested in him even more."

"How so?"

"For a British billionaire, sounds to me like he handled himself a little too well. About as well as any LCR operative. There's got to be more to him than just inherited wealth and a keen eye for the next moneymaking venture."

"Think he has military training?"

Noah shook his head. "Records show that he spent most of his years collecting degrees and prepping himself to take over his family's empire. No military training mentioned."

"Perhaps he had someone train him. As high-profile as he is, maybe he felt he needed to know how to defend himself."

"Could be. That's where you come in. I want your impression. I may be biased."

She smiled. "That's because you're protective of McKenna."

"I'm protective of all my operatives."

"True, but whether you want to admit it or not, you have a special fondness for McKenna."

Noah couldn't deny it. He did feel much more like McKenna's big brother than her boss. Not that he was technically her boss, since she still wasn't officially employed by LCR.

Though all active LCR operatives were freelance and could work when they wanted, he considered them full-fledged employees. McKenna, not so much.

LCR's first encounter with McKenna had been unusual. One day, during the middle of an op involving the rescue of a young teenager, McKenna had just shown up. One of his operatives had been injured, unable to assist. McKenna had gone after one of the kidnappers, jumping on his back and taking him to the ground. Dylan had been on the op, along with Shea and Ethan. All three had regaled him with accounts of her bravery. Problem was, she'd disappeared as soon as the rescue was complete.

The second time she had assisted was in Paris. Based upon the description he'd been given, Noah had known this was the mysterious rescuer he'd been told about. He had cornered her before she could disappear. She hadn't liked being trapped. Had been almost feral in her fear. They'd talked—or at least as much as he could get her to talk. That's when he'd learned her name, McKenna. He'd also learned enough to know that not only was she incredibly brave and surprisingly skilled, she was also the most alone person he'd ever met. And he'd met a lot of alone people since starting LCR.

Though McKenna had never officially become an LCR operative, most of his people thought she was. Noah gave her that support and allowed her the anonymity for one very important reason: McKenna needed to feel that she was part of this organization, whether she realized the fact or not. Even though she turned him down every time he asked her to become an operative, he had high hopes that someday she would change her mind.

When LCR operative Gabe Maddox's wife, Skylar, had been abducted, McKenna had contacted Noah with the offer to assist. It was during that operation that she learned that Lucas Kane had been abducted by the same man. McKenna had assisted in Skylar's rescue and then stayed back to rescue Kane, too.

No one knew where McKenna came from or even where she lived. Though Noah was more than aware that he could do his own investigation, he continued to refrain from it. At some point he might have to. For right now, he wanted to allow McKenna the anonymity she obviously needed.

Samara had gotten to know her better than anyone at LCR. One of the many reasons he wanted his wife to meet Lucas Kane. The man had not stopped looking for McKenna from the moment he arrived home after his rescue. Noah wasn't about to give up any secrets on McKenna, but he wanted Mara's opinion on Kane. He trusted his wife's judgment over anyone's.

"So McKenna has no idea he's looking for her?"

"She knows he's looking. As you know, she's got good instincts about that." He and Samara both believed McKenna was hiding from someone. But until she was ready to ask for their help, all they could do was wait until she chose to trust them. "I just don't think she knows how determined Kane is to find her."

"Why do you think he is so determined?"

Noah shrugged. "Could be as simple as he wants to thank her; somehow I think it's more. With his contacting LCR, he either suspects we have an association with McKenna or he's desperate and wants us to do something we don't do as a rule. He knows we only search for people who are endangered in some way. . . . I'm in-

terested in your observations. What you think he's looking for."

The buzzer sounded, alerting them that Kane was on
his way. When he'd called Noah, requesting LCR's assistance, the man had given the vaguest of descriptions and
reasons why he was searching for the young woman.
When pressed for more information, Kane had insisted
on a face-to-face meeting. Since Noah was more than
aware that Kane didn't have additional information to
give him, he'd agreed without much argument. Discov-
ering why Kane wanted to find McKenna was Noah's
primary concern.

That he was being allowed to come to LCR headquarters was almost unprecedented. Only LCR operatives,
or those Noah knew he could trust, were aware of this
location. But Noah had an instinct for people. He'd met
Kane years ago at a social event and had never forgotten
that meeting. There was more to Lucas Kane than the
man allowed most people to see.

Noah didn't worry that Kane knew where LCR headquarters was. What did concern him was his unusual fix-
ation on McKenna. He wasn't known to be obsessive . . .
so why this time?

McKenna had given Noah the barest of facts on her
rescue of Kane, just that all three men holding him
were killed. She'd reported that Kane was shot, but
only slightly wounded, and she'd left as soon as Dylan
Savage, another LCR operative, had picked him up. She
also indicated that Kane had assisted in his own rescue.

Noah hadn't pressed McKenna for more details. If she
were officially with LCR, he would have. However, with
McKenna he treaded softly. Yes, he wanted to hire her as
a full-time operative when she was ready, but that
wasn't the biggest reason. He greatly feared that if he
pressed she would just up and disappear. The young
woman needed LCR even if she wasn't aware of it.

After the rescue, Dylan had dropped Kane at a local hospital before he regained consciousness. The story had been that Kane had been in Brazil on business and had been jumped by some thugs. Having no publicity was better for LCR and, for that matter, Lucas Kane.

If one ignored nuances and went only on words, McKenna's rescue of Kane had taken less than an hour. Noah sensed there was more. Something had happened in that time frame that had her even more skittish than usual. Even more reason to want to meet with the man.

At a knock on the door, Noah went around the desk and stood by Samara.

The instant Lucas entered Noah McCall's office, he knew he'd get little or no cooperation from the head of Last Chance Rescue. And the petite, dark-haired woman at his side looked just as reticent.

Didn't mean he wouldn't try to persuade them otherwise. Lucas held out his hand. "Thank you for seeing me, Noah. It's been a few years."

As Noah shook his hand and introduced him to his wife, Lucas felt Samara McCall's eyes assessing him. He was being given some kind of test, and apparently the lovely Mrs. McCall would be issuing the final verdict. *Interesting.*

He settled onto the overstuffed chair McCall indicated, and waited. As expected, Noah led the interrogation, while his wife observed.

Seated across from him, McCall leaned forward. "You said you were looking for a young woman?"

"You may have heard that I had a bit of trouble in Brazil a few months back."

McCall's expression didn't change as he nodded.

"Truth is . . . I was in Peru on business, abducted from my hotel room there, and ended up in Brazil. With help from the authorities, I kept it quiet . . . conducted my own investigation. The people who assisted in the abduction were caught. However, there was a young woman there. She rescued me, but disappeared before I could thank her."

"This young woman . . . what was her name?"

Frustration and admiration dueled within Lucas. Going on nothing but instinct, he was almost certain his ghost had some sort of association with LCR. McCall was apparently going to pretend otherwise.

"She gave no name . . . other than Ghost."

McCall's mouth quirked slightly. "Ghost?"

"Yes. Unfortunately, I lost consciousness before I could inquire further. When I woke in the hospital, she was nowhere to be found. I was told a man brought me there, leaving no information other than my name."

"I'm surprised you came to us. You know we only search for those who have been abducted or are missing."

"I'd like for you to make an exception in my case."

"And why would I do that?"

"I think she may be in trouble."

McCall's expression didn't change, but his wife's shoulders stiffened, confirming Lucas's suspicions. They did indeed know her.

"What sort of trouble?" McCall asked.

Lucas shrugged. Even as much as he wanted to find her, he felt an odd loyalty to his ghost. Describing the expression in her eyes . . . how do you describe a look that on one hand had the innocence of a fawn but at the same time revealed a stark hell?

His innocence was long gone; he had a familiarity with hell. That look was something he'd seen in his own eyes from time to time. Along with hollowness, emptiness. Extreme sadness. He would mention none of these. Odd, really, but he felt as if a secret had been shared between them. He was loath to break their silent bond.

Those naked moments with his ghost would remain theirs alone.

Aware that McCall was waiting for an answer, Lucas shrugged. "She looked as though she needed a friend. I'd like to be able to help her in whatever she needs."

"I'm sure you've hired your own investigators to find her. Why come to us?" McCall asked.

"For one, LCR is the best at finding people. My investigators have come up dry."

"And the other reason?"

"I thought perhaps she was affiliated with your organization."

"Why would you think that?"

Lucas shrugged. "She rescued me."

McCall frowned. "We are hired to rescue. We rarely become involved unless asked."

While Lucas knew that was true, he also knew that LCR would and had rescued when they saw a need, whether they would be paid for it or not.

"How did your rescue go down?"

This was the first time Samara McCall had asked anything. Her question surprised him. He had figured Noah would be the more direct interrogator. So far, McCall had been subtle; Samara McCall cut to the chase. Did her question hold a secret agenda?

Nevertheless, he described how he'd been abducted from his hotel room while he was on business. He glossed over the disgusting details of his sickness and the infuriating information about the beatings he'd endured while he'd been ill. He explained his first meeting with the young woman who had rescued him, along with her apparent association with Victor.

"Could this woman have not just decided that she'd had enough of Victor and turned on him?" McCall asked.

That's exactly what he'd told himself many times since

then. She was just one of Victor's people who'd decided to betray him and Lucas happened to benefit from that. None of that rang true. She'd let him go instead, saved his life. Seemed genuinely concerned for his welfare. And she'd asked for nothing in return.

Lucas lifted his shoulder in a casual shrug. "It's possible. However, I'd like the opportunity to talk with her, ask her myself."

McCall shook his head. "I'm sorry, but I don't think LCR can help you."

With a nod, Lucas stood. Noah McCall wasn't known for changing his mind once a decision had been made. Lucas saw no point in trying to persuade him. However, he'd gotten at least a piece of the answer he'd been searching for. This woman did indeed have some sort of connection with Last Chance Rescue. Unfortunately, that was apparently the only thing he was going to get.

Holding out his hand, he shook Noah's hand and then Samara's. As he walked to the door, Samara McCall's soft voice stopped him. "Mr. Kane, if you don't mind my asking . . . if you were given a chance to see this young woman again, what would you say to her?"

He turned and gave her the truth, hoping that it would get to his ghost. "I would thank her and tell her that if at any time she ever needs my help in any way or for any reason, I would be there for her."

With a slight smile, she said, "Very nice to meet you, Mr. Kane. Have a good trip home."

Lucas nodded again and walked out the door.

Noah waited several seconds until he was sure Kane had gotten on the elevator, then turned to Samara. "So what do you think?"

"I think he'll keep looking until he finds her."

"Did you also get the impression he knew we weren't exactly truthful?"

She scrunched her nose. "My fault. He surprised me

when he said the words that you and I both feel about McKenna. That she needs help in some way."

"Don't worry about that. His knowing she has some kind of association with LCR won't get him any more information than he had before."

"Something else is bothering you, though. What?" Samara asked.

"I just think it's interesting that Kane picked up on McKenna's vulnerability. When she's on an op, she's excellent at hiding her true self. Which makes me even more curious about what really happened during the rescue. When she gave me the details, I sensed she was disturbed about something."

Samara nodded. "I talked to her a couple of weeks after it happened. She glossed over the entire event, but I got the feeling she has a distinct admiration for Lucas Kane."

"He's done some admirable things since he took over his family's dynasty. Did you get a feel for why he's so intent on finding her?"

A smile curved his wife's mouth, and Noah couldn't resist the opportunity to feel it under his. After several breathless moments, he pulled from the kiss and said, "Sorry, got distracted . . . you were saying?"

Her smile now even bigger, she said, "I think in the short amount of time that Lucas and McKenna spent together, they both felt a strong attraction for each other."

"You may be right." He picked up the phone. "Now let's see if McKenna wants to do anything about Kane continuing his pursuit."

McKenna hung up the phone. Refusing to acknowledge the racing of her heart at the knowledge that Lucas Kane was in Paris searching for her, she went to her closet. Pulling her duffel bag from the top shelf, she immediately began to pack.

His hunt for her had gone further than she'd anticipated. She'd become aware of questions being asked about her in Brazil. Based upon the physical description the people searching for her had given, she had known they were Kane's people. She hadn't expected him to expand beyond Brazil, nor had she expected him to go to LCR. That was a little too close to home.

Why did he continue? Did he believe she was involved in his abduction? Was that the reason, or was there more? Noah had indicated that Kane wanted to thank her. Perhaps that was all. She hoped so. Silly, really, but she hated for Lucas Kane to think badly of her by believing she'd actually been in cahoots with Victor.

She'd had plenty of time to relive those moments from his rescue. *His rescue?* How laughable. Other than taking out Victor, she'd done very little. Pretty damn bad when the victim becomes the rescuer. Of all the times to pass out. Any other time she'd been forced to kill someone, she would become nauseous. Not pleasant, but at least she was usually able to function to finish the rescue. Passing out was not only embarrassing, it was damn dangerous. They both could've been killed.

When she woke, one man had been dead. Thankfully, she'd managed to distract the other one, but Lucas Kane had still been able to take care of him, even with a bullet hole in his shoulder.

After the excitement had passed and she'd been far enough away from Kane to think straight, she acknowledged that if she had never shown up, Lucas Kane would have gotten out of the situation all by himself. Which made her fascination for him even larger. Something she definitely hadn't needed.

McKenna rushed around her little apartment, collecting the few things she wouldn't leave without. She'd stayed here longer than she did most places; it was past time to leave, anyway. No use looking around and be moaning the frilly little curtains she'd hand-stitched herself or the painting she had found at a flea market that reminded her of home. She'd hung it over the television and found herself looking at it more than at what was on TV.

She would leave those things, of course. Taking the minimal belongings was the only way she traveled and the only way she'd survived this long.

Being hunted wasn't a new thing for her; she just had a new predator. No, she could never call Lucas Kane a predator. Noah's words continued to whirl around in her head. "He wants to thank you . . . wants you to know if you ever need anything, you only have to ask."

McKenna snorted as she grabbed a handful of underwear. Maybe she should just go to Kane, tell him that for years she'd been hunted by a crazed maniac, and would he mind hiring an army to kill him? She could just see his handsome face as she gave him her request. He probably wanted to give her a box of chocolates or a basket full of bath salts as a thank-you, not a paid assassin.

No, she would never ask someone to do something she would one day have to do herself. There would be a final confrontation. And she would be the one who would end his sorry life. If she had to lose hers in the process, that was only fair. At some point she would stop being such a chickenshit and do the deed.

Standing on her rickety kitchen chair, she opened the cabinet above the refrigerator. Moving aside the bargain-sized jar of peanut butter, she pulled at the loose board behind it and opened the small area she'd created only hours after moving in. She took the nylon pouch, unzipped it, and checked its contents, though she knew nothing had been moved. Six passports, five driver's licenses, twenty-eight thousand dollars, and a small black wallet with three photographs. She no longer looked at the pictures—they were carved into her mind, seared into her soul—but she would never go anywhere without them.

She stepped down and returned the chair under the table. Zipping the pouch, she dumped it in with her clothes and toiletries. Placing her notebook computer on top of everything, McKenna closed the bag and straightened. With a long, silent sigh, she took one last glance at the landscape above the television, grabbed the duffel bag, and walked out the door.

Lucas Kane needed to stop looking for her. There was only one way to ensure that he did.

two

"We believe we've found her."

The Paris traffic was almost deafening in its exuberance; Lucas held the phone closer to his ear. "Say again."

"We've found her."

Stopping in the middle of the sidewalk, he ignored the creative curse of a bicyclist who almost rammed him. "How? Where?"

"We spotted a woman matching her description two days ago. We followed her but lost her in the crowd. Then we spotted her again this morning, hailing a taxi."

"Where?"

"Paris."

His heart thudded and that strange shiver he'd felt the first time she was near swept through him. "Does she know you're following her?"

"No. Her ride is about three cars ahead of us . . . wait, she's stopping."

"What street?"

"Rue de Morat."

Lucas looked up at the street sign above him: Rue de Morat.

"She's getting out."

An odd, surreal feeling washed over him as Lucas slowly turned. There, not ten feet away from him, stood his angel, his rescuer . . . his ghost.

The cacophony of an overcrowded city became silent;

the busy Paris sidewalk disappeared. Lucas had only one focal point as he began a slow walk toward her. If he moved too quickly, would she disappear like the ghost she claimed to be? He didn't want to take the chance.

She looked the same, yet different. Her hair was still short and bleached a platinum blond. Faded, ragged jeans covered her slender legs; the olive green T-shirt and black leather jacket she wore were probably supposed to make her look tough and boyish. Instead he thought they made her look sexy as hell.

The real difference from the last time he saw her was her face. Her skin wasn't coated with inches of heavy makeup, and her expression was a mixture of vulnerability, determination, and defiance.

She didn't move, just watched him with those lovely but oh so wary eyes. He knew people were passing by him, and if his former commander could see him now, he'd have blasted Lucas for having no concept of his surroundings. He didn't care. This woman had haunted his dreams nightly. Damned if he'd let anything get in the way of seeing her, including watching his back.

Within a foot of her he stopped and murmured, "And the ghost reappears."

A small, enigmatic smile tilted her lips. "I think we need to talk."

Lucas held out his hand. She stared at it for the longest time. Just when he was about to drop his hand, she brought hers up in an awkward, shy way and her fingertips touched his. At that touch, his heartbeat skyrocketed.

"I'm staying here." He shot a glance over his shoulder at the hotel behind him.

"Yes. Room 2304."

He didn't bother to question how she knew where he was staying or his room number. It didn't matter. Pulling her with him, he turned and walked the few yards to the hotel entrance. She didn't say a word, just went along with him, that mysterious smile still in place.

Still holding hands, they went through the lobby and stepped into the elevator without talking. He felt her give him several glances out of the corner of her eye, but she didn't speak. More surprising than anything, she didn't let go of his hand.

Since he was in the penthouse, he used a special key to take them to the top. He knew her eyes watched him; heard her swallow hard a couple of times. He felt the tension in her body, the coldness of her hand . . . but still she didn't let go of him. Something about the trust in that one small gesture did strange things to his heart.

The elevator opened and they walked out together. Standing in front of the penthouse door, she pulled her hand from his and said, "Before we go in, I'd like to ask you something."

"What?"

"Why am I here?"

"You mean, am I going to expect something from you by coming into my hotel room?"

Wariness. Vulnerability. Curiosity. They were all there in her expression. But her answer was one small nod.

"I don't expect anything from you," he said.

Her eyes searched his; she was looking for a trick, a lie. Lucas held his breath, feeling as though this was one of the most important moments of his life. Somehow he felt that if she gave him her trust, she would be giving him a gift of major proportions. He waited for her verdict. If she turned around and walked away, he wouldn't try to stop her, but he knew there would always be an ache inside him that he could never fill.

Finally she said, "Okay."

He opened the door before she could change her mind. She walked through; he followed behind her.

As the door closed them into the luxurious penthouse,

McKenna told herself this was probably the third dumbest decision she'd made in her life. The first one had gotten her entire family killed; the second one had landed her in jail. Both times it had been because she'd trusted the wrong people.

Somehow, even knowing how stupid this was, she refused to regret it. Lucas Kane had been on her mind well before she met him. She'd seen him on a television interview once and hadn't been able to resist Googling his name. And had become an instant admirer. Several of the causes he donated his wealth to were her favorite charities. Ones she supported as much as possible.

Since meeting Lucas, the fascination had only grown. During his rescue he had handled himself like a pro. Lucas Kane was more than just a wealthy businessman from England.

She couldn't deny that another reason for her fascination was the incredibly odd connection she'd felt the instant their eyes met. As if he'd not only seen straight into her soul but had liked and approved of what he saw.

She had to see where this would lead. Nothing permanent, of course. Permanency no longer existed for her. But she had to see what happened.

"Would you like something to drink or eat?"

She shook her head. Odd, since she was known to have a healthy appetite and had never turned down a meal. Nerves weren't usually an issue for her, but if she put anything into her mouth right now, chances were it'd come right back up. Her stomach was filled with giant butterflies.

"Have a seat."

Instead of sitting on the elegant sofa he indicated, she went to the giant floor-to-ceiling window and stared out at the sprawling city below. What was she doing here? She shouldn't have come. In a city this size, there was no reason she couldn't have disappeared, and he would

never find her. In her heart she had known that. Telling
herself she had come to him before he found her was a
lie. And McKenna had long since stopped lying to herself. She had come to Lucas Kane because he intrigued
her on so many levels. For one brief moment in time, she
wanted to indulge that fascination. And then she would
leave and never see him again.

"I've been looking for you for so long, I hardly know
what to say to you."

She turned to him and once more tried to pinpoint her
fascination. Tall, maybe around six-two; muscular, but
not overly so; thick, golden blond hair that held just
a hint of a wave; clear silver-gray eyes; stubborn chin.
Elegant with an underlying ruggedness. A ruggedness
that caused all sorts of interesting shivers throughout
her body.

His khaki pants and navy shirt should have looked
ordinary, even bland. Lucas's physique and air of confidence made them appear stylish and classic.

Was Lucas Kane a handsome man? Absolutely. Best-
looking man she'd ever met? No. That title belonged to
a monster. But this man had something that drew her to
him. Moth to a flame. Magnet to steel. Every cliché ever
created to describe an indescribable attraction.

Direct as ever, she asked, "Why have you been looking for me?"

"I wanted to thank you for saving my life."

She couldn't prevent the smile. "Is that what I did?"

"Yes." He lifted a brow. "Why would you ask that?"

"Because you're more than capable of taking care of
yourself. I may have taken out Victor, but the other two
men were all your doing."

Lucas shrugged. "I was angry enough and they were a
bit out of shape."

That was true. Victor's MO had always been to hire
his people locally, and he'd never worried whether they

were trained. As long as they could halfway shoot a gun and had no conscience, they'd filled his qualifications. She had been one of the few people who had ever worked with him more than once.

But still, an elegant Briton with billions in the bank and aristocracy stamped on his face should have had a bit more trouble than he'd had. He'd been shot and yet that hadn't stopped him from taking out the shooter. McKenna had been shot before . . . hard as hell to think with a bullet hole burning into your skin.

"You handled them quite well. Where did you train?"

It was the first personal question either of them had asked. She chose to go first. He would have his own questions. She would answer what she could. And expected the same from him.

"I took some private training." He grimaced. "Getting pulled out of bed in the middle of the night was a bit of a surprise."

Heading to the sofa he'd pointed to earlier, she asked, "What happened?"

He dropped into a chair across from her in an effortless, graceful way that was somehow all masculine. Her gazed zeroed in on the slight curve of his mouth. A man's mouth had never even drawn her attention before, but she wanted to stare at his. It was masculine but also well shaped, almost beautiful. It had been years since she'd willingly kissed a man. How odd that she wanted to kiss him.

She jerked back from her fantasy when he said, "I was in bed with food poisoning."

"I'm guessing that's not a euphemism for a nasty-tasting woman?"

Another twitch of that beautiful mouth. "No, the real gut-wrenching, vomit-inducing kind."

"What happened?"

"Victor's friends gave me food poisoning."

Stupid, really, but that was about the funniest thing she'd heard in months. She tried to disguise her amusement, but he must have seen it in her face because his eyes twinkled with laughter.

"I'm sure waking up to Victor's ugly face didn't help."

"I hoped I was hallucinating."

She could see that his noble, masculine nose had been set to rights. "How's your shoulder?"

"Fine . . . just a twinge now and then. You did save my life."

McKenna shrugged. Gratitude wasn't something she was comfortable with. One of the reasons she never stayed with a rescued victim. After she'd secured the rescue, someone else took over their care and she would disappear. That was how she preferred it. Last Chance Rescue and Noah gave her the opportunity to help without personal involvement. Having even a hint of interaction with the victim would be more than she could handle. Personal involvement had to be avoided at all cost.

"You're more than capable of taking care of yourself. I'm assuming you had a plan for escape?"

He shrugged. "I had a plan . . . didn't know if it would have worked. I managed to loosen one of the wooden posts on the bed. If you hadn't come along, it would have become my weapon."

"He didn't intend to kill you." She grinned slightly and added, "Although your little comment about tongue might have changed his mind."

Humor glinted in his eyes, turning them to gleaming silver. "I've been known to be a bit of a wiseass at inconvenient times." His expression went solemn. "He deserved to die."

McKenna slammed the door on the memory. Regretting Victor's death would do no good. Lucas was right. Victor had deserved to die. Not only for what he had done to Lucas and Skylar, Gabe Maddox's wife, but for what he'd done to countless others through the years. Just because he hadn't intended to kill Lucas didn't mean he wouldn't kill. There had to be true evil in Victor. What he had done to her while she'd been pretending to be his employee was something she didn't bother to regret. Rescuing the victims would always come before her own personal comforts. That decision had been made years ago.

"I was disappointed that you disappeared," Lucas said.

She had been disappointed, too. Leaving Lucas lying on the sidewalk had been difficult. Though Dylan had been there and an ambulance was on its way, she'd wanted to linger. Had wanted to see him wake up, hear him talk to her. That had scared the hell out of her, so she'd run away, faster than she'd run in years.

So what the hell am I doing here now?

McKenna shut down the voice, but it would be back. That was the damnedest and most irritating thing about a conscience. It could only be ignored for so long.

"Can I ask you some questions?"

She nodded but went on high alert. Questions were expected, but she couldn't be distracted when she answered them. Having Lucas know her was one thing; having Lucas know about her was something altogether different.

"Where do you live?"

Odd question to start with, especially since she had no definitive answer. "Wherever the job takes me. I don't have a permanent address."

"And what is your job?"

She shrugged. Hell, she hated sounding evasive, but there was no real answer for that one, either. "Whatever happens to be available when I need the money."

"So were you working with Victor after all?"

That was something she couldn't lie about. For many reasons, she didn't want him to know very much about her, but damned if she'd let him think she really was one of Victor's employees. "No. I was working undercover."

"For whom?"

"Victor had another woman, just a few miles from where he'd stashed you. He was holding her for ransom. I helped her escape and heard that you had been taken, too." She shrugged. "Thought I'd see if I could assist you, too."

"How did you know about my abduction?"

Now that was something she couldn't talk about. Her underground contacts would shut off all communication if she revealed anything but the most basic information. "I heard some chatter."

He looked briefly frustrated, then changed tactics. "How old are you?"

That she had expected. And one of the few questions she didn't mind giving the full truth about. For some reason, people were always intrigued with her age. She knew she looked younger than she was, but even if she was the nineteen that they sometimes assumed, what was the big deal?

"Twenty-six," she said.

"How long have you been in the business?"

She wrinkled her brow in a deliberate frown of confusion. "What business is that?"

A slight flare of temper in his eyes told her he hadn't liked her answer. Tough. There were only certain things she could tell him.

"The rescuing business."

"I'm not in the rescuing business. Whatever gave you that idea?"

"You rescued me, for one. Helped the young woman you mentioned. You obviously know the head of Last Chance Rescue, since barely an hour after I leave Noah

McCall's office, asking for his help in finding you, you appear before me."

"I know many people. That doesn't mean I'm in their line of business. I'm acquainted with Mr. McCall and I've assisted his organization on a few occasions. However, I'm not in the rescue business and am not employed by LCR."

There. She'd told him a version of the truth.

He looked at her for the longest time without speaking. McKenna once again felt those nerves she really didn't know she still had. This man made her feel way too much. Emotions and feelings she hadn't been aware of in years, if ever, were surfacing. Maybe coming here had been a bigger mistake than she'd thought.

"No. Don't leave. I won't ask anything more personal. I promise."

Shit. That was scary. She hadn't moved, hadn't changed her expression, yet somehow he'd guessed. His ability to read her thoughts put her on even higher alert.

The promise not to ask anything more personal was also a surprise. Not the words themselves, but his attitude. He seemed nervous, almost vulnerable. Her stupid, irresponsible, unwise heart thumped harder in her chest. Stiffening her body, she forced herself to ignore the urge to go to him and soothe him. Just how dangerous would that be?

"I don't mind questions . . . I just don't like certain questions."

"Fair enough. I'll ask one more and then you can question me."

"All right." She tensed. Would it be the one to make her get up and leave this insanity?

"What's your name?"

Laughter burst from her before she could control it. After all that had happened, she realized, that was one thing she hadn't told him. She could give him one of the names she had on her passports, or even make up a new one. She could, but she wouldn't. Having him say her name in his beautiful, crisp British accent was an indulgence, but one she desperately wanted.

"McKenna."

"McKenna." He said it like a caress, and warmth flooded her again. "It's a beautiful name. I'm assuming you're not going to give me a last name?"

When she just looked at him without answering, he nodded his agreement. "Okay. Your turn. Ask away."

She stared at him for several seconds more. If this were the last chance she'd ever have to get to know a man who had fascinated her from the moment she'd heard of him, then she would take advantage of his openness as much as possible.

"You're British, but you seem to have some very American mannerisms and language."

He nodded. "Two of my stepmothers were from the States. They were with me during my most impressionable years."

"Two stepmothers?"

"All totaled, six."

"Wow."

"Exactly."

"Do you have siblings?"

"No. Closest I came were step-pets."

"And your parents?"

"My father died a few years back. My mother died only a few weeks after I was born."

"So your father was always trying to replace her?"

"Doubtful. The photos of her look nothing like the exceedingly attractive and, shall we say, voluptuous women my father married."

"Oh."

He smiled then, and McKenna caught her breath before she could sigh. His smile was like sunshine. Not only was it beautiful, it created a warmth that permeated her entire body. Only a deeper, more intense warmth went to certain areas and heated them even more. Something fluttered deep inside her. *Oh, my.*

"Are you okay?"

She shook herself, suddenly becoming aware not only of his concerned gaze but that she was almost lying on the couch. Maybe she was hungry. Her croissant and coffee had been hours ago.

"I'm hungry. Can we have lunch?"

He laughed, but McKenna cringed. Blurting out her thoughts was a side effect of being alone too much. Social skills eroded quickly.

He stood and walked over to a table that held a phone. "What would you like to eat? Any preferences or things you dislike?"

"Anything is fine."

Lucas picked up the phone and gave an order that sounded large enough to feed ten people. Either he was very hungry or he was under the impression that she could eat like a linebacker. And that bothered her again, because she did indeed have an extraordinarily large appetite.

Lucas returned to his chair. "It'll be here in about fifteen minutes. While we wait, tell me all of your favorite things."

"Why?"

"Because you won't tell me anything personal about yourself, but I still want to know you. Just tell me the things you don't mind me knowing."

She didn't know why the question made her uncomfortable. He was asking for innocuous things that meant nothing to her, yet somehow she felt that if she told him anything at all, he could see everything.

"Okay, let's see . . ." Her mind searched for something that was insignificant but didn't sound completely lame.

Apparently understanding her difficulty, he asked, "What's your favorite food?"

"Cheeseburgers."

"Good, since that's one of the meals I ordered."

He seemed so approving, McKenna suddenly felt stupid for not wanting to tell him trivial things. What would it hurt? So, one by one, she began to name her favorites, from flowers to movies, from songs to books.

Lucas settled against the cushions of the sofa and watched a wonder unfold before him. McKenna's eyes gleamed and her face became animated, beyond beautiful. She looked like an angel . . . as he'd often thought of her. He felt as if he were being given a gift. There was no trickery involved; she didn't seem to realize that naming these favorites of hers gave him a tremendous amount of information.

His mind formed a profile of McKenna, and while he enjoyed learning these things about her, he acknowledged it also made him want to know more. Such as why would someone so young seem to have no family, no one to care for them? She was clearly American. Her mannerisms and speech pattern gave that away. When he'd first met her, he'd thought midwestern, and he hadn't changed his mind.

She had an artful innocence about her. If he hadn't witnessed it himself, he would never have believed that she could swat a fly, much less take out a psychopath like Victor Lymes. How had this McKenna come to be?

The things she liked were very American. From food to movies and books, all reflected her American heritage. How long she'd been in Europe he didn't know, but her core desires and heart were still with her native country. So why was she here in Paris, seemingly all alone?

A chime at the door indicated their lunch had arrived.

And with it, her wariness returned. Lucas felt a punch that went straight through to his gut. In that instant he realized something deeply disturbing. The captivating and enchanting McKenna was not only wary, she was absolutely terrified. Question was, *What was she terrified of?*

Palm Beach, Florida

Damon Hughes stared at the glittering water of his Olympic-sized swimming pool. Loneliness and rage made an odd combination, but it had been part of his life for so long, he had become used to its burning presence. This pool was for her. He'd had it built just for her, because she loved to swim. He remembered taking her to the lake when they first started dating. She'd been so sweet, so cute in her new bikini. The one her mother had told her she couldn't buy. He'd given her the money and she'd gone back the next day and bought it. She hadn't liked being told what to do. He'd loved that hint of defiance and independence. Had seen it as a challenge.

The emptiness of the pool taunted him. She should be swimming in it, enjoying herself. Instead, she continued to run from him. When would she learn her lesson? When every person she cared for was gone? Why hadn't he seen that selfishness in her when they first met? When would she understand that he would never give up looking for her, wanting her, loving her? Years might have passed, but his love for her would never die.

Her defiance against her parents had been funny. He'd encouraged it, nurtured it. It had worked so completely with his plans. However, her defiance against him had been another matter. Something he hadn't been able to tolerate.

"Mr. Hughes, the investigators are here."

Damon stood, resigned to hearing yet another of their failed reports. If he hadn't been quite sure that everything was being done to find her, he would have had every one of the bastards ripped apart and fed to the sharks. But he believed them. The last couple of years, she'd become excellent at hiding. Where she'd gotten the help and the training to do such a thing bothered him almost as much as not being able to find her. If he ever found out who had assisted her, they'd be screaming for death long before he granted it to them.

As he headed to his offices, he paid little attention to the opulence that surrounded him. He'd become accustomed to such things in the last few years. Though he had worked hard for his money and stature, they hadn't brought him the happiness he sought. Happiness couldn't exist until she was back in his arms, where she belonged.

Delaying the inevitable, Damon bypassed his office and headed upstairs. His investigators would wait . . . they worked for him. He had a need to feel close to her for just a short period. If he were to hear, as he fully expected, that there were no leads, he wanted to have this peaceful memory in his head.

He pulled the key from his pocket. He and his trusted housekeeper, Margret, were the only two who had access to this room. No one else dared come in here; they knew their lives would be over. He stepped inside and leaned against the closed door. He inhaled deeply, the scent of light floral perfume washing his senses in memory. Her favorite. He had it replaced each month so it wouldn't lose its fragrance. Each day Margret would come in and dust the room, and before she left, she would spray just a hint so he could come in and enjoy it when he pleased.

The room was pink and feminine. An exact replica of the bedroom she'd had as a teenager. And it was such a representation of her. Fair and delicate as a flower. That was one of the things he loved the most about her. She was all girl, pure femininity. No bows or frills, nothing silly. Just a soft, lovely fragility that literally made him ache.

The first time he'd seen her, at a theater in Omaha, Nebraska, his heart had raced. He had sneaked in to watch the movie and had ended up watching her instead.

She'd worn a blue sundress with white flowers on it. Her soft, golden brown hair had been long, reaching just above her beautiful bottom. She hadn't giggled like so many other girls her age. She'd seemed serious, mature but oh so innocent. And though she was only sixteen, he knew from the moment he saw her that she was his dream come true.

As usual, he was drawn to the photograph of her he'd had enlarged and framed. It was the first thing he'd put in this room; the only thing that was different from the original room. Sometimes he'd come in here and stand for hours, just gazing at her loveliness. Often, knowing no one was around to see him, he would let his tears flow freely. Tears of heartache; tears from her betrayal.

Sighing, Damon turned from the portrait and gazed about the room again. A shrine to her. Out of his love, he had replaced everything she had lost. This was what she'd had before all the troubles started. Before her family intervened and ruined everything. Before she broke his heart.

He had few regrets in his life. They were useless and insignificant, and they changed nothing. However, if he had to admit to one regret, he might have told her to leave the house. Years ago, he'd had a volatile temper and little discipline. Now he could control his rage and react with reason. Still, he had no remorse for what had happened. It had to be done.

No, he would never regret killing McKenna's parents. They'd deserved to die. He did, in his weakest of moments, wish that he hadn't made her watch.

three

Careful not to touch her, Lucas replaced the blanket around McKenna's shoulders that she'd knocked off during one of her nightmares. Settling back into the chair he'd sat in all night, he watched as she seemed to sleep peacefully. *Seemed. Ha.* When was the last time McKenna had slept in peace? In the three hours she'd been sleeping on the sofa, she'd tossed and turned, mumbled and cried. He had only understood a few of her mutterings. The words had made little sense, but the emotion in them had broken his heart.

Before she'd fallen asleep, they'd talked for hours . . . most of the night. He'd told her things he'd never told another living soul. Concerns and worries he'd always kept to himself came out of him as though she were his therapist. Of course, he'd kept some vital information back. He hadn't told her about his once secret life.

When he'd joined the agency, he'd sworn an oath, and when he'd left the agency, he'd sworn the same oath. Never talk about the organization few people in the world knew existed. Having her know his background wasn't pertinent to the here and now except for one tiny detail. He wanted to know who she was running from, because he wanted to find him.

Would telling her make her trust him? She'd told him many things but almost nothing about where she'd come from or why she was so frightened. The information he'd gleaned about her had come from her likes and dislikes and reading between the lines. She was young, afraid, trying so hard to be strong and brave. And the obsession he'd had since meeting her had grown.

She'd fallen asleep around four. He'd been in the midst of describing a sunset he'd experienced the last time he was in Tangiers. And like that setting sun, she'd sunk into the cushion of the sofa and drifted into slumber. It was one of the sweetest sights he'd ever witnessed. And one of the most humbling. She trusted him. If she hadn't, she wouldn't be lying on his sofa, vulnerable and open.

Lucas closed his eyes as arousal surged. Hell, having her trust him was one thing; having her trust him enough to make love to her would be altogether different. His angel would probably turn into a tigress if he made one move in a romantic direction. He'd have to take it slow, lure her with cheeseburgers and ice cream.

Arousal surged harder. He'd watched her devour both, and it'd been a stimulating sexual experience beyond his understanding. Watching a woman who looked as ethereal as a specter consume a massive amount of food brought an unexpected lust to the surface. The pleasure she seemed to derive from eating made him wonder if she would make love with the same amount of energy and enthusiasm.

He shifted in his seat again. Thinking about that was getting him nowhere. Lucas closed his eyes. A fifteen-minute snooze, then he'd resurface to stare and to figure out how the hell he could hold on to a woman he knew would never willingly be held.

McKenna blinked, returning from the deepest sleep she'd had in years. Used to bounding out of bed and getting the hell out of wherever she was, this feeling of lethargic contentment was unprecedented and scary as hell. Nevertheless, she savored the sensation.

Shifting her head on the pillow, she saw Lucas sitting across from her. His eyes were closed, their silver-gray depths hidden from view. Oh man, was she in trouble. Lucas was the only man she'd ever met that she would love to just sit and be with, talking about anything, everything, or nothing. She just wanted to be near him.

He'd talked about his childhood, about the various schools he had attended, and about Kane Enterprises. He had seemed open, no shadows apparent. And then she'd asked about his father. He hadn't minded talking about him, but the shadows had emerged. Dark, ominous, and full of pain. There was love there and a hell of a lot of guilt.

She wanted to know more; she wanted to know everything. He was a dangerous lure. One she damn well could not afford.

Regret pulling at every cell and muscle in her body, McKenna put her feet on the floor. She would refresh herself in the bathroom and then get the hell out of here. She wouldn't leave without saying goodbye. Not because it wouldn't be the polite thing to do. Politeness had disappeared from her life long ago. However, they needed to get one thing straight before she disappeared from his life for good. He had to stop looking for her.

Stepping quietly into the bathroom, she gazed around at the temptation. Lavish and expensive toiletries filled the room. Cursing herself for her one major weakness didn't stop McKenna from taking advantage of such luxury. Though she refrained from taking a bubble bath in the giant Jacuzzi, she showered, taking advantage of the fragrant shower gel, expensive shampoo, and wondrously decadent body lotion.

Twenty minutes later, she emerged from the bathroom, feeling like a new woman. Though she'd had to put on the same wrinkled clothing, beneath her jeans and T-shirt she felt feminine and pretty for the first time in years.

The fragrance of breakfast assailed her senses the moment she opened the door. She'd told Lucas many things about herself last night. Nothing that would give him any real knowledge of her past, but he'd learned more things about her than anyone else on this earth. And from the scents of the breakfast he'd ordered, he had made use of that knowledge.

Breakfast was her favorite meal. Her mom had been a wonderful cook and her father had been a breakfast lover. Every Sunday the family had shared what her dad referred to as a good old-fashioned country chowdown. Her heart clutched as she remembered what she'd once taken for granted, rolled her eyes at, and disdained. Oh God, how she wished she could take it all back. She would give anything and everything if only she could.

"Breakfast is ready."

McKenna jerked to attention. She was thankful she was long past the days of shedding tears for the massive mistakes she'd made. Explaining those tears to this man who seemed to be able to see straight into her soul already wasn't something she could deal with.

He was standing in the elegant dining room, beside a food-laden table. She'd learned many things about Lucas Kane last night. One she hadn't expected was his need to take care of her. Despite the knowledge that she was treading on the most dangerous ground with him, she couldn't prevent the little thrill that went through her. That this beautiful, golden Adonis of a man wanted to do nice things for her filled her with all sorts of warm tingles.

She ignored her heart's warning that reminded her the last man who'd filled her with those feelings had brutally betrayed her in the worst possible way. That man and Lucas had nothing in common. Besides, after today she would never see him again. What could one breakfast hurt?

"Hungry?"

Before she could speak, the loud growl of her stomach provided the answer. McKenna gave into a small grin. She could lie without blinking an eye, but her stomach always told the truth.

Apparently hearing the growl, he laughed. "Good. It just got here."

Her eyes widened as she surveyed the feast he'd ordered for them. They were in Paris. This kind of meal shouldn't even be available in this country, much less in the most elegant city in the world.

The scraping of the chair on the hardwood floor pulled her from her lustful staring at the massive meal. She plopped inelegantly into the chair he'd pulled out for her and watched as he proceeded to heap a plate with eggs, smoked ham, fried potatoes, and biscuits.

"Where did this food come from?"

A small enigmatic smile played around his mouth. "I made a call to the chef after you fell asleep. He was kind enough to create the masterpiece you see before you."

Oh hell. Emotions clogged her throat and tears stung her eyes. Trust her to cry over something as silly as the mental image of a French chef running all over Paris looking for someone who could sell him a smoked country ham or perusing a cookbook for a biscuit recipe.

Obviously recognizing the signs of an overwhelmed woman, Lucas urged softly, "Eat."

McKenna took a sip of strong French coffee, pulled herself together, and dived into a breakfast fit for a Nebraska farmer. Her father would have loved it.

Lucas ate, because if he didn't, it would make McKenna self-conscious. However, he enjoyed watching her eat much more than he enjoyed the meal. He needed to get over this odd fascination of watching her consume food. Not only was it making him as hard as a rock, it was damn freaky.

His taste in women had always been a bit on the eclectic side, but the things he found physically attractive were, for the most part, predictable and traditional. A pretty face, a beautiful smile, a shapely ass. McKenna had all those things, but she also had a way of eating food that made him want to push that food away, pull her onto the table, and devour her the way she devoured her meal.

She leaned back into her chair with a groan of apparent fulfillment, and he gripped the table. His erection pressed against the zipper of his pants—painful, inconvenient, and embarrassing as hell.

"That was wonderful, Lucas. Thank you."

"Where are you from?"

Shit. Shit. Shit.

Her eyes flaring with fear, she stood. "I think it's time for me to go."

Lucas remained seated. The knife in front of him was tempting. Hell, never had he thought to wish that Victor had gotten the chance to cut out his tongue. Why the fuck had he asked the one question that was guaranteed to put every radar and defense mechanism she possessed on the highest of alerts? *Damned idiot.* His mind had been on other things and he'd blurted his thoughts.

Having no choice, Lucas tried to dig himself out of the hell pit he'd just thrown himself into. "I apologize, McKenna. I know that was out of the bounds of our agreement. Don't leave."

She sighed. "No, I'm the one who should be apologizing. You've been incredibly kind . . . fed me like a queen." Her lips tilted into a tiny smile he had become very familiar with. It was an endearing little gesture she was probably not even aware of, and it made her look so incredibly vulnerable and alone. Once again, Lucas gripped the edge of the table, this time to keep from jumping to his feet and pulling her into his arms.

"But I really do have to go."

Lucas stood then. The erection that had been throbbing for release had disappeared. His stupidity and her fear had effectively doused it.

"Last night was . . ." Hell, what could he say? Amazing? That would scare her out the door before he got in another breath.

"Nice," she said. "I haven't talked like that in ages." Another tiny smile. "Thank you."

"Do you know where I live?"

Her brow wrinkled. "London?"

"Yes, but . . ." Ah hell, he might as well say it and get it over with. "I don't want to say goodbye." When she opened her mouth to speak, he held up his hand. "No . . . I can see it in your eyes. You're going to tell me we can't see each other again."

Her slender shoulders lifted in a helpless little shrug. "We can't."

"McKenna, we're two adults. We can do what we damn well please."

"Sometimes adults don't always get what they want."

He watched as she turned toward the door. The small bag she'd brought with her was still beside it, where she'd dropped it yesterday.

He reached into his pocket. "Here's my card."

She turned then and looked at it briefly. "No . . . thanks." For just an instant, the vulnerable, alone expression flashed in her eyes as she said, "You're a very special man, Lucas. Thank you for a lovely night." She grabbed her bag and went through the door.

Lucas followed her but stopped at the door and watched as she stood at the elevator. He felt almost numb, as if she was taking life and energy from his body.

Suddenly she turned and dropped her bag. Lucas's heart stopped. And then she was running toward him. Two feet from him, he saw in her face what he was feeling in his heart. Opening his arms, she ran into them.

He allowed her to show him what she wanted.

Standing on her toes, she put her mouth on his and kissed him. It wasn't a peck, it wasn't soft, and it wasn't neat. Her lips covered his and she pressed her tongue deep into his mouth.

Instinct took over. Pulling her against him, he lowered his head and dove into the kiss. She tasted like strawberries, coffee, and honey. This was not an invitation. This kiss was probably the only one she would allow, the only one she planned to ever give him. He knew that about her.

With that thought, he drew back slightly from the kiss. He didn't plan for this to be the only kiss they ever shared, but he damned well intended it to be the best one either of them had ever had. Which meant turning down the heat to a simmer instead of a full boil. Keeping his mouth on hers, he decreased the pressure and played with her lips, feathering, retreating, savoring.

Under the roar of passion and lust in his head, he heard a groan. Surrender. Arousal. Need. Though everything within him wanted to press her against the wall, strip her pants down, and love her till neither of them remembered their names, he knew that'd be the biggest mistake of all.

Finally, knowing she needed to breathe, Lucas pulled slowly away and looked down at the aroused, heated woman in his arms.

Panting slightly, she whispered against his lips, "I couldn't have lived without ever knowing your taste." Then, before he could respond, she jerked away. As if on cue, the elevator dinged, announcing its arrival. She ran toward it.

"McKenna!"

At the entrance to the elevator, she looked at him again.

"If there's ever anything you need, you only have to ask."

Her smile one of sheer beauty, she whispered, "You just gave me more than I ever expected." And then she disappeared.

Lucas stood staring at the closed elevator door. The only thing that hurt worse than the unappeased arousal pounding through him was the gaping hole in his chest that used to hold his heart. McKenna had taken that with her.

four

McKenna made it out to the street without crying, which she thought was pretty damned good considering she wanted to crawl into a corner and bawl like a baby. She hadn't felt this bad in years. How could she have thought she could have just one kiss and it would satisfy an eternity of want?

Lucas Kane had morphed from a golden hero of her dreams to a flesh-and-bone mortal, and the fascination for him hadn't diminished as she had hoped.

A harsh curse brought her attention back to her surroundings. Holy crap, here she was lusting after a man in the middle of a busy Paris sidewalk without any concept of time and place. Damon had spies everywhere, and if he found her in Paris, which was the closest place she had to a home, she was screwed.

Holding her head down, she draped the strap of her bag across her shoulder and started down the sidewalk. She needed to get out of Paris for a few days. Her bags were at a small storage facility she'd set up when she'd first arrived in Paris. She'd go there, grab some things, and head toward Lyon. Hopefully, Lucas would be gone by the time she returned. Being in the same city with him was too much of a temptation.

Her mind back into total awareness, McKenna kept her head down, her eyes avoiding contact with anyone she passed. She had to be aware, always on guard. It had been over two years since Damon's people had spotted her. But he hadn't stopped looking. She wasn't stupid enough to believe that. The man had killed everyone she loved, taken everything she held most precious.

Thinking herself free of him would be dangerous not only to her but to those around her, too. The last time she'd felt safe, she had learned a hard lesson. And a sweet, elderly lady had paid the price.

Damon had a way of teaching lessons. She had learned more than her share. Unfortunately, she wasn't the only one to suffer when Damon was of a mind to teach her something.

No way in hell would he give up until she gave him what he wanted: her freedom, her body, and her obedience.

Palm Beach

"We may have found her."

Damon shot up in bed. Morning blues had kept him in bed for hours longer than he normally stayed there. His investigators' news a few days ago had depressed him more than usual. But at those words his adrenaline spiked.

"Where?"

"Little Rock, Arkansas."

Damon swung his legs around, his feet dropping to the floor. She was from a small town in Nebraska, but a bigger city might suit her better since she was hiding from him. The last time his investigators had found her she was in Memphis, Tennessee. After the unfortunate but necessary incident with her neighbor, she'd disappeared.

"Do you have a picture?"

"Yes. I just sent it to your cellphone. Take a look and let me know what you think."

Damon looked at his cellphone screen and pressed a key for his photographs. And there she was. She looked somewhat different than he remembered. He rubbed his eyes and peered closer. The picture had been taken from a distance, but he would recognize her anywhere. Long brownish blond hair, the same full lips, pert little nose, baby-soft skin. Yes, it was his McKenna!

Tearing his gaze away from the screen, he put the phone back to his ear. "Has she seen you?"

"No. She acts a bit shy and wary, but not abnormally so. We followed her all day yesterday while she was doing errands. Was totally oblivious."

"What name is she going by?"

"Jamie Kendrick. She works two part-time jobs, one at a dry cleaner's, the other at a real estate office."

Fury exploded inside Damon. Dammit, she wouldn't have to work at all if she just did what she was supposed to do. If she were with him, she would never have to lift a finger again. Why couldn't she understand that?

"She have any relationships?"

"None that we've seen so far. She lives in an apartment complex . . . kind of ratty. Since we've only just found her, we don't know that much about her yet."

"I expect that will change." He kept his voice mild. His investigators knew that just the initial news that she'd been found wasn't enough. In a few days, they should know what the last pair of shoes she bought looked like and whether they pinched her feet. They were that good and he had that much money.

"Yes. We'll report more soon."

"Very good, Carlos. I'll make sure you're amply rewarded."

"Thank you, sir." There was no pride or smugness in his voice. The man knew Damon didn't stand for that.

Damon closed his phone and dropped his head back to his pillow. His love had been found. Years ago, he'd given her the choice to come to him on her own and she had defied him. Killing the old lady had been an unfortunate by-product of McKenna's defiance.

The elderly woman had fallen down the stairs . . . okay, admittedly she'd been shoved a little, but he'd been trying to get into McKenna's apartment and the old bitch had caught him. She had been going to call the police. He'd tried to explain to her that he was an old friend, and she hadn't believed him. The little struggle on the stairway had lasted not even a minute. He'd pushed her away and she'd fallen down the entire flight of stairs and broken her neck.

And he'd never gotten to see McKenna. Instead, he'd had to send her a damn letter explaining what had happened and how it was once again her fault. If she had come to him as he'd asked, the old biddy would still be alive. He had expected the letter to produce a good result. That hadn't happened. Instead of coming to him and admitting her mistake, she had disappeared again, and he'd been looking for her for two years.

At some point he had hoped she would come back on her own. That had been his ultimatum. *Come to me of your own free will or everyone you care about will die.* She hadn't taken him up on his offer, so he really didn't have a choice in the matter, did he? Now that she'd been found, he would never let her go again.

He'd had to tame her into submission several times before, and though it would pain him to do it again, he would have no choice. With the right amount of discipline, along with all the love he had for her, he was sure that this time he could change her mind. This time he would convince her.

And very soon, he would have that opportunity. Excitement rushed through him. McKenna would soon be his again!

Marseille, France

McKenna sat on the park bench across from a sleazy hotel. Sipping coffee, she tried to pretend she wasn't freezing her ass off . . . pretty damn hard since she *was* freezing her ass off.

Right before she'd gotten on a train to Lyon, Noah had called with a possible job. He never said he had a job for her—just a possible job if she was interested. She'd yet to turn down any possible jobs. Not only did she need the money, but working with LCR was the most worthwhile thing she'd ever done. She was just lucky she got paid for it.

The hotel was a known operation for prostitution. If that's what a person chose to do, that was their business. Being forced into prostitution was another matter. Noah had gotten word that several young girls had been taken off the street in various parts of the city and had ended up here in this skank hole.

Only one LCR operative was working the job with her. He had gone into the hotel for a brief look-see. On his word, she'd either know they needed more help or this was something they'd do on their own.

"Got ourselves a bit of a problem."

If anyone else heard Dylan Savage's lazy voice, they'd think he was about the most laid-back person in the world. McKenna had worked several ops with him. Beneath that slow, lazy drawl, she heard the underlying tension in his tone.

"What?"

"Don't have time to get additional help. We got ourselves a serious issue."

McKenna stood and crossed the street. Making her way slowly to the entrance, she tried to appear as unconcerned as Dylan always did. Inside, her heart was triple-timing with adrenaline. Dylan would never be authorizing her to come in without backup unless some major shit was taking place.

"Can you give me an idea?"

"Got four of them going on right now. All of them sound pretty damn rough." He stopped and added, "And damn young."

The sheer grimness in his voice had her picking up her pace. Four young women were being raped. He was right. No waiting for backup.

"I'm at the entrance," McKenna said.

"Lobby should be deserted. Gorilla behind the counter will be out for a while. I'm on the third floor. I got rooms six and eight. You take rooms thirteen and fifteen."

"Got it." Before she went through the door, McKenna pulled her knife from its sheath under her pant leg and slid it into her jacket pocket. Taking the gun from her shoulder holster, she held it down at her side. It was doubtful she'd need it until she got to the room, but she'd take no chances.

Entering the small lobby, she scrunched her nose at the repugnant smells that hit all at once: musky sex blended with the stench of urine, vomit, and other excrements she didn't even want to think about.

Dylan was right: the lobby was empty. The long counter that served as check-in or whatever the hell they called it in a prostitution house had no one standing behind it. On her way up the stairs, she glimpsed a pair of jean-clad legs sticking out from behind the counter and figured they belonged to the aforementioned gorilla.

Her gun at the ready, McKenna ran up two flights of stairs. Stopping at the top of the third-floor entrance, she held her breath to listen. All sorts of sounds emanated from several different areas. Groans of pleasure and beds squeaking didn't cause alarm. Screams and cries of pain did. McKenna took off running toward the sickening sound.

Her heart racing, she stopped at room thirteen and eased the door open. Peeking inside, she decided to hell with stealth. She shoved the door open and it thudded hard against the wall. The grunting man on the bed whirled around and yelled, "I'm not finished."

Gun steady in her hand, she stalked over to him. "Yes, you are."

Cursing, he pulled away from the girl on the bed and turned around. "You want some of this, too?"

Since shooting off a certain body part would hold too much appeal, she refused to look down at him. Instead, she motioned with her gun. "Get on the floor."

Sneering, he turned back to the helpless girl on the bed. "Go to hell."

"If you don't think I'll shoot you, think again."

Apparently even with a gun pointed at him, her threats didn't impress him. The young girl was crying; McKenna refused to look at her. Getting rid of the raping bastard was her first priority. Since subtlety hadn't worked, she went with a more aggressive move. Drawing closer to the bed, McKenna jumped and delivered a hard, controlled kick to the man's flabby arm. He tumbled off the bed, landing with a nice, satisfying thud on the floor.

Backing away from him, she taunted, "Now do I have your attention?"

With a roar, he lurched to his feet and took a step forward. Pulling her knife, she threw it, hitting him in the meaty part of his shoulder. The knife wasn't long enough to do major damage, but she expected it to hurt like hell and slow him down. It did. He howled in pain, his eyes wide with shock.

Taking a pair of handcuffs from one of her pockets,

she threw them at his bare feet. "Handcuff yourself to the bedpost."

His hand holding his wound, he continued to stare at her, not moving to take the handcuffs.

Arching her eyebrows, McKenna lowered her gun and pointed it at his naked crotch. "It's a small target, but I think I can hit it."

That got him moving. Bending down, he picked up the handcuffs and put them on, attaching one end to a bedpost.

She finally turned to the young girl, who was now sitting up, her arms wrapped around a pillow to cover her body.

"You okay?" McKenna asked softly.

Tears pouring down her young, ravaged face, she nodded.

An agonized scream came from the room next door, piercing the tense silence. Pulling her knife from the man's shoulder, McKenna ignored his vicious curse of pain. She shot a glance at the girl again. "Wrap the sheet around you, go out to the hallway, and wait for me."

Not waiting for a reply, McKenna dashed out the door and ran to room fifteen, where horrific screams of pain continued. She shoved the door open. What she saw had her rushing into the middle of the room before she knew it. A girl lay facedown on the bed, her long blond hair hanging over the side. She was spread-eagled and nude, each limb tied to the bed. Two men stood on either side of the bed. Both were nude and held whips. And both were taking turns using them on the girl's bare back.

The scene before her morphed into a scene from eight years before. McKenna's mind went into shutdown mode. Raising the gun, she shouted over the young girl's screams, "Stop!"

Neither man appeared to have heard her. Her eyes

went to the larger, older one. Not only did his eyes gleam with an unholy lust, but he was fully erect, sexually excited by whipping the girl.

With a low growl, McKenna sprang, taking him to the floor. She heard the other man shout. The roar of fury in her head was so great, she barely felt the stings of the whip on her back. She knew the other man had turned on her. Right now, her priority was the pervert she was choking to death. The stranger beneath her had Damon's face. She tightened her grip, barely conscious of the pain on her back or the purplish tinge of the man she choked.

"McKenna! Let go." Hands pulled at her arms. Reality returned. Her breath coming in ragged spurts of panic, she rolled off the man and crawled away from him. She turned to see that the other man was on the floor across the room, apparently unconscious. Dylan had taken care of him. The man McKenna had almost choked to death lay wheezing several feet from her.

With silent efficiency, Dylan rolled the gasping man over and handcuffed him. Then he went to the girl and untied her.

McKenna sat frozen on the filthy floor and watched it all take place. She'd never had a flashback. For eight fucking years she'd been able to suppress that humiliating and physically painful event. And today, for some reason, the memories had returned as if it had just happened.

"You okay?"

Dylan stood several feet away. Most male LCR operatives treated her that way. Early on, they'd sensed she had a problem being physically close to anyone. And today Dylan had more reason than before to stay away from her. She'd behaved like a maniac. And an amateur.

Unable to articulate a word, McKenna managed a nod. She had known that at some point her past would catch up with her. She just hadn't expected it to happen this way. Somehow she'd always thought that Damon would find her and she'd have to take him out. Or she'd finally find her backbone and go after him. Never had she considered that a flashback would throw her for a loop. Not only had she almost killed someone in a rage, but the victim had still been in danger. While she'd been whooping up one guy, the other one could easily have killed the woman. And it would have been her fault.

She watched as Dylan spoke into a cellphone. The authorities would be here soon. Her mind told her she needed to get up and move. Her body refused to listen.

"McKenna?" Dylan said quietly. The concern in his eyes almost undid her again. He knew she'd lost it. If she hadn't been so numb with shock, she would have been mortified. She never, ever showed the real McKenna. No one was allowed to see the scared little girl behind her façade of toughness. Today Dylan had seen that and so much more.

A furious inner voice snarled: *Get off your ass!* Hands pressed on the floor for balance, McKenna got to her feet. Her legs felt like soggy pretzels. Her teeth gritted and her jaw tight, sheer determination alone made her move forward.

"The police will be here soon. You need to get going."

Another bit of information LCR knew about her, though no one ever talked about it. Being seen by the police, by any government official, was something she avoided at all cost.

She took a trembling breath, feeling the need to at least apologize. "Dylan, I'm sorry I—"

"Hell, little girl, if you're going to go all sloppy on me, I might just have to carry you out of here."

If her mouth hadn't been stiff, she'd have smiled. Dylan only called her "little girl" when he wanted to piss her off. It usually worked like a charm. Today it just made her want to sit down and cry. Damned if he'd see that, too.

"What about the other victims?"

"They're comforting each other. They'll be fine till we can get them medical attention." He shot a look at the young woman on the bed. Wrapped in a sheet, her hands covering her face, she sobbed softly. He turned back to McKenna. "I'll stay with her. You need to go."

McKenna nodded and forced her legs to move toward the door. Before walking out, she stopped and looked back at Dylan. "Tell Noah that—"

"Noah will be in touch with you for another job. This was a glitch. Got it?"

Gratitude brought unexpected tears to her eyes. She turned away before he could see. "Thank you."

Feeling as though she'd been whipped all over again, McKenna trudged through the hotel, not seeing anything but the blankness of her own thoughts. She would go back to the tiny hotel she was staying at, hole up for a few days. When she reemerged, she would be McKenna once more. No longer broken, no longer defeated. No longer a victim.

five

London

Lucas stared down at the numbers before him. When he'd taken over his family's empire, he'd had some lofty goals. Reading mind-numbing numbers sure as hell wasn't one of them. But in this case he had no choice. Someone was stealing a considerable amount of money from Kane Industries.

Five years ago, he'd assumed control of Kane Enterprises. Taking over that early hadn't been in his plan, but it had been his only option. And he had the deepest regrets that he hadn't come on board sooner. Not because he wanted to run a multibillion-dollar organization, but because it was what his father had wanted.

Phillip Kane had been a healthy, robust sixty-four-year-old. With his zest for adventure, fine food, and young women, he should have had many more years to enjoy himself.

From the time he was in diapers, Lucas had known he was expected to take over his family's business at some point. He'd never questioned if it was the right thing for him. It was what it was. Until he'd been given another choice.

His interests had always been eclectic. Sharpshooting and martial arts were two hobbies he not only enjoyed but excelled in. Never had he considered that his skills would catch the eye of anyone, especially an ultra-secretive government agency called IDC, International Deep Cover. He'd been instantly intrigued.

His father had taken some convincing, mostly because of worry for his only child. But he'd been proud, too, knowing that his son was serving the country he loved. Having his dad proud of him had meant a hell of a lot.

Lucas had taken to life as a government agent as if he were born to it. The training had been intense and grueling. Bruises, dehydration, sleep deprivation, and exhaustion were the norm and should have made him question his decision at least occasionally. Not once did he regret it. No, the job wasn't always fun, but damn, it had been challenging. He'd been a natural and would still be in the service if not for one major, heart-wrenching snag: his father had died.

He'd known all along he'd have to leave the agency eventually. His father expected it of him, and despite his love for his country and his belief in the cause, he'd been prepared to do the necessary thing for his family. Circumstances had worked differently.

He had planned to serve ten years and then would leave to work alongside his father before he took over completely. Instead, five short years later, his father was dead and Lucas had to take over leadership.

Lying beneath one of his latest bunnies, Phillip Kane had just stopped breathing. A barroom joke to many; a devastating blow to Lucas, who'd adored his father.

Like most people, Phillip Kane had both good and flawed features. Bringing home a new wife every few years, his father had confused his son. As he grew into a man, Lucas had seen the depth of loneliness in his father's eyes. He never really knew what his father was searching for. Sadly, his father didn't seem to know what he was searching for, either. Saddest part of all was that he never found it.

The first year after his father's death had been horrific.

Stocks had been plunging already, but with Phillip's sudden death and his son's unproven record, few people believed Kane Enterprises could survive. Five years later, not only had they survived, they'd doubled profits in some areas and many of the companies were now bigger than before. Kane's vast interests throughout the world had made them a household name. Lucas always tried to keep ego out of his success; however, he knew that his father would be proud of him. And that gave Lucas some measure of happiness.

Yes, he missed the day-to-day challenge of the agency. He couldn't deny that, but his loyalty to his family's empire had to come first. Kane Enterprises employed thousands throughout Europe. He might not be saving the world, but putting people to work, food in their bellies, and children through college was a worthwhile endeavor. Just because it wasn't fun didn't mean it wasn't worthwhile.

Though Kane Industries was just one part of Kane Enterprises, it was a healthy, thriving part. But now someone was stealing without having earned it. Since Lucas had taken over the reins, Kane Enterprises had become known for its charitable endeavors as much as its moneymaking ventures. By stealing from Kane Industries, this person was literally taking food out of the mouths of needy people. Lucas didn't take too kindly to that.

After seeing the ugliest as well as the most beautiful of humanity in his undercover work, Lucas's goals for Kane Enterprises were simple: take care of his employees, help the helpless, and make the world a better place for having lived in it. Idealistic? Yes. Lucas made no apologies for his beliefs. He was both hated and loved for the way he lived his life and ran his business. Opinions didn't matter. He didn't live to please people; he lived to be able to face himself in the mirror. If he had the means to help but didn't, just what kind of lowlife did that make him?

McKenna would understand that kind of philosophy. *McKenna*. Lucas raised his gaze from his desk and looked out the window. Canary Wharf was spread out below him, but all he saw was the vulnerability and beauty of the woman he couldn't forget. Where was she? How was she? He had done as she requested. He had stopped trying to find her. She knew where he was. Knew he cared for her. The rest had to be up to her.

He tried not to think about the danger she constantly put herself in. He, more than anyone, knew that one wrong decision could end her life. She was well trained and she'd chosen this life. He respected her decision and admired her. In a way, he worried more for her mental stability than he did for her life. She was hiding something deep within her. Something traumatic and life-changing. He only wished she had trusted him enough to share it.

When he'd kissed her . . . Lucas closed his eyes. As usual when he thought about that kiss, his heart raced and his body hardened. But when he'd kissed her, he'd recognized that not only was she inexperienced in the art of kissing, she was also terrified. Yes, the shaking of her slender body could have come from arousal, but the fear in her eyes was something else. She'd been afraid of him, but she was also attracted to him.

Having McKenna fear him cut deep. Someone had hurt his angel, and whoever it was, Lucas wanted to tear the bastard apart. But until she came to him, allowed him to help her, he could do nothing. He respected her too much to ask her for something she wasn't ready to give. She knew where he was . . . he just hoped she would come back to him, and soon.

With a sigh, Lucas looked back down at the glaring discrepancies in the latest quarterly reports. Knowing he had no choice, he picked up the phone. Time to call in the culprit and have him explain why he'd pilfered over a million dollars from company funds.

*   *   *

McKenna opened her eyes and blinked at the bright light streaming in from the high window across from her. Her bleary gaze took in her surroundings. Single bed, ratty chair, cheap desk, ancient television. Hotel . . . she was in a hotel in Marseille. What day was it?

She moved and then groaned at the stiffness in her limbs, the dull throbbing on her back. How long had she been out this time? From the ache in her sore muscles, it had been at least a day, if not more. Hell, it had been two years since she'd had that kind of breakdown.

With effort, McKenna got to her knees and looked around. She didn't remember much of what had happened once she got to the room. Apparently she'd collapsed as soon as she was inside. Thank God she'd at least had enough sense to close the door before she passed out.

From past experience, she knew her legs wouldn't hold her yet, so she crawled toward the bathroom. Emptying her bladder was the most important issue at the moment. When she was done, then she would think about the other stuff she had to face.

She reached the bathroom and managed to grab hold of the sink and pull herself up. Taking care of the most important matters first, she relieved the pressure on her bladder and then stripped off her clothes. A shower. She had to get clean. She could feel his hands on her, his breath on her . . . she had to scrub him off. It didn't matter that the event had occurred eight years ago. It felt recent, like it had happened only moments ago. She had to get his stench off. Now!

Stumbling to the shower, she pushed aside the curtain and stepped inside. She twisted the knob and gasped. Ice-cold water gushed over her, chilling her in an instant. She didn't back away. Not only did the shock of freezing water wake her up, but the icy crispness immediately began to cleanse something inside her. The something that had felt defiled and corroded with filth every time Damon put his hands on her.

At some point, rationality would return. This might have been her first meltdown in a while, but she used to have them all the time. She knew how to deal with them. Perseverance was key. Just like any other hell. You hung on with all your might, gritted your teeth, and survived.

Hot steaming water finally emerged. McKenna peeled the paper from the cheap hotel soap and scrubbed her body vigorously. Sharp stings from the whip marks on her back wanted to pull her into that dark abyss of memory. She forced back the graphic images that flitted into her mind. After she was clean, the memories would once again be vanquished and she would be fine again. Seeing the young girl whipped was the only reason they had returned so vividly. It was nothing more than that.

Seeking solace, McKenna pictured Lucas in her mind. And amazingly, peace came almost instantly. His beautiful smile that made her think of sunshine. Those silver-gray eyes that mesmerized and enticed. The integrity and honesty that seemed a natural part of him. And the actual caring and empathy she could see in him. All of those things and so much more were Lucas.

And his kiss. That she'd had the nerve to kiss him was one thing; the reaction she'd had was something else. Most of her actions in life were born of sheer bravado. She did what she had to do and refused to think too much about it. And that's why she'd kissed him. Bravado had put her in his arms; the incredible feelings the kiss evoked had kept her there. She had never felt like that before. She'd heard and read enough to know that other people did, but she'd never thought she could be one of them. Lucas Kane had made her feel like a sensual, sexually healthy woman.

Realizing the water was cold once again and the

soap almost gone from her rough usage, McKenna turned the water off. Shivering, her limbs weak, she grabbed the sheet-thin towel and briskly dried her body.

Her mind was back in automatic mode again as she pulled clothes from her duffel, barely noticing their wrinkles. Looking attractive or even halfway presentable had ceased to be important years ago. Dressing down not only helped her disappear into a crowd more easily, it was a rebellion against Damon. How many times had he told her he loved her femininity, her girly ways? When she'd finally escaped him, she became the complete opposite of what he admired about her. The fact that she couldn't be easily recognized had been a small but satisfying snub to the monster. Not that he couldt see the result, but looking so plain had given her spirits a boost. Besides, looking attractive to anyone wasn't something she wanted anymore.

Except for Lucas.

Lucas Kane was the first man in years to stir that kind of emotion in her. Sure, there had been men she'd found attractive. Gabe Maddox had caused a flutter of her heart every now and then, and Dylan Savage would be somewhat amused to know she'd found him attractive, too. Finding a man physically attractive was light-years away from what she felt for Lucas.

There was nothing about Lucas that she didn't find appealing. Not only his looks but his commitment to making the world a better place. It might sound trite unless you put something behind the words. Lucas did that. How could she not admire a man who had every opportunity to be a spoiled, careless playboy but chose to do something good and worthwhile with his fortune?

Dressed now, she took a deep breath, knowing she needed to face some facts. There was another man she admired, and she had let him down mightily. Noah McCall was one of the few people she trusted in this world. She pulled her cellphone from her purse. Now she needed to check to see if he still trusted her.

She had one voice mail message . . . from Noah. McKenna pressed the key to retrieve it, refusing to back away or flinch as she waited to hear McCall's hard, grim voice telling her she'd never work for him again.

Holding her breath, McKenna listened intently: "Call me."

Noah wasn't much on long messages or conversations, so she wasn't really surprised at the brevity. However, he didn't sound pissed, so that was a plus.

Speed-dialing his number, she waited, her heart a dull thud of dread.

" 'Bout damn time you called in," McCall's gruff voice answered.

"Been busy."

"You up for a job?"

Her heart leaped. Maybe she hadn't totally screwed everything up. "Yes."

"Good. Come here first." He ended the call.

This wasn't the first time he'd asked her to come to LCR headquarters before he offered her an assignment. But it was the first time he'd asked her after she'd majorly screwed up the last one. His voice sounded as though nothing had happened. No way Dylan hadn't told him. Not only would he have to file a report, something Noah required on all ops, but it would be totally unprofessional of him not to give Noah full details.

Despite the fact that she hated for Noah to know what had happened, she'd be royally pissed if Dylan hadn't told him.

No, she was sure McCall knew. Question was, what would happen when she arrived in Paris? Noah had asked if she wanted a job, but doubt kicked in again. Would she be booted out after all?

There was only one way to find out. Gathering her few belongings together, she headed out the door.

McKenna stood at the entrance to Noah's office. She told herself that life wouldn't be over if he no longer wanted her to work with LCR. After all, she had rescued a couple of people before she came across the operation that led her to working with LCR. She could do that again. But she couldn't deny that it would be a huge blow. Working ops with LCR was the first time she'd been a part of something . . . part of a team. By necessity, she was alone in all other areas of her life; this had been one area where she'd felt she belonged to something larger. Now, because of her weakness, that might be lost.

Spine straight, shoulders back, McKenna opened the office door, determined to weather whatever was to come. She stumbled to a halt when she saw who sat behind Noah's desk: Samara McCall, Noah's wife. *Oh shit.*

Samara stood and came toward her, her beautiful smile both welcoming and compassionate. "McKenna, it's good to see you."

McKenna stiffened her spine even more. Noah had played this well . . . he'd brought out the big guns. She could be belligerent and sarcastic with McCall. He'd just shoot it right back at her. She couldn't do that to Samara. Not only was Noah's wife a genuinely nice person, but McKenna felt that if her life had been different, she and Samara could have been good friends.

McKenna said somewhat stiffly, "Where's Noah?"

"He's at home with Micah." She wrinkled her nose in a humorous grimace. "There was some sort of monster truck marathon on television. Apparently it's a guy thing."

And McKenna would like nothing better than to be watching mindless television with them, instead of being in a meeting with Samara. Not because she liked big trucks, but because Samara could see through her. Noah might be able to see through her, too, but she could tell him to fuck off and he'd grin. With Samara, she couldn't wear her façade.

"Come in and sit. I just made some hot chocolate." She headed to the small kitchenette against the wall. "It's instant, but still pretty good."

McKenna slumped down in a chair across from the giant cherry desk. Dammit, she didn't want to be nice to the woman. Why couldn't it be Eden or even Shea? They were two female LCR operatives she could be a bitch with and they'd give it right back.

A mug of steaming chocolate topped with whipped cream appeared before her. McKenna took the offering, more for warmth and comfort than anything else. She didn't have to question why Samara wanted to see her. She was a former social worker and was in charge of LCR counseling. *Social worker.* Those two words caused a deep churning in her stomach. McKenna's one experience with a social worker had been hellacious. Somehow, though, she almost wished to have that bitch in front of her instead of the lovely and compassionate woman now sitting across from her.

"McKenna, relax. I'm not going to bite you."

Knowing she had no choice but to suck it up and get this over with, she said, "I'm assuming Dylan told Noah about the meltdown I had the other day. Now you're here to try to figure out just how screwed up I am."

"Dylan did tell Noah . . . you knew he'd have to. And you're not any more screwed up than any other LCR operative."

A smile attacked her lips before she knew it. Samara's straightforward way was something she'd always enjoyed. She called it like she saw it, but always in the kindest way possible.

"So what's the drill?" McKenna asked.

"We talk."

"About what?"

"Anything you like."

"And after we have our talk, do you decide whether or not I work with LCR again?"

"Good heavens, no. I have no control over whom LCR hires or fires. If I did, I'd get rid of anyone who's ever looked at my husband in the wrong way, which would be just about everyone on board." A chagrined grin. "I have a tendency to be overprotective."

Since Noah McCall was six-four and more than two hundred pounds of arrogance and cold-minded reasoning, the thought of tiny Samara being his protector should have been laughable, but it wasn't. The love shining in her aqua blue eyes said it all. Noah's wife might be small in stature, but her love and devotion to her husband were a mighty force.

"Okay, so what happens after we talk?"

"The same thing that would happen if you walked out of here right now without talking to me. Noah will ask you once again if you'd like to come on board full-time with LCR."

I will not cry. I will not cry. And she didn't. But she did look away from those compassionate, perceptive eyes and swallowed a giant lump in her throat. Noah had asked her previously if she'd like to work for LCR full-time, but that had been after a successful operation. One where she'd behaved the way she should and had actually helped. No one in his right mind could term the op she'd handled the other day as successful. Sure, the women had been rescued, but that was due to Dylan's professionalism and skill. If she'd been the only one on the op, she'd be either dead or in captivity along with the young girls she'd failed to save.

Still looking for a catch, McKenna asked, "Does being

an LCR operative mean I have to go through a psych evaluation or something? Is that why he wants me on?"

"LCR doesn't do psych evals. I talk to new recruits when they come in; I also talk to LCR operatives when they need to talk. Other than that, I don't get involved."

It couldn't be that easy. "So you're saying if I just get up and walk out of here, Noah will call me later and still tell me he wants me as an operative?"

"Yes. Want to try it?"

McKenna drew in a breath. "Then why the hell am I here with you?"

"Because you need to talk and I'm a good listener."

"And then you go tell Noah?"

Samara shook her head. The kindness in her eyes almost undid McKenna. Having people be nice to her was so damned difficult. Not only because it was rare, but because she wanted to be nice back. *Shit.*

"Noah doesn't hear anything from me. I'm here to support LCR operatives, not spy on them or rat them out to my husband."

"So anything I say to you stays with you?"

"With one caveat. If you, for instance, told me you planned to kill someone, I would have to consider telling someone else."

Testing her, McKenna leaned forward and asked softly, "And what if I told you that at some point I do plan to kill someone?"

Without blinking an eye, Samara asked, "Does he deserve it?"

"Yes."

"Why?"

"Because he killed my family."

"Why isn't he in prison?"

"He escaped."

She was surprised when a faraway look came into Samara's eyes. After several seconds, she refocused on

McKenna and said, "If it comes down to you and him, would you allow LCR to assist you?"

For some reason, Samara understood where she was coming from. How or why, McKenna didn't know. This woman didn't look like she could have a vindictive bone in her body, but she saw something in the other woman's expression that said she understood exactly how McKenna felt.

Something shifted inside McKenna. An easing, a lessening of a giant burden. "Maybe . . . I don't know."

"Can you talk about it?" Samara asked.

Could she? She hadn't spoken of that devastating day in years. And when she had, so few had believed it happened the way it did. Though she knew she had been responsible for bringing the devil into her home, what he had done was something she would have died to prevent. Would Samara be any different from the others?

How odd that twice in the last few days she was considering telling someone else her story. During that wonderfully comfortable night with Lucas, she had thought several times about sharing her deepest secrets but couldn't do it. Even the slightest flicker of disapproval in Lucas's eyes would have been devastating. Knowing his opinion meant that much to her scared the hell out of her.

Taking a plunge she never thought she'd willingly take, she asked, "What happens if I tell you?"

"Same thing that happens if you don't."

McKenna believed her. There was no hidden agenda, no subterfuge, and, most important, no judgment. And because of that, McKenna opened her mouth and began to speak of the day her world collapsed on top of her.

six

London

Lucas swung a right cut and connected to the hard jaw of his opponent. He followed with a quick full-body twist, and then side-kicked the man's broad chest. The man stumbled, stayed on his feet, and responded with a series of quick, hard jabs. Lucas blocked each one until the man backed slightly away, whirled, and kicked, aiming at Lucas's head. A second before impact, Lucas grabbed the size-twelve foot and twisted, throwing the man to the floor.

Standing over his opponent, Lucas grinned. "Getting slow in your old age."

Jared Livingston grimaced up at him. "Somebody must've pissed you off today. Last time you knocked me on my ass was the day your favorite rugby team lost the championship."

Backing up, Lucas held out a hand to his friend to help him up. "Now that day I was mad. Today I'm just frustrated."

"The blond ghost again?"

There were few things Jared didn't know about him. Learning he'd fallen for a beautiful, blond ghost had probably surprised his friend more than just about anything.

"Actually, no. I fired Humphries today. Felt like shit but had no choice."

Jared grabbed a towel and threw it at Lucas. Then, grabbing one for himself, he wiped his face and torso. "Glad you finally called him on it, since we've suspected him for a while. What made you finally do it?"

Lucas shrugged. "Last deal he brought in. Bought and sold at a different price than he reported, took the extra for his own."

"And I already know you didn't press charges."

Lucas took two water bottles from a shelf and tossed one to Jared. "Man looked miserable enough. Didn't see the need to compound it."

"You know, if all your employees start screwing you over, you won't have the companies to employ them."

"Hell, Jared, he's worked for Kane Industries for thirty-five years. The man's sixty-three years old, with four grandchildren."

"So what'd you do, give him an early pension and that's it?"

Lucas shrugged back into his shirt. Jared understood him better than just about anyone. They had served in IDC together. Though Jared was from the United States, International Deep Cover was a global agency with fifteen different countries participating. Since the goal of IDC involved preventing terrorism worldwide, borders weren't an issue for the organization.

After Jared left the service, he hadn't returned home to the States because he'd fallen in love with a young woman from England. Since he had no family in the States, he'd made England his home.

Jared had been the first person Lucas hired to work at Kane Enterprises. When you've been in the trenches with a man, saved his life and he yours, you learn a hell of a lot about his character. Jared was now Kane Enterprises' main investigator.

Slugging down the water in one long swallow, Lucas threw the empty bottle into the recycling bin. "Over his career, Humphries probably made the company a thousand times more than what he stole. He apparently got into online gambling, lost most of his savings, and didn't know how to tell his wife that the comfortable retirement they'd been planning was gone."

"So you gave it back to him?"

"I couldn't let him destroy his family."

Jared snorted and shook his head but didn't try to argue with him. When Lucas made a decision, he wasn't one to change his mind. Jared knew any argument would be pointless.

Lucas headed up the stairs, knowing his friend would follow. They practiced beating the shit out of each other four times a week. Only recently had it morphed into dinner afterward. Ordinarily when Lucas whipped up this much adrenaline, he had a woman waiting to take the edge off. Since he'd returned from his abduction, that had changed. Since Jared's wife, Lara, was an emergency room doctor in the largest hospital in London and worked nights, Lucas told himself it was a kindness to invite his friend for dinner.

A troubling thing about Jared was that he had an uncanny ability to read Lucas's mind, so he wasn't surprised when the question came. "So when are you going after her?"

Lucas nodded his thanks to Conrad, his butler, who, formal as ever, pulled out a chair at the dining table for him.

After taking a sip of his favorite cabernet, he answered, "I'm not."

Jared pulled out his own chair before Conrad could get to him, causing poor Conrad to look insulted and Jared to grin. He looked at Lucas as his words registered. "What do you mean, you don't plan to go after her?"

"Just that. Next move is hers."

He hadn't told Jared anything other than he'd seen her

again. What he and McKenna had shared was between them. But he could understand Jared's surprise. Lucas wasn't one to sit back and wait.

Ignoring the concerned look on his friend's face, Lucas dove into his meal. Just because he sounded calm and sure that McKenna had to make the next move didn't mean he liked it or was even sure she'd come to him. She was teaching him patience. If he had pressured her or continued his pursuit, she would disappear and he'd have to start looking all over again. He hadn't found her the first time; she'd come to him. And he hoped she would again. Waiting might not be comfortable, but he damn well couldn't risk spooking her and having her run from him again.

That one kiss had almost blown his head off and destroyed his plan. More than anything, he'd wanted to pull her back into his suite and show her how good they could be together. If he had, she might have stayed for a while, even let him make love to her. But he'd seen the look in her eyes. She wasn't ready for what he wanted from her. Until she was, he'd pursue her from another country.

Some people might call him either delusional or overly optimistic. Lucas knew it was sheer determination and nothing more. They had something. He recognized it; at some point, McKenna would, too. He just hoped it didn't take her too much longer to realize it.

McKenna waited for Noah to arrive. She felt emptied out, almost clean. She'd poured her guts out for an hour. Samara had listened and nodded occasionally, and never once did McKenna see judgment. Compassion hadn't been a part of McKenna's life in years. Hell, after what she'd caused, she had never felt she deserved it. But she had wanted justice, not for herself but for her family. That had been denied her.

Now Noah was due in to talk with her. She trusted

Samara not to tell him about her past. But McKenna had already made the decision to tell him herself. If she came on permanently as an LCR operative, he deserved to know her damage. She knew enough about LCR operatives to have seen that most of them were wounded in some way. Having experienced hell gave extra incentive to rescue those who were in the midst of their own.

She stood and turned when McCall came through the door. Since Samara had only left a few moments before, she doubted they'd had much of a conversation. Would he be surprised she had changed her mind? Probably not. Noah McCall saw more than most people—more than most people were comfortable with, too.

"McKenna, thanks for staying." He stalked over to the bar, took a couple of water bottles out of the fridge, handed her one, and then sat in his chair at his desk.

Dropping back into her chair, she blurted the words out before he could speak. "I screwed up the op in Marseille."

He didn't say anything for the longest time, just looked at her with those piercing black eyes. She met his gaze head-on. Taking responsibility for her actions had come at a high price. She'd once blamed everyone else for her problems. No longer. She knew exactly when she fucked up and she didn't back away.

McCall nodded. "You're right. You did. The girls could have been killed. You and Dylan, too."

"I know."

"Is it going to happen again?"

"No."

"Good. You ready to come on board as an operative?"

"You're sure you want me?"

"You've proved yourself over and over again, McKenna. I don't expect perfection from my operatives. You learn from your mistakes and you move on."

"Then yes, I'll come on board."

"Good." He stood. "Stop by and see Angela before you leave. I know we usually send your payments to an account. Let her know if you want to continue with the same arrangement."

"And that's it?"

"You got something else to say?"

She took a breath. "I'd like to tell you what I told Samara."

"You know that's not necessary, don't you?"

And that was one of the biggest reasons she was going to talk. She had trusted few people in her adult life, had trusted the wrong people as a teen. It was time to spread her wings, and that meant trusting her instincts. Noah and Samara had given her their word and their trust. She could do no less.

"I was raised in Traylor City, Nebraska. It's a little town, maybe seven thousand people then. About twenty miles outside of Omaha. My parents were part-time farmers and had a hardware store in town. I had a little sister, two years younger than me."

She took a breath. Telling it the second time was no easier than the first. "When I was sixteen, I met a good-looking guy at a movie theater. He was older, told me he was nineteen. I had only just been given permission to date, so to my parents, a nineteen-year-old was too old. I didn't know until much later that he was actually twenty-three. Anyway, they didn't approve of me dating him, told me I couldn't. I ignored them, didn't listen to them . . . thought they were too old, too backward to know what they were talking about."

Noah leaned back into his chair and watched McKenna open herself up. After seeing Samara briefly before he came in, he knew whatever McKenna had gone through was bad. He hadn't expected her to share it with him, and as she talked, he was somewhat surprised that she was. As a teenager, she'd made a horrendous mistake in judgment; she and her family had paid the highest price possible. What boiled his blood even more was the way McKenna had been treated after the fact. No wonder she trusted so few. The very people she should have been able to depend upon had betrayed her.

Dylan had told him the circumstances of the operation and how McKenna had reacted. The man hadn't liked sharing that information but knew it had to be done. Knowing his operatives' weaknesses and fears was just as important as knowing their strengths. When a victim's life is on the line, having an operative unable to function can cost lives. Noah had needed to know.

After hearing the details, he'd made a decision. McKenna needed LCR as much as LCR needed her. No employee of Last Chance Rescue was infallible and few operations went off without some kind of glitch. Noah himself had made some terrible decisions during operations. Perfection wasn't expected. Guts, determination, and the fierce desire to help others were. McKenna had those characteristics and then some.

Breath shuddered through her as she finished her heartbreaking story. She'd shed no tears, but her deathly pale face and the dark hell in her eyes told him how haunted she continued to be.

"Where's Damon Hughes now?"

"I haven't heard from him in a couple of years. After he killed my neighbor, Mrs. Winston, I left Memphis. I managed to hook up with a good counterfeiter before I left. I got a new name, new social security number . . . new everything. I changed my appearance as much as possible. Came to Paris." She shrugged. "The rest you know."

"Where did you get your training?"

A hard look crossed her face for an instant. "I was staying at a shelter in Baltimore. A couple of guys roughed me up . . . tried to rape me. I fought back, but it wasn't enough. Just before they got started, a man interrupted them. Beat both of them to a pulp, then turned on me. Yelling and screaming at me for being such a stupid idiot." Her mouth twisted. "He was right. I was stupid . . . and untrained. Having him yell at me was the right thing to do. If he'd been nice, I probably would've just melted in a puddle. Instead I got pissed."

"And he's the one who trained you?"

"Yes, he and two others. They own a private gym called Three Brothers. Two of them were former Special Forces. The other one, the one who saved me, had been in and out of jail for various things in his youth. He'd turned his life around and was the one who opened the gym."

"They did a good job. How long did you train with them?"

"For about a year. They gave me a job there. I got an apartment . . . things were going well."

"What happened?"

"Damon's people came. My friends gave them the ass-kicking of a lifetime, but I knew if I didn't get out of there, Damon would find a way to hurt them. I disappeared the next day." She shrugged. "It's best that I don't form attachments."

"Do you plan to confront him at some point?"

"Yes."

"Are you actively looking for him?"

She clenched her jaw, and he saw the fear behind the bravado she always showed. "Not yet."

She would at some point. Each person had their own timetable in facing their demons. She would decide when the time was right. Right now it was easier for her to have no life than to deliberately take another. He could understand that mentality, but at some point she would come to the end of her rope.

"If he ever finds you, will you allow us to help?"

A stubborn expression, one he'd seen too many times to count, crossed her face. Often when it came to confronting their demons, people wanted to do it on their own. He couldn't fault her for that. He understood it, too, better than most. But she needed to remember she was part of a community of people who'd been to hell and back in their own right. Not only were LCR operatives committed to rescuing victims, they were damn good at banding together to help one another.

She gave a slight nod. "If I think you can help, I'll let you know."

He would let himself be satisfied with that. If he pushed, she'd push back. He'd have to trust her to make the right decision. McKenna needed to learn to trust, and one of the best ways was for her to know that she was trusted.

Noah stood and held out his hand. "Welcome to LCR officially, McKenna."

Her hand felt delicate and small in his, and Noah had to remind himself that she might look like she was too young, too fragile, but physical appearances were often deceptive and rarely had anything to do with courage. Samara was even smaller than McKenna and was one of the gutsiest people he knew.

"Thank you for your trust, Noah. I won't let you down again."

Noah nodded and watched as, head held high, she walked out the door. After she closed the door behind her, he slumped back into his chair.

Lucas Kane had his work cut out for him. She'd given her trust to LCR, but giving her trust to another man would be even more difficult for her. A smile played at his lips. Actually, Kane might be the one man who was up to the challenge.

But there was still the worry of this Damon character.

No. h could only hope she'd give LCR an opportunity to help when the time came. The man was well past insane. From the sound of it, once he found McKenna again, he'd never let her go, not even if he had to kill her to keep her.

Palm Beach

The call woke him from a restless sleep. Since learning McKenna might have been found, he hadn't been able to rest well or concentrate. His business would soon suffer. Since there were few people he trusted, he was a hands-on businessman. People were less likely to screw you over when they knew they were being watched. In his early days, he'd had to eliminate some of his people to show them how things were to be done. It'd been years since he'd had to kill anyone for business reasons, but his people knew he would have no qualms if it became necessary. Keeping your employees on their toes and scared as hell had gotten him where he was. He couldn't slack off.

But McKenna was more important to him than any business venture. He had the wealth, but he needed the woman to share it with him. The only woman who mattered.

The phone rang again. Groggy and pissed, he kicked the woman beside him. "Get out."

She mumbled but didn't move. He grabbed the phone and barked, "What?"

"Sir, I have more news."

"Hold on." Damon rolled over. Inches from the woman's face, he shouted, "Get the fuck out of my bed!"

Sleep disappeared from her face as her eyes went wide with fear. She slipped from the bed and slunk out of the room. *Stupid bitch*. He'd get rid of her tomorrow.

He put the phone back to his ear. "Talk."

"It's her. She fits the description perfectly."

"Tell me about her."

"As I told you, she goes by the name Jamie Kendrick. The photograph you gave us from her high school portrait is almost identical. No one really seems to know much about her or where she came from."

"You've talked to people who know her?"

"Just in passing. Not enough to cause suspicion."

"I would be quite upset if she found out and disappeared again."

There was a long pause and then the man said, "Yes sir. I realize that."

"Has she seen you at all?"

"No."

"Does she have any friends?"

"Not that we've seen."

Good; perhaps she had learned her lesson. However, he was tired of waiting. He'd given her time and she had gone off and made a new life for herself. A life without him? Totally unacceptable. It was time for her to come home. Time for her to become what she was meant to be. *His.*

"Bring her here."

Damon hung up the phone. Anticipation stirred in his body. He wouldn't force her this time . . . not at first. He would woo her, as he had when they first started dating. She would get to know him again. See how much he still loved her. He had fallen in love with her when she was sixteen and had never stopped. She had been young, fresh, innocent. So malleable. And then she'd started listening to her parents. That had been her mistake.

Their relationship had never been as peaceful as he had hoped it would be. Time and again she had defied him. She thought he enjoyed punishing her. Had even screamed that terrible accusation at him. Those words had hurt and infuriated him. Enjoy causing her pain? He'd almost cried that day. How could she accuse him of that? Everything he had done, he had done for her so they could be together. And had she ever appreciated it? Not once had she thanked him. Not once had she told him she understood. Instead she had tried to escape in the most heinous way possible. And when that hadn't worked, she had done something even worse. She had betrayed him.

The more he thought about her constant betrayals, the angrier he became. He had to stop thinking about them. Reliving the past would get him nowhere. Once she was home, everything would be forgotten. They would start all over again.

She would accept her new life and everything he wanted to give her. He would forgive her and she would be his again. And if she said no again? Then there would be the need for more lessons . . . perhaps harsher ones. This time it would take; this time it would be permanent.

seven

London

She stood on the other side of the street, across from the gate to his estate. She told herself she was crazy for being here. Just because they'd talked for hours one night and shared that one amazing kiss didn't mean there should be anything more than that. She was now officially an LCR operative. Any other time Noah had asked for her help, she'd had the option of turning him down . . . not that she ever had. But as a full-fledged operative, she was on call 24/7.

Most likely Lucas had wanted her to know his address as a courtesy. She'd rescued him from Victor; he felt that he owed her. The kiss? Well, admittedly it had been wonderful, and yes, she'd felt his arousal, but reading more into it than that could only create problems. Besides, she'd thrown herself into his arms. What was he supposed to do? Lucas was a normal man with a healthy sexual appetite. He wouldn't want a woman who was neither normal nor healthy when it came to sex. Damon had made sure she was too damaged for anyone else.

She should go back to Paris, wait for a job. But she didn't want to. She wanted to see him. Stupid? Absolutely. Damon had no idea where she was. But thinking he'd stopped looking for her would be foolish and dangerous. And if he did ever find her, he'd make sure that whoever she cared about was hurt.

She had learned a lesson with Mrs. Winston in Memphis. McKenna had ignored everyone in the apartment complex, wanting to make sure she caused no one problems. Mrs. Winston had been an elderly widow. One day McKenna had come home to find the woman struggling to carry in groceries and McKenna had carried them up for her. As a thank-you, the elderly lady had baked her some cookies and brought them to McKenna's apartment. That was it. She hadn't invited the woman into her apartment. She'd accepted the gift and said thank you. Just as she was about to close the door, she'd caught sight of Mrs. Winston's crestfallen expression. The elderly lady had looked so eager to please and so lonely . . . a loneliness McKenna recognized in herself. In a reckless moment she would forever regret, she had hugged the old lady for her kindness. Then she had closed the door. That was it—that's all she had done.

The next day Mrs. Winston was dead. The police and medical examiner had ruled that she'd slipped on the stairs, fallen, and broken her neck. The woman's death had saddened her; she'd been a nice old lady.

Never had she suspected anything else. Then the letter came.

Damon had made sure she knew who was responsible. He'd written out a full confession. Admitting to the deed, but blaming her, of course. McKenna hadn't bothered going to the police. What was the point? Damon Hughes was supposed to be dead. Accusing a dead man of a murder would be a sure way to get herself locked up.

Besides, they hadn't believed her years ago when she'd had physical proof of Damon's evil; why would they believe her now? The bruises and scars from months of abuse hadn't elicited anything from them other than disgust and contempt. A few had looked at her like she'd put them there herself, or at the very least like she deserved what she got. How could she argue with that reasoning? In many ways, she *had* deserved them.

Wrapping her arms around herself, McKenna turned away. No, she couldn't face Lucas. There was nothing she could give him. She would go back to Paris and wait for a job.

"Don't go."

Lucas! She whirled around. He stood on the other side of the street, in front of his home.

"How did you know I was here?"

"I looked out the window."

It shouldn't have been that easy. Had she stood here subconsciously, hoping he would see her? That he would take the choice out of her hands? She sure hadn't tried to hide. Was she setting herself up for a major heartache? One she would never recover from? Having her heart broken didn't concern her. Having Damon find out about her fascination for Lucas frightened her more than anything she'd known since she'd lost her family. If he hurt Lucas, she wouldn't survive it.

"I don't know why I'm here," she confessed.

"You don't have to have a reason to see a friend."

Her heart melted. *Friend.* It had been so long since she'd had one. "I can't stay long."

He held out his hand. "Stay as long as you can."

Without consciously telling her body to move, she crossed the street. It was as if he summoned her with just one lift of his hand. Not in command, but in welcome.

When she reached him, she stood and let her eyes roam over his face. It had been two weeks since she'd seen him. Somehow she thought he looked older, tired.

"It's good to see you again."

Silver-gray eyes gleamed as he pushed a strand of hair behind her ear. "And you."

"Are you well?" she asked.

His smile, more glorious than any sunrise, brightened his face and with it her soul. "I am now."

Her heart pounding with a multitude of emotions, McKenna took his hand. "I am, too."

Palm Beach

His heart pounding in his chest, Damon looked down at the unconscious woman lying in the trunk of the car. So long . . . it had been so long since he'd seen her, touched her. He wasn't surprised to see his hand trembling as he gently pushed aside the silky, golden brown hair covering her delicate face. She looked different, yet the same. A bit older, but still so innocently sweet.

"Did she give you much trouble?"

The large man beside him grunted. "Not much. She was doing laundry in her basement, middle of the night. We got her, took her clothes and personal stuff from her apartment. Made it look like she left town."

"Good." He leaned down again, caressed her neck, his fingers trailing over her firm breast. Anticipation and arousal zinged through him. "Has she woken yet?"

"A couple of times." He shrugged his massive shoulders. "Last time she woke, we injected her with that stuff we got from that doctor you told us to contact. Worked great. Knocked her out, fast as lightning."

"Did she say anything?"

"She tried. Figured it was best to keep the tape over her mouth until we got her to you."

"Did you touch her?" He asked the question mildly, but it was the most important question of all. And the man knew exactly what he meant.

"Of course not. Only to subdue her. She's yours. I know she's not one you'd share."

He was right about that. Damon was known to be a

generous employer. Other women he'd shared, given away, sold at below market value. He wasn't in the human trafficking business, but when he had some tasty merchandise he knew his friends and employees might enjoy, he'd always been generously accommodating.

But not McKenna. She was his. Had been his from the moment he saw her. Anybody who got in his way, who tried to take her from him or dared to touch her, would experience an instant and painful death.

No longer able to wait, Damon scooped her into his arms and lifted her from the trunk. He looked at the man beside him. He owed him a debt of gratitude. Money was a no-brainer, but Carlos had been wanting something else. Though he had never asked for it, Damon had seen the fire in his eyes.

"The guesthouse is yours for the night. As is Lilly."

A wide grin covered the man's big face. "The whole night?"

Damon nodded. "Yours to do with as you please, my friend. Enjoy. You've earned it."

Carlos needed no more information. He turned and started down the path to the small guesthouse on the other side of the estate. His giant body moved faster than Damon had ever seen it move. The man was so eager, he wondered if Lilly would even survive the first hour.

Lilly had been a tasty treat he'd planned to enjoy a few more months before he offered her to a friend in Spain. Delicate and lovely, she had been a little something he'd purchased at a bargain price the last time he was in Mexico; she had provided him with hours of immense pleasure. But he'd seen Carlos eyeing her more than once. Now she was his for a short period.

Damon turned away from watching the eager man head for his reward. If Lilly made it through the night, he knew of an older couple who'd been seeking a companion such as her. Perhaps he would offer her to them.

Business decisions could wait. What he held in his arms couldn't. He'd waited too long already. Tightening his arms around his prize, Damon carried her into his house. He had so much time to make up for; he couldn't wait to get started.

London

Lucas hadn't taken her inside his home yet. Stupid, but he felt if he pushed her, she'd try to run. How the hell had he come to this state? He'd killed more than his share of evil men, helped bring down insane dictators, prevented terrorist attacks, and once went through a weeklong bravery test in a culture few people knew existed. And yet never once had he felt the fear that he did when faced with this one small woman.

"Your grounds are beautiful. How many acres?"

Gazing around the estate that had been in his family for seven generations, he tried to see it through her eyes. It was nice, but he took it for granted. Gently rolling hills, meandering brooks and bubbling springs, large expanses of woods, and two giant lakes. His father had loved the untamed, less manicured look, and Lucas had wanted to maintain it the way his father would have wanted. To Lucas, though, this was a place where he entertained friends and had sometimes played football on Sundays. "I think it's about five hundred acres, give or take a few."

"Wow." She shot him a small smile. "Bet it takes you days to cut the grass."

He grinned. "Yes, but I have a riding mower, so it doesn't take so long."

She wrapped her arms around her body and gave him another tight smile. "I'm nervous."

"Would it help if I told you I am, too?"

Cocking her head slightly, she squinted into the sun to look up at him. Lucas moved so that the sun wasn't in her eyes. "Better?"

"Yes, thanks . . . but why are you nervous?"

"Because I'm afraid if I say the wrong thing you'll leave."

She looked up at him for several long seconds, and Lucas was beginning to think that had been the wrong thing to say after all. Finally, with one of the most vulnerable expressions he'd ever seen on her face, she whispered, "I shouldn't have come."

"Why did you?"

"I don't know."

"If I invite you in, will that make you more nervous?"

She gave a small little laugh. "I don't know that I can get any more nervous, so I guess the answer is no."

"So you'll come in?"

"Yes . . . for a little while."

Holding out his hand again, Lucas led her down a brick sidewalk to the back patio of his home. So odd to be holding her hand again. He'd never been a hand holder, had actually thought it a somewhat odd custom. Now, with the feel of her delicate hand in his, it conveyed something. Trust, friendship . . . a need to be close.

He opened the back door and pulled her inside. She stopped abruptly and looked around.

"Oh . . . wow."

Again, Lucas tried to see through her eyes. One of three living rooms in the house, it held four sofas, several chairs, two tables, and a grand piano. Expensive Persian rugs covered the hardwood floors; bright chandeliers hung with regal splendor from the sixteen-foot ceilings. To him it was a room he went through to get to the side patio. He rarely came into the room for any other reason.

"Mr. Lucas, do you or your guest need anything?"

Lucas swallowed a chuckle. *Conrad.* No matter where the man was in the house, he somehow always knew what was going on.

"McKenna, I'd like for you to meet Conrad. He's been with my family for years."

McKenna stuck her hand out. "Nice to meet you, sir."

Conrad didn't blink an eye as he shook McKenna's hand and returned the greeting. He looked at Lucas again, and though the man's stoic expression was often impossible to read, Lucas saw a spark of approval in his eyes.

"Think the kitchen can put together a tea for us?" Lucas asked. "Perhaps in the north parlor."

"I'm sure we can arrange that." With another nod to McKenna, Conrad walked in his usual silent way out of the room.

Thinking to use McKenna's healthy appetite to his advantage, he'd ordered the tea before he asked her. But since politeness was written in the DNA of his family, he asked, "Are you hungry?"

And as before, she couldn't give a verbal answer before her stomach growled. "Seems like you're always feeding me."

Telling her that watching her eat turned him on might be the truthful response, but damned if he'd say anything to scare her off. He could barely believe she was here. It was a challenge to avoid any verbal trip wires. If nothing else, this woman definitely kept him on his toes.

"Let's go to the parlor and get comfortable."

Her heart pounding with a dozen different emotions, McKenna followed Lucas as he entered a giant marble foyer; she swallowed another gasp. The house she grew up in would have fit in the foyer, with room to spare.

Gawking was rude and she tried her best not to do it, but Lucas's home made her realize just how out of reach he was. Their differences probably should have made her feel awkward, and in a way they did. But she also felt relief. Lucas wouldn't be interested in someone like her. Humble background notwithstanding, their worlds were on different spheres, which made him even safer. She would stay for a quick visit and then be gone. He need never know that her heart was thumping so loudly in her chest, she feared he would hear it. Or that in the deepest recesses of her mind, the only place she allowed unrealistic fantasies to exist, he was the man of her dreams.

Lucas led her into a small, cozy room with a sofa, two chairs, a table, and a roaring fire. She could imagine him coming in here after a long day at the office, putting his feet up, sipping a brandy, and staring into the fire. Her imagination went further than it should have when she pictured herself sitting in a chair beside him, holding his hand and gazing at the fire, too.

Such a stupid dreamer, McKenna.

"Have a seat."

Lucas's voice jerked her out of her idiotic fantasy. She dropped into the closest chair. Nerves were attacking her limbs, and she needed to get control of herself before she either ran from the room or kissed him again.

"Are you here on a job?"

She shrugged. "Not really. Just had some free time on my hands."

"I'm glad you came."

"Me too." She didn't add that she hoped she didn't regret it.

The silence that followed should have been awkward but it wasn't. There was peace in being here—a dangerous peace, because she couldn't stay. The longer she was here, the longer she would want to stay. She would enjoy the meal with him and then leave.

A distant sound drew her attention. She looked up to see Conrad open the door and push in a tea trolley laden with enough food for a half dozen people. Apparently Lucas had somehow shared the information that she had the appetite of a teenage boy.

"Thanks, Conrad," Lucas said with a smile. "I'll take it from here."

"Very good, sir." He went through the door, closing it behind him and leaving Lucas and McKenna alone again.

A delightful fragrance wafted through the air and her stomach growled in welcome.

Lucas smiled and said, "Let's eat."

Oh man, this was a full-fledged meal and looked delicious. McKenna had never been shy about food before and she wasn't about to start now. She dove in, prepared to enjoy every bite.

Lucas couldn't eat. Hard as hell to eat when one was as hard as hell. McKenna ate with the same gusto as she had before. And once again it turned him on.

She looked up at him, gray-blue eyes wide and guileless as a doe's. "Aren't you hungry?"

Oh, the answer he would love to give her, but she would run and he'd do just about anything to keep that from happening. So he shook his head and said, "Had a large lunch."

With a small grin, she looked only slightly embarrassed as she said, "I did, too."

He smothered a laugh; he loved her honesty. Hoping she wouldn't mind talking while she ate, he asked something that had been on his mind since they first met. "When we were together in Paris, you said you'd worked undercover before and helped some people escape from Victor. How did you get in with Victor in the first place?"

She swallowed a bite of turkey and answered, "Coincidence, mostly. I saw him carry an unconscious man into a house. That was odd enough; I knew something was up. So I followed him around for a few days. Talked to him in a bar he liked to hang out at . . . got to know him. Victor was careless about stuff like that. He hired local people and didn't check them out thoroughly. I lucked out when he asked me to work for him without needing to know me better."

"How many jobs did you do with him?"

"Four or five."

"And those you helped escape . . . he never caught on?"

Her eyes took on that faraway expression, and Lucas suddenly realized how she'd kept Victor from catching on. "You slept with him." The words came out before he could stop them.

She got to her feet. "I think I'd better go. It's getting late."

"McKenna . . ." Hell, what could he say? The fact that she'd had to lie under the sweaty, barbaric body of Victor Lymes sickened him to the point of nausea. But to know she'd done something like that to save a life? Hell, there was courage and then there was courage. McKenna's kind of courage wasn't black and white, nor was it pretty. She had done things she wasn't proud of and hadn't wanted to do. But she'd done those things to save lives.

"Thanks for the tea . . . I'll—"

He caught her by the upper arm before she could turn away. "No. You're not running away when things get uncomfortable."

Whirling, she shot her fist toward his face. He caught it with his hand and brought it to his mouth.

She looked stunned. He didn't know if it was for the kiss or the fact that he could move faster than she could.

"I can't believe I almost hit you."

Ah, another reason. She was surprised at her anger toward him. "Anger and passion have much in common."

Turning away again, she avoided his gaze and said, "So you don't think I'm a slut for sleeping with Victor?"

Suddenly angry himself, Lucas pulled her around to face him. "Do not put that word and your name together . . . ever. I think you're incredibly brave."

"I'm scared most of the time."

"That just means you're smart. Being scared keeps you alive."

"Were you scared when Victor kidnapped you?"

"I think I was too furious to be frightened. I'm sure if you had been the crazed lunatic you pretended to be and managed to cut off my fingers, I would've changed my attitude."

Instead of smiling at his teasing words, she whispered, "You need to be careful. There are more people like Victor out there than you might think."

Hoping he wasn't making a mistake, Lucas drew her into his arms. She didn't resist as he had feared. Instead she leaned her head on his shoulder as if it belonged there.

"I promise to be careful, but will you promise me something in return?"

She tilted her head to look up at him. "What?"

"You'll be careful, too?"

"Always."

"Good."

He leaned down and pressed a soft kiss to her mouth. Her gasping sigh was captured and treasured as he slowly and carefully showed her what she was coming to mean to him. She moved more fully into his arms, her fingers weaving into his hair as she pressed deeper into the kiss. His body demanded that he take things further; his conscience and brain told him something different. If he pushed, she would run. He couldn't take the chance.

With a regret-filled sigh, Lucas lifted his head from her sweet lips. Her eyes had been closed. She opened them and, just for an instant, he saw what he longed to see. McKenna was beginning to feel the same things. Damned if he'd scare her away.

"Want to take a walk?" he asked.

"Yes."

"Good. Then we'll watch a movie in the theater room. I have a popcorn popper I've never even tried out."

Not giving her time to answer, Lucas took her hand and pulled her with him. If she had time to think, she would leave. He knew she would at some point, but he wanted to delay the inevitable as long as possible. There was no trickery involved in trying to keep her. She could say she was leaving and he wouldn't try to stop her. But he was beginning to see that McKenna's need was almost as strong as his own. There was something between them, but he knew damn well she would deny it. Until the day came that she accepted and acknowledged that, he would do his best to create a sense of safety for her. If she felt she could come to him at any time, chances were that at some point she would begin to trust him with everything.

And when that day came, he would get her to tell him what she was so terrified of, and he would do everything within his power to eliminate the threat.

eight

Palm Beach

Terror and fury gleamed in her eyes as she stared up at him. Tears poured down her face, and his heart ached for her. If her hands weren't tied to her chair, Damon knew, she would be clutching her throat. That always seemed to be the first place people touched when given the drug.

Damon pulled up a chair to sit across from her. "Don't be afraid that you can't speak. While you were sleeping, I gave you an injection. Your vocal cords have been disabled for a few hours. I have several business associates in the medical profession. One of them supplied me with the drug. Quite a breakthrough, really, since it doesn't impair breathing. Though it is quite expensive." He gently caressed her arm. "But when it comes to you, I spared no expense." When tears continued to well in her eyes, he said, "Don't worry, baby, it's not permanent."

And just like most people, she opened her mouth to speak anyway. When no sound emerged, she sobbed silently and the tears fell harder.

"Now, darling McKenna, I know you have things you want to say to me, but I felt it necessary to get a few of the most important things out of the way first. You have the ability to nod your head to tell me you understand."

More anger emerged through her tears. He had expected that. His McKenna was a fighter. One of the reasons he loved her was the incredible spirit she had within her. But that spirit needed to be contained, then shaped and molded. Otherwise their relationship would not succeed. Damon had worked too hard, waited too long, to fail. This time she would succumb, become what he needed her to be. It would just take some time.

"Acknowledge what I told you with a nod, McKenna."

A mutinous expression, and then she glared at him.

Rising to his feet, he got in her face, leaned his forehead against hers, and shouted, "Nod your damn head!"

Her head jerked with a quick nod, and Damon felt as if he'd won a small victory. Taking a breath, he seated himself again and said in a more even tone, "I don't want cross words between us. When I say something, I want you to acknowledge your understanding with a nod. If there's something you don't understand, then shake your head and I'll explain further." He raised a brow. "Understand?"

She nodded again. He was pleased to see that fear had replaced the earlier anger. Once she was trained, he wouldn't have to use harsh words with her. With a touch or a mere look or gesture, she would be able to understand and do what he asked. Until that happened, he would use a firm but controlled hand.

"Good. Now, this wasn't the way I envisioned our reunion, but you really gave me no choice."

She continued to stare at him with those accusing, terror-filled eyes. The fear was good; it would help her focus. The accusation would fade once she accepted the way things would be.

Her gaze moved from him to roam around the room. He waited to see the recognition, the happiness. When her eyes looked back at him, he saw nothing but anger.

What the fuck was wrong with her? "Don't you recognize the room?"

She stared at him for several seconds, then shook her head.

He tamped down his temper; his McKenna was sometimes dense about certain things. "The room is identical to your room when you were a teenager. Remember? When we first met?" When she just stared at him, he sighed with frustration. "On Sundays, when you and your family went to church, I would sneak in and sit in your room for hours. I remembered every detail of your room and replicated it perfectly."

Tears fell from her eyes again. Damon ignored her for the time being. There would be plenty of opportunity later to discipline her if she continued to be stubborn. For now, he needed to say what he'd been planning for years to tell her.

He stood and began pacing around the room as he recited all the things he had done for her. "I created an empire for you, amassed a fortune. Built this mansion with you in mind. The swimming pool, too." He turned around suddenly to see that she was once again shaking her head. "Dammit, stop that. All of the things I've done for you, and yet I still see no appreciation."

Damon drew another breath and started again. "I know we've had our differences. Our time together, after your parents' death, wasn't what I wanted it to be. You were rebellious and I was angry. You deeply disappointed me and I had no choice but to punish you until you complied. But the way you handled things, McKenna . . ." He shook his head. "That was so very wrong. And then your betrayal . . . if not for the friendships I made, I would still be in prison."

Damon closed his eyes as he felt the anger try to reemerge. No, all of that was in the past. He needed to forget about how much she had hurt him. "I know you were angry with me. You didn't approve of the way I handled the situation with your parents. But they were trying to keep us apart, McKenna. You broke up with me because of them. I couldn't allow that. Don't you understand? I couldn't let you go, baby. From the moment we met, I knew we were meant to be together."

He sat down across from her again. "I was angry and let my temper get the best of me. I should have sent you out of the house before I took care of them." He smiled. "See, I'm not too proud to admit my mistakes." Leaning forward, he caught her gaze. "But you need to understand that it wasn't all just me. There were so many things you did, too."

Tears filled his eyes as he remembered the things she'd done to hurt him. "You tried to leave me in the cruelest way possible. And then, when that didn't work, you betrayed me." He wiped at his face, a little embarrassed that he'd let her see his weakness. A strong man did not cry, even when those he loved tried to destroy that love.

"But I've forgiven you, McKenna, for all of those things, and I'm ready to move forward. All of that is in the past, where it belongs. You're here to stay. And we'll be happy. I'll make sure we're happy this time.

"When we were together before, I realize my punishments were painful, but I only did it to help you understand how much I love you. I had no choice but to teach you a lesson. That's what love is . . . punishment and then forgiveness. You understand that, don't you?"

She closed her eyes and tears slipped through her closed lids. He knew she was probably exhausted. He would let her rest soon. "Look at me when I'm speaking, McKenna."

In an instant, her eyes flew open.

Her immediate obedience pleased him immensely. "Good girl. I want you to be happy. Everything I do . . . it's all for you, baby. Now, nod your head like the good girl you know how to be and I'll get you some water and food and allow you to rest."

She nodded frantically.

Damon smiled his approval. Yes, she was coming around very quickly now. To show her how considerate he could be when she obeyed him, he explained, "I know it's been a while since we've seen each other and you might be feeling a bit shy, so my housekeeper is going to help you freshen up. I must warn you, though, Margret has a black belt in karate and has my full permission to restrain you by force. Whatever bruises she's forced to give you, I'll have to add to them. Do you understand?"

When she nodded again, he smiled his pleasure. Things were going splendidly. "Tomorrow we'll start rebuilding our relationship."

Pressing a kiss to the top of her silky head, he walked out the door. Margret stood in the hallway, ready to take care of his woman. She had been his loyal servant for years and was totally devoted to him and his happiness. She would make sure McKenna had everything she needed and would ensure she wouldn't leave.

Tomorrow he would show McKenna around his estate and share the most exciting news of all. What woman wouldn't be thrilled to know that in a few days from now, she would have her dream wedding?

London

"It's getting late. I need to go." The words sounded much more sure than what she felt. She didn't want to leave. It had been the best day of her life, without exception. Lucas had showed her around the grounds, then she'd sat with him in a darkened theater room, held his hand, and watched an old Cary Grant movie she'd never seen. They'd eaten buttered popcorn and drunk icy sodas; McKenna felt as if she were on a real date. After the movie, dinner had been served in a room overlooking a lake. Moonlight had turned the water into a shimmering lake of diamonds, and McKenna knew she would return to this night in her memories for years.

Lucas had done nothing other than allow her a day without pressure. She hadn't once wondered if Damon would be waiting for her behind a door to pounce on her. She hadn't felt this safe in forever.

"I have several bedrooms. You can take your pick."

She shook her head. The temptation was too great. And it was one she absolutely couldn't indulge. If she stayed one night, she'd want to stay the next and then the next. Years ago, she'd sworn never to be on more than a first-name basis with anyone. They had gone eons beyond first names. If Damon knew about Lucas, he would kill him.

"Tell me what you're thinking."

The question made her smile. If he had voiced those words hours ago, she probably would have left immediately. Now the question seemed as natural as his smile. There was no pressure to tell him anything. And that made her want to tell him all the more. Another reason she had to leave.

Standing, she pulled the strap of her purse higher on her shoulder. "I can't stay. Thank you for a lovely day."

He stood and held out his hand. She took it and allowed him to draw her closer. "Will you come back?"

Knowing the answer should be no, she said what she shouldn't: "If you like."

Pulling her against him, his breath soft against her lips, he whispered, "I'd like very much." And then his mouth was on hers.

McKenna leaned into him, wrapped her arms around

his neck, and allowed herself forgetfulness for several magical seconds. Only this man had the ability to make her forget who she was, what she had done, and why a future was impossible.

Heat washed over her. She moaned beneath the delicious, masculine mouth eating at her lips. Desire and need were rare enough, but she recognized them. What she could barely comprehend was the level of trust she felt with Lucas. The arms that wrapped around her felt wonderful . . . strong and exciting yet safe. There was nothing she wanted more than to lie down with him. The rigid erection pressing against her stomach should have terrified her. Instead, she wanted to touch him, taste him, and feel that hard length inside her. Arousal shuddered through her; with that thought, she knew she had to pull away.

Leaning her forehead against his chest, McKenna tried to slow her heavy breathing and thundering heart. She could feel Lucas's heart pounding just as hard. He wanted her . . . she wanted him. How easy it would be to just let go. Indulge herself. And how much more difficult that would make it when she said goodbye for good.

"I have to go."

"Stay, McKenna."

The husky thickness in his voice almost melted her resistance. She imagined how he would sound as he made love to her, how that beautiful, crisp accent would sound in her ear as he moved over her, inside her. A hot flush of heat spread throughout her body. Nipples peaking and desire pooling between her legs, McKenna jerked away. "I can't."

His grip on her arms tightened for barely a second, then he let her go completely. McKenna almost whimpered at the loss of his warmth, the magnificent feeling of his body pressed against her.

"Go, McKenna, before I try to convince you to stay."

The frustrated anger in his voice grounded her. Leaving him was difficult for her; why would she think it was less so for him? Lucas had gone out of his way to show her she meant something to him. He had been kind and considerate. And she'd done nothing but take advantage of his wonderful hospitality.

That thought stiffened her spine. Typical, selfish McKenna.

Refusing to back away from the anger she was sure to see in his expression, she looked up at him. "Thank you for a wonderful day."

"And I was about to say the same thing to you."

The husky want was still in his voice, but his expression held nothing but amusement and tenderness. And there wasn't a hint of anger.

"I don't want to use you." The words burst from her mouth before she could stop them.

He cocked his head. "Use me . . . how?"

Ignoring the nausea in her gut, she refused to back away from the truth. He had to know where she stood. "There can never be anything permanent between us." She cringed at those words. They sounded so egotistical, and she hadn't meant them that way at all.

"Friends don't use each other, McKenna. They lean on each other. Support each other. And they're always there for each other. That's not using."

McKenna's heart melted. For so many years, she'd felt so alone. Now Lucas was telling her that not only did he understand her, but he was also her friend.

"And you can lean on me, too, right?" she asked.

"I'm counting on it." He pressed a tender kiss to her lips, her nose, and then her forehead. "Go, sweetheart. Come back when you can."

Before she could change her mind and ask him if she

could stay forever, McKenna took one last look at his face and then ran out the door.

Lucas waited until he heard the front door slam before he picked up the phone. The nice thing about having a private investigator on sole retainer was that day or night, he was on call.

"I have her fingerprints and some information. Can you be here in an hour?"

"Yes." The male voice sounded groggy, but Lucas knew when the man arrived, he'd be alert and ready to do what needed to be done.

Lucas dropped into the chair and stared at the fire. A part of him knew and accepted the betrayal she would feel; the other part didn't give a damn. This woman stirred more in him with one small look or soft sigh than any woman he'd ever met.

If he hadn't known for damn sure that she felt something just as strong, he might have considered not doing what he was about to do, but he doubted it. The fact that there were very intense feelings drawing them together was one reason, but not the only one. This woman was terrified of something or someone. She was in hiding, and whether she wanted to admit it or not, she was vulnerable. He intended not only to find out what or whom she was afraid of, but to remove the threat from her.

He hadn't asked her because not only wouldn't she have told him, she would have been on the run again. Lucas wouldn't stop her from running, but he could damn well find out what or whom she was running from. Did she fear the law? Something told him she did, but not because she'd done anything illegal. He sensed a lack of trust more than anything else. Besides, Noah McCall might bend the rules frequently, but LCR didn't get involved in illegal activities. And McCall wouldn't be associated with someone who did.

The day had been full of delightful surprises and a frustrating lack of information. For every step he had taken to get to know her, she'd retreated two steps back. In anyone else, he might have suspected coyness, but McKenna was totally lacking in that area. She was straightforward, direct, and as evasive as hell.

Hearing a noise, Lucas turned. Conrad stood at the door. Standing beside him was Myron Phelps, the Kane family private investigator. The man had gotten here faster than Lucas had expected.

Getting to his feet, he held out his hand in welcome to Myron and then turned to Conrad. "Go on to bed. I'll see our guest out when he leaves."

His face stoic as ever, Conrad nodded and turned away. But before he did, Lucas saw something in his eyes he'd never seen before: disapproval. Conrad knew why Myron was here and he didn't like it. Lucas felt a twinge but ignored it. He was doing this for McKenna, not for himself. Conrad didn't understand that yet. When this was over, he'd explain it to him. And to McKenna. Somehow he got the feeling that Conrad would be much more understanding.

Determined to go forward, no matter what, he turned to Myron and began explaining exactly what he wanted him to do.

nine

Palm Beach

Damon unlocked the bedroom door and eased it open. The enticing scene of his woman lying on the bed he'd bought for her, sleeping in the nightgown he'd chosen for her, brought fresh tears to his eyes. How long had he dreamed of this day?

Treading softly, he went to the bed and pressed a kiss to her forehead. "Wake up, my love. It's time to start our new life together."

She blinked sleepily and then her eyes opened wide. Making an odd little sound in her throat, she shrank away from him as if terrified.

"Dammit, McKenna. I thought we were over that." A healthy fear was good, it would keep her in line, but she acted as if he was going to kill her or something.

Damon took a breath to control the mass of conflicting emotions McKenna always created in him. All he had ever wanted to do was love her, and when she didn't appreciate what he had done for her, hurt and anger blended into a mass of volcanic emotions he had difficulty controlling.

Drawing a breath, he reminded himself that she had been here just one day. He had rushed her before, gone a bit overboard in his discipline. It would take her some time to adjust. There was romance to be had, and they had all the time in the world.

He stepped back several feet. "I want you to join me for breakfast. There's a blue and white dress in the closet . . . it has little flowers on it. Put it on and come down."

Would she remember it was identical to the dress she'd been wearing when they first met? Would she appreciate the time and effort it had taken to replicate every single thing, down to the very clothes she wore? He had re-created it all just the way it was before their difficulties had begun. And he'd done it all just for her.

When she merely looked at him with those accusing eyes again, Damon huffed a frustrated sigh and walked out the door. Impatience, especially with McKenna, had always been his downfall. That's what happened when you loved someone more than they loved you. Expecting her to fall in with his plans was unrealistic. In time, McKenna would see what he had done for her, what he would do for her. And then all would be well.

Margret stood in the hallway, waiting for him. "Louise Stenzel, the wedding planner, is here, sir."

A burst of optimism shot through him. Soon McKenna would be wholly and legally his. Then she could never leave him, never deny him.

"Have her meet me in my office. I want to go over a few details with her before McKenna comes down. Have breakfast ready for us at the pool in half an hour. Give McKenna ten minutes to dress and then bring her down to me."

Margret nodded, her face expressionless as always. When they'd first met, he had wondered if Margret had any emotions in her at all. But the longer they were associated, the more he realized that he and Margret had much in common. They loved fiercely. He loved McKenna and would do anything to have her. Margret loved Damon. And because of that love, she would do anything to see that he was happy. He had never asked her to kill for him, but he knew that she would.

Funny, he was almost tempted to ask her to kill someone, just to see her reaction. It would be an interesting experiment to see how she would carry out the deed. Shrugging off the odd but intriguing idea, he headed downstairs to see the wedding planner. He couldn't wait to get started.

Damon entered his office and sat down at his desk. When the door opened, he stood and waited for the woman to come to him. She needed to be alerted to certain facts before his bride-to-be arrived. He'd been assured the woman was discreet and would look the other way as long as she was handsomely compensated. He intended to make sure of that before he allowed her to meet McKenna.

"Thank you for coming, Louise. You come highly recommended."

She seated herself in a chair in front of his desk. "And it's a pleasure to make your acquaintance, Mr. Hughes. You come highly recommended as well."

"As you know, I'm an eager bridegroom, so by necessity, the wedding will need to take place quickly. That doesn't mean, however, that I want to skimp on the wedding itself. It must be as spectacular as my bride."

"I have ten individuals who at a moment's notice can create a masterpiece." She pressed several buttons on her BlackBerry, apparently looking at her calendar. "What month and day do you have in mind?"

"This weekend." His expression one of utmost seriousness, he waited to see if she would pass the first test. Though her head popped up and her eyes widened briefly, she nodded as if it was a reasonable request, then looked down at her calendar again.

Damon knew his request wasn't reasonable. Putting

together a fairy-tale wedding in three days would take a miracle. Since he had the money and power to order a miracle, he fully expected her to do what was necessary to make sure he got what he wanted. If she didn't, she would pay a hefty price.

He handed her a detailed plan. It included everything, from the specific flowers he wanted to use to the design of the wedding cake. After years of imagining this in his mind, it had taken barely an hour to put everything down on paper. "This is what I want, down to the smallest detail. See that I get it and your commission will be beyond your wildest dreams. Fail me and you will regret it."

Her throat worked as she swallowed, but she nodded again. The woman had dealt with some of his associates, so she knew exactly what he meant.

"Another issue. My fiancée has only recently returned to me and we still have a few issues to iron out. She may seem a bit reluctant. I want your assurance that this will not concern you."

A slight smile. "And you have my assurance. You and your fiancée's relationship problems are none of my business and will be of no concern for me. My only goal is to give you both the wedding of your dreams."

"Excellent." Damon stood at the knock on the door. "That should be her right now. I will warn you that she has a bit of laryngitis, so she won't be able to interject anything into the conversation. However, I did want to introduce you so you can understand why I want this day to be so special."

His love entered the room and his heart almost stopped beating. The simple little summer dress she wore brought back so many wonderful memories. Though she had filled out a bit more and her facial features had changed a little with age, she still looked so much like the girl he'd fallen in love with.

Turning to the wedding planner, he said, "Leave us. I will be in touch."

He had no idea, and didn't care, what she might have seen in his face or heard in his voice. Apparently it was enough to have her stand up and walk out the door without a word.

His legs shakier than he could ever remember them, he held out his hand and said softly, "Come."

Though she still looked terrified and defiant, he was beginning to see a gradual softening of her features. He'd known it would take some time for her to accept being here with him, and he was glad to see it was happening even faster than he'd hoped.

Unable to wait any longer to taste her, he pulled her into his arms and kissed her. He heard a gasp and plunged his tongue into her mouth. Yes, this was what he had missed. This connection. All the women he'd had since the last time he'd been with McKenna disappeared into oblivion. They had been nothing but a way to satisfy a hunger. Holding McKenna in his arms was nothing like touching those other women. This was all about love; the others had been lust.

She stood stiffly in his arms. Tension raced through her body, but she didn't fight him. Didn't respond, either. That would come eventually. Just the taste of her in his mouth gave him a certain amount of peace. Their wedding would be this weekend. And then their honeymoon would commence. He had been waiting this long . . . he could wait a little longer.

Paris

McKenna stifled a yawn, surprised at the effort it took to put her hand over her mouth. She couldn't remember ever being so tired. Since officially joining LCR, Noah had insisted she receive more specialized training. He and two other operatives had been coaching her in everything from self-defense to shooting a long-range rifle while running at maximum speed. She was by no means an expert at anything, but Noah had told her more than once that her skills were good and her instincts were excellent. Despite the weariness that tugged at every muscle and sinew, the praise gave her a lift.

In between the trainings, she'd worked two separate rescues. Previously she had rarely worked more than one a month. Not only did a rescue take enormous energy, but in her case, undercover was often involved. Building trust with people who trusted no one took time and finesse. The two jobs she'd worked hadn't required undercover; they'd been straight-up rescues. However, between the training and the rescues, exhaustion had crept into her bones, and now just climbing the stairs to her apartment seemed like a major feat.

And she was lonely. There, she'd admitted it—not that the truth would do any good. Before she met Lucas, she had been alone and hadn't really given it a lot of thought. It was what it was. But now, after being with him, talking with him, and getting to know him, she wanted to be with him again. It was crazy insane. She needed to get over the need. This want and ache would lead nowhere, and even allowing herself the fantasy was so damned dangerous it scared her.

Finally reaching her apartment, McKenna unlocked and opened the door, forcing her mind back to the present. Staying aware kept her alive and out of Damon's clutches. Gun at the ready, she eased her head in. Heard and saw nothing wrong. Taking no chances, McKenna closed the door behind her and went from room to room, checking every place a person could hide. She released a tired sigh. All clear.

Placing her gun and keys on the coffee table, she collapsed onto the sofa. She should eat—she needed to eat—but she wasn't hungry. She was tired and she was lonely and that was that.

Maybe she should just get it over with and confront Damon. Even as exhausted as she was, a surge of adrenaline-drenched fear shot through her at the thought. Stupid? Absolutely. She who had confronted kidnappers, rapists, and every other kind of conscienceless person in the universe was scared to death of this one man.

Was he the most evil man in the universe? Probably not. She knew her fear came from something else, somewhere else. Memories of what he had done. What he was capable of and what he would do if he had the chance. No, he wasn't the most dangerous person to others, but to McKenna, who had seen him screw with her mind until she barely knew her name, he was evil personified.

Curling up on the sofa, she wrapped her arms around a soft throw pillow for comfort and closed her eyes. A nap . . . she just needed a nap. Then she would feel better. Her eyes closed.

"You look pretty. Where are you going tonight?"

McKenna whirled around from the mirror. She'd been so into her thoughts, she hadn't heard her mother come up behind her. Taking a breath, she said, "Tina is babysitting her sister. Since we both have history finals on Monday, we're going to have an all-night study fest."

Something flickered in her mom's face and McKenna waited for her to call her on her lie. Though it wasn't technically a lie. She was going over to Tina's house. Tina was babysitting her sister. And they did plan to study. Of course, the studying would come after McKenna got home from her date with Damon.

"Are Tina's parents out of town?"

"No, they're going to some kind of concert."

"*And this is really studying? No boys?*"

Ignoring that ever-increasing bite of conscience, McKenna huffed a sigh. "*Mama, I wish you would start trusting me.*"

Tears filled her mother's eyes, and McKenna felt lower than a slug.

"*Honey, I want to. Your dad and I both want to. But you betrayed our trust before. Saw that Damon character when we told you not to. How do we know you're not going to do it again?*"

Tears filled her own eyes. "*I'm seventeen, Mama. Almost an adult. You have to trust me sometime.*"

Her mom's raised eyebrows told her the tears were useless. Jane Sloan was no fool. Tears had always been one of McKenna's tools to get her way, but they rarely worked anymore. Which was stupid, because this time they were real. Her mother and father were finally getting their way. Tonight she would tell Damon she couldn't see him again. And it was breaking her heart.

McKenna whirled back around and faced the mirror. What did she care that her mother didn't believe her? She was breaking up with the man who was the love of her life all because her parents thought he was too old for her. After months of sneaking around and pretending, it had become too much.

They thought Damon was bad for her. She didn't agree, but the constant lying was getting to her. Despite the way she had treated them lately, she truly loved her parents and hated having this rift between them. They used to be so close. Since she'd met Damon, that closeness had disappeared. More than once, McKenna had screamed at them for their lack of understanding, for their backward thinking. And now they were finally getting what they wanted.

Damon would be hurt, but she had an answer for that, too. She would be eighteen in a few months; a full-

fledged adult. Then she could see Damon and her parents would just have to accept him. It wouldn't be pleasant, but they'd come around eventually. They just hadn't given Damon a chance. Thanks to Amy, who'd ratted on her before she could tell them about him, they already disapproved. And the minute she told them that he was nineteen, they'd immediately demanded she stop seeing him. But they didn't know him like she did. He'd had terrible parents, and because of that he'd been in trouble with the law. Damon just needed someone to love him and take care of him. Once they saw that beneath his tough-guy image a really sweet boy existed, they'd come around.

But that would have to wait until she turned eighteen. Then she'd show them. Once they got to know the Damon that she knew, they would love him, too.

With a jerk, McKenna woke. What had woken her? Sobbing noises came from her throat. That wasn't unusual. She was used to waking up crying, with tears on her face. After eight years of nightmares, this one was no different.

No. Wait. Was that a noise outside her door? Grabbing her gun, she crept to the door and looked out. She did indeed have a visitor. Dylan.

"McKenna, you there?"

Lifting the hem of her T-shirt, McKenna scrubbed her face clean of tears. Taking a breath to compose herself, she opened the door and Dylan meandered in. And *meandered* was the correct term. For a man who could move faster than just about any person she'd ever seen, Dylan Savage didn't look as though he'd move quicker if his clothes were on fire. There was laid-back and there was very laid-back. Dylan was very, very laid-back.

McKenna had often wondered if he saved all his energy for rescuing. There was no one she'd rather be on an operation with because the man could move like lightning when it was necessary. Any other time, he was like a sloth. A big, masculine, and very handsome sloth.

But just because she liked working with him didn't mean she wanted him here in her apartment. "What are you doing here, Dylan?"

His broad shoulders moved in a lazy shrug. "You left the job even quicker than usual. Just wanted to make sure you were okay."

"I'm fine. Just tired." She wrapped her arms around herself. Dylan didn't really make her uncomfortable, but having him in her apartment and being this near to him made her nervous. Lucas was the only man she felt comfortable being close with. At that thought, a sigh burst from her before she could stop it.

She detected a flash of compassion in his expression before it went blank again. Sympathy was the last thing she wanted from anyone. "You need to go."

Instead of leaving, he walked deeper into her apartment, then turned to face her. This time she recognized the look in his face; he didn't try to hide it. Anger. "You live in a shithole, McKenna."

Her lips twitched. "Tell me what you really think."

He ignored her amusement, his eyes glittering with anger. "Why? I know you've got your damage. Hell, we all do. But why the fuck do you live like this? LCR pays you well."

"What I do with my money is my business."

"You're right, it is. I just hate seeing you live like this."

Oh hell, there it was. She knew he'd been overly protective of her lately and now she knew why. What was it about her that everybody wanted to be her big brother? Even Noah, in his gruff, bossy way, was protective of her.

"I live the way I choose to live, Dylan. Just like you do."

"At least I enjoy what I've earned." He gestured around at the bare walls and shabby furnishings. "No one in their right mind would enjoy living like this."

"Never said I was in my right mind."

"Why do you punish yourself? We've all screwed up, McKenna. You couldn't have fucked things up any worse than I have."

She knew nothing of Dylan's background. Knowing him better would put their relationship on a whole new level. One she couldn't afford. Having any kind of relationship, friendship or otherwise, was out of the question. So she didn't ask him to tell her more. She hated that because Dylan would be a good friend to have. Not only was he an excellent operative, he was also the kind of person who would be easy to be with. No expectations of anything happening between them. Friendship. How she would love to take up the offer that was so obvious on his face. She couldn't.

Seeing no reason to prolong the pain, she made it quick. "How I live my life and what I've done to fuck it up is none of your damn business."

Instead of snarling at her that she was a bitch, he gave her a quick grin. "You're right, squirt. It's not." He headed toward the door, stopping on the way to give her an affectionate pat on the head. "I'll be around if you need to talk."

The door closed behind him, and McKenna fought the need to call him back. She did so much better when people weren't nice to her.

Knowing Dylan better would be dangerous. If she knew more, she might feel as though she should reciprocate. Telling her story to Noah and Samara had been one thing. Noah was her employer and deserved to know the truth. Actually sharing it as part of a budding friendship was altogether different. Sharing was an intimacy she could give to no one. If she were to share her past with anyone, she wanted it to be with Lucas. But she couldn't. Because if she did, he'd know the real McKenna. The selfish, egotistical, and stupid bitch who'd gotten her entire family killed.

Returning to the couch, McKenna curled up and forced herself back to sleep. This time, pray God, she could escape the nightmares.

ten

Palm Beach

Damon frowned at the almost full plate across the table from him. "Are you not hungry, my love?"

Staring down at her plate, she said, "No."

He sighed. "McKenna, look at me when I speak to you." He waited until she lifted her head. "You used to have such a healthy appetite. Was it not to your liking?"

Though her expression was stiff, her words were polite. "It was delicious. I . . . I just don't have as much of an appetite as I used to."

While that could be true, something odd flickered in her face. A look he'd seen before, as if she were keeping something from him. He knew it would take some time for her to trust him again, but he didn't like that she had secrets. It had been eight years since they'd been together. She had eight years of secrets to share with him. He wanted to know them all.

Earlier today, her voice had returned. Damon had used the drug on a few women before, just as an experiment to see how effectively it worked. He knew it was best that she rest her vocal cords as much as possible. This evening he'd allowed her to speak for the first time. Not that she'd had much to say.

"You managed to elude me for two years. Where did you live during this time?"

Again that look of secrecy, then she shrugged. "All over the country."

He frowned again. Something in her voice wasn't right. "You have a southern accent. Why?"

Her eyes lowered to her plate again. "I've lived in a lot of southern states. It's an easy accent to pick up."

"You've moved around so much . . . I still can't believe I finally found you after all this time."

She looked up at him then. "How did you find me?"

Delight filled him. It was the first question she had asked of him. They were finally sharing. "I have an entire investigative agency totally devoted to finding you. I've had men scouring the country for years. Cities everywhere are installing surveillance cameras these days. With the right kind of skills, you'd be surprised at how easy it is to hack into them. My people are excellent at getting into some of the most sophisticated systems in the world. I knew it was only a matter of time before you were spotted."

"What do you plan to do?"

"What do you mean?"

"There must be a reason you brought me here."

Genuine shock held him speechless for several seconds. "What a ridiculously odd thing to say. Why would you ask such a question? I've already admitted to my past mistake. It's time that you do also." Feeling unusually tentative, he touched her soft hand, caressing it gently. "I want us to start all over again. Forget about the past. There's nothing and no one standing in our way now. What's done is done. I'm willing to forgive you for your betrayals and for running from me. Can't we get past what happened and look to the future?"

She was silent for the longest time. Damon was beginning to think he'd have to shake a response from her. Finally she nodded and gave him a trembling smile. Damon felt all his anxiety melt away.

"Good. Now, I know that you haven't had a chance to look around since you returned. I'd like to show you your new home." He stood and held out his hand. "I remember how you loved warm weather—that's the reason I moved here to south Florida. You'll be able to enjoy summer year round."

As she stood beside him, he felt another odd sense that something was wrong. He'd held her in his arms earlier but desire had blurred his thoughts. Now, standing so close to her without touching, he felt that something was off. What? She seemed like the old McKenna, yet not. He reminded himself that after eight years, it was only normal that people change. Nothing more than that.

Shrugging off the feeling, he led her out the door to the patio. He had focused so much effort on finding her, his brain was having to readjust. Soon they would settle into their lives and everything would be as it should be. She still seemed so uneasy around him, but that would change soon. She had another couple of days to get used to him again and then she would be his forever. Of course, she would have to endure the punishment he planned because of her betrayal and abandonment, but that would take place after they returned from their honeymoon.

Once that punishment had passed and she had full knowledge of the boundaries and guidelines, they could enjoy the peace and harmony of a happily married couple.

London

Lucas reread the incredibly thorough report. He'd complimented Phelps and his team of investigators on being so detailed, but the man admitted it had taken almost no effort to come up with all the facts. Everything was on record, out in the open for the world to see.

McKenna Sloan. She hadn't even bothered to change her name. He wondered about that for barely a second before he concluded that it was just one more way McKenna punished herself. Anyone, anywhere, if they wished, could read about the atrocious things that had happened to her family. Things that McKenna no doubt blamed herself for. And why shouldn't she when the state of Nebraska had done their best to prosecute her for the crimes?

What the bastard had done to her family was horrific, but what he had done to McKenna made Lucas want to rip the bastard apart. Too bad he was dead. Dying in a fire caused by a prison riot had been too good for him. He had escaped his punishment through death, but McKenna continued to punish herself even today.

That was why she didn't want to form a relationship. Why she refused the slightest bit of companionship. She didn't feel as though she deserved to be happy. He recognized the guilt. Lucas had lived with his own for years. It was something he had come to accept. McKenna hadn't come to that point yet.

But there had to be more than that. Why did she seem so terrified? She wasn't hiding from the law for the crimes. Though they had tried to prosecute her, all charges had eventually been dropped. So why the hell did she act as though someone or something was chasing her?

"So are you going to go after her now?"

He looked up to see Jared in the doorway. The man was determined to marry him off. Jared had married a year ago. Since then, when he wasn't investigating something for Kane Enterprises, he was a harassing matchmaker.

"Nothing's changed."

"Like hell nothing's changed. You now know the reasons she acts the way she does. From the looks of it, she needs you even more than you need her."

"And what would you suggest I say to her when I find her? 'McKenna, I've investigated your past and I want to fix your hurts'?" Lucas shook his head. He knew what he had done wasn't something she would easily forgive.

"You don't have to tell her anything, but now that you know, you can show her she's safe with you."

That wasn't an issue. Lucas didn't bother telling Jared that he knew for a fact that McKenna felt safe with him. That wasn't what worried him. Trust wasn't the problem. It was the fact that McKenna so obviously felt she didn't deserve happiness. And how the hell could he explain that she deserved to be happy without telling her that he knew about her past? Damned if he would show her that her trust had been breached. If she knew, her faith in him would be completely gone.

Guilt niggled at him for having this information, but despite that, he'd do it again. She was clearly not going to tell him, and until he knew her problems, how could he fix them for her? Now he knew her problems—and, dammit, still had no idea how to fix them.

Aware that Jared waited for an answer, Lucas closed the file and stood. "McKenna knows she's safe with me. That's not an issue."

"What is the issue, then? The damnable guilt?"

Lucas wouldn't answer that question. Wouldn't do any good. Jared's parents had died when he was a child. Having been raised in orphanages and foster homes, he had welcomed working for IDC.

For Lucas it hadn't been that simple. His father had expected Lucas to take over years ago. Because of his commitment to the agency, he hadn't been able to do that. Though Phillip Kane had been proud of his son for serving his country, Lucas knew he'd also been disappointed.

Lucas hadn't understood his father's reluctance. What was the big deal of coming a little late to the company? It wasn't as if Kane Enterprises would just disappear. It hadn't; but his father had. To this day, Lucas would blame himself for not taking over sooner. If his father had been able to retire earlier, might he still have been alive today?

"Maybe if you go to McKenna and tell her about your own guilt, it will help her with hers."

"You know I can't tell her about the agency."

"I'm not saying you have to tell her everything, but you can tell her enough to help her understand you know where she's coming from."

"Have you told Lara about your experience?"

Jared's eyes widened, as if shocked Lucas had even asked. "Hell, no. That'd scare the shit out of her. Having her think of me as her loving and slightly geeky husband is exactly what I want . . . because it's what she wants."

Lucas studied his friend. Was that the way it should be? Secrets to make sure the other one stayed happy? Was that a real marriage? Hell, he hoped not. Jared claimed to be content, but how was that possible when the real you is hidden? Sounded like a miserable way to live.

Lucas shrugged off his disquiet. Jared's life was his own. Talking about this stuff with anyone, even his best friend, was something he just wasn't comfortable with. "Tell me what you've come up with on Humphries."

"Not much more than what we knew before. Doesn't appear to be gambling anymore, unless he's doing it under an alias. Are you sure you don't want to reconsider pressing charges for embezzlement?"

Lucas nodded grimly. Another thing Jared wouldn't understand. Humphries had been a friend of his father's. The older man's resentment of Lucas had been vague at first but had grown as policies had shifted from his father's old-school philosophies. Phillip Kane had been a good businessman and Lucas admired him tremendously. That didn't mean Lucas didn't have his own ideas. Humphries didn't approve of those and apparently felt little loyalty toward him.

"We'll just leave it as it is for now."

Jared blew out a frustrated huff but didn't pursue it further. He knew Lucas wouldn't change his mind.

The opening of his study door brought his head around to see Conrad standing just inside the room.

"You have a visitor, sir."

Lucas's heart slammed against his chest. Conrad wouldn't disturb him unless it was one particular visitor. "McKenna?"

"Yes sir."

The frown on Conrad's face wasn't normal. "What's wrong?"

"She doesn't appear well, sir. I took her to—"

Lucas shot out the door and headed to the north parlor. After that day last month, he had begun to think of it as McKenna's room.

Stopping at the entrance, his eyes took in the wet and bedraggled-looking waif standing at the fireplace. "McKenna?"

She whirled around and reached out to grab the mantel as if she were having trouble standing. "I shouldn't have come."

Lucas stalked toward her, noting not only her soaked clothing but also the bright glaze of her eyes and the hot flush covering her pale cheeks, indicating a fever. Holding out his hand, he said, "This is the only place you should have come."

She looked at his hand and shook her head. "I have a slight cold. I may be contagious."

Cold? He doubted it. She had the flu, maybe worse. "I'm as healthy as an ox; I don't catch colds. Have a seat and let me get you some tea."

What he wanted to do was strip off her wet clothes, wrap her in blankets, and haul her off to a hospital. Even as sick as she was, she would resist him. So he would ease her into bed and call his family doctor. If she had to go to the hospital, he'd deal with her resistance then.

Before he could turn, he knew Conrad was there. "Would you mind getting us a cup of hot tea?"

"Not at all, sir," Conrad said.

Her teeth chattering, McKenna sank onto the sofa. "It's raining outside. Did you know?"

"It does that quite often here."

"Yes, I suppose it does." She blinked at him as if she were trying to stay awake. "Are you well?"

"Yes." He looked down at her soaked feet. "Let's get those shoes off so Conrad won't fuss about getting the carpets wet."

As he had suspected, if she thought she was causing any kind of problem, that became an immediate concern. She slipped off her soaked running shoes. Lucas went to his knees, pulled off her wet socks, and held her slender, icy feet in his hands. Other than kissing her, this was the most intimate thing she'd ever allowed him to do. Stupid, but he suddenly felt a giant surge of arousal. Hell, if he ever got all of her clothes off, he'd explode immediately.

"Everything okay?"

Lucas looked over his shoulder at Jared, who stood in

the doorway. Should've known his friend wouldn't be able to resist meeting the woman Lucas had been obsessed with.

He turned back to McKenna to gauge her expression. The last thing he wanted was to alarm her. Jared's dark scowl had frightened more than one person. Thankfully, McKenna didn't seem to see his friend as any kind of threat.

"McKenna, this is a friend of mine, Jared Livingston. Jared, this is McKenna."

McKenna gave a halfhearted smile to Jared and then looked down at Lucas, who was still kneeling. "I should have called first."

"You did exactly as you should have."

The sound of a rolling tea cart brought Lucas to his feet. Conrad placed it beside a small table and poured a cup. Without asking, he sweetened it with three sugar cubes and then gave it to Lucas.

Lucas sat beside McKenna and handed her the steaming liquid. "Drink."

Her hands were shaking so badly he thought he might have to hold it for her. When he was assured that she could hold it herself, he shot Conrad a look. The man knew him well. With a small nod of understanding, Conrad walked out the door. Lucas's doctor would be here within the half hour.

McKenna sipped the hot, soothing liquid and let the warmth seep into her bones. Both men stared down at her as if she had two heads. She probably looked like crap but couldn't make herself care. She felt like crap.

She tried to ignore them as she concentrated on maintaining her grip on the cup in her hand. Taking slow, careful sips, McKenna willed herself to feel better. Coming here had been a stupid thing to do, but she didn't know where else to go. She'd been in Northampton on a job and had suddenly felt so ill she knew she wouldn't make it back to her apartment in Paris.

Stupid not to go to a hospital, but if she did, she might say something she didn't want anyone to hear. She had fake identification, but if she was out of her head and said something incriminating to the wrong person, then everything could start all over again. She couldn't bear that. Probably should have just gone to a hotel here and sweated it out. A nice one with room service that would deliver chicken soup or whatever it was she needed to get her well again.

She had called Noah but had given him only the barest of facts. Just that she had a bad cold and was taking a few days off. If she had told him how ill she was, he would have sent someone for her. Made sure she was taken care of.

Yes, she could have done any of those things, but she hadn't. She had wanted to see Lucas. He was her safe haven. Whether she wanted to admit it to him or not, being with him gave her a feeling of completeness she'd never felt before. But that had to stop. Once she was better, she would leave. Maybe she should consider moving out of Europe. She only knew how to speak English and French, but that didn't mean she couldn't learn another language. It would be a new challenge.

Italy. She liked Italy . . . no, wait, that was still Europe. Where could she move? McKenna searched her foggy brain, her mind grappling for another country she could move to. For the life of her, she couldn't come up with one. Were there any left?

"McKenna, I'm going to put you to bed now."

Her head heavy on her shoulders, she looked up and blinked at the man standing in front of her. Lucas? Where had he come from? Her eyes tried to focus as his features blurred. "Lucas?"

Strong arms lifted her and she felt herself being carried somewhere. She didn't care where Lucas took her as long as he didn't let her go.

"I'm not going to let you go, McKenna. Ever."

His voice, gentle and masculine at the same time, strummed through her senses like warm honey. A bout of shivering attacked her, dispelling the warmth. "So cold."

"We'll get you warm soon enough. Just hold on."

She felt masculine hands tugging at her wet clothes. *No . . . should try to stop them.* No one had the right to touch her without her say-so. Then she heard Lucas again. His voice, soft but insistent, told her to relax; she had nothing to fear. Yes, everything was all right again. As long as Lucas was here, everything was all right. Sighing, she drifted into oblivion.

Fastening the last button of the shirt he'd managed to get on her, Lucas covered her still-shivering body with two blankets and a comforter. As he had undressed and then dressed her again with his shirt, she had struggled only a little. Now she was barely conscious.

He ignored his rampaging emotions and focused on his movements, his purpose. The doctor would be here soon. McKenna's fever felt dangerously high . . . probably well over one hundred. The tea she'd drunk had temporarily stopped the shivering, but it had returned full force within minutes. He'd stupidly been about to ask her if she wanted another cup when she dropped the cup and almost crumpled at his feet. He'd been trying to be careful with her and had learned his lesson. No more.

He heard the door open and Dr. Scott's brisk voice say, "I heard we have a very sick young woman here."

Without taking his eyes from the sleeping McKenna, Lucas said, "She's got a high fever, her pupils are dilated, and her breathing is labored. I think it's either a severe case of flu or pneumonia."

"Hmph. Sounds like you're ready to make a diagnosis, young man. Mind if I take a look first?"

Normally he would have smiled at the doctor's humor, but at this moment Lucas didn't know if he'd ever smile again. He needed to get out of the room for just a moment. The fury was about to explode within him. For a short while he needed to be by himself. Then he would return and do what needed to be done.

Turning, he finally moved his gaze from McKenna to Dr. Scott, a man he'd known all of his life. "Absolute privacy is a must," Lucas said quietly.

Though the doctor's eyes held questions, he simply nodded and said, "Of course."

Lucas swallowed. The words needed to be said because he couldn't have the doctor questioning her later. He forced them from his frozen mouth. "She's had a difficult life. I know you have to examine her, but when she wakes, I want no questions asked about the markings on her body."

Compassion replaced the normal humor usually lurking in Dr. Scott's eyes. "I wouldn't dream of it, Lucas."

Nodding his thanks, Lucas took one last look at the small, delicate-looking woman on the bed, then turned and stalked out the door. Closing it softly, he leaned against the wall and inhaled ragged breaths. Fury was bubbling, and he didn't try to hold it in check. Before he went back, he would be in control again. But for now, he let it boil.

McKenna's health came first. But once she was well, they were going to talk. She wouldn't like some of the things he planned to discuss with her. For starters, he was going to ask two direct but very simple questions: Who the hell had put the scars on her body? And who the bloody fucking hell had branded her bottom with the letter *D*?

He already knew the answer to the second question. Damon Hughes, the sick dead fuck, had done it. But had he put the scars there also? If not, if whoever it had been wasn't already dead, they would be, and soon. This he vowed.

eleven

Palm Beach

Damon paced back and forth beside the pool. Tomorrow was their wedding day. He had yet to tell her. He'd planned to reveal his surprise last night, but she'd still seemed so stiff and uncomfortable with him. Fear was healthy, as it would breed respect. But he was damn tired of her looking at him like he was some kind of monster. After everything he had done for her, how could she continue to look at him that way?

Perhaps they needed to connect physically after all. He had planned to wait until after their vows were exchanged. Now he was thinking that was a mistake. Not only because he wanted to fuck her—he needed it and it was his right—but because she needed to see who was in charge. He had been too gentle with her, too loving. It was clear she was taking advantage of him. This he could not allow.

After they were married, she would have ample time to fall in love with him again. He had been charming, attentive, and generous, and it had gotten him nowhere. Tomorrow was their wedding day, but today he would show her exactly what she had to look forward to.

Maybe they could take a walk on the beach beforehand. By necessity, a brick wall enclosed his mansion, but only a few yards outside the wall was a beautiful beach she had yet to see. Yes, they would walk, and when they returned, he would wine her, dine her, and show her how wonderful their life would be. And tomorrow they would marry.

Hearing a sound, he looked up to see her walk toward him. She was still so very beautiful, and she was all his. Though her breasts were larger than they'd been when she was a teenager, she seemed more slender than she had years before, but that was because he hadn't been there to take care of her. He would make sure she stayed healthy.

Beneath her short cover-up, he could see she wore the most modest of the swimsuits he'd given her. Still, it revealed her luscious body, and that pleased him, so he refrained from chastising her. He held out his hand for her to come to him. Her mouth stretched slightly as if it was an effort to smile; there were still shadows and doubt in her eyes.

His patience holding by a mere thread, he gestured at the sparkling water. "I had this pool built for you. I remember how you loved to swim."

For just an instant uncertainty flickered in her eyes. Then she smiled and said, "It's beautiful, but we just ate breakfast. . . . I'll just lie in the sun for a while."

"Come now . . . that's an old wives' tale." He pulled off his robe, revealing that he wore his swim briefs. He saw her eyes sweep over his body and he hardened with arousal. Two hours a day in his gym, honing his body to peak condition, and it was all for her. Early in his youth, Damon had realized he was extraordinary-looking; age had only improved him. He was proud to be able to show his masculinity off to her. "Let's swim, and then I'll let you rub sunscreen on me."

A visible shudder went through her body. Yes, the waiting had been worth it. The anticipation had built and now she would welcome him.

She dropped the short robe and his mouth went dry.

This was the most he'd seen of her body. She was so beautiful. The few times he'd burned her with cigarettes, her fair skin had glowed hotly as if he'd set her on fire. Odd, he didn't see them anywhere. Her breasts were covered, but he remembered creating a cluster of burns on her stomach. It had been eight years. They must have faded with time.

Singeing her lovely skin had been painful for him. She had been so defiant back then, so resistant to the inevitable. Things were much better now. All of that was ancient history.

Holding out his hand, he led her to the steps of the pool. It was late morning, so it should be heated to just the right temperature. Stepping down, he turned to pull her down to him, then stopped and froze. Once again, he felt as if something was not right; something was missing.

"The scars . . . where are they?"

"What?"

"Your scars. They're gone."

Her eyes widened and he saw absolute terror in them. "I . . ." Her throat worked convulsively. "Th—they must have faded."

Lies. Her words said one thing, her face something else. A horrible, incredulous feeling swept through him. He told himself he was crazy. This had to be his McKenna. Not only did she look just like her, but she had acted as if she were McKenna. Why would she do this if she wasn't? Why wouldn't she have told him?

There was only one way to make sure. He had given her his brand. Why the hell hadn't he checked before?

"Turn around."

"What?"

Fury geysered through him. "I said, turn around."

She made a little stumbling turn and then gasped when he pulled the bottoms of her swimsuit down. Her

ass was unblemished. There were no marks; there was
no brand.

She's not McKenna.

He pushed her hard; she fell forward onto the concrete, catching herself on her hands and knees. Her
smooth, bare bottom pointed up at him. Mocking him.
Damon looked around for something, anything to hit
her with but could find nothing. Unable to control the
fury long enough to go find a weapon, he pulled down
his briefs. She might not be McKenna, but she was
about to learn a hard, painful lesson.

Pushing her down, Damon fell on top of her. Fury and
lust roared in his head, drowning out the screams of the
woman who wasn't McKenna.

London

The hospital had been necessary after all. Fortunately,
she'd been so out of it, she hadn't known she was being
taken to a hospital. And with Lucas's money and contacts, almost no one knew she was there. Another blessing in knowing Lucas Kane.

"Are you ready to go home?"

McKenna looked up as Lucas stood in the doorway.
The first time she'd seen him, she'd likened him to a
golden Adonis. Everything about him was bright and
golden. He was a light . . . her light.

"More than ready."

"Good. You still need some recuperation time, but
you can do that at home much better than here."

He took her hand and helped her to her feet. She
should be thanking him for his help and explaining that
she could recuperate just as well in Paris. McKenna
knew she needed to leave. She should leave. And she
would . . . soon. But not yet.

Wobbling slightly, she grasped Lucas's arm to steady herself. Odd how she'd avoided touching people, especially men, for years. Now, touching this man felt so natural, so right.

"Want me to carry you?"

Her heart said yes; her independent, no-nonsense brain said no. She shook her head. "I need to build up my strength as much as possible."

"The car is around back. No one will see us, but just in case, I'm going to put this jacket and hood over your head. Okay?"

She had yet to tell him anything of her past, but somehow Lucas recognized her need to remain anonymous. Telling him would come soon. He had done too much for her not to be totally honest with him. And he needed to understand the reasons she absolutely had to leave once she was well.

Holding on to his arm, she walked the short distance to the elevator. In most hospitals, a wheelchair was usually a cardinal rule. Another perk of knowing a man like Lucas. Certain rules could be ignored.

By the time she made it out of the elevator and through the door that led to a back alley, she was so weak she was beginning to wish she'd taken Lucas up on his offer to carry her or at the very least that she had a wheelchair. Thankfully, the limousine was only a few steps away. The door opened, and McKenna practically collapsed into the backseat.

Lucas settled beside her. Wrapping his arm around her shoulders, he brought her head to his chest and whispered, "Rest, love. We'll be home soon."

Home. McKenna closed her eyes and savored the warmth and comfort she knew she'd only ever find in this man's arms.

Holding close the treasure in his arms, Lucas let go of the tension that had strung him tight for days. She was going to be all right. He'd thought he was going to lose her. Considering McKenna's desire to stay anonymous, taking her to a hospital had been risky. He'd had no choice. She had needed the most up-to-date equipment to save her life. He could have gotten the equipment into his house, but that would have taken time, and time was one thing they'd almost run out of. The pneumonia had almost taken her from him.

For a man known to be one of the most unflappable operatives in IDC history, he'd come close to losing it several times. When she'd been struggling for every breath that came from her tortured lungs, he'd been breathing with her, willing her to live.

Now that he knew she was going to be all right, he had another battle on his hands—one he intended to win also. She would want to leave soon. He'd seen it in her expression earlier. She had considered telling him she wouldn't go with him. He was thankful she had changed her mind. Having an argument with her while she was still so weak wouldn't have been enjoyable. But he would have had it out with her if she had tried to leave. Fortunately, that hadn't been necessary, but it would be soon.

Most of the things he knew about her were still the things he'd learned from the investigators' reports. When she'd been feverish and restless, she'd mumbled a few things. Not a lot, but enough to confirm his suspicions. She was hiding from someone. He needed to know who and why.

Though Damon Hughes was dead, perhaps it was someone he had been associated with. A relative or friend? The police were no longer looking for her. So why the fear and the secrecy?

She snuggled in his arms and Lucas felt his heart pound faster. Of all the women in the world he had known, and there had been many, why did this one small woman create such a mass of unrivaled feelings within him? He wasn't an emotional person. It had just never been in his makeup. His father had been the fiery, emotional one in the family. Lucas was known more for his cold, objective reasoning.

Growing up with a man like Phillip Kane, Lucas had sometimes felt more the parent than the child. He'd loved his father, but seeing him look for something all his life and never find it, Lucas had determined early on that to have those kinds of wants and needs only led to heartache.

And he was more than aware that the woman lying in his arms had broken through those barriers.

Common sense told him to get his head together. From the moment he met McKenna, he'd felt this odd connection with her. While he willingly admitted that, it didn't mean that he had to behave like a complete idiot. A man could have affection for a woman without going completely crazy over her. McKenna was a special woman and he would do everything in his power to make sure not only that she stayed safe but that she knew he cared deeply for her. That sure as hell didn't mean he had lost his mind over her. He was a grown man, not a pubescent teenager. One who had control of his body, his mind, and his heart.

She stirred suddenly. Sleepy eyes blinked open and were unfocused for an instant. Then, as if she realized where she was and who held her, she smiled. His chest tightened almost painfully, and Lucas gritted his teeth, reminding himself of his self-lecture barely five seconds before.

"I'm so glad you're here with me," she whispered.

Holding her closer, Lucas looked out at the green and brown landscape speeding by as the vehicle headed to his estate. Perhaps he was more like his father than he thought.

Palm Beach

Damon stood over the body of Carlos Ortez, his former, and now very dead, investigator. It had taken days to hunt down the bastard. He'd apparently heard about his enormous mistake and had gone into hiding. While Damon waited for him to be found, his fury had built to monstrous proportions. When Carlos had stumbled from the van that carried him inside the compound, Damon had detonated.

His favorite knife, the one he always carried clipped at his waist, had been in his hand and then deep inside Carlos's gut before the man knew what was coming. It had been years since he had enjoyed a killing as much as this one. Carlos was soaked with blood. Damon didn't have a speck on him.

Years ago, he had killed in violence, without regard to either the consequences or the mess. Now, not only was he more controlled in his kills, they were some of the cleanest. It was a challenge he liked to give himself. The bloodiest of killings without a spot on him. He was a perfectionist, and looking down at his pristine white shirt and pants, he realized he had reached perfection. What made it even more amazing was he'd never killed anyone when his mind had been fueled by so much fury. Not even McKenna's parents had caused such anger.

The man had died in excruciating agony. Damon only wished he could do it all again but make it even more painful. The idiot had kidnapped the wrong fucking woman. Not only had Damon treated the bitch with kindness and hospitality, he'd been ready to marry her. Carlos had received his just deserts. And so had the woman.

He hadn't killed her, as he'd wanted. Though he'd been about to wring her scrawny neck, she had whispered an apology for her deceit. That had saved her life.

Besides, killing her would have been too easy, so he had sold her to one of his clients. Since she had been a bit hideous-looking when he had finished with her, she hadn't brought the price he would have gotten otherwise. But money hadn't been important. It was her punishment he wanted, not a profit. Just because he'd spared her life didn't mean she didn't deserve great punishment.

He hadn't bothered asking her why she hadn't told him at the beginning. What good would that have done? What was done was done. She might have apologized, but her apologies hadn't made his pain disappear. He made sure she sincerely regretted her deception.

The woman would eventually heal and the man she belonged to would get good use of her. Or she would be sold to someone else. It didn't matter. She didn't matter.

McKenna. She was what mattered. He had thought he had her back with him. But she still eluded him. His heart cried out for her. His body ached to feel her warm, soft body beneath him. Now he had to hire a new team of investigators and they had to start all over again.

Fury refueled and washed over him; he kicked viciously at the bloodied, lifeless body. Pulling his foot back, Damon cursed violently. He'd gotten blood on his shoe after all.

London

McKenna blinked sleep away. Sitting up, she leaned against the headboard, pleased to realize that for the first time in days, she was clearheaded and felt halfway human. She was still weak, but a few good meals should take care of that.

Decisions had to be made soon. Lucas had been so wonderful to her, and she had taken advantage of him.

She couldn't do that much longer. The longer she stayed, the more she wanted to stay forever. Forever with Lucas was an impossibility, and the time had come to accept that. She'd been living in a dream for almost two weeks. In a few days she would be well enough to leave. And leave she must. That was the only forever in her future. Leave Lucas forever.

Oh God, it hurt to admit that. Lucas was everything she'd dreamed of when she was a teenager. A knight in shining armor, gallant, kind, and devastatingly handsome. Every young girl's dream. And then had come Damon and all of her fantasies disappeared. Damon had replaced them with horror, death, and destruction. Abuse. Everything hell consisted of was inside Damon. He had destroyed those girlhood dreams. She had never thought to have anything like those feelings back inside her. Lucas had returned them to her, and she would be forever grateful to him. There were true white knights in this world.

But she was no damsel in distress and she was most certainly not a princess. She had a role and a purpose. She rescued people and she saved lives. Her purpose and life were important. Even if she didn't have a maniacal murderer hunting for her, Lucas's world and hers could never be the same.

"You appear to be feeling much better."

She smiled as Lucas came into the room. "Almost one hundred percent, thanks to you."

He sat on the edge of the bed. "Feel like getting up and having breakfast with me?"

"Absolutely. For the first time in days, I'm ravenous."

"Good. I told the cook you were feeling better, so I think you'll be pleased with her offering."

A knock on the door had Lucas stalking toward it. She heard his deep voice thank Conrad for the delivery, and then Lucas rolled in a loaded cart filled with enough food to feed a family of six.

Her stomach growled in approval. "It smells wonderful."

"Come eat."

McKenna got to her feet. She knew Lucas watched her to make sure she was steady, but she appreciated that he allowed her to stand on her own without trying to hold her up. She needed to regain her strength as soon as possible. The reason behind that need dampened her spirits, but McKenna refused to acknowledge it. For the here and now, she was with Lucas. She would face what she had to do later.

The nightgown was a bit skimpier than she would have liked, and she was thankful for the robe lying at the end of the bed. She knew Lucas had undressed her . . . knew he had seen the scars. It was time to answer those questions gleaming in his eyes.

First breakfast, then the truth. Lucas needed to know everything. Who she was and what she had done. And then he would understand why, very soon, she would have to leave him forever.

twelve

Lucas had concurrent feelings running through him as he watched McKenna slowly make her way across the room. On one hand, he was enormously relieved to see the color in her cheeks and the sparkle in her eyes. She was beginning to look like the old McKenna. On the other hand, dread and sadness swept over him. McKenna was gearing herself up to leave.

She didn't know that every expression on her face had been open for him to read from the moment he met her. If he told her, she'd try to mask her thoughts. It was hard enough that McKenna had secrets; damned if he'd give her another way to hide from him.

Filling a plate with some of her favorites, Lucas handed it to her and then sat down, ready to be exquisitely tortured. Watching McKenna was incredibly sexy. The way she ate, the sounds she made, everything about her consumption of food turned him on. It was the oddest thing, but no way in hell did he plan to deprive himself of those moments, no matter how torturous they were.

She took one bite of toast and then dropped it back on her plate.

He frowned at her bent head. "Something wrong?"

"My full name is McKenna Sloan and my entire family was murdered because of me."

He didn't say anything. Whatever he said wouldn't be appropriate, so he waited.

When she lifted her face to look at him, Lucas's chest

went so tight it hurt—a reflection of the pain brimming in her eyes.

"We lived in Nebraska, in a little town outside of Omaha. My mom, dad, my little sister, Amy, and me. Amy was two years younger." A small smile. "She followed me around everywhere . . . drove me crazy. She's the one who told them about Damon."

"Damon?"

The pain in her eyes became even starker. Lucas saw hell—pure, unadulterated, life-destroying. "I met him at the movies. He seemed so grown-up, so much cooler than the other boys. He was already out of school. I was sixteen, almost seventeen. Damon told me he was nineteen. Turns out he was really twenty-three. I didn't know his real age until much later.

"I told my parents about him, but they told me he was too old for me. That I couldn't date him." Her gaze went unfocused. "We met each other secretly for a few weeks." She shook her head slowly. "I hated the sneaking around. Had decided to go to my parents and confess everything. Before I could work up the courage to talk to them, Amy spilled the beans.

"My mom and dad were loving and incredibly supportive but also strict. I hoped, once they got to know Damon, they'd see him the way I did. They were furious, of course, but they finally agreed to meet him. Meeting him didn't change their minds. They were so much wiser . . . saw through his façade. He was an older man trying to take advantage of their teenage daughter. Our age difference seemed insignificant to me, but to them he was a child predator. They told me I couldn't see him again."

She wrapped her arms around her body and began rocking. He recognized the signs of grieving, the need for comfort. And that was why he was here. Standing, Lucas pulled her into his arms; carrying her to an overstuffed chair beside the fireplace, he sat down.

As usual, when she sat in his lap, she snuggled her head against his chest. He waited. This was her story, her hell. He could do nothing but let her expose it the way she needed to.

"I once again disobeyed them . . . for several months. Snuck out when they were in bed. Said I was going to a friend's house but instead went out with him. Then it got to be too much. I despised lying to them. We were always so close, but I felt this gap between us and it was eating at me. Even though I still didn't agree with them about Damon, they raised me to be honest.

"So I decided to tell Damon we needed to stop seeing each other. I didn't plan for it to be permanent. Once I turned eighteen, which was just a few months away, I planned to start seeing him again. It would have hurt my parents, but at least I wouldn't have been sneaking around. I thought if I was a legal age, it would somehow be different."

She paused and took a long trembling breath. "He took the news better than I thought he would. He said he didn't like the fact that I was lying to my parents, either. That I should do what was right. He kissed me, told me everything would be all right."

She stopped again. Lucas held his breath, waiting for what had to be the most horrific event a young girl, or anyone, could experience.

Closing her eyes, McKenna saw it all as if it happened yesterday.

Eight years earlier
Traylor City, Nebraska

A soft sound woke her from a deep sleep. Drowsy, she rolled over in bed and snuggled deeper into her soft, warm pillow. Squirrels again—trying to get into the attic. They did that this time of year. Daddy would have to run them off tomorrow. On the edge of sleep again, she heard another sound.

"McKenna."

Someone was calling her name. McKenna sat up, her heart thundering in her chest. She gasped to see a tall, dark figure in the middle of her room. *Damon!* "What are you doing here? How did you get in?"

"Your window was open."

Keeping her voice barely above a whisper, she said, "My daddy will kill you if he sees you in here. You have to leave."

He laughed. It wasn't a laugh she'd ever heard from him before. It sounded almost nasty, not like the Damon she knew and loved.

She put her feet on the floor; she had to make him leave. Daddy would never understand this and would never forgive Damon for sneaking into her room.

Before she could stand, Damon pushed her down and then came down on top of her. Though fearful of having him in her home in the middle of the night where her parents might hear, she wrapped her arms around him to kiss him. Instead of the passionate yet tender kisses she was used to and expected, he ground his mouth onto hers. He was hurting her. She tasted blood and knew he'd cut her lip.

She pushed at his shoulders, trying to dislodge him. Why was he acting this way? Finally managing to get him to move his mouth from hers, she whispered, "You're hurting me."

"I'm about to show you what real hurt is, McKenna. You've cock-teased me for the last time." He pushed her nightgown up; she felt his hands on her bare legs and then extreme pressure between her thighs as he thrust deep inside her.

*   *   *

A harsh sob jerked her out of her memories. Lucas's arms held her as she shuddered against his chest. "I was a virgin. I thought he understood that I wanted to wait. He had never pressured me before. I didn't realize I screamed until the light in my room came on and I felt him being pulled off me. Oh God, why did I have to scream? If only I hadn't screamed . . ."

Swallowing hard, she returned to her memories.

"Bastard! Get off my daughter!" her father shouted.

Sobbing, McKenna lay on the bed, unable to move. Damon had raped her . . . why? How could he have done this to her?

Damon's harsh laughter woke her from her shock. "She ain't your little girl anymore. She's mine."

The slamming of a fist into flesh caused her to sit up. Her father was on top of Damon, pummeling his fist into Damon's face. She screamed again. Her father jerked his head around and looked at her; tears swam in his eyes, and she saw love and compassion in his beloved face.

Her body and heart aching, she held out her hand and whispered, "Daddy?"

A loud blast pierced the silence. Her daddy's face changed from shock to pain, and then in an instant he fell onto the floor.

McKenna shouted, "No!" and threw herself onto her father's lifeless body. Damon pulled her away from him and dragged her out of the room. Her mother stood in the hallway, a phone in her hand. McKenna barely registered her mother's pale, panic-stricken face before Damon raised the gun and fired. A red stain suddenly appeared on her mother's white nightgown; she dropped the phone and fell to the floor.

Screeching her pain, McKenna whirled around and

clawed at Damon's face. He slammed her against the wall; her head struck so hard she literally saw stars.

"Nobody comes between me and what belongs to me," he growled. "You were mine the moment we met. Your parents were too stupid to realize that. Don't you make the same mistake."

Sobs tore through her. She was crying so hard she could hardly breathe. Her mama and daddy . . . *Oh dear God. Mama. Daddy. Amy!* She had to protect Amy!

"You have to go," she babbled. "My mama called the police. They'll be here soon."

"Police ain't coming. I cut the phone lines before I came in. You think I'm stupid or something? Now, where's that sister of yours?"

"No. You can't hurt Amy. I won't let you. Please, Damon. I'll do whatever you want, but you can't hurt Amy."

"You do what I tell you to do and I won't. Understand?"

Barely able to stand, she leaned against the wall and nodded.

"Good. Go get some clothes and let's grab your sister."

"You said you wouldn't hurt her."

The smack of the back of his hand against her face busted her lip, but it woke her up, too. No longer faint, she straightened and said woodenly, "What do you want me to do?"

"Get some clothes. I'll get your sister."

"If you hurt her, I'll kill you." She said the words softly, but he heard them.

Instead of reacting like the maniac she now knew him to be, he smiled and said, "You can try."

She ran, stuffed some clothes into her bag, and then ran back out. She would be crazy to take him at his word. Rushing down the hallway to Amy's room, she found him kneeling on the floor, trying to coax her sister out from under the bed.

"No!" McKenna flew at him, pushing him away. "Leave her alone."

Damon backhanded her in the face, knocking her down. Lying on the floor, she could see Amy's terrified eyes gleaming at her. *Oh God, please help me save her.*

Getting back on her knees, she tugged on Damon's arm. "Please, Damon. I'll do anything . . . *anything!* I swear. Just don't hurt her."

"I ain't going to hurt her. I'm just trying to get her to come with us." He looked back at Amy. "Come on out here, little girl. I'm not going to hurt you."

Amy didn't utter a sound; McKenna knew she was too terrified to move.

"Tell her to come out or I'm going to shoot her under the bed."

"Dammit, Damon. Leave her alone." She was sobbing, pleading . . . she didn't care what she had to do. She'd already lost her mother and father—she couldn't lose Amy, too.

Damon grabbed McKenna by a hank of hair and jerked her down till she lay on the floor. "Tell your fucking sister to get out here or I'm going to shoot your head off."

McKenna gritted her teeth. She didn't care if she died. She deserved to die for bringing this monster into her home. No matter what she had to do, she would save Amy.

But Damon's threatening words had worked. McKenna heard her little sister's trembling voice say, "No, I'm coming . . . don't hurt Kenna . . . I'm coming."

"Amy, please, no."

"There ya go," Damon coaxed. When Amy came within reaching distance, he grabbed her arm and dragged her the rest of the way out.

McKenna pulled Amy away from Damon. Getting to her feet, she placed Amy behind her. "Let me lock her up in the closet or something. She won't call the police, I promise."

Damon got to his feet and grabbed McKenna by the shoulder. "Shut the fuck up!"

Swallowing a sob, she nodded.

"Did you get your clothes?"

She nodded again.

"Then let's go."

"But Amy—"

"She comes with us."

"Why can't she—"

He pointed the gun toward Amy's head and snarled, "She either comes with us or I shoot her. Your choice."

As much as she wanted to get Amy away from him, she had no choice. Willing herself calmness so she could try to figure something out, she turned and said, "Amy, pack some clothes."

Her little sister stood shivering, obviously in shock. McKenna took her hand and walked with her to the closet. "Here, I'll help you."

Taking some of her summer dresses and shoes, they dumped them into Amy's backpack, lying on the closet floor. No one spoke but both were more than aware that Damon stood behind them, the gun pointed at Amy.

Zipping the bag, McKenna turned. "What now?"

He gestured with the gun. "Let's go to your parents' room. Get what cash they have, get their ATM and credit cards. We'll use them till they're canceled."

Acting on automatic, careful to keep Amy at her side, she walked the short distance to her parents' bedroom. Her eyes focused on the bureau where her father kept his wallet. She refused to look around, to think about all she had lost, what she had caused. She took the wallet from the dresser and turned.

Damon grabbed the wallet from her hand and pulled out several bills and credit cards. "Okay. Where are the car keys?"

"Hanging on a hook in the kitchen."

"Get them. Then let's get out of here."

"Damon, please . . . let Amy—"

The gun pointed at McKenna this time. "Every time you argue or disobey me, you're going to pay for it. Now, either get your sister in the car with you or I kill her here. It makes no difference to me."

Knowing she had no choice, McKenna put her arm around her sister and led her through the house. They stopped in the kitchen and McKenna grabbed the keys. Refusing to allow herself one last look at the life she had destroyed, she took her sister's arm and went out the door.

Amy was crying now. Soft, silent tears. Did she know what Damon had done to their parents? McKenna hoped not . . . but feared that she did.

Her father's vehicle was a small, old truck he used to drive back and forth into town. Her mother's car was newer, larger.

Damon pointed to the car with his gun. "Get in the car. Put your sister in the backseat. You sit up front with me, where you belong."

Opening the back door for her sister, she helped Amy in and put the two bags she'd packed in with her. She got into the passenger seat and watched as Damon came around and settled himself into the driver's seat.

He turned and smiled at her. "Now we can be together like we were meant to be."

Returning to the present again, McKenna found herself curled into Lucas's strong arms. Her face was hidden against his chest, and ugly, soul-deep sobs tore through her. This was the first time in years she'd completely let go. The first time in years she had allowed herself to recall everything that had happened.

Lucas held her, pressed kisses to her head from time to time, and allowed her to cry. Finally there were no tears left. She lay in his arms, exhausted and so sad she could barely think straight.

"And Amy?" Lucas asked softly.

Breath shuddered through her body. "We were about fifteen miles out of town, going down the highway. I don't know why she did it. Maybe she thought she could get help; maybe she realized Damon would kill her when he got tired of having her with us. She never said anything, never gave any warning. I had my head against the window, kind of going in and out of consciousness. The next thing I heard was the door opening."

"She jumped out?"

McKenna nodded.

"And?"

"I screamed at Damon to stop. He refused. I turned around and she was lying in the middle of the road . . . just lying there. Still in her pink pajamas. Not moving. I couldn't just let her lie there . . . I jumped on him, determined to make him stop. He hit me in the head with his gun, knocked me out. When I came to, we were miles from home."

She swallowed. "I listened to the news on the television when we stopped at a motel. She was found, taken to a hospital. She told them what Damon had done . . . about my parents. And then she died."

Lucas had no words to convey his sorrow for what she had gone through. Just losing one parent was bad enough, but to lose both parents, along with your sister, and to hold yourself responsible? Beyond hell.

Would she tell him the rest? He knew most of it, but she didn't know that and the last thing he wanted was for her to know he'd dug into her past. That would come later when they were able to talk about this openly. Until then, he'd wait and see if she could bear to tell him the other horrific parts. He didn't have to wait long.

"He took me to somewhere in Kansas. A friend of his had a place there. I knew I had to get away from him, but I couldn't think straight. My head was splitting open; I kept passing out. He locked me in the bathroom with no windows. Told me I had to stay there until I learned obedience. Finally he let me out." She shook her head and added, "I have no idea how many days went by."

She was silent again. He risked asking her a question, one he had to know. "Where did the scars come from?"

"Mostly from Damon . . . though I've picked up a few over the years."

"The cigarette burns?"

"Damon," she whispered. "He'd come into the bathroom, light a cigarette, and talk, telling me things would be better once I learned obedience. Then, when he was through with his lecture and his cigarette, he would force me to the floor and put out the butt on my skin."

Lucas closed his eyes. He had to hear everything. "And the thin scars on your thighs and back?"

She took a shuddering breath. "He came in one day, said he was going to test me, give me some freedom. I had to do it . . . I had to try to leave. At that point, I didn't care what happened—I had to get away from him, even if he killed me. So when he let me out of the bathroom, I shot out the door. I even made it halfway across the yard before he caught me. That was the first time I'd been outside in weeks . . . the first time I realized we were at a small ranch." She shook her head quickly. "Anyway, he took me back inside. His friend, the one who owned the ranch, helped Damon tie me to the bed. Then Damon used a whip on me."

"The brand on your bottom?"

"Damon was gone one day, or outside or something . . . I don't know where. Anyway, I was chained to the bed. Butch, Damon's friend, came in and he . . ." She took a deep, trembling breath; Lucas held her tighter. "Damon came in and pulled him off me before he could get inside me. Damon beat him . . . literally beat him to death. Slammed his head against a windowsill over and over again until there was almost nothing left. There was blood everywhere . . . the stench gagged me. I started throwing up. Damon unchained me."

She gave a half laugh, half sob. "Stupid, really, but I thought he was going to comfort me, or at least let me go to the bathroom and throw up."

"He didn't?"

She shook her head. "He dragged me to the barn. I was so damn weak, I couldn't fight him. He told me the reason Butch went after me was because his brand wasn't on me. He tied me to a stall and branded the *D* on my bottom."

One thing . . . just one of the atrocious things that had happened to her would have broken many people, but not McKenna. Yes, she might be broken in some ways, but God, she had so much good in her, so much strength and courage.

How he hurt for her. Lucas wished with all his heart that Damon hadn't died in prison. Because if it took every bit of his wealth and he had to pay with his life, he would have taken the man apart for what he had done.

Silence once more. Would she tell him the rest or wait for another day? Then she whispered, "I didn't expect them to think I was in on it."

Already knowing, he asked, "Who?"

"The police. They thought I helped him . . . that I was an accomplice. That I actually aided him in killing my parents."

"How do you know?"

As if she couldn't be near him when she told the rest of the story, McKenna moved to get up. Lucas wasn't having it. "Stay, McKenna. Whatever you have to say . . . we'll deal with it together."

She stopped resisting then, but didn't relax as she had before. "Damon kept me locked up. If I wasn't locked in the bathroom, it was the bedroom. Wherever he kept me, I was chained. I got sick a lot, had no appetite. He raped or beat me almost daily. Said I had to learn obedience and this was the only way to teach me.

"I found some sleeping pills way back in the medicine cabinet. I had seen them before but kept hoping I could escape alive. Then one day I realized the only way I could escape him was to die. I swallowed all the pills. Damon found me on the bathroom floor, tried to get me to throw up, but I couldn't. He had to take me to the hospital to get my stomach pumped out. When he was talking to the doctor, I snuck out of the hospital. The police picked me up as I was walking down the road. Since all I had on was a hospital gown, I guess I looked suspicious."

She swallowed audibly. "I was so glad to see them . . . I thought they would help me. And they did at first. They were really kind and sympathetic. Then they checked their records, or whatever they check. There was a warrant out for Damon and me. They arrested me. And then they went and arrested Damon.

"They didn't believe me when I told them I'd had nothing to do with Mama, Daddy, and Amy's deaths. They locked me up and then sent me back to Nebraska. Fortunately, I had a public defender who believed me. Everybody else either didn't believe me or thought I got what I deserved."

"I'm assuming you got off?"

She nodded. "The public defender made a deal with

the DA's office. If they got Damon to confess that I had nothing to do with it, they'd drop the charges against me. They tricked him into admitting I wasn't involved. Damon was furious . . . or so I was told. I didn't see him again."

"Then what happened?"

"Damon went to prison. By that time I was eighteen . . . an adult. I tried to restart my life, such as it was."

"Did you have no other family?"

The little hitch he heard in her throat gave him a preview of the heartbreak of her next words. "Just my aunt . . . my dad's sister. She was at the jail when they brought us back to Nebraska. We were never that close—she was years older than my daddy and lived in another state. Anyway, she made a point of being there that day to tell me I was responsible for her brother's death, and as far as she was concerned, they could give me the death penalty."

Lucas cursed softly. No wonder she held herself responsible for everything. Everyone she should have been able to count on had betrayed her and let her down.

"And now Damon Hughes is rotting in jail?" He knew the bastard had burned to death in some kind of prison riot, but asked the question since it was the reasonable one to ask.

"No, he escaped."

Everything stilled inside him. "What do you mean, he escaped?"

She sighed and moved to get up again. This time he let her. He needed all his faculties about him to hear this. Having McKenna in his arms affected his thinking.

She sat down on the edge of the bed and faced him. "He was sentenced to thirty-five years to life in a maximum-security prison. About a year or so after he was convicted, there was a prison riot. Several inmates died. . . . It was reported that Damon was one of them."

"Why don't you believe that?"

"Because I've heard from him."

"Heard from him how?"

"A few months after I heard he died, he sent me a letter. It wasn't signed, had no return address, but it was full of facts. Facts only Damon knew. He told me he would forgive me if I came back to him. Said that he was leaving it up to me this time, but he knew where I was and could get to me anytime. He said if I made any kind of friend, had any kind of relationship, he would kill whoever it was. That he was the only person I should love."

"Did you go to the police?"

Humorless, painful laughter burst from her mouth. "Oh yes, I made a fool of myself. Gave them the letter, told them it had to be Damon. They told me I was probably having psychotic episodes from all the drugs I'd been on or that I was imagining things because of a guilty conscience. They acted as if I was the one who wrote it."

She shook her head. "I walked out the door and didn't try anymore. I left town—this was in Seattle . . . I think." She frowned as if confused. "I've lived in so many places, it's hard to remember. I lived a year or so in Baltimore, worked at a gym. One of the men there gave me some street-fight training. But then Damon's people found me again." A small smile. "The guys who owned the gym beat the hell out of them. I left the city . . . I knew they'd be back."

"Have you heard from him since?"

"I didn't for a long time. Almost three years went by. I thought I was safe . . . thought he'd finally really died or had forgotten about me. I was living in Memphis, Tennessee. I still had no friends, worked part-time jobs to be able to eat and have a place to stay. I was too afraid to talk to people . . . I couldn't take the chance."

She released a shaky breath. "But there was an elderly lady in my apartment building. I came home one day and saw her trying to carry groceries up three flights of stairs. The elevator rarely worked. I helped her carry them to her apartment. The next day she came to my door with a plate of cookies.

"It was the nicest thing anyone had done for me in the longest time." Her eyes were desolate as she whispered, "I hugged her, thanked her. That was it. Nothing else. The next day she was found dead at the bottom of the stairs. She was eighty-one years old and it was decided that she tripped and fell down the stairs."

"But you don't think so?"

"Damon sent me a letter. Told me I was responsible. Said he pushed her down the stairs to punish me. That he had warned me I couldn't have friends." She shrugged. "I didn't bother going to the police. No one had believed me before—why would they believe me then? They still claimed Damon was dead. I was afraid they'd lock me up as some sort of crazy person or, even worse, accuse me of killing her myself."

She sat there for the longest time without speaking. Finally she started again. "I disappeared once more. This time I did it right. I had made some contacts in Memphis in case Damon ever did try to get to me again. I had fake driver's licenses, fake passports. I cut my hair off, bleached it, and started wearing tons of makeup. I changed the way I walked and talked, and dressed like a boy. Everything that used to be McKenna, I changed. And then I left the country."

"And you've not heard from him since?"

"No. But I know he's still out there looking for me."

"That's why you stay on the move. Don't have relationships."

He didn't speak the words as questions. He knew that was the reason she refused to allow anything permanent between them. Now that he knew the truth, he planned to make a significant change in her outlook. First he had to find the bastard. And he would.

"It's just best that I don't invite trouble. I don't think he knows where I am, but I can't risk anyone's life."

He wouldn't argue with her. After what she'd seen, she had no reason to think otherwise. And she was correct. If Damon knew where she was and she had any kind of relationships, he would see those people dead. The bastard had proved that to her.

But there was one thing he had to say. She wouldn't believe it, but it had to be said. He just hoped to God he wasn't the first person to say it to her. "McKenna, you know that you're not responsible for your family's death, don't you?"

Her expression was one of shocked disbelief as she shook her head. "Of course I'm responsible, Lucas. I brought that monster into their lives."

Lucas went to her, kneeled at her feet, and took her hand. "No, Damon Hughes committed those murders. Not you. You were just as much a victim as your family."

Her head continued to shake. He knew he wouldn't be able to convince her with that one statement, but he hoped that at some point she could see that she hadn't been responsible.

Getting to his feet, he pulled her into his arms and whispered, "Thank you for telling me."

As her head snuggled against his chest, a plan began to form in his mind. One that he knew McKenna would not approve of and would be furious if she knew about. However, if it worked, it was worth the risk. It was damn time Damon Hughes got a taste of his own medicine and received the justice he had coming to him.

thirteen

"I'm glad you're feeling better," Noah said. "When will you be ready for a new assignment?"

Her grip on the phone tightened; McKenna chewed her lip in indecision. Truth was, she could handle an assignment now. Other than the need for a couple of extra hours sleep each night, she was completely recovered. She hadn't worked an op in weeks. She needed to get back on the job before she got rusty. So what was keeping her from telling Noah that she was ready now?

Lucas.

She didn't want to leave him yet. Yes, she would have to go very soon, but she wanted to wait just a few more days. She had already determined that once she left, she couldn't come back. It was too dangerous . . . not only for Lucas but for her heart.

"You there?"

"Yes . . . sorry. I should be ready in about a week. Will that work for you?"

"Anytime you're ready, we'll be ready to have you back. Just give me a call." The phone went dead.

There had been no censure, no accusation in Noah's voice. He was telling the truth. Noah didn't say things he didn't mean. One of the many reasons she admired him. She might be an official LCR operative, but she was still a free agent. She worked when she wanted to work. All LCR operatives did.

Still, there was guilt. She pushed it away. One week—

that was all she had. In seven short days, she would be saying goodbye to Lucas for good.

"Want to take a run?"

McKenna whirled around, no longer startled when Lucas appeared without her hearing him. She used to pride herself on being able to hear a spider approach— her hearing was nearly that perfect. But Lucas could appear as if from a fog, his footsteps so quiet. She had asked him how he did that, and he had just shrugged it off. Not that it mattered, but she hoped it was because she trusted him so much that he could come upon her without her knowing, as opposed to her skills being less sharp. Staying aware had kept her safe from Damon for eight years and had saved her ass on numerous occasions during ops. She couldn't afford to lose her advantage.

"Are you all right?"

He had drawn closer to her, and without even knowing she was going to do it, McKenna took a few steps forward, rose up on her toes, and pressed a soft, quick kiss to his beautiful, masculine mouth.

Delight gleamed in his eyes. "What was that for?"

"For everything and for nothing. You're one of the finest men I've ever known, did you know that?"

Something like guilt flickered in his face. She told herself she was being silly. Guilt for what? Maybe her instincts *were* getting dull. She used to be able to read people very well. Though Lucas was one of the few people she'd had difficulty reading from the beginning. He was so controlled that few emotions were revealed in his expression. Until he smiled . . . how she loved his smile.

"Your words almost sound like goodbye."

"You've been so generous with your hospitality. I don't have to leave yet, but I will soon."

"Why?"

"Because I have a job and you have a life that I can't be part of."

"And why can't you be part of my life?"

She held back a huff of exasperation. The man wasn't dense. He knew exactly the reason she couldn't be part of his life. But she gave it to him anyway. "Because you're a high-profile businessman and billionaire. You're in the news all the time. I can't even be seen out in public."

"So you're going to be on the run for the rest of your life because of one prick that you don't even know is still alive?"

"He's still alive, I'm sure of it. And the last thing I'm going to do is get anyone else involved in my problems. I'd like to stay for a few more days, if that's okay with you. Or I can leave now."

Lucas snorted. "But either way, you're going to leave and you don't plan on coming back, do you?"

She wrapped her arms around herself, a defensive move she recognized but couldn't prevent. Lucas had never really questioned her or argued with her. She wasn't afraid of him, but neither did she want anger between them. Yet she wouldn't back away from his statement. She couldn't because it was true.

"That's right. After I leave here, I won't be coming back."

His face was harder than she'd ever seen it as he stared at her for several seconds. Unflinching and resolute, she returned his stare. He might not like her words, but she wouldn't lie to him. If he wanted her to leave, she would. The thought wrenched her heart, but she refused to put him in any more danger than she already had.

It had been selfish of her to come to him when she was sick; it was even more selfish to stay any longer than she already had. Now it was up to him to decide if she would leave even sooner.

His face relaxed into the beautiful smile she loved. "Stay. I'm sorry I'm such an ass. I know you're doing what you think is right. I have no right to question you."

The relief was overwhelming—so much so, she feared she might cry. To prevent that, she said, "How about that run? I'll go upstairs and change. Be right back." And run she did, up the stairway before he could see how much he had come to mean to her. How much it was killing her to know she would soon leave him for good.

Lucas watched her disappear up the stairway. Part of him wanted to shake her for being so damned stubborn. The other part wanted to hold her and tell her she never had to worry about Damon Hughes or anyone hurting her ever again. That he would slay every dragon that threatened her safety and happiness. He hoped, one day soon, to be able to give her that assurance.

She would be furious when she discovered his plan. McKenna might have many vulnerabilities; she also had many strengths. One of those strengths was her determination to not involve anyone in her problems. Lucas had tremendous admiration for her courage, but damned if he would just sit on his ass and not help her. Not when he knew he could do something to stop her pain. McKenna had been running from the bastard for eight years. The man had to be stopped.

Opening the French doors, Lucas went out onto the patio. While he waited to be able to implement those plans, he had one other plan. And that was for McKenna to enjoy her time here. Not only was she still recovering from her illness, but he wanted to see her face light up with happiness. The constant worry and sadness in her eyes tore at him. Had she ever taken time off, had a holiday? He already knew the answer. Hell, she refused to go out in public except to get from one place to the other. No way would she go someplace to actually enjoy herself.

He was limited to entertaining her here at the estate. Yesterday they had gone horseback riding. The day before they had played tennis. Today they would take a run and have a picnic on the grounds. Tonight he planned a romantic dinner on one of the private patios facing the lake. McKenna had mentioned it was one of her favorite spots.

They had talked little about her past since she had revealed everything. He had a vague suspicion that McKenna actually knew Damon Hughes's location but hadn't told him for fear that he would hire someone to go after him. He wouldn't do that. McKenna didn't yet know that he didn't need to send someone to do the dirty work. Lucas was more than capable of taking care of the dirty work himself.

Minutes after she had told him that Hughes was still alive, Lucas had called his investigator. Myron Phelps's previous assignment had been to investigate McKenna; his new job was to find Damon Hughes. Once he knew his location, Lucas would then introduce himself to the bastard who had made McKenna's life a living hell.

Lucas would deal with McKenna's anger once Hughes was no longer a threat to her. What he absolutely refused to do was sit on his ass and wait for the bastard to finally make a move for her. It was way past time for the stalker to become the stalked.

She took one last bite of her sumptuous dinner, then leaned back into her chair with a sigh. "That was the absolute best meal I've ever eaten."

"You're sure you're through? You've only had three servings of everything."

McKenna laughed. "You're only jealous because I took the last of the potatoes."

"Not true. I'm upset because you took the last piece of chicken."

"Hey, I'm still recovering. I need to get my strength back."

He smiled. "I'd say you're well on your way."

She looked out at the beautiful night, the lake gently glittering under the bright moonlight, the soft sounds of nature in the background. Everything was lovely. The man across from her made it all the more so. She turned back to him and asked, "Why are you so good to me?"

"Because you deserve the best of everything. And because you're very easy to be good to."

"How so?"

"Simple things please you. A good meal, a walk in the rain, a warm fire, and a challenging game of chess."

She laughed again. "You've just described the most boring person in the world."

"No, not boring. You like the simple things in life. You take joy in them."

"Tell me about growing up with this kind of wealth. Is it difficult?"

"That's another thing I like about you. Most people might assume that since my family was wealthy, things were easy."

"I don't think anyone gets through this life easily. Some might have more advantages here and there, but we all struggle in our own way."

"You're wise beyond your years."

"And you're prevaricating."

Accepting that she wouldn't let it go, Lucas sighed and began speaking in a reflective tone. McKenna couldn't help herself—even as she listened to his words, she had to close her eyes and enjoy his voice. How she loved to hear him talk.

"I loved my father. He had his faults, but he was a good man. Losing my mother was difficult for him. Even though she died long before I was even aware of anything, I sensed a deep loneliness in him. We were close, but I always knew there was something missing in him, an emptiness I couldn't reach. A void he could never fill. There were so many times I'd find him in his study just staring at her portrait displayed over the mantel."

McKenna had seen the portrait. Merry Kane hadn't been a beautiful woman so much as she'd had a liveliness about her. Her name had been apt. Even though it was a portrait, the artist had captured the mischievousness and love of life in her eyes. She looked not only spirited but also as though she would have been a delight to know.

"Do you think that's why your dad married so many times?"

"I actually think he was looking for the exact opposite of my mother because he knew no one could ever replace her in his heart."

McKenna sighed. That was just about the most romantic thing she'd ever heard.

"You're not going to sleep in the middle of one of my stories, are you?"

She blinked her eyes open. Too embarrassed to tell him that his voice made her want to melt onto the floor in a pool of sheer want, she shook her head. "No, just feeling extremely relaxed."

"Take a walk with me?"

"Only if you don't mind if I take my shoes off."

"Are your shoes bothering you? Did I get the wrong size?"

Lucas had not only taken care of her and fed her but clothed her. She had arrived with a pair of jeans, three T-shirts, underwear, and running shoes. That was almost three weeks ago. After much haranguing, she had agreed to let him get a few things for her. And what had he done? He had bought her a new wardrobe. Dresses, skirts, blouses, and pantsuits. And shoes, all different styles and kinds of shoes. McKenna hadn't been this dressed up in years. She felt so feminine, so girly.

"The shoes fit fine. It's just been years since I've worn anything other than sneakers. I think my feet are in shock."

"Then take them off. We'll just walk along the path. If you stumble, it'll give me an opportunity to carry you."

Her heart turned over as another body part throbbed in anticipation. After everything she'd gone through with Damon, never had she thought to feel desire. But with Lucas it was a whole new day, a whole different way of looking at life. He made her feel like a beautiful, desirable woman. And he made her feel normal. When was the last time she'd felt even the slightest bit normal?

Slipping off her shoes, she took the hand Lucas held out for her. Instead of moving away, he stayed still and McKenna found herself within inches of him. His expression revealed admiration, desire, and affection. All the things she felt herself. Afraid she'd blurt out her thoughts, McKenna leaned into him and wrapped her arms around him. He took it as the invitation she meant it to be. Lowering his head slowly, his lips touched hers and the world disappeared.

She allowed him to devour her mouth. When she opened to him, he plunged inside; McKenna moaned at his taste, groaned at the desire throbbing for release. Lucas pressed his hands on her hips, pushing her against his erection. His desire should have scared her; it didn't. She wanted him as a woman wants a man, in every way, in every form. Her body didn't care that they had no future together. Her heart didn't listen to her warnings, either. She was in love with Lucas Kane, forever. And despite the knowledge that forever couldn't be in her vocabulary with this man, she ignored those warnings and let nature takes its course.

Lucas lifted his mouth slightly and whispered, "I want you, McKenna."

Emotions coursed through her: pride, gratitude, desire, and an incredible, life-altering need to know this man in every way possible.

"I want you, too, Lucas."

Letting her go, he took her hand and led her inside the house.

Lucas fully acknowledged he'd never been more scared in his life. He'd lost his virginity at the age of sixteen and had had more women throw themselves at him than he liked to remember. Without ego, Lucas knew he was attractive and because of his wealth was sometimes considered even more so.

None of that mattered right now. He was about to make love to McKenna for the first time. Once again, he felt like that sixteen-year-old virgin who'd almost exploded at the first touch of soft, supple skin under his hands.

"You don't have to if you don't want to."

Hell, for a man who had trained in hiding every thought from others, she had read his hesitancy. Except she'd read it all wrong. It wasn't that he didn't want her . . . he wanted her too much.

"You won't laugh if I tell you something?"

"I don't laugh at people and I especially would never laugh at you."

His chest tightened at the sheer sweetness and honesty of that statement.

Nudging her up the stairs, he led her to his bedroom. He had never had a woman in this room before and was glad. Whenever he slept with someone, he usually slept at the woman's apartment, or if she stayed here, he went to her room. The fact that he was leading McKenna to his bedroom was of great significance. One she wouldn't know, but he certainly did. McKenna was special.

Closing the door behind him, he said, "I'm nervous."

"Why?"

How did he tell her that her experiences of sex made him nervous because he wanted to take away those memories? He wanted to imbue only good things in her head when she thought about lovemaking in the future. What Damon had done to her, what she had felt forced to do while on a job, those didn't matter. Only tonight mattered.

She was still waiting for an answer, an expression of nervousness on her expressive face. The perfect answer came to him, one that he wasn't so sure wasn't true. "I've never made love to a woman who could kick my ass."

She burst out laughing, as he had hoped she would. "If I promise to be gentle with you, will that make you feel better?"

Drawing her close, he whispered, "Yes," and then forgot all trepidation as his mouth closed over hers.

McKenna groaned into his mouth. If he was nervous, she was terrified. Suddenly hands that had always been gentle and tender were caressing her, filling her with a need she barely recognized as her own. Panting, she pulled back. "I think I'm more scared than you are."

A tender smile lifted his mouth. "Let's be scared together, shall we?"

"Yes."

His eyes watched as she pulled the dress over her head. Standing in a nude-colored bra and bikini panties, she would have shivered, but heat infused every particle of her body, blazing like an inferno.

With a tenderness she had only ever seen in this man, he unclasped the front closure of her bra, and she let him look at her. Nipples tightened as his eyes roamed over her with so much want she almost cried out in need.

Lowering his head, he licked lightly at her nipple; electricity blended with the fire and McKenna thought she might explode from the pleasure.

His mouth still on her breast, his hands glided down her body and hooked his fingers at her panties, drawing them down her. In seconds she was completely naked.

McKenna shuddered and he pulled back to ask, "Still scared?"

"No."

Another smile, sexy and hot. "Me neither."

Suddenly his eyes went serious and grave as he gently touched the scars on her stomach and her breasts. Some were scars from fights she'd had, close calls during rescues. Most had come from Damon's hands, but under Lucas's tender hands, they seemed to disappear. Despite those marks, he treated her as if he was touching something precious, something special.

Going to his knees before her, he looked up at her. "From the moment I met you, I've thought about tasting you, loving you. Will you let me?"

She nodded, unable to deny him. No man had ever behaved this way with her. Each time with Damon had been a violent rape. A few times when she'd been on a job, she had endured a quick screw to gain trust or ferret out information for a rescue. She was so glad no man had ever touched her like this, made love to her. At least in this she was a virgin.

Lucas's golden head lowered as he pressed soft kisses to her mound. McKenna melted, her legs going weak. He took advantage of the loosening of her legs and pushed them apart. Then, when he had her in the position he wanted her in, he looked up at her again. "Thank you, McKenna."

She didn't know why he said that. She was the one

who should be thanking him. And then she stopped thinking. Her mind, her very being, was focused on his tongue as he licked, then delved deep. Not thinking, only feeling, McKenna cupped his head in her hands and pressed him against her. When he groaned, the vibration on her clit had her growling his name. The throbbing between her legs increased, and apparently Lucas knew she was close. He groaned again, pulled her closer, and tongued her over and over, lapping, sucking, and licking. And with a wild flash of blinding light, McKenna screamed and came against his tongue.

Still panting at the incredible sensation she'd never felt before, she barely comprehended that Lucas came to his feet. When he began to rip at his clothes, she watched him in wonder. The coolly, controlled Lucas Kane was no more. He seemed feral, almost wild, yet nothing about his action frightened her. He wanted her and he intended to have her . . . that was the way it should be. What she had known and read about happening to others was happening to her. She was about to make love for the very first time.

When Lucas made a grab for her, McKenna held a hand out to stop him. Yes, she wanted him, but she also wanted to look at him. He had seen her, admired her despite her imperfections. And Lucas? He had none. She wanted to devour him with her eyes, and then with her hands and her mouth.

He was as beautiful as she had imagined him. Broad shoulders, smooth golden skin, the furring on his chest darker than the hair on his head. His taut belly looked as hard as a rock and his erection jutted upward, almost reaching his navel. Her mind told her she should be scared. She had felt the violence, knew what pain that appendage could cause. But with Lucas, she knew he would never hurt her. His penis was a beautiful part of his body. She knew it would give her pleasure, and for the first time ever, McKenna wanted to give it pleasure. She went to her knees before him.

"McKenna, you don't have to—"

She closed her mouth over him. Oh yes she did. She absolutely had to taste him, pleasure him, give him everything he had given her. This was what physical love between a man and a woman should be. No fear, no pain, no dread. Only pleasure.

She took him to her throat and groaned at his taste. With what sounded like a curse, Lucas jerked from her mouth and lifted her in his arms. Dropping her on the bed, he kneeled over her.

"But I was enjoying myself," she murmured.

"As was I . . . way too much."

"How can you enjoy yourself too much?"

His mouth whispered against hers, "Let me show you."

McKenna loved how he kissed. As if she were a canvas and his mouth the paintbrush, his total concentration was on her pleasure, creating and building until she was almost crying with her need. His lips feathered softly, gently over hers. A hot flush of heat speared through her and then she moaned in protest when his mouth lifted from her.

Lucas's heart, his entire body, felt as if they were about to explode as he looked down at the beautiful woman before him. Passion-swollen lips, nipples distended, begging for his hands, his mouth. He wanted to savor her and devour her at the same time. If he went too fast, he might frighten her; too slow and he would explode. His gaze went to her face again, and he knew that no matter how badly he wanted to explode, he wouldn't. This was for McKenna . . . he would prolong her pleasure, give her everything she had been denied.

If it killed him, when she left this bedroom, she would know that what happened between a man and a woman could be beautiful and satisfying, with absolutely no pain involved.

"Lucas?"

"Easy, love . . . just enjoying the moment."

Her smile nervous and sexy at the same time, she whispered, "Could you enjoy it down here with me?"

"Definitely." Lowering his head, he whispered kisses all over her face and neck, then stopped at her breasts because he had to. They were small, lovely, infinitely kissable and suckable. He could spend hours enjoying them. Keeping his mouth closed over one nipple, he let his hands roam up and down her body, loving the way she writhed beneath him, her soft little pants and gasps firing his blood and burning through to his soul.

Unable to wait any longer, he grabbed a condom from the bedside table and slid it on. His jaw clenched for control, Lucas moved between her legs. Watching her face for any expression of fear or pain, he eased into her wet warmth and groaned at the tightness. When he heard the hitch in her breath he stopped. "Are you okay?"

She nodded. "Yes, you feel so good . . . it feels so right."

His heart pounding, everything within him begging for release, wanting to pound inside her for satisfaction, he ground his teeth together as he eased further in and then buried himself deep.

"Oh."

That one soft word was loaded with meaning. The expression of wonder and awe on her face stripped every bit of control away from him. Covering her mouth with his, Lucas began to move. And McKenna was right there with him. She wrapped her legs around his hips and met every movement, arching her body to drive him deeper within her.

Propping himself on his elbows, he watched her eyes

glitter as he thrust and retreated. She was close. The look on her face, the tightness of her body, and the clenching of her channel told him she was within seconds of climax. Wanting to make it as spectacular as possible, Lucas pressed deep within her and held still, allowing her to reach for the pleasure she sought. Her eyes widened and a long, low wail left her mouth as she tightened and spasmed around him.

Unable to stop, Lucas let go, pounding deeper, and then felt the quickening of his body as he came full force inside her. Several seconds later, his breath still rasping from his lungs, he shifted to move off of her. She clasped her arms around him and buried her face against his chest.

"McKenna?"

"I don't want to let go yet. Okay?"

"I'm too heavy for you."

Her face still hidden, she shook her head. "No, you're fine."

Knowing he had to be smothering her, he rolled over onto his back, keeping her as close as possible. Something told him he needed to stay quiet and just hold her. He didn't think he'd hurt her; he'd watched her reaction every step of the way until the very end, when he'd lost his mind. Had he somehow hurt her then?

A soft sound that sounded like a sniffle pierced his heart like a dagger. "McKenna? Sweetheart?"

When she still wouldn't look at him, he pulled away. He had to know the truth. Had he injured her somehow? He looked down at her face and his heart hurt even more. McKenna wasn't a crier. The only time he'd seen her cry was when she'd told him about her past. Any other time, she faced things with sheer bravado and gritty determination.

"Did I hurt you?"

She shook her head but seemed unable to speak.

"What is it, then?"

A long breath shuddered through her. "I never knew how beautiful it could be or how good it would feel to have you inside me."

Relief at her word mingled with sorrow at her previous experiences. "It was special for me, too."

"Really?" She looked up at him with such hope, he was tempted to spill his guts. He couldn't. She wasn't ready to hear it, and he honestly didn't know what he felt other than a myriad of emotions he could barely comprehend himself, much less explain.

"Yes, very special."

Dammit, he sounded like an idiot, but she seemed happy with the words, so he let it go. If he started talking about commitment or anything remotely related to her staying, she'd be out of his bed and into a taxi before he could speak.

He kissed her softly and said again, "It was very special."

A stomach growl was her response.

He looked down at her in mock horror. "No way."

She giggled, and he delighted in the carefree sound.

Bounding from the bed, he held out his hand. "Let's go."

"Where are we going?"

"To raid the fridge, of course."

She stood and looked around the room. "Where are my clothes?"

Pulling a sheet from the bed, he wrapped it around her slender frame and gave her the end of it to hold.

"What are you going to wear?"

Grabbing his underwear, he pulled it over his hips. "Let's go."

"What if Conrad gets up in the middle of the night?"

"Conrad has his own apartment on the other side of the estate. There aren't any servants in the house."

For some reason that statement seemed to delight her. She held the train of her sheet in her hand and said, "Let's go clean out the kitchen."

Feeling more lighthearted and happy than he could ever remember, Lucas led her down the stairs to the kitchen.

Lucas stood at the window of his office. He'd left McKenna sleeping deeply and had come into the city. Though his plans had been to work from home today, the urgent phone call he'd received from Phelps changed them.

The man was due in a few minutes and would expect some direction. He'd been furious at the news Phelps had given him and had been determined to give an earful to the editor of the news rag. Now he was rethinking those plans.

A knock at the door and then Myron stuck his head in. "Is it safe to come in?"

Lucas almost smiled. His initial reaction had been less than calm. "I've cooled down considerably."

Myron strode in, placed a packet on Lucas's desk, and dropped into a chair. "We only have a limited amount of time before it will be too late to stop them."

Lucas picked up the packet and emptied it onto the desk. There were only five photographs. All taken the day she'd come to his estate, the pictures only showed two people staring into each other's eyes, holding hands. In one photograph, Lucas had pushed a strand of hair behind her ear, a tender, affectionate gesture he'd never planned to share with the world. As celebrity photographs went, these were mild, even anemic displays of affection. But for Lucas Kane, who avoided as much publicity about his love life as possible, they might as well have been caught in a passionate kiss.

Dammit, he'd been so careful. Had even hired two

extra security personnel to patrol the outer grounds, all in an effort to protect their privacy.

"Any reason why they're just now surfacing? The photos were taken weeks ago."

Phelps shrugged. "I don't think anyone thought anything of them at first, but you've become more elusive than ever. You used to appear in public, at least occasionally, with some beauty hanging on your arm. That hasn't happened in a while. Some enterprising reporter found the photographs filed away and decided there was more to them than what was first thought."

Lucas stared down at them again. Only two of the photographs were clear enough to show their faces. He wasn't so much disturbed as surprised by the expression on his face. Though Lucas had spent years learning to hide his thoughts, the photographer had somehow captured naked emotion as he gazed down at McKenna. And McKenna's face was even more revealing, showing vulnerability and tenderness. Dammit, they'd been so busy gazing into each other's eyes, they had let their guard down.

"What do you want me to do, Lucas? It's going to cost some money, but I think we can buy them off or at least buy some time."

Lucas didn't respond to that. Money wasn't even an issue. However, while he'd been waiting for Phelps to arrive, he'd had some time to think. What was done was done. Was this an opportunity he could use?

Uttering a silent prayer that he was making the right decision, Lucas said, "Delay them . . . but don't stop them."

Myron's eyes went wide. This was clearly not the answer he expected. "You want them to run the story?"

His gaze unfocused, Lucas saw McKenna as she'd been this morning when he'd left her in bed, asleep and vulnerable. Awake, she was so determined to be tough and invincible, but underneath that bravado was a fragility. Damon Hughes was obsessed and would never stop looking for her. The only way to protect McKenna was to get Hughes out of her life forever.

"What do you think a man like Hughes would do if he saw what he considers his property being touched by another man?"

"Explode," Myron answered.

"Exactly. He wouldn't be able to stand that another man has been in possession of what he believes is his."

A frown of confused concern replacing his surprise, Myron gave a cautious nod.

"He'll come after me."

Myron surged to his feet. "You're crazy, Lucas. Do you know what the man would do to you?"

Having been in the Kane family's employ for many years, by necessity Myron knew a little about Lucas's past. However, he didn't know the extent or specialization of his employer's training.

"I can handle the bastard."

Staring hard for several seconds, Myron apparently saw the determination in Lucas's eyes. He dropped into his chair with an explosive, resigned sigh. "What do you want me to do?"

fourteen

"I can't believe you've never competed."

McKenna grinned at him. This was the second swimming race they'd had and she'd beat him each time. He looked so incredibly proud of her, as if he had discovered a national secret.

"I tried out when I was in junior high but I didn't have the reach I needed. My arms were too short. Then, when I got to high school, the swim team had pretty much disbanded. The school ran out of money and it was one of the first things they cut."

"That's too bad. You could've been one of their stars."

She didn't answer that it probably wouldn't have worked out that way. She'd met Damon and her life had not been her own from the moment she saw him. Why had she not seen his possessiveness sooner? What she had thought was romantic and sweet had really been obsessive and sick. Her parents had seen it, and because of her stupidity, they'd paid the price.

"Stop it, McKenna."

"Stop what?"

"Reliving the past. You can't change it, but you can change the future."

She didn't want to think about it or dwell on it. There were just a few days left until her self-imposed deadline. Thinking about Damon would destroy the joy, and he had destroyed too much already.

"Race you to the end," she challenged.

"Not on your life. I think I pulled a muscle during that last stretch."

"Poor baby. Want me to rub it?"

"Yes . . . in fact, I think I pulled several muscles."

Sputtering with laughter, McKenna swam away from him. One thing Lucas could do was make her laugh. Every day was a new adventure with him. It had been so long since she'd felt so lighthearted, so free from burdens. Lucas had given that to her and she would be forever grateful to him.

There was that word again. Forever. When would she get it through her head that forever was out when it came to them?

"Ready for lunch?"

Turning her mind away from those dark thoughts, she smiled up at him. "Do you even need to ask that question?"

Holding a towel for her, he said, "Come on up here, then. I might even allow you a second dessert."

As she walked slowly up the steps, air hit her wet, naked skin, but it was the heated look in his eyes that caused the goose bumps to form all over her body. She loved it when he looked at her as if she were the most beautiful, desirable woman in the world.

Allowing him to wrap the towel around her, she put her arms around his neck and pulled him down for a slow, languorous kiss. Then, leaning away slightly, she whispered, "And I might just ask for thirds on that dessert. What do you think about that?"

"I think I'm damn glad this is an indoor pool, and that I gave everyone the afternoon off." With those words, he pulled the towel from her and then unhooked the top of her swimsuit, dropping both to the ground. His mouth went to her breast.

Gasping at his hot mouth on her water-cooled skin,

she held his head as he suckled. Finally she managed to ask, "What about lunch?"

Without lifting his head, he muttered, "Dessert first." His mouth moved to her other breast and gave it the same treatment.

"Mmm. Yes, definitely."

As his mouth worked at her breast, his hands swept down her body and removed the minuscule bathing suit bottom. McKenna's hands were equally busy as she tugged at his swim trunks. They were more difficult to get off and she grunted her frustration at the effort.

Chuckling at her impatience, Lucas lifted his head and pulled his trunks down with one jerk. His erection sprang out and McKenna sighed at the sheer beauty of him. In her life before Lucas, she would never have acknowledged that a fully aroused man was anything but an atrocious, evil demon. Lucas had made her fall in love not only with the man inside but with the body that housed the man.

Her hands went to the hard, throbbing erection pressed between them. Lucas's mouth had gone back to her breast and he growled in approval of the firm strokes she gave him. While one of his hands held her close, the other glided down her stomach and pressed against her mound. McKenna opened her legs, knowing what he wanted. At the first touch of his fingers on her clit, she went wild, arching into his hand. Lucas thrust three fingers into her and she screamed at the suddenness of her release.

With a fierce growl she'd never heard from him before, Lucas lifted her in his arms and carried her to a lounge chair. Thinking he meant to drop her on it, she was surprised when he pulled the mat from the frame and threw it on the ground. Then she forgot to think at all because he lowered her onto the mat, positioned himself over her, and then was inside her.

She was about to wrap her legs around his waist, but Lucas grabbed her ankles, stopping her. She watched as he slowly pushed her legs up and wide until she was totally exposed to him. Following his eyes, she looked down to where they were joined. And together, they looked as his penis slid in and out, stroking deep, over and over again. McKenna almost screamed at the sheer eroticism and earthy sexuality.

"Lucas . . . ," she groaned, and closed her eyes.

"Open your eyes, love."

His gaze was hotter, his expression wilder than she'd ever seen. Pulling out of her completely, Lucas bent down and licked her slowly, softly. As if he were licking a melting ice-cream cone, savoring her taste, her essence, he swirled and licked her inside and out. McKenna didn't know whether to sob, scream, or explode. When his tongue plunged deep and his teeth nibbled delicately on her clit, she did all three as she came in a long, earth-shattering sensation of ecstasy.

Before she could catch her breath, Lucas was inside her again. With her ankles wrapped around his neck, he pounded into her with more force than he'd ever used before. McKenna hung on, enjoying his wild, untamed lovemaking just as much or more than the tender, sweetness of their earlier times.

Another growl, this time deeper and more guttural, came from his throat as he stiffened above her and then exploded.

McKenna loosened her legs and let them fall on either side of him. Holding him close in her arms, she cherished the gasping breaths of her lover. The golden man of her dreams.

A soft sound woke him. Without opening his eyes, he pulled McKenna's body closer. She lay on her side, spooned against him. Reaching down to kiss her neck, he had to move her hair aside, and for the first time he realized how much it had grown since he'd known her. When they first met, her hair had been almost as short as his. Now it fell just below her ears. And since she'd been here, she hadn't colored it, which meant the light golden brown of her natural color was showing.

Lucas didn't question why her appearance was changing. He knew the reason. Here she felt safe. Here she knew there was no way Damon Hughes could find her. His heart jerked at the deception he was playing, but he couldn't back away.

So far his investigator had been unable to ascertain Damon's location. If he didn't have it soon, Lucas would go with his second plan. The photograph and a small teasing caption under the photo should more than satisfy Damon that McKenna not only was alive and well but had a lover. Once the bastard saw the pictures, the ball was in his court.

He'd had to pay a tidy sum of money for the delay in printing them, but if this worked, he'd pay ten times over. Though he wasn't giving up hope that Damon's location could be determined before the photographs were printed, he wasn't counting on it. The pictures would ensure that Lucas got the results he wanted.

McKenna planned to leave him soon. He'd seen the truth in her eyes. She didn't believe there was a future with him and she would do what she thought was the right thing. To protect him, she would leave him. Little did she know that not only did he not need her protection, he would soon be luring a demon out of hiding for a confrontation. One that Lucas planned to win, assuring McKenna she need never be afraid of anyone again.

She groaned softly, wiggling her round bottom against him. Despite the pleasure of having her silken body in his arms, fury at the marks the bastard had made reignited in him. Each scar was a badge of courage. She had thought they would repel him. The only thing they made him want to do was rip the head off the creature who'd put them there. McKenna's outer scars didn't pain him nearly as much as the scars he knew she had on the inside. Damon had damaged so many things inside her. Things Lucas didn't know if she'd ever be able to reclaim. He only hoped that once the threat was over, she could find the innocent, trusting, and loving woman who had been smothered by the freak.

Another bottom wiggle told him she was waking up. Unable to deny such a lovely invitation, Lucas lifted her left leg up and pressed his erection into her soft warmth. She moaned in approval. This time it was soft and sweet. Arousal built like a campfire, small, unassuming, until soon a cinder would catch and a blaze would burst forth, out of control. Lucas surged and retreated, thrust deep, slowly withdrew, again and then again. Heat bloomed . . . building . . . building . . . building. The blaze flared, turned into an inferno. He could wait no longer; turning McKenna onto her stomach, he simply, passionately, and lovingly mated with her.

Paris

Noah stared at the computer screen, an ominous feeling spreading through him. Though he wasn't much of a cursing man, every curse word he knew came to mind as he studied the photo of the missing woman. Jamie Kendrick had been missing for weeks, maybe more, and it was just now being reported. How the hell did this happen in today's society, when a fucking celebrity can kiss someone in public and in seconds it's spread like a wildfire on the Internet?

"What's wrong?" The concern on Samara's face told him she'd sensed his rage.

"Take a look at this picture." He turned the screen so she could get a good look.

"Oh, Noah," Samara breathed. "It's McKenna."

"No . . . just looks an awful damn lot like McKenna." Using the eraser end of a pencil, he pointed out the differences. "See, the nose is tilted up a little more than McKenna's. Her eyes are more rounded, less oval. And her chin is squarer."

She peered closer. "You're right, but the resemblance is uncanny." She looked at him then, concluding what he had only moments ago. "You think Damon Hughes took her, don't you?"

"It's a damn good possibility. What fries my ass is that no one reported her missing. Apparently she'd just moved to Little Rock, Arkansas, a few months ago and hadn't made any friends. The part-time jobs she had were low-level positions and the people assumed she had just decided not to work there anymore."

"How did they finally decide she was missing?"

"She missed a court date in Baton Rouge, Louisiana. Seems her husband, now ex-husband, had abused her and was in jail, awaiting trial. The woman had moved away but with the obvious intent of going back to testify. She never showed up."

"But couldn't it have been her ex-husband who arranged her disappearance?"

Noah nodded. "That's what the authorities are going on. He's made several threats against her. They've not named him as a suspect since he was in jail at the time of her disappearance; however, they're speculating that he hired someone."

"That's a reasonable assumption."

"Yes, and I'd be the first one to agree with them if she didn't look almost identical to McKenna."

Samara sat on the edge of his desk, pressed her fingertips to Noah's temples, and rubbed. From experience,

Mara knew that if there was any tension in his body at all, it resulted in a slight ache in his temple. And dammit, yes, he had tension.

"What are you going to do?" she asked.

"What I don't want to do, but there's no choice. If Hughes has this woman, McKenna needs to know."

"She's been with Lucas for almost a month."

Noah blew out a sigh. Standing, he took his wife in his arms, drawing comfort from her warm, enticing body. Holding Samara always helped.

"Have you talked with her since she's been there?" Noah asked.

Samara nodded against his chest. "Only once. She sounded . . ."

She trailed off, and Noah knew why. She didn't want to say the words because it would reemphasize what he knew and would only make calling her doubly hard. McKenna had sounded happy. For the first time in her young life, she was feeling safe and secure. And without a doubt, she was falling in love with Lucas Kane. Dammit all to hell, he didn't want to have to do it, but he didn't have a choice.

McKenna gripped her cellphone in her hand, afraid if she let go of it, she would throw it across the room. Refusing to flinch from what she knew she had to do, McKenna stalked jerkily to her laptop. She hadn't had it on in days. Just how freaking irresponsible could she be?

She went to the website Noah had set up for LCR, typed in her code word, and hit enter. And there she was. A face that wasn't hers, but looked too much like hers not to mean something.

Jamie Kendrick looked like McKenna, yet she didn't. This woman still had a wholesome, innocent quality about her. McKenna could no longer claim either. And if

Damon had taken her, she wouldn't be wholesome or innocent for long.

If? She snorted under breath. Of course he had taken her. She wasn't into lying to herself. The woman's ex-husband might be the only suspect, but McKenna knew in her gut he had nothing to do with her disappearance. Damon had somehow found the woman and had taken her. What had he done when he realized she wasn't McKenna?

Physically, she had changed many things about herself. However, she still had one identifying emblem that was almost impossible to demolish. Long ago she had tried to have the brand on her bottom removed. The *D* had been burned into her skin so deeply and was so large that it would take several skin grafts to repair the damaged area. And even if she had the brand removed, the doctors told her, she'd still have scarring. Either way, if this woman didn't have scars or a giant letter on her bottom, Damon would know.

Would he kill her? Years ago, Damon hadn't minded killing. He'd done it as easily as some people swatted at an insect. If someone irritated him, he killed them. Was she now responsible for one more death?

"What are you doing?"

McKenna closed her laptop and looked over her shoulder at Lucas, who stood at the door of her bedroom. A bedroom she hadn't used since they'd become lovers. "Checking my messages."

Standing, she went toward him, willing herself the courage to do what she had to do.

"Something wrong?"

"No." She grimaced. "Well, other than I have to leave earlier than I planned."

"Leave?"

She sighed. "Yes, I had hoped to stay a couple more

days, but Noah McCall just called. He needs my help with a job . . . sounds really intriguing."

"Just like that, huh?"

"Just like what?"

"You can leave with no regrets?"

"I didn't say I wanted to leave, Lucas. But you knew I would have to eventually. We've talked about it."

"We talked about it before we became lovers."

"Nothing's changed. I can't stay permanently."

He turned and walked away. "You're right."

Well, what the hell did that mean? She followed him as he headed down the landing toward his bedroom. "Where are you going?"

He turned and gave her a mild look. "Taking a shower. Want to join me?"

Jerking to a stop, she could only stare at him. Though she hadn't wanted him to be angry or upset when she left, she had expected a different kind of reaction. McKenna didn't know if she should celebrate, cry, or stomp her feet with frustration. Had she misread him? Did he not care as much as she thought?

"That's it?" The words were out of her mouth before she could stop them.

"What exactly do you want me to say, McKenna? Please stay? Of course I want you to stay, but I've known from the beginning you were here only temporarily. Why should I waste time on an argument when I know it will do no good?"

Hell, he was right. She should be glad there were no harsh words said between them. Their time together had been so special and he had been so wonderfully good to her. She forced a smile to her frozen mouth. "You're right. And I wouldn't want to spoil anything by arguing."

She looked down at her hands, surprised and disturbed to see them clenched. Acting indifferent came with her tough-girl persona. She damn well needed to get it back before she confronted Damon. Taking a breath to center herself, she said, "I need to leave within the hour. Would you mind asking Conrad to call a taxi for me? I need to go to a car rental place."

"Take one of my cars. I have several I never use."

"Thanks, but then I'd have to arrange to have it returned. I'll just rent one that I can return to a rental agency in Paris."

She sensed he was about to argue, but all he said was "Fine" and continued walking.

"Lucas!"

He turned once more to look at her. McKenna swallowed past a mountainous lump of emotions in her throat. "For what it's worth, thank you for giving me the best days of my life."

He stared at her for the longest time. She didn't know what she wanted him to say. Whatever he said wouldn't change what she had to do. Finally he said solemnly, "Thank you, McKenna, for sharing them with me." He then continued toward his bedroom.

As she watched him disappear from view, she told herself it was better this way. No anger, no recriminations, no tears. Wiping at her damp face, she shrugged. Oh well, two out of three wasn't bad.

fifteen

Duffel bag in hand, McKenna stood in the foyer. She'd left the clothes Lucas had bought her in the closet. Though she would need stylish clothes for her new assignment, she couldn't make herself wear the things Lucas had given her when she faced Damon. She refused to taint them with the stench of that bastard. She would buy clothes before she contacted him.

"I see that you're ready to go."

Whirling around, she faced Lucas. He was several feet away, in the shadows, so she couldn't see him as clearly as she wanted . . . as clearly as she needed. Why couldn't he be in the bright light so her last glimpse of him could be something to remember?

She wanted to go to him, see him, touch him, taste him one last time. Her toes curled into her shoes and she forced her entire body to freeze. If she went to him, touched him again, she wouldn't leave. She might be tempted to tell him things. Things that could get him killed. She'd die before she let anything happen to Lucas. She'd lost too much already.

"Will you be back?"

"No."

"So this is goodbye forever."

Gripping the handle of her bag so tight she almost drew blood, she whispered, "Yes."

He continued to just look at her, not saying anything, just looking. Why didn't he move closer? Even as she wanted him closer, she needed him to stay at a distance. She wanted to remember him as she'd seen him this morning, when he'd woken her with a soft kiss and made slow, delicious love to her.

Since she was the one leaving, it only made sense that she head toward the door. Legs stiff with the desire to walk in the opposite direction, she turned and made herself move forward.

"McKenna."

She stopped. If she turned . . . no, she couldn't. Facing the door, she asked huskily, "Yes?"

"I know you think you have to leave. I'm not sure why now, and I won't ask. But no matter what happens in the future, you'll always be welcome here."

Tears came before she could stop them. Leaning her forehead against the door, she drew in a breath and said, "You're the finest man I've ever known, Lucas Kane." Before she could say anything more, she opened the door and ran.

"Damn, that was intense."

His chest so tight he could barely breathe, he turned to Jared, who stood at the entrance of the library. He raised a brow at the man's rudeness. "I believe I asked for privacy."

Jared grinned. "See, that's where you made the mistake." When Lucas didn't respond, Jared sighed. "Why the hell did you let her leave?"

"Because she thinks she has no choice. I intend to see that she has choices. What do you have?"

"Come into the library. I have it all laid out. With what Phelps has uncovered for you also, I think we're going to be able to pinpoint the bastard rather easily."

Lucas forced himself to follow Jared, though every part of his gut was telling him to go after McKenna and tell her he'd slay every dragon and demon that even looked at her cross-eyed. She wouldn't let him. Her independence was one of the things he admired most about her. It was also one of the things that infuriated him the most. Dammit, he had the wherewithal to take out the bastard.

Again he questioned whether he should have told her about his past. Would that have made a difference? His gut told him no. McKenna was bent on protecting those she cared for. She wouldn't want him going after Damon, whether she knew about his background or not. Therefore, he had no choice but to remove Damon and then tell her. He refused to consider the betrayal she might feel. Better she feel betrayed than someday end up in the bastard's clutches again.

Lucas dropped into a chair and faced his friend. "Tell me."

Deadly serious now, Jared sat across from him and told him what he knew about Damon Hughes. "He's about as bad as they come. Drugs and gambling are his mainstay."

"First, explain to me how the bastard escaped from prison and somehow everyone believes he's dead."

"I don't have names, only off-the-record suppositions, but they sound feasible." Jared pulled several pages from a folder. "Here are statements, all unofficial, by prison guards, an administrator, the jail warden, and two doctors. They won't testify in court and will deny everything if approached by any person in law enforcement, but they all indicated that Hughes had some influential friends before he went into prison, and made even more while he was there. Powerful friends. When the riot broke out, some prisoners escaped. It was reported that they were all apprehended. Several prisoners were killed in the fire caused by the riot. Damon's friends greased some hands and got him declared dead."

"That's some damn powerful greasing."

"Mafia money can be quite slick."

"Mafia? In Nebraska?"

"Hell, the Mafia's got connections everywhere. Though apparently this was a cousin of a cousin. Still, it got him what he wanted. Freedom without anyone looking for him."

"So what did he do once he got out?"

"What he promised to do. He went into business with the people who helped him. Unfortunately, he became more powerful, and they had a parting of the ways. A few people conveniently died. Hughes continued to gain more power and money. Eventually he killed off his enemies and became the big honcho."

"Do we know where he is?"

"That's the kicker. Probably in the southeastern United States, but that's as close as we've been able to pinpoint."

"Why do we think the Southeast?"

Jared grimaced. "Apparently he's told more than one person that his fiancée loves the warm weather."

"And I'm assuming this fiancée is supposed to be McKenna?"

"No one has seen her, but his story is they met when she was a teenager and he's the love of her life. She plans to join him as soon as she graduates from law school."

If Lucas had a sense of humor left, he would have laughed. Seeing McKenna as an attorney would be interesting. She was so bluntly honest.

"Anything else?"

Leaning forward, Jared said, "He's damn dangerous, Lucas."

"I've been acquainted with quite a few damn dangerous people."

"You've been out of the game for a while, mate. Just don't go off half cocked because of what he's done to your girlfriend. He's going to be surrounded by the most conscienceless people around."

"For just one of the things he did to McKenna, he deserves to die. But he not only destroyed her life, he wiped out an entire family. And judging by the things you've learned, he's still killing. The man needs to be stopped."

"Agreed. Just make sure you don't go down with him."

Lucas nodded but didn't reply. What could he say? He had no intention of dying, but if he did, it would be after Damon Hughes drew his last breath. That he could swear.

There was something else eating at Jared. Knowing the man's penchant for detail and follow-up, Lucas asked, "What's Humphries done now?"

"He's gambling again. Using his son-in-law's name and credit cards."

Shit. He didn't need this now. "Can you get to his son-in-law without tipping him off?"

"Probably."

"Go to him, tell him what's going on. If he wants to press charges, I'll go along with it. However, if he thinks he can pull him in without informing the rest of the family, I'd like to try it."

"Bloody hell, Lucas. Why?"

There were certain personal things few people knew about Phillip Kane. Lucas would never defile his father's memory, but Jared deserved to know why he was so reluctant to punish Humphries. "After my mother died, my father went off the deep end. He had a drinking problem not many people knew about. Humphries was one of his closest friends. Every time my father ended up in a ditch, Humphries was the one he would call. My dad finally cleaned himself up. Exchanged his love for alcohol for an obsession for beautiful women, but he never forgot what Humphries did for him. And neither can I."

His expression grim, Jared nodded. "I'll talk to the son-in-law."

"Good."

"Have you made a decision about the photographs Phelps showed you?"

"I had hoped to find the bastard before now. Since we still have no real idea where he is, I don't have a choice but to proceed with the lure."

Jared stared hard at him for several seconds, then sighed and said, "When are you going to start the game?"

"Tomorrow. Phelps will release the gag on the tabloid, with the understanding they get to run the photo first. Then it'll go viral. All major newspapers will run it the next day, with a small, tantalizing story regarding my new love interest. I'll go to the States, make myself open and available. Hopefully by this time next week, Mr. Hughes and I will become acquainted."

"Have you considered the man might just kill you outright, no questions asked?"

Lucas shrugged. He had considered it. "It's a risk I'm willing to take."

"When I told you that you needed to stop playing around and settle down, I had hoped you'd fall for a nice, calm English girl. Not a wild child from Nebraska."

"My feelings for McKenna don't even enter into this. Damon Hughes is the kind of man we used to fight against. Even if I didn't know McKenna personally, I'd still go after the man."

"Just be damned sure you stay alive." Jared's smile was one of grim humor. "The Millington Award is just a few weeks away. I'd hate to have to accept for you posthumously."

Paris

Running on determination, nerves, and a gallon of caffeine, McKenna entered Noah's office. Yesterday he'd only given her the bare facts of Jamie Kendrick's disappearance. Today she hoped to learn more. With LCR's assistance, she would rescue the woman. Noah undoubtedly already had a scenario planned, but McKenna had her own ideas. She only hoped Noah would go along with them.

Noah stood as she entered the room. "You're looking well, McKenna."

She nodded. "I'm one hundred percent again."

"Good." He gestured to the small conference table. "We're ready to get started. I'm assigning Dylan as your backup, with an assist from Aidan Thorne. I've asked Samara to sit in with us, too."

McKenna spared a small smile for Dylan and a larger one for Samara. Since she'd never worked with Aidan before and had only met him once, she gave him a nod and seated herself at the table.

"Okay, here's what we know. Jamie Kendrick disappeared weeks ago. No one reported her missing because she was new in town. The part-time jobs she had were the kind that people often quit without giving notice. Her apartment rent was paid through the end of the month. Mail was stopped at the post office. Someone stuck a postcard in a mail slot asking that the mail be held. Since she knew so few people, it was assumed she had just left town."

"What about her apartment? Anything left behind?" Dylan asked.

"No. Whoever took her wanted it to look like she'd moved. Nothing, not even a dish, spoon, or square of toilet paper, was left. The apartment was a furnished rental. So it looked as though she had just moved out."

"And the reason she's considered a missing person now is that she failed to show up for a court date?" McKenna said.

Noah nodded. "Her ex-husband had been charged with abuse. Bastard is in jail, so they know he didn't take her. They think he might have hired someone. From the sound of it, he's pretty torn up."

Aidan snorted. "Yeah, sounds like a real prince of a guy."

"Point is, police are treating it as a missing-person case now, but they're still looking at the obvious, which is that her ex-husband had someone abduct her to keep her from testifying."

McKenna shook her head. "That's because no one knows she looks identical to a woman being stalked by a maniac."

"I've talked to one of our FBI contacts, Honor Stone. She knows the special agent in charge of the investigation." He met each person's gaze, then his eyes settled on McKenna. "You remember her? She worked on Keeley Fairchild's missing children case."

"Keeley Mathison now," Samara added.

He smiled at his wife, then looked back at McKenna. "I told Honor our theory. She's checked Hughes out and the story of his death still stands. Whoever helped the man disappear knew what they were doing."

McKenna shrugged. No big surprise there. Why wouldn't they believe prison officials instead of one helpless, seemingly drugged-out teenager? Especially when it had been so expedient.

Noah leaned forward to lock gazes with her. "We all agree that there's an amazing resemblance between you and Jamie Kendrick. And the fact that she's mysteriously disappeared is suspect, but it could all still be a coincidence. Are you sure you want to risk it?"

A long sigh escaped. "My gut tells me he has her. And

since we're the only ones who even know he's alive, no one will be looking in his direction. He can dispose of her, sell her . . . whatever he wants to do with her."

McKenna refused to acknowledge the ice-cold fear that raced through her veins as she remembered some of Damon's favorite punishments. This wasn't about her any longer. This was about saving a woman whose only crime was the misfortune of looking like someone else.

She took another breath and said, "But even if he doesn't have her, I'm ready to confront him."

Noah and Samara exchanged a concerned look. "Confront him? How?"

Knowing that she would see censure in their eyes didn't stop her from looking around the room as she explained. Fear had kept the truth hidden for too long. "I know how to contact him."

"How's that?" Noah asked.

"When he left me that last message, telling me he killed my neighbor, he gave me a phone number. I know I should have gotten it over with, confronted him then. I was too scared . . . a coward." She straightened her shoulders and set her jaw. "I'm not scared anymore."

Noah shook his head slowly. "There's not a person at this table or in this world who would ever call you a coward, McKenna. You've endured things no one ever should have to experience. And you've saved a lot of lives, so don't ever use that word again."

Since she continued to be scared, she couldn't agree with Noah's assessment. However, the words were a balm to the ragged edges of her mind where her conscience had chiseled condemnation.

"Since you know where he is, I'm assuming you have a plan?"

"Yes. I'm going to trade myself for Jamie."

Three men cursed simultaneously. Samara was the

only one who didn't seem surprised. "What happens if you can't find her?" Samara asked.

"I'll stay until I find her. Once I do, I'll get her to safety and then . . ." She took a breath and finished. "I'll take Damon out."

"We don't, as a rule, take people out," Noah said.

McKenna snorted softly. "I'll be glad to try to make a citizen's arrest, but I doubt he's going to come quietly."

"You misunderstand. Damon Hughes dying would be no big loss. However, you've got two LCR operatives and me on standby, just waiting to help you." Noah's eyes narrowed as he stared into space for a moment. Then he looked around the room. "Perhaps we could do this without an exchange."

"What do you mean?" McKenna asked. "He's not going to give her up without getting me."

"We could trick him into giving her up, but before he got to you, we could get him."

McKenna was shaking her head before he finished his sentence. No way in hell was she putting LCR people at risk for something that she could have prevented. If something happened to one of them . . . horror twisted her gut. She couldn't live with that on her conscience.

"Don't shake your head till you hear the plan, squirt." Dylan's lazy voice interrupted her thoughts.

Her mouth was so frozen, she couldn't even come up with the half smile his nickname usually caused. "I can't allow—"

"McKenna, you're part of a group now. We work together to save others and we band together to help each other. Understand?"

Emotion lumped in her throat unexpectedly. Damned if she would give in to the silly emotional tears that were pounding behind her eyes. For someone who'd been on her own for so long, having these people treat her like family was overwhelming. And then her conscience snarled a warning: *Remember what happened to your last family because of you.*

Since everyone's eyes, including Samara's, were staring at her with the conviction of Noah's words, McKenna didn't bother to argue. If it came down to it, she would protect these people in any way she could. Telling them this wouldn't help.

Since she hadn't spoken, Noah apparently believed he had her agreement. "Once we have Jamie safely in our sights, you back away and we'll do what needs to be done. If we can take Hughes peacefully, we will. I think we can ensure that the next prison he's taken to will hold him."

She didn't know how she felt about that. For so long she had dreamed about killing Damon. Of course, that was always once she got up the courage to actually confront him. But now that she would soon confront him, how would she feel if the man didn't die? She needed to think on that a little more.

"So the plan is for me to contact Damon, tell him I'll exchange myself for Jamie. We set up the meeting. As soon as she's safe, I get away and you guys come running."

Noah nodded. "He'll probably expect a setup, so you'll need to make it convincing. Make him believe that this is just something between you and him . . . no one else is involved. You saw a news report, saw Jamie's photograph, and immediately knew. Let him think you've changed your mind . . . say whatever you have to say to make him believe this is what you want."

Since she knew what Damon wanted, what Damon liked, that shouldn't be a problem. There were things he liked to hear her say and he had done things to her to make her say them. Hearing the words without coercion would be like an aphrodisiac to the lunatic.

"I'll be convincing." What else could she say? They

would know the truth tomorrow. Giving them details today wouldn't do any good.

When everyone nodded, she said, "I need to go shopping . . . get my hair done. Damon doesn't know about my training. I need to look as unchanged as possible. Feminine and weak. If he thinks I'm the same person I was years ago, he'll be less likely to suspect anything."

"Your hair has grown out in the last few months, but it's still much shorter than Jamie's," Samara said. "Getting it back to your original color should make a big difference, though."

Noah checked his watch. "Why don't we meet back here tomorrow afternoon?" He glanced at McKenna. "Will that give you enough time to shop and get your hair colored?"

"Yes. I'll only get a few things."

McKenna started toward the door. She stopped and turned when Noah said, "What about Lucas Kane?"

"What do you mean?"

"Does he know about any of this?"

"No. He needs to stay out of it."

She waited for him to say something else, but instead he just gave her the small, enigmatic smile he was famous for and said nothing at all.

McKenna went through the door and thought about all the things she needed to do. Shopping for clothes to wear to lure a killer. Gee, that sounded like such fun.

"Want some company?"

She turned to see Samara standing behind her. Relieved that she didn't have to face this alone, she nodded. "Love some."

Samara pulled her cellphone from her purse. "I'll call my hairdresser and see if she can squeeze you in. She's a whiz with color."

The elevator doors opened and McKenna entered, listening to Samara talk in broken French to her hairdresser. A surreal feeling washed over her. It was about to happen. She was finally going to face the man who'd killed her family. She had dreamed about it, had nightmares about it, and even fantasized about the actual deed. Deep down she had never believed she'd have the courage to really carry it off. Now she had no choice. She had to do it, to save a young woman's life. And in the process, she might lose her own. That seemed only fitting. Because of her, the monster had taken the most important people in the world to her. Dying to avenge them seemed only fair.

sixteen

"I know you're nervous, but you look wonderful."

Aware that Samara was only trying to boost her confidence, McKenna managed a small smile. Yesterday, at the salon, the stylist had turned her chair around so McKenna could look at the final results of her hard work. A slap in the face couldn't have had more impact. Seeing the old McKenna Sloan staring back at her wasn't something she had been prepared for.

Last night she'd spent a sleepless night convincing herself she could do this. This morning, determined to go forward, she had dressed in her new clothing and practiced being McKenna in the mirror for several hours. After changing everything about her persona for so long, she'd felt the need to relive who she had been back then. The experience hadn't been pleasant but had been necessary.

This afternoon she'd walked into Noah's office as the old McKenna but with a few important changes. She might look the way she had years ago, but there was a core of strength she hadn't had before. She could and would rescue Jamie Kendrick and in the process deal with Damon Hughes one last time.

If yesterday had been difficult, today would go several steps beyond. And despite what she'd told herself, she could feel the panic rising again. Giant winged gargoyles had replaced the butterflies in her stomach. She was about to make a call to her worst nightmare, the man she feared above all people, and now she didn't know if she had the courage to go through with it.

"McKenna."

Noah's voice snapped her out of her terror. She lifted her gaze to see his expression of compassion and concern. *Oh hell.* Seeing Noah McCall worried grounded her and brought her back to where she needed to be. The man was rarely blatant in showing his concern for an operative. The fact that he was allowing her to see it turned the job back to what it was. A job. Nothing more. She'd taken down evil bastards before; this was just one more.

"You don't have to do this," Noah said. "We'll find another way."

"No. We have no other way of getting to him without me."

Noah handed her a small plastic bag holding a ring. "One of our designers came up with this. If something goes wrong and you get taken, the ring has a GPS device in it. We can track you up to a thousand miles."

McKenna pulled the silver ring from the bag. Celtic in design, simple yet intricate. Since she had never worn a lot of jewelry, she was glad the ring was unpretentious. It shouldn't attract Damon's attention.

"You'll be wearing an earpiece. We'll hear everything and you'll hear us. That way, as soon as Jamie is safe, we'll be able to alert you." Noah looked around the room, his eyes stopping on everyone. "Are we ready?"

When there was a round of head nods, McKenna took the disposable cellphone that had been purchased just for the occasion. Trying to act like this was any other op, she took a breath and punched in the number she'd memorized long ago, then pressed the speakerphone key so everyone could hear.

Damon answered on the first ring. "McKenna."

The familiar oily voice knotted her stomach even more. "Yes."

"At last, my darling. I'm so pleased you called. Are you ready to come home?"

"Yes. On one condition."

"Condition?"

The anger in his voice didn't surprise her. Damon didn't like conditions. He insisted on total control. She'd learned that the hard way.

"I know about the woman you took."

"What woman?" The words were a denial, but she heard the shock in his tone.

"The woman who looks like me. Her name is Jamie Kendrick. You took her from Little Rock, Arkansas. What did you do with her?"

There was a long pause. It seemed everyone in the room had stopped breathing. When he spoke again, collective soft breaths were released.

"Say I did take a woman who looks like you. What about it?"

"Is she still alive?"

Another long pause, then he said, "Yes."

Praying he was telling the truth, she said, "Good. I want an exchange."

"An exchange?"

"Yes. If you'll release her, I'll come back to you."

Fury filled his voice. "Are you working with the police? Because if you are, you will fucking pay for it and so will the woman."

"No, this is between you and me, Damon. I saw her picture on the news. She looks just like me. I don't want her to pay for my mistakes. This is all my fault. If I had done what you wanted me to do . . . given you what you wanted . . ." She trailed off.

Knowing that all eyes were on her, McKenna turned slightly away. Every word dripping with submission, she continued, "I'm ready, Damon, to be what you want me to be. You were right . . . we were meant to be together. I'm nothing without you."

There was such a pregnant silence, McKenna felt as if the entire world were holding its breath. Finally Damon said, "You'll submit to me? Be what I need you to be? Give me everything I want?"

"Yes."

"I want to believe you, McKenna. I want to believe that you've learned your lesson. How do I know this isn't a trap?"

"How could it be a trap, Damon? You convinced the authorities that you were dead. No one would believe me if I went to them."

He chuckled. "That is true. The beauty of having greedy friends in high places."

"So you'll agree to the trade?"

"If you've learned your lesson, why should I have to give something up?"

"Because you love me . . . and I know you want to make me happy." Her stomach clenching, she forced even more submission into her tone. "I'm begging you, Damon . . . as a favor for me . . . please."

He sighed. "I don't know why I'm so good to you . . . but yes, I'll let the woman go."

"Thank you, Damon. I'll make it up to you. I promise."

"Yes, you will."

"When can we make the trade?"

"I ask the questions, McKenna. Have your forgotten your lessons?"

"Yes, Damon. I'm so sorry."

"Monday afternoon, three o'clock. Mandeville Wharf isn't far from my home in Tampa. I'll be waiting at the end of Pier 77. As soon as I see you walking toward me,

I'll let the woman go. If you try to trick me, she gets a bullet in her back. Got it?"

"Yes. Thank you, Damon."

"We're going to have a wonderful life together, McKenna. Once you've proven yourself and I know I can trust you, we'll start out brand new. I'll forgive your betrayals and we can finally be together the way we were always meant to be."

"That's what I want, too."

"See you soon, darling."

McKenna closed the phone and turned back around. Unable to face the people at the table who'd heard every groveling, sniveling comment she'd made, she kept her head down as she put the phone in her purse.

"McKenna, look at me." The compassion in Noah's voice almost crushed her. She looked up, surprised to see that only Samara and Noah were still there. The other operatives were gone.

"Dylan and Aidan left. They knew this wasn't something they needed to hear," Samara explained.

"You have nothing to be ashamed of . . . nothing to hide from," Noah said. "Damon Hughes is the monster."

Working to keep her emotions on lockdown but unable to articulate her feelings, she gave a small nod of thanks. "I guess it's best if they come back in so we can discuss any last-minute details."

Samara went to the door and opened it. Both men returned and sat down. Dylan shot a glance at Noah. "When and where's it going down?"

"Monday. Tampa, Florida. But I doubt he really lives there. There's no reason for him to tell you where he lives other than to throw off anyone he thinks you're working with."

"You're right," McKenna said. "I'm sure he expects us to trick him. That's why we can't."

Dylan leaned forward. "What are you talking about?"

"Until Jamie is completely safe, we have to make it seem as though I'm the only one involved."

"Agreed," Noah said. "But don't think for a moment that you're alone, McKenna."

She nodded, reassured but feeling oddly disconnected from everything. The feeling wasn't unusual for her. When she worked an op, she often put herself into that kind of mode. One where she felt as if she were acting on automatic pilot and saw everything from a distance. A coping mechanism she'd learned during the worst of Damon's torture, it had kept her halfway sane during her time with him and had kept her alive for the last several years.

She only hoped she could stay disconnected. Just hearing Damon's voice after all this time, every word tainted with evil, brought back the old fears and insecurities she thought she had conquered.

She stood. "When do we leave for Florida?"

"Tomorrow morning. Ten o'clock."

McKenna headed to the door. "We can go over scenarios on the plane."

She hurried out before anyone could stop her, needing to be by herself for a while. She'd been so busy gearing herself up for what she had to do, she hadn't even allowed herself to grieve over Lucas. Once that was done, she would return to the hell she faced. But just for a few hours, she wanted to relive the wonder of what she had found with him. And then she would put all of that behind her and do what she should have done years ago.

Palm Beach

Excitement beat within Damon as he closed the phone. The one he'd kept specifically for McKenna to call him on. And she had finally called. McKenna was coming home! The real McKenna. Not that slut of a fake he'd gotten rid of.

After all these years, his McKenna had called him. So what if it was to make a trade? The reason didn't matter. What mattered was that she would be with him. Once that was accomplished, he'd make damn sure they never parted again. She had said she was ready to accept her place, her role. He would soon see.

Was she working with someone? She had said she wasn't, but how could she not be? McKenna might be the love of his life, but he knew her well. She wouldn't be able to conceive of making a trade all by herself. She would need someone guiding her, telling her what to do. His McKenna was an innocent in the art of deception. One of the many things he loved about her. She couldn't lie worth a damn.

If she tried to double-cross him, she would pay a high price. Either way, he was determined to have her back. This was the closest he'd been to having her back in years. He'd damn well not fail.

His body hardened at all the ways he intended to ensure that she would stay with him forever. All the things he'd done to her when they were together before had been to train her, but they hadn't worked as they should have. The years they'd been apart had given him plenty of time and opportunity to study and practice how to create a perfect submissive McKenna.

He would reinitiate her to the pleasure of exquisite pain. Once her training was over, she would finally be everything he had dreamed.

Willing his body to settle down, he picked up another phone. To show her the depth of his love, he would even attempt to keep his promise and return the woman. The man he'd sold her to might still have her. If not, there were plenty of substitutes he could use. One whore was just as good as another.

Either way, soon McKenna would be back where she belonged. And he would kill anyone who got in his way.

London

The photographs strewn across his desk were better than he remembered. The photographer might be a sleaze, but he was a talented sleaze. Of course, McKenna was an exquisite subject to photograph. The elegant lines of her face, the lovely tilt of her chin when she spoke, the unbelievable but much too rare smile that could brighten her entire face to a beauty beyond description . . . the ache he'd had since she left increased.

"Which ones do you want to use?" Myron Phelps asked.

Lucas slid two photographs across the desk—the two that clearly revealed their faces and that they were only aware of each other. "Do you have the wording?"

"Yes, I typed it up this morning." Myron handed him a sheet of paper. "Just to make sure it was exactly what you wanted. Then I'll send it to *Tattles*."

The handsome, mysterious, and oh so wealthy Lucas Kane is apparently holding out on us once again. Who is this new lovely? Insiders report the first name McKenna. Can it be that one of England's most eligible bachelors has finally been snared?

Lucas inwardly winced at the over-the-top description, but it sounded similar to other things that had been written about him. No one should be able to detect that the message was a lure for a killer. "This gives just the right amount of information. And you're sending it to the major newspapers tomorrow?"

"Yes. *Tattles* will run it tomorrow in their paper, and

then the rest will have it by the next day. Are you sure you don't want to go with just the newspapers in the southeastern U.S.?"

"No. Even though it's likely he lives there, I want to do this only once. If we hit them all, he'll be certain to see it at least once." Lucas shrugged. "And if he sees them several times, that will only make him more anxious and determined to come after me as quickly as possible."

"Once they're printed, other countries will have them, too."

Meaning McKenna would see the photos as well. That was inevitable. He just hoped to hell she saw them *after* he got to Damon. Either way, his course was set; he wouldn't change his mind. "Damon needs to see the photos as soon as possible. Making them widespread will ensure that."

"If he's got eyes out, he should know about them within forty-eight hours."

"Perfect. I want to make the abduction as simple for him as possible, but not so easy that his suspicions are aroused. Put out another news notice the day after the photos are published. I'll be in the U.S. all week. Give an itinerary with as much information as you can without it screaming that I want him to know where I am."

"Anything else?"

"Yes. Once I'm taken, you should be able to track me with the GPS in my watch. However, I'm not certain he'll leave that on me, so I've asked my dentist to implant a small one in one of my back teeth."

Myron grimaced. "I've heard about the procedure. Sounds painful."

Lucas shrugged. He fully expected more than just pain in his mouth. When Damon's men took him, he'd have to endure some abuse. If he acted as though he could handle himself, they'd keep a closer watch on him. If he acted like the untrained, wealthy man most of the world thought him, they'd be less on their guard.

"After the implant, I'll fly to Atlanta. If he *is* in the Southeast, being that close to him should make it easier for his people to get to me."

Phelps stood and shook Lucas's hand. "I wish you well, Lucas."

"Thank you."

As Conrad saw his investigator out, Lucas mentally reviewed his plans. Tomorrow he would clear up anything urgent at his office. If he didn't return, provisions had to be made. His attorney had been round that morning already and Lucas had initiated some key changes. If the worst did happen, McKenna would be a wealthy woman. Most important, she could finally live in peace, because if there was one thing he would ensure before he took his last breath, Damon Hughes would have breathed his last, too.

He was counting on Damon wanting to be the one to kill him. Yes, he was making some dangerous assumptions, but his life had once been full of risks and he'd never been personally invested in doing more than achieving his goal and surviving. This was completely different. He was risking everything for McKenna for one reason only: because she was worth the risk.

Palm Beach

Damon stood in the middle of his dressing room and observed himself in the triple full-length mirror. Odd, but he suddenly felt a bit nervous about seeing McKenna again. The fake bitch who claimed to be McKenna had looked at him like she thought he was attractive. And the other women he'd been with over the years had all assured him with their lust that he still had the kind of looks that made a woman wet and ready. But this was the real McKenna. Eight years had passed. Would she still find him attractive? He'd been twenty-three years old when they met, twenty-four when they were torn apart. Would she think he had changed much?

Turning side to side, Damon examined himself. He'd gotten the best features from both his parents. Dark brown eyes. Good hair—thick and medium brown with a hint of auburn highlights. The hair had come from his mother; his height and physique came from his old man.

In high school, all the girls had panted after him; he'd taken the good-looking ones up on their offer. McKenna had been different from any other girl. She hadn't fallen all over him, but she'd been so cute and sweet, so incredibly innocent, he'd practically fallen all over her.

Drawing closer to the mirror, he examined his face. No doubt about it—he had only gotten better-looking with age. McKenna had fallen for him when he was a good-looking young man. Now he was older, handsome, ultra-sophisticated. He had the money to buy her anything and everything a woman could want.

In a couple of years, he'd allow her to have a baby, maybe even two if the first one didn't spoil her figure. Though he kind of liked the idea of McKenna swelling up with his seed. She'd have a boy and Damon would raise him right. Wouldn't leave him to go out drinking or partying the way his mama had, or beat the shit out of him like his old man had. He'd teach him all the things it was important for a man to know. Things Damon had learned the hard way. His son would have what he'd missed out on.

A knock on the door had him turning. He was expecting some news of the bitch who'd faked being McKenna. Elliott, one of the men who'd been with him for years, stuck his head in and reported, "They don't want to give her up. Said they're very pleased with their purchase and hope you understand."

Pleasing a business associate was much more important than returning some whore, especially since she had lied to him. Damon shrugged. "One's as good as another. Can Lilly stand up yet?"

"Yeah, I saw her walking yesterday. Kind of slowlike, but she was moving."

"As long as she's able to walk, that's good enough. Get a wig about the length and color of that woman's hair. We'll put it on Lilly. She's no good to me now, anyway. Hell, I doubt I could pay anyone to take her off my hands after what Carlos did to her."

A smile of admiration lifted the man's thick lips. "Will do." He turned to leave.

"Oh, and Elliott, make sure Lilly doesn't give us away. McKenna may have some people with her. Make sure they have no reason to doubt her identity. Explain that a bullet in her back would be a hell of a lot worse than the rough ride she got from Carlos."

Another nod and Elliott went out the door.

Damon turned back to the mirror, his smile even brighter. McKenna's little ultimatum hadn't sat well with him, anyway. Why should he have to give up anything? If she'd done what she should have, none of this would have been necessary. She thought she had him right where she wanted him, but she would soon learn that Damon had more than a few tricks up his sleeve.

Laughter burst from him. He couldn't wait to see her face when he put his plan in place.

McKenna sat across from Noah on the private jet. Dylan and Aidan were at the other end of the plane talking quietly. Samara and Micah were lying down in the small bedroom.

They were bound for Tampa, where she would finally

face her past. She and Noah had gone over the scenario three times since she'd come onboard. The flight was a long one, but she knew Noah. He would want to go over it with her at least twice more before they landed. He was that thorough. And that worried.

He hadn't voiced his thoughts, but she knew he had doubts. Not necessarily about her abilities, just about this being the right thing to do.

She couldn't deny the uncertainties herself. She wasn't naïve enough to believe their plan would go off without a hitch. But this was the only way she knew to ensure the safety of Jamie Kendrick, as well as finally end the horror of what she'd lived with for so long.

If only she'd been brave enough years ago to have figured out a way to get rid of Damon. But she hadn't, and now a woman had been tortured, probably raped, and at the very least traumatized . . . all because of her own lack of courage.

"Stop it, McKenna."

She looked up at Noah's grim face. "Stop what?"

"Stop blaming yourself for the acts of a perverted maniac. You're not responsible."

"Hard to not blame myself. If I had faced him years ago, this woman would never have been abducted."

"Damon Hughes is the monster. You should never have had to face him at all."

McKenna took a breath. She'd had time to think some things over, and though she hated to admit what she considered a major weakness, her boss needed to know. "I've killed bad people before, Noah. Men who raped, murdered, tortured—done despicable things. It made me physically sick to do it, but I knew I didn't have a choice."

"And?"

"Damon has done all those things . . . not only to me and my family but to others. He deserves to die." She swallowed and admitted softly, "I just don't think I can do it."

His brow furrowed, Noah shook his head. "It was never my intent for you to kill him."

"But if there's anyone I should kill, it's Damon. He murdered my family, destroyed my life." She swallowed again. "I don't want to kill him, though."

"Why is that, do you think?"

She hated telling him this, but she needed to talk to someone. "Because the thought of killing him terrifies me." She laughed humorlessly. "Isn't that the craziest thing? A demon that I want to see dead more than anyone else on this earth, but I'm so afraid of being the one to do the deed."

"That's not crazy at all. The other men you killed, you didn't do it out of hatred or revenge. You did it to survive or save a life. It was your job. But if you kill Damon, it will be personal. For revenge." He shook his head. "Killing for revenge isn't in you, McKenna. You're not a killer."

As Noah's words sank in, something eased inside her; McKenna felt a lightening of the burden she'd carried since her family died. For so many years, her entire being had ached for Damon's death. And for so many years, she'd called herself a coward for not confronting him.

And now another person was suffering. Yes, she hated what had happened to Jamie Kendrick, but Noah was right. Placing the blame where it belonged was not only correct, it helped lessen the terror of facing him.

She would view Damon as a monster who needed to be put away, but the responsibility of killing him was no longer on her shoulders. Her parents wouldn't have wanted her to avenge their deaths in this way. She would see this through to the end. Damon would go to jail, where he belonged, and this time he would stay there.

And McKenna would finally be at peace.

Lucas's image instantly came to her mind. Without Damon and her fear hanging over her head, could she have something with him? She knew he cared for her. What his true feelings were she couldn't begin to guess. Lucas was a master of not revealing how he really felt. But the way he had made love to her, cared for her when she was sick, been so compassionate when she told him about her past . . . he had to have strong feelings for her.

Despite what lay ahead, McKenna suddenly felt an optimism she never thought she'd have. She would survive this one last experience with Damon and then she would go to Lucas. Her life had not been simple for so long. But this was simple. She was in love with Lucas Kane, and in a week, maybe less, she would return to England.

Was she being overly confident? Perhaps, but she had put her life on hold for too long. She had a lot of catching up to do. And whether Lucas knew it or not, he had helped her reach the point where she wanted to have a real life.

She closed her eyes and imagined his beautiful smile when she appeared on his doorstep again. He would be so surprised.

seventeen

A warm breeze floated gently over her skin, soothing McKenna's ragged nerves. When they'd left Paris, the weather had been damp and cold. Here, the sky was the blue of a bird's egg, the sun blazed like a beacon, and everything seemed peaceful and nonthreatening. She hoped it was a portent of how the operation would go down.

They all stood on the long pier together. Noah was in front, facing her; Dylan and Aidan stayed several feet behind him. For men who often looked as though they chewed bullets for fun, all three had the same worry in their eyes. Their concern was touching, but it also made her even more determined to succeed.

As she expected, Noah reviewed the plan with her again. "Remember, the ring has a GPS radius of a thousand miles. If something happens and you get taken, we'll find you. Your earpiece has a microphone, too. We'll be able to hear you, and you can hear us. You see anything suspicious, anything strange, let us know. We'll abort and go after him another way. Okay?"

Touching the plug in her ear lightly with her fingertip, she nodded. It was in place and working fine—it had been tested three times to make sure. She was as ready as she would ever be.

"As soon as Jamie passes you, drop down, lie flat on your face. We'll start shooting. The tranquilizers should incapacitate him immediately. I don't want you anywhere near Damon, not until he's under lock and key. As soon as I call an all-clear, you run the other way. After he's in custody, if you want to see him, that's your choice."

If she never saw Damon in this lifetime or any other, it would be too soon for her. However, she did look forward to seeing him in leg chains and handcuffs. The mental image of him shuffling around in chains, wearing an orange jumpsuit, was so enticing she could barely keep from laughing.

A glance down at her watch increased her heartbeat. The time was close. "We're within an hour of his scheduled arrival. You guys better get out of here."

Noah put his hand on her shoulder. "Just remember, we're only a few feet away. Dylan will hide behind that post over there. Aidan is going to be stooped behind a rock on that incline." He pointed to another giant post. "I'll be behind that one. If anything goes wrong, seems out of place, I'll say abort and you haul ass. Got it?"

"Got it," McKenna said. She winked at Dylan, nodded her thanks at Aidan, and—in a move completely unprecedented for her—hugged Noah. If she'd ever had a big brother, she would have wished him to be just like Noah McCall.

Noah returned her hug and then backed away.

Taking several deep, even breaths, she strove for calmness and prayed for courage. In less than an hour, she might well be looking into the eyes of the one man she hated and feared above all others. She needed some alone time, away from everyone, to prepare. Whenever she was on an op, her conscious mind—at least the part where fear and nerves existed—shut down, enabling her to do her job with efficiency and determination.

Oftentimes, when the job was over, she would realize how scared she should have been. Nerves would attack her then. And occasionally, when she'd had to kill someone, she got sick. It wasn't something she was proud of, and few people even knew about her problem. Actually, Lucas was probably the only one who knew. After she'd killed Victor, she'd passed out. Embarrassing, yes, but dangerous as hell, too. Thankfully, Lucas had been more than able to handle himself.

His face appeared once more in her mind, his image giving her peace as always. What was he doing now? Staying with him had given her insight into his daily routine. Today was Monday, so he would be at his office in London. He always met with his top executives on Mondays.

An interesting aspect she'd discovered was that Lucas had a routine and rarely veered from it. Silly, but she loved that about him. After living on the edge for so long, having a routine seemed so normal, so gloriously safe. God, how she would love to feel that safety. That security.

The sound of a speedboat caught her attention. McKenna straightened her shoulders. "Noah?" She uttered his name without moving her lips, if they were using high-powered binoculars, as Noah was, she didn't want them to see her speaking.

"I see them . . . four men . . . don't see a woman yet." Noah's calm, even voice came through as though he were standing next to her.

Several tense seconds passed. McKenna was about to ask for an update when Noah said, "Okay. They're docking. I see what looks like a small woman. About your size. They've got a hood over her head."

McKenna turned to see the speedboat putter into the narrow area between two small piers. She brought her hand up to her mouth as if she were coughing. "I'm going to get a little closer."

She took slow, careful steps toward the boat, noting the four large men, along with a smaller person. From her vantage point, she couldn't tell if the small person was a woman. McKenna continued to move toward them.

"Stop . . . wait, McKenna," Noah said. "Do you see Hughes yet?"

Squinting, she carefully examined each man. Damon was about six feet tall, but these men appeared to be taller, bulkier. That was odd. Having what he considered to be his prized possession collected by his flunkies wasn't really in keeping with Damon's obsessive personality. That, along with his supreme arrogance, made her think he would take part in this event.

Pretending to push a strand of hair behind one ear, she covered her mouth and said, "No, I don't see him."

"I don't like . . . Wait. She's walking toward you. They removed the hood. Her head's down, so I can't see her face, but her hair is about the right length and color."

McKenna breathed a relieved sigh, even as she felt a crushing disappointment. Damon wasn't with them. They wouldn't be able to get him. His men would be captured and questioned. Hopefully one of them would be willing to give up Damon's location.

A harsh gust of wind ruffled the approaching woman's hair; McKenna saw ink-black hair beneath. It wasn't Jamie! Dammit, they'd been tricked!

Simultaneously Noah shouted, "It's not Jamie. Get down, McKenna! Get down!"

The men in the speedboat jumped back into the boat and took off.

Before she could move, McKenna heard an odd noise. *Wop, wop, wop.* A fiercely loud whirring sounded overhead. She looked up, her breath catching on a gasp. A helicopter hovered above her; a large man she'd never seen before hung from a ladder with his arm outstretched.

Holy crap!

Noah shouted, "Dammit, run, McKenna. Get the hell out of there!"

Blanking out all noise and distraction, she made a split-second decision. Jamie was still missing. McKenna might be her only hope. She had no choice but to let Damon take her.

"I have to go with them, Noah. I have to find her." Holding out her hand, she allowed the man hanging from the ladder to grab her. In an instant, her feet left the ground and she was soaring through the air.

Hanging on tightly to the man's massive arm, McKenna looked down. The pier below grew smaller and smaller, but she was relieved that it remained empty. Noah and the others were still hidden. Anyone looking down would assume this exchange was something she'd done all by herself.

She could hear Noah's voice in her ear. Although the sound of the helicopter was deafening, she was able to pick up quite a few swearwords. And then his voice lowered to its normal calm tone. "We're tracking you, McKenna. We'll find you."

Despite the terror flooding through her, she knew this had been the only way. If Damon hadn't killed Jamie, he had her stashed somewhere. McKenna owed it to the woman to find her.

Hanging on to the arm of the man who held her over the ocean, she closed her eyes and tried to find that center of calm once more. It was harder this time because she would be seeing Damon after all. And she would be in his lair. Surrounded by his people. People who would do exactly what he told them to do.

Closing her eyes, Lucas's face appeared before her, reminding her what she had promised herself once this was over: a possible future with the man she loved. Resolve stiffened her backbone; she had too damn much to live for to panic now.

The game might have changed, but the end would still be the same. She would rescue Jamie Kendrick and they would both be safe.

Noah had gone ominously silent in her ear. The microphone range wouldn't reach this far. Pretending to push her hair out of her eyes, McKenna pulled the earphone from her ear and let it drop to the ocean below. If Damon was to believe this was her idea alone, explaining an earphone would be impossible.

The man holding her started climbing. McKenna had no choice but to hang on to him. If she let go, she'd fall to her death. Massive muscles bulged as he held her with one arm and climbed upward. At last they reached the top and he threw her face-first onto the floor of the helicopter.

McKenna rolled over onto her back.

"Hello, darling." Damon stood over her.

Forcing her lips into what she hoped was a believable smile, McKenna stared up at her worst nightmare. The smile must have worked. With an approving expression on his wicked face, Damon held out his hand to help her up; before she knew it, she was in his arms, his mouth over hers.

Nausea bloomed and bile surged; McKenna jerked away. "I'm going to throw up."

"What?" he snapped.

"Heights . . . I'm afraid of heights." Heights didn't bother her; she was a certified skydiver. Damon didn't have to know that his sloppy, disgusting mouth on hers had caused the nausea.

Damon released her and drew as far away from her as he could in the small compartment of the helicopter. She almost laughed. Good to know the freak had a weak stomach. Knowledge like that might aid her again.

She perched on the edge of the seat across from him

and closed her eyes, pretending to try to control the nausea.

"Better?" Damon asked.

Opening her eyes, she shook her head. "Not yet."

"It'll get better. Take your clothes off."

Astonished, she couldn't control the question that blurted from her mouth. "What?"

"Do not question me. I said strip. Now."

Knowing she had no choice, McKenna shifted so she could pull the dress over her head. Left only in her bra and panties, she shivered.

"Everything. You come to me completely bare. Everything you need, I will provide. Understand?"

She shot a glance at the man who'd grabbed her. He was sitting with his back to her, looking out the small window.

"Don't worry about Simon. He knows if he turns around and sees you naked, he'll die."

Having no choice, she removed the bra and panties, then her shoes. Completely nude, she stayed seated and waited for further instructions.

The slimy look on his face as his eyes roamed up and down her body made her want to spew the bile in her throat all over him. His gaze stopped at her hand. "The ring, too."

Dread filled her. *No.* If she lost the ring, Noah couldn't track her. She covered the ring with her other hand protectively. "It was my mother's . . . it's all I have left of her."

"Poor baby." He held out his hand. "Can I see it?"

She held out her hand to show him. Taking a hard grasp of her wrist, he pulled the ring from her finger and held it up to the light. "It's lovely."

Her smile trembling with nerves, she said, "Thank you," and stuck her hand out for him to return it.

He opened a small window beside him and tossed the ring out. "Bye-bye, Mama."

The sheer cruelty of that one simple action shouldn't have shocked her, but it did. She barely paid attention as he bundled her clothes and shoes together and threw them out, too. Though she couldn't show her anger, it gave her just the right amount of determination. She'd been scared before, but fury was quickly taking over.

His smile one of smug arrogance, he said, "Stand up."

Gripping the leather strap over her head, McKenna stood. When his fingers circled the cigarette burns on her stomach and then her breasts, she stared out the window, determined not to show her disgust. She could do this; she had no choice.

"Turn around."

She turned her back to him, knowing exactly what he wanted to see. His hands cupped and kneaded her bottom, then his finger traced the letter he'd branded her with. When she felt his wet tongue there, she closed her eyes and willed her churning stomach to settle down. Throwing up on him might give her a moment's satisfaction, but it would most likely get her a beating as well. She had to stay healthy as long as possible.

"Yes, that's my McKenna."

Knowing he wouldn't want her to turn around until he said so, she remained standing and waited for his command. One of the many things Damon liked was to be able to order her every movement.

"Very good. Now turn around."

She turned and was immediately enveloped in a soft blanket. Holding the covering tight around her body, she went to sit down. Damon had other ideas. He pulled her down onto his lap. McKenna had no choice but to let him have his way.

She dared a look up at his face. He had changed in

the eight years since she'd seen him. There were lines around his eyes and mouth, and when he smiled, the tooth that had once been slightly crooked was now even more so.

Once, long ago, she'd thought Damon the most handsome man on earth. And while her mind acknowledged that he might still be physically attractive, evil was beginning to have a negative effect on his face. In fact, he was looking more like the demon she'd often believed him to be.

Odd, but she was suddenly completely unafraid. She was facing the devil once more, and though she wasn't safe, neither was she terrified, as she had thought she would be. Damon's hold on her was truly at an end. He was just another perverted monster who had kidnapped someone. She'd dealt with this kind of filth before. He was just one more.

That settled in her mind, she could fully concentrate on finding Jamie Kendrick. Pray God she was still alive.

Tampa, Florida
LCR field office

Noah sat at his desk and reviewed the new information they'd gathered on Hughes. He refused to think that McKenna wasn't all right. She had made the decision to go with Damon. While he understood her reasons, he was still furious she'd taken that risk.

McKenna was a professional. He'd been impressed with her from their first meeting, and that hadn't changed. And the conversation he'd had with her before they landed in Tampa reinforced that confidence. If she could maintain the perspective that this was just another job for her, she would succeed. Didn't mean he didn't intend to help her out.

Her mic had stopped working within minutes of her being taken. That hadn't worried him; the range wasn't that long. What did concern him was the ring she wore. The GPS signal had disappeared ten minutes after the helicopter left their view. Getting inside Damon's head, Noah surmised he'd made her take off anything that might have a tracking device in it. McKenna was resourceful. She would find a way to contact LCR when she could.

From what he'd been able to glean from his new informant, and based upon Damon's suggested meeting place, he was betting that Damon did live in Florida. Which was why he and his team were still in Tampa. When McKenna called, they could be at her assistance within hours.

He looked up when the door opened. Samara came in looking angrier than he'd seen her in years. Though she was concerned for McKenna, Noah knew most of the anger stemmed from what Damon had left them: a young woman, barely out of her teens, named Lilly Francis, ravaged, beaten, and damaged so badly internally, the doctors were stunned that she was able to walk upright.

So far, she'd only been able to give them her name and could supply little information on Damon's whereabouts other than to tell them there were palm trees everywhere and she had often heard the ocean. Two years ago, she had arrived at Damon's residence unconscious and had lived at his giant estate all this time without any idea how to get out or where she was.

Damon had used her to entertain himself or the occasional businessman. The man who'd raped and almost killed her was one of Hughes's employees named Carlos. Apparently Lilly had been his reward for something.

Despite the little information she'd given them so far, Noah had hopes that, given time, she'd be able to provide them with something they could use. And that it wouldn't be too late.

"How's Lilly?"

Samara came around the desk, and by the tears in her eyes, he knew the news wouldn't be good. Holding out his arms, he pulled her into his lap. "Tell me."

"She started hemorrhaging about an hour ago. They're doing an emergency hysterectomy. We won't know for a few hours if that will completely stop the bleeding."

Noah held her close. Mara's sorrow only increased his determination. If McKenna didn't manage to destroy Damon Hughes, Noah would make sure he did. The sadistic bastard should not be allowed to take another breath.

Samara took a shuddering breath. "Any news?"

"Not a lot. Based upon the little that Lilly could tell us, I believe he's here in Florida. I've got investigators running all over the state trying to dig something up. It's just a matter of time."

"But will it be too late to save McKenna?"

"Hughes won't kill her. And he's certainly not going to be expecting that McKenna can and will kill him if it comes down to it. He's used to fragile women who can't defend themselves. My money's on McKenna."

"Do you think Jamie Kendrick is still alive?"

"I don't know. Once Hughes realized his people got the wrong woman, his temper may have got the best of him. However, if he didn't kill her, my guess is that he sold her. He wouldn't want her around, reminding him how stupid he'd been."

"Sad that we're sitting here hoping that he sold her to someone."

"You're right, but at least if she's alive, there's hope."

She pulled quickly from his arms and turned to face him. "I can't believe I haven't told you this. With the news of Lilly's surgery, it flew right out of my mind." Turning, she looked down at one of his computer monitors. "Can you go to the website for one of the newspapers?"

Frowning, he cleared his screen. "Which one?"

"Try the *Tampa Times.*"

Noah clicked on their main website. "Now what?"

"Go to the business section."

Noah clicked on the business section and scrolled down. The image that appeared brought a vile curse to his lips: Lucas Kane and McKenna holding hands, looking into each other's eyes. They looked every bit the besotted couple. The brief and uninformative caption speculated on whom the billionaire businessman was now romancing. McKenna's name stood starkly out in the small paragraph.

It took barely a second to determine Kane's motive. "He's luring Hughes."

Samara's shocked gasp told him that was something she hadn't considered. "You think so?"

Holding off on answering her, Noah clicked onto the sites of three other newspapers and came up with the same photo and wording. "These are fairly obscure newspapers. Even as famous as Kane is, it's doubtful they'd run anything with an international slant without good reason. And Kane's got enough money to stop every scandal rag from printing this. He's setting Hughes up."

Samara's eyes grew wide as she realized the ramifications. "Oh, Noah, he might ruin everything."

With a grim nod, Noah picked up the phone. He had to get to Kane before he did anything else. There was no telling what Damon Hughes would do to McKenna if he saw the pictures.

Lucas Kane might have had the best intentions, but if Hughes's temper got the best of him, McKenna might well pay for Kane's ploy with her life.

eighteen

Palm Beach

Damon carried a still-bundled McKenna into the house. Though she was still such a small, delicate thing, the solidity of her slender body was a bit of an unpleasant surprise. Years ago she had been soft and firm, but now that firmness felt almost muscular. He detested women who marred their body with muscles. Was she into bodybuilding or something? How disgusting. A woman should be soft and feminine, relying on her man to be the strong one in the household.

She was covered from head to toe as he stalked up the stairway to her bedroom. Tomorrow he would give her a tour of her new home and grounds. He didn't want her to see anything until he showed her his special surprise. When she saw what he had done for her, she would realize how much she meant to him.

Margret stood outside the room, waiting for him. He gave her a small nod and she immediately unlocked the door. The instant the door swung open, Margret vanished, as he had instructed her earlier. He wanted no one around to witness this grand homecoming.

"Close your eyes. I have a surprise for you."

Damon uncovered her face, pleased to see that her eyes were closed. Anticipation building, he dropped her feet and allowed her to stand. Whipping the blanket from her body, he stood back for a few seconds and absorbed the moment. McKenna standing nude in the middle of the room he'd created for her. It was as if eight years ago had never happened.

"Open your eyes."

Blinking rapidly, her eyes opened. Damon watched her focus on her surroundings. He spread his arms out, so moved by the moment that he couldn't speak.

Her eyes roamed around the room and Damon waited for her to voice her enthusiasm. He could see the surprise, but where was the gratitude? Where were the tears? Did she not recognize the significance? Was she that dense?

"Well, what do you think?" He hated asking, but she was apparently not going to say anything.

She looked at him then and he saw the surprise and wonder in her expression, just as he'd been expecting. He watched her throat move convulsively as if she were too overcome to express her joy. Yes, his McKenna had always been a bit on the emotional side. She was probably close to tears, feeling overwhelmed by all he had done for her.

Finally she said softly, "It's my bedroom."

Damon nodded eagerly. "See, everything's going to be the way it should have been."

Whirling around, she took in everything, then turned back to Damon and whispered, "Oh, Damon, it's beautiful. Thank you so much."

Overcome by his own emotions, Damon knew he had to leave before McKenna saw how moved he was. Showing her how this homecoming was affecting him would make her think he wasn't the strong disciplinarian he had been years ago.

"I knew you would love it. And this is only the beginning. Every day will be better than the one before. I'll leave you to get settled. I know you must be exhausted. Everything you need is in this room. There are clothes in the closet and the dresser. If you need anything else at all, you only have to ask."

Her mouth trembling with a smile of gratitude, his McKenna looked close to tears.

Drawing her into his arms, he closed his mouth over hers, groaning at her taste. Yes, this was his McKenna. How could he have mistaken that whore who was here before for McKenna?

Pulling away reluctantly, he said, "Margret, my housekeeper, will bring you dinner. Tomorrow I'll show you around your new home."

"Thank you, Damon, for being so good to me."

Her words, the deference and sincerity in her voice, were music to his ears. A new wash of tears stung his eyes. Stepping away from her, he stalked to the door. Before walking out, he turned back around and said, "We're going to be so happy, McKenna. It's going to be the way it should have been."

She nodded and smiled. Relishing her trembling, grateful smile, Damon closed the door, then turned the lock. Tomorrow they would begin their courtship all over again.

The night had been a sleepless one, long and agonizing. Now McKenna stood in the middle of the bedroom Damon had led her to last evening. Eyes closed, she drew in deep, even breaths, preparing her mind for what she had to face today.

Their arrival last night had given her little information about her whereabouts. After landing on a helipad obviously belonging to him, she'd been hustled from the helicopter to a gated entrance. Her eyes barely caught a glimpse of anything other than a sandy beach and a few palm trees. The ocean had been close because she'd heard and smelled it, but other than that bit of information, she still had no real knowledge of her location.

The instant she entered the compound, the loud and ominous clang of the lock told her that any possibility of escape had been relinquished. Damon allowed her to look around for a scant few seconds, enough to see that the giant courtyard was surrounded by a high brick wall and cameras were everywhere. Whatever she did while she was here, she would be seen.

The surprises hadn't stopped. Damon had picked her up and carried her into the mansion, still wrapped in the blanket. Before they'd walked through the door, he had covered her head. She hadn't asked why. Asking questions would bring out his ire faster than anything.

She'd heard a door open and close, then Damon had dropped her to her feet and told her to open her eyes. A wide grin on his face, he had spread his arms out as if to say, "See what I've done for you."

As she had looked around the room, a chill of revulsion shuddered through her. He hadn't said anything; he hadn't needed to say anything. He had just waited, apparently expecting delight and gratitude.

It took a lot to shock McKenna and a whole lot more to make her speechless. She had been both. Not because of what he had done, but by his attitude. Yes, she recognized that he had replicated her bedroom. What stunned her was that Damon seemed to think giving her an identical bedroom to the one she'd had as a teenager somehow made up for what he had done. Just how freaking crazy was the bastard?

McKenna had struggled somewhat to pull herself together, knowing Damon's eyes would pick up any hesitancy or antipathy. He needed to think he had her where he wanted her. Reminding herself that she was damn good at undercover and pretense, she went into automatic mode and became what Damon wanted.

Whirling around the room like the silly, naïve sixteen-year-old she'd once been, she had forced delight and wonder onto her face as she thanked him. All the while the bile built in her throat.

His words told her she had convinced him. "I knew you would love it. And this is only the beginning. Every day will be better than the one before."

It had taken every ounce of her control not to respond with *Yes, you freak. As long as I obey your every command and never have another independent thought.*

He had pulled her into his arms. Unable to use her fear of heights to explain the nausea churning in her stomach this time, she reminded herself that this was no different from any other job. She had closed her eyes and accepted his mouth on hers.

Finally he had let her go. Before walking out the door, he'd given her a sickening smile and a promise. "We're going to be so happy."

The instant the door closed behind him, she had dashed into the bathroom and vomited.

An hour later, after McKenna had scrubbed herself raw in the shower and brushed her teeth three times to get the taste of Damon out of her mouth, Margret, the housekeeper, had entered the room. The dour-faced woman had brought her a large meal and absolutely no sympathy. She clearly didn't want McKenna here.

For an instant, McKenna had thought she might be able to use Margret's obvious resentment to her advantage. If the woman didn't want her there, what better ally could she have? She quickly changed her mind when she saw the jealousy gleaming in the housekeeper's eyes. No way in hell would Margret betray Damon.

Sleep had been nonexistent. Much of the night had been spent pacing and trying to come up with a way to get Damon to talk about Jamie. She hadn't revealed that she knew the girl he had returned wasn't Jamie Kendrick. She might have to at some point. For right now, she needed Damon to think all was well. Chances were, at some point, he'd let his guard down. Until then, she would continue to be the helpless, trusting McKenna he wanted.

Though she was surprised he hadn't tried to force himself on her last night, in a way it made sense. To Damon, this was romance. He was wooing her again, as he had when they first started dating. And as long as she acted like the sweet simpleton he wanted her to be, he wouldn't take it any further . . . yet. That wouldn't last, so she needed to act as quickly as possible to figure out not only where Jamie was, but how the hell to get out of here in one piece. Was Jamie still here or had Damon sold her? Hell, was she even alive?

Since the bedroom door was locked, she hadn't been able to snoop last night. The room was on the third floor with nothing but a steeply sloping rooftop outside her window. Trying to escape through the window would be pointless; breaking her neck would help no one.

Her only option was to gain Damon's trust and hopefully get some freedom to snoop around.

The click of the lock told her she was being released temporarily. She turned to see Damon standing there. The adoration gleaming in his eyes made her want to run to the bathroom and throw up again. Instead she forced a glowing smile and headed to him with her arms outstretched. "Good morning, Damon."

Damon stood at the bedroom door and allowed himself once again to revel in the happiness he felt at having McKenna back with him. Last night had been an exercise in patience. He'd gotten out of bed at least half a dozen times to come and stand outside the bedroom door, just to make sure she hadn't somehow escaped. It had taken all of his considerable willpower not to unlock the door and show her exactly how much he'd missed her. Each time his hand had been on the door, he had reminded himself of his promise to woo her back into his arms.

As he opened his arms, allowing her to come to him, he was glad he'd waited. His McKenna was coming around already; just by allowing her this extra time, he was already reaping the rewards for his patience. Another couple of days and he'd have her exactly where he wanted her.

Wrapping his arms tightly around her, he pressed her close against him. "Good morning, my love. Did you sleep well?"

She snuggled against him, but then he felt her stiffen suddenly as his hard dick pressed into her belly. Damon smiled. Yeah, let her get used to feeling it again. Eight years had passed since she'd felt something that good. He wouldn't take her to bed yet, but it wouldn't hurt her to know what was coming and what he could do to her anytime he wanted. Not only would she realize that he was just as virile as he had been years ago, she should be grateful he still felt this way about her. Eight years was a long time to stay horny for a woman. Damon pushed against her, giving her a good, solid rub to reinforce his message, then stepped away from her slightly.

Her smile was one of shy gratitude as she answered his earlier question. "I slept wonderfully, thank you, Damon."

"And did it feel good to be back in your old room again?"

"Oh yes, I'm sure that's why I slept so well."

"Excellent." His eyes swept over her, noting she'd put on one of the short, feminine dresses he'd purchased for her. Many of them were identical to the dresses she had worn years ago. The one she had chosen today wasn't one of his favorites since it covered her more than most of the others, but since he had provided it for her, he decided he couldn't complain.

"Are you ready for breakfast?"

One of the many things he knew about McKenna was her enjoyment of food. Though her excessive appetite had always disgusted him a bit, he indulged her since she never appeared to gain weight. If it ever came to the point that her body showed signs of overindulgence, that would change in an instant. Having her change the least little bit wasn't something he would tolerate. Which brought him to a concern he hadn't addressed yet.

"You've cut your hair."

Her eyes widened as if she was startled by the difference in his tone. He refused to soften the statement, though. She needed to realize that making any kind of change to her appearance without consulting him wasn't something he would allow.

Giving him a tentative look, she admitted, "Just a bit."

"Don't do that again. I want you to let it grow to just above your ass like it was before. Understand?"

"Yes, Damon. I'm sorry I had it cut."

Her apology pleased him so much, his erection grew harder. Knowing that if he didn't get her out of the room soon he'd throw her on the bed and screw her senseless, he held out his hand. "Come. Let's go down to breakfast, then I'll give you a brief tour of your new home."

Looking both relieved that he'd allowed her some slack about her hair and grateful for his patience, she put her hand in his and followed him out the door.

Yes, he was playing this as he should. Very soon she'd be filled with awe over the grandness of his mansion and his wealth. With his good looks, abundance of money, and obvious adoration, McKenna would soon realize she was one of the most fortunate women in the world. Any woman would be grateful, but a farm girl from Nebraska with nothing going for her but a pretty smile and a nice ass? Yes, McKenna was damn lucky he loved her.

And very soon he intended to show her just how grateful she should be.

Standing at his mirror, Damon admired how the new tailored shirt emphasized his broad shoulders and the way the trousers called attention to his long, muscular legs. During the tour of his mansion this morning, he'd seen McKenna stealing a glance at his physique more than once. The attraction was most definitely still there.

At the knock on the door, he turned from his reflection. "Come."

Elliott entered; Damon eyed him closely. The man's usual ruddy complexion was almost pale. He looked like something had scared the shit out of him. His massive neck jerked as his throat moved convulsively, but he still didn't speak.

"Well, what is it?" Damon snapped.

"I just got an email. . . ." He trailed off to look down at the small device in his hand.

Somewhat surprised that Elliott's hand seemed to be shaking, since the man was usually devoid of emotion, Damon said, "What's wrong?"

"There's a picture you need to see."

Afraid of nothing, especially a fucking email, Damon grabbed the iPhone from the man's hand and looked down at the screen. It was a picture of a man and woman standing on a sidewalk, holding hands and gazing into each other's eyes. Even without reading the caption, he knew who they were. He'd seen photos of Lucas Kane. The man was almost as famous as a rock star. And the woman—he knew her, too. It was McKenna. His McKenna. Her hair was even shorter than it was now and seemed much lighter, almost white. But he'd recognize that face anywhere.

When had this been taken? And what was Lucas Kane doing with his woman?

The caption below the photograph hinted of a relationship. Perhaps a secret romance. McKenna had been with Lucas Kane? Impossible. The man had a whole harem of women he dated. No way had his McKenna been one of his many followers.

"There has to be some mistake." He glared at Elliott. "Where did this come from?"

"Maury, one of our investigators. It was in the gossip column of the local newspaper this morning."

"Leave me."

"Do you want—"

"I said get out. Now!"

Elliott moved as fast as his big body would allow, closing the door behind him.

Damon took one more look at McKenna's betrayal and then with a roar threw the iPhone at the mirror. The fracture in the glass matched the crack in his heart. Both McKenna and Lucas Kane would pay for this.

He hadn't asked her if there had been other men in her life. Hadn't believed there was a need. Long ago, he'd told her what would happen to anyone she became close to. If he'd killed her fucking neighbor, just what the hell did she think he would do to a man who'd been between her legs? A place no man but Damon belonged?

Why would Lucas Kane even be interested in McKenna? Yes, she was beautiful to Damon, but that was because he loved her. The scars on her body aroused him, but only because he had put them there; they were marks of his love, his devotion. Lucas Kane should have been repelled. Besides, though he adored McKenna's sweet innocence and slight dim-wittedness, why would a powerful, wealthy man be attracted to her? She should be a nonentity to other men; to Damon, she was everything.

Something didn't add up. Either way, Lucas Kane was a dead man.

The bastard might be one of the wealthiest men in the

world, but he didn't have the contacts or the drive Damon did. The man had inherited his wealth; Damon had earned every penny and had killed more than a few to get what he had. He would use every bit of that wealth to get Lucas Kane.

Breathing in and out several times to control the rage, Damon began to plan. He would have Kane brought here. As the plan took on substance, the familiar anticipation swept through him. He'd killed many people but had only enjoyed a few. The kills he enjoyed, though, had brought him a rush he'd never experienced from anything else, except disciplining McKenna.

Lucas Kane was famous, wealthy, and powerful. Killing him would be a rush of monumental proportions.

Taking his cellphone from his pocket, he hit the number for one of his investigators. Once Kane was secured and brought here, McKenna would receive a lesson in obedience and faithfulness she would never forget; Lucas Kane would be his weapon.

nineteen

Her steps silent, McKenna began her own tour of the mansion. After breakfast, Damon had given her a cursory tour, pointing out what he was obviously most proud of, which included a massive gym, Olympic-sized swimming pool, and some sort of art collection in the giant courtyard that seemed to be mostly of naked women with big breasts. She'd oohed and ahhed, smiled and lied until her jaws ached. *Ostentatious* and *pretentious* were two apt descriptions for Damon's home. *Ugly as hell* would be another.

After the tour, he'd suggested she put on her swimsuit and take a dip in the pool he told her he'd had built especially for her. Grinding out one last grateful smile had hurt, but she'd managed it. Then, thankfully, he'd left her with a kiss on her forehead and a warning not to get too much sun.

Over breakfast, she'd heard him tell Margret that he had to leave the compound for a while. His statement had given her a much-needed lift. Staying in character as the sweet, clueless, and ever so grateful McKenna was exhausting. The freak was buying her act but having a reprieve for a few hours away from him was a huge relief. Not only could she stop with the fake sweetness for a while, she now had the chance to explore on her own. If she was caught by anyone, she would merely explain that she was just becoming more acquainted with her new home.

An hour later, she had drawn two conclusions. First and foremost was that Jamie was not inside the mansion. She'd been through every single room. Surprisingly, no door was locked, but since there didn't seem to be anything to hide, perhaps she shouldn't be surprised. And though Damon had only given her a quick tour of the grounds, McKenna doubted Jamie was anywhere on the estate.

The second conclusion was that Damon Hughes had a hell of a lot of money coming from somewhere. When she'd first met him, he had worked as a mechanic at a garage in town. Where he'd gotten his wealth she could only speculate, but she was quite sure none of his activities were legal.

Taking a breath, McKenna eased the door open to a room she'd made a quick search of a few minutes before. Damon's office. This was one place where it would be difficult to explain her presence. That couldn't be helped; she had to take the risk. There were no landline phones in the house. Everyone used cellphones and she hadn't yet found one she could steal.

Noah and his team were probably going crazy, not knowing where she was. If nothing else, she needed to find a computer so she could email him. If she got caught, she got caught. Damon wouldn't kill her, although it was the only thing she was sure he wouldn't do. Just about anything else was still possible.

Until she found Jamie's whereabouts, she needed to stay healthy. Once she found her, she'd turn the tables on Damon. He didn't yet know that she could kick his pampered ass and those of just about all of his employees. She looked forward to the opportunity to show him what she could do.

Damon's office was as gigantic, cavernous, and pretentious as the rest of his mansion. In the middle of the room was a giant oak desk with almost nothing on it other than a laptop and a large dictionary. For some reason, the image of Damon looking up a word like a regular person was amusing.

The desk drawers opened easily and revealed nothing more than ordinary office equipment, although the silver-plated letter opener was too enticing not to grab. She looked down at her clothes, cursing the silly, feminine dress. In the closet of clothes Damon had provided were only dresses—short, revealing, and completely lacking in places to hide a weapon. Deciding she'd have to come back for it, McKenna returned it to the drawer. If she was caught with it, there was no way in hell she could come up with a reasonable explanation.

She sat down at the desk and opened the laptop, relieved to see that he did have a wireless connection. Quickly accessing one of her email accounts, she typed a message to Noah:

I'm fine. Still looking for the girl. Don't believe she's here. Don't know where I am. Hear the ocean. See palm trees and tropical flowers. We traveled south for about an hour in the helicopter. Believe I'm still in Florida. Will contact you ASAP.

She stared at the screen for several more seconds. What else could she say that would help them? Shaking her head, she added: *Don't worry.* She hit send.

Damon's desk was so neat, his records were probably on the laptop. They were sure to be password-protected, but she had to try anyway. She pulled up a list of documents and clicked on one captioned "Merchandise." The password screen came on. Taking a chance, she typed in "McKenna." The error screen came up. Dammit. What did a narcissistic psycho use as a password? She typed in several random words but still came up empty.

Blowing out a frustrated curse, McKenna exited the program and closed the laptop. Damon might be coming back soon; she'd have to return when she had more time. Before leaving, she used up precious minutes walking every inch of the office, pressing on walls and pulling books from shelves, hoping for a hidden door to open and reveal some secrets. Disgusted, she gave up. If there was anything here, it was well concealed.

Opening the door as quietly as possible, McKenna crept out of the office and closed the door behind her. She turned and swallowed a scream. Damon stood in the hallway. He had seen her walk out of his office.

Looking only mildly curious, he asked, "What are you doing, my love?"

She had no answers for him, so she went with her sweetly innocent smile. "Just looking around."

"Looking around for what?"

She shrugged, offered an embarrassed little laugh. "I still know so little about you. It's been almost nine years since we were together. All you've told me about yourself is that you have diverse interests in a lot of different things."

"And you thought you'd be able to figure it out all by yourself just by looking through my office?"

Swallowing a snarl at his obnoxious superiority, she went with what usually worked for him. "I'm sorry, Damon. I was just curious."

"Come here."

Reminding herself that he might bring her pain but he wouldn't kill her, she went to him. She'd dealt with pain before; she could deal with it again. Still, her movements were jerkier than she would have liked.

He took her hand in his. "What is it you wish to know, my love?"

"Everything, Damon. When we were together before, you weren't rich. But in a relatively short period of time, you've been able to amass a fortune?"

He pulled her hard against him and spoke against her

mouth. "How I earn my money is really none of your business, is it?"

"I just thought—"

"Don't think, McKenna. You'll get wrinkles and I'll have to throw a sheet over your head to fuck you."

She said nothing, kept her face expressionless. He was getting meaner now. She could see it in his eyes. Was it because he'd caught her snooping? Or was this just a natural progression for a sadistic murderer?

Either way, she needed to soothe his ire. Having him suspect her of anything would get her nowhere. She lowered her head and whispered humbly, "Please forgive me."

He was silent for several seconds; she could feel his eyes scrutinizing her. Would he buy her act? McKenna didn't dare raise her head. She'd done that once without his permission and had ended up on the floor with a bloodied nose.

"Look at me."

Her head popped up obediently.

"Do not for a moment think I will forget this. However, since this is your first day here, I'll forgive your little indiscretion." He tightened his grip on her arm until she winced. "You won't be snooping again. Will you, McKenna?"

"No, Damon. I won't."

He smiled at her, but it wasn't the condescending indulgent one from this morning. There was cruelty there. "Come. We'll have cocktails by the pool. Then I really think you need to take that swim I suggested to you this morning. You're looking a bit pale, not nearly as attractive as I prefer in my women. Then perhaps a nap before dinner." His smile grew broader, his anger apparently over for now. "We have an exciting week ahead of us. You're going to need all of your energy."

"We do?"

"I've allowed you several questions already. I really don't believe you want to push your luck, do you?"

Properly meek, she said, "No, Damon, I'm so sorry."

There was the smile again, but the cold, hard gleam in his eyes remained. Something had definitely changed. Ice surged through her veins. She'd seen that look in his eyes before. It was usually followed by severe punishment.

His words, though condescending and cruel, revealed nothing. "That's a good bitch. Besides, I don't want to spoil the surprise. Let's just say that the upcoming events will be something we'll both remember for a very long time."

More uneasy than she'd been since she had seen him again, McKenna nodded absently and let him lead her down the hallway. What the hell was he talking about? Damon's surprises usually meant intense pain for her and extreme enjoyment for him.

Since he hadn't tried to rape her since she got here, she could only assume that was in the plan. She tried to ignore the nausea crawling at her insides at the thought of having sex with Damon. While it was true she'd had sex on jobs before to maintain her cover, that was before she'd met Lucas. Not only would Damon's touch remind her of what he was and what he had done, the thought of being with any man other than Lucas was abhorrent. When she'd made the decision to let Damon take her, she had known having sex might be a possibility but hadn't allowed herself to think about it. Now that it was a very real probability, she honestly didn't know if she could go through with it.

One thing at a time, McKenna.

She drew a long, shallow breath. She would face that nightmare scenario when she had to. For right now, she had more than enough to think about. Whatever she could find out about Jamie, she needed to do it soon.

* * *

Lying in a cramped car trunk with his hands bound, Lucas stared up at the monster who'd tortured and raped McKenna. Odd—he actually looked like a normal man. Attractive, early thirties, with an air of hard-edged sophistication that many women might find attractive. And those women who were unfortunate enough to catch his attention were no doubt horrified to realize they'd hooked up with a maniac.

"Welcome to my home, Mr. Kane. Did you have a pleasant trip?"

Since tape covered his mouth, Lucas let his eyes speak for him. He may have lured the bastard for this meeting, but the fury he felt was real. Besides, he had to act as surprised as possible, even fearful. Having Hughes suspect any kind of setup would not only destroy his plan, it could damn well backfire and get Lucas killed instead.

"I have to admit to a bit of a disappointment that you were so easy to grab. I had thought it would take weeks to get to the famous British stud. Instead, in just over one day my people managed to abduct you and bring you here." His smile one of supreme superiority, Hughes shook his head. "Doesn't say a lot for your intelligence, now, does it?"

Lucas would have laughed if he could have. Damon's people had passed him on the street three times before he could attract their attention. He'd ended up having to walk down a dark alley by himself just so he could make it as easy on them as possible. Poor stupid fools had looked so damned proud of themselves; he hadn't even bothered putting up a token resistance. What was the point when they were taking him exactly where he wanted to go? A gun poking in his side had gotten him to their car. The tap on his head had given him a headache, but it was the frustration of having to feign unconsciousness for hours that had worn him down. If

nothing else, he was glad he didn't have to pretend anymore.

Hughes's gaze roamed Lucas's scrunched-up body.
"I'm assuming you would like to know why you were
taken?"

Lucas nodded.

"McKenna, of course." A cold smile twisted his
mouth. "Ah, I see the acknowledgment in your eyes."
He stooped down till he was inches from Kane's face.
"You have been in possession of my most treasured
asset. She may have been just another woman to you,
but to me she's everything. You dared to touch what
belongs to me only. For that, you will pay the highest
of prices." He straightened and backed away. "Since
I expected it to take longer to get you, the show unfortunately can't start as soon as I would have liked.
However, I'll make sure you're comfortable until the
arrangements can be made. The event might not be as
elaborate as I had planned, but the entertainment will be
off-the-charts fun, I assure you."

At a nod from Hughes, two big lugs pulled Lucas
from the trunk. His legs were numb from hours of being
crammed in a small space, and he fell to his knees. The
time he'd been locked up hadn't been wasted, though.
The ties around his wrists were almost loose; in seconds
he could be free. That, however, would have to wait
until the circulation returned to his limbs.

One man grabbed him under his arms and pulled him
to a standing position. Since he could do nothing about
the sting of pins and needles that racked his entire body,
he ignored it. It would be gone soon enough and then he
could act. His eyes appearing to dart fearfully around,
Lucas leaned against the car and took in his surroundings. The estate was small compared to Lucas's, but the
obvious opulence of his surroundings assured him that

Damon Hughes was making a fortune on his illegal activities.

When he was pushed forward, Lucas didn't have to pretend to stumble. Damn his legs . . . he willed them to work. He didn't know how many men were at the estate but he needed all his parts in working order before he got started on getting rid of them.

Hughes stood several feet from him, still smirking. "Why don't you take Mr. Kane the long way around, Simon? Show him some of the scenery."

One of the giants behind him grunted, apparently Simon. As he was pushed forward again, Lucas tried to get a sense of where he was. The courtyard was round, filled with statues, large plants, and small trees. The statue of a large-busted nude woman stood in the middle of a giant fountain. The mansion was a three-story massive structure of brick and stucco. Lucas wondered what mortuary designer had built it.

Lucas stumbled again, then shuffled forward like a whipped, terrified man. Hughes chuckled beside him. As they made their way toward the side of the house, his legs regained their strength. Taking the men out before they reached their destination seemed the wisest course. Adrenaline surged within him. One good tug on the rope and he would be free.

"Stop." Damon's voice was low.

Lucas turned slightly. Were they planning on shooting him here? No, that would be too anticlimactic, not in keeping with Damon's earlier comments about an event.

"This is an excellent place to get a glimpse of my most prized possession," Damon said.

Lucas shot a glance at the giant swimming pool. *This* was Damon's most prized possession? As pools went, he supposed it was nice, but it certainly wasn't—

Breath shuddered from Lucas's body in a giant gasp of air. A woman emerged from the pool, dripping from her swim and barely covered by an almost nonexistent bikini, her golden skin glistening beneath the blaze of the sun. He had no trouble recognizing the lovely female form. He'd held that body in his arms, made love to it for endless hours, and dreamed of it nightly.

Just what the hell was McKenna doing here?

Before he could come up with a reasonable answer, he felt a small prick at his neck. Whirling, Lucas turned to see Damon holding a hypodermic needle. The bastard had an even broader smirk on his face. Dammit. Drugs. His gaze went back to McKenna. She was drying her body, apparently unaware of the audience she had attracted. Her image wavered and blurred in front of him. His limbs loosened, taking on the feeling of melting wax, and he collapsed on the ground. Lucas had one last urgent thought before darkness covered his mind: McKenna was in danger.

Caressing the handle of the favorite knife he always carried at his waist, Damon watched Lucas Kane being hauled into an outbuilding he'd had designed for this type of guest. Oh, how he wanted to begin the carving immediately, but that would spoil the upcoming event. Patience had brought McKenna back to him; that same patience had to be exercised here. The anticipation of the kill would only increase the pleasure of the act.

McKenna thought her secret was safe, that he didn't know about her lover. She thought everything was settled between them. He had wined and dined her, treated her with the utmost gentleness. Given her clothes and all the luxuries a woman could want. He'd asked nothing in return. Had barely even touched her other than a few kisses and caresses here and there.

Last night, instead of joining her for dinner, he'd had Margret deliver a meal to her room. If he'd spent any more time with her, he would have lost his temper and showed his hand too soon.

Admittedly, he had allowed a little of his anger to show yesterday afternoon, but she had shocked him. Why had she gone into his office? That seemed so un-McKenna-like; he'd had difficulty maintaining his role of gentle lover.

Now that his plans were working so well, he could go back to being the charming, loving Damon. Showing her what she could have was an excellent precursor for the coming events. When he punished her for her unfaithfulness, she would be able to see the difference. The contrast would be so apparent, even her little mind could comprehend the distinction. And then they could move on. All of this would be in the past. Lucas Kane would be dead and Damon would never worry that McKenna would even think about straying again.

How many men McKenna had been with over the years he refused to contemplate. One was one too many. All these years, he'd thought that even though she was far from him, she would remain celibate until they reunited. After all, it wasn't as if she enjoyed the sex act or was even very good at it. How many times had he had to tie her down and tame her into submission? But that was his right. To know that she had willingly spread her legs for this man and who knows how many others sickened him.

When McKenna once more understood her place in his world, her final and most important lesson was to see her lover mutilated and dead. That vision in her mind would ensure she never roamed again. Lucas Kane would be gone for good and McKenna would know she was once more responsible for another person's death.

And then life would be what it should have been eight years ago, before McKenna destroyed everything. She would pay for her mistakes and then they would go forward together as they were meant to be.

twenty

The house held a deathlike silence as McKenna eased open her bedroom door. It was three in the morning, and she hoped the men patrolling the house would be nodding off, or at least inattentive. If she had to, she would disable them and hide them somewhere. Depending upon what Damon had planned for what he called the upcoming "big event," this might be her last chance to get information on Jamie. She had to take the risk.

Damon had joined her at the pool this afternoon and smirked the entire time. Twice at dinner he'd startled her by bursting out in laughter. Questioning him wasn't something he liked, but she did ask him once to share the joke. He'd only smiled and said that tomorrow all would be revealed. Just what the hell did that mean?

She knew she was damn lucky he hadn't locked her in again. Last night, when he'd had Margret deliver a meal to her and lock her door, she'd been sure he was on to her. Figured catching her coming out of his office had put him on alert. Apparently that wasn't the case.

Tonight, after spending the evening together, he'd escorted her to the bedroom door and kissed her. The minute she entered the room, she'd expected to hear the click of the lock. It never came. Questioning the reason would do no good. She had to find information on Jamie. Time was running out.

She was dressed a little differently tonight. One of the dresses Damon had supplied her with had a thick lining, so she'd ripped a hole in it, figuring the slot would be a good place to hide the letter opener.

On silent feet, she crept down the hallway to the top of the stairs and looked around. The giant foyer was empty. Most of the men were posted outside, but two stayed inside and walked constantly through the interior of the mansion. Fortunately, there was a lot of house for them to cover. The key was to time it so that they were in a different part of the house than she was.

Easing downstairs, her ears and eyes alert for any shadow or sound, she saw and heard no one. Damon's office was on the first floor, at the back of the house. At the bottom of the stairs she stopped and listened. Nothing. Running as quickly and quietly as possible, she reached the closed door of his office in less than a minute. She turned the knob and then almost sobbed her frustration out loud. The door was locked.

Dammit, it hadn't been locked yesterday. This was no doubt his attempt to keep her out. She'd just see about that.

Thinking of all of the tools she could have used to unlock the door would do no good. She had to find something to improvise with. *Think, McKenna, think!* She stood in a largish hallway. To her right was a small sofa and table. On her left was nothing other than a landscape hanging from the wall.

An image of the landscape she'd left in her little apartment in Paris came to her mind. Not the picture itself, but the wire that had been on the back to hang it. Telling herself this one would be too expensive to have a thin wire in the back, she looked anyway. As she had figured: hooks only, no wire.

Refusing to give up, she turned and considered the table and sofa again. A vase full of some kind of exotic-looking flower sat in the middle of the table. The flowers looked fresh and had a rich color . . . they had to be real. She crept closer and touched them. Silk!

Wasting no time, McKenna plucked one of the flowers; using her teeth and fingernails, she stripped the plastic off the stem wire.

Heart pounding with trepidation and exhilaration, she inserted the wire into the lock, jiggled for several seconds, and heard a soft click. Voilà!

McKenna slipped inside, went straight to the laptop on Damon's desk, and clicked on his document file again. Several different file names caught her attention; she tried "McKenna" for every password and finally got into one file.

Her eyes quickly perused the contents: all the different transactions Damon had been involved in this year. Apparently his business interests were quite a diverse collection of illegal activities, including gambling, drug smuggling, bribery, and . . . Her breath stopped. Women. Dollar amounts were beside each name. Had he sold these women? Her eyes read through them, looking for Jamie Kendrick. She wasn't there. Memorizing the names and places as best she could, she exited the program and started searching again.

She heard a soft noise. Someone was coming! Closing the laptop, she ducked under the desk and held her breath. Voices just outside the office door. She couldn't hear what was being said or who it was. They sounded as if they were standing in front of the door.

She waited for several more breath-holding seconds. The talking continued. Cursing silently, McKenna reached up and pulled the laptop down on the floor with her. If they were going to stand there and block her only exit, she might as well take advantage of what time she had left.

Each file she clicked on was no help. She found nothing more than entries showing the amazing amounts of money he had made and spent. She went back to the file of names showing women being sold, hoping she had somehow missed Jamie's name. No, there was no mention of her.

Another sound. The men were moving away. Sighing because she'd gotten nothing helpful, McKenna stood and replaced the laptop back on the desk. Her next option was to explore the grounds. The estate was large enough for small guesthouses, perhaps a place he had hidden her. She couldn't give up. Her last option was to confront Damon and force him to talk. Which meant she would have to get him alone, away from the mountainous men who protected him.

Her feet soundless on the carpeted floor, she went to the door and listened. Heard nothing. Taking a breath, McKenna opened the door. And there stood Damon, apparently waiting for her. His eyes gleamed with evil; the expression on his face was that of a predator on the verge of taking down its prey.

The pretense was over.

The mother of all headaches pounded at Lucas's skull. Willing his body to absorb and then deny the agony, he took several deep, even breaths. Deciding the slight lessening of pain was the best he was going to get, he pushed himself up to look around. Several thoughts hit him at once. He wasn't restrained, meaning they thought he wasn't a threat. The room was dark, but he had good night vision, so he could see that he was in a bedroom. Not much of a bedroom, since all it had was one bed and nothing else. The room was stripped clean. Not a weapon to be found anywhere. Not that that was a problem; he'd come prepared.

The men who'd nabbed him had checked his pockets and nothing else. They had most definitely been hired for their brawn, for which Lucas was immensely grateful.

Taking his belt from his pants, he stripped the leather

away from the buckle and pulled out a five-inch Peace-maker knife. Tearing further into the leather, he slid out thirty inches of piano wire. Removing his left boot, he slid his Kel-Tec .380 from the small holster that held it in place. Pulling off the other boot, he took out the extra cartridge of bullets.

The dark navy shirt hanging loose covered the gun he slid into one pocket, and the knife was hidden in the other, along with the cartridge. He slipped the piano wire into his waistband, within easy reach.

Feeling reasonably ready to face Damon and his men, Lucas stood and perused the room for an escape. They might be coming for him soon, but he'd just as soon get out on his own if he could.

Ears and eyes alert, Lucas walked the perimeter of the room and finally allowed himself to think of why McKenna was here. Two options came to mind. One, Damon had kidnapped her again. Or two, she had finally decided to confront him and for some reason decided to take a swim first.

He was going with the first theory. Damon had kidnapped her again and she hadn't been able to escape. The thought of how and when that had happened pounded in his skull. What had the bastard done to her while she was here?

McKenna's being here upped the danger quotient a hell of a lot more than he would have liked. Though he knew she could handle herself about as well as anyone, he didn't want her endangered if he could prevent it. Killing Damon needed to be done as quickly and efficiently as possible. Then he'd deal with the explanation she was sure to demand of just how and why he was here.

Her mind racing, McKenna faced Damon, more than aware she was in deep shit. Yesterday he'd let her get away with being in the office with almost no questions. At this time of night she had no answers, lame or otherwise.

"Have you been a bad girl, McKenna?"

His taunt surprised her. Years ago he would have just knocked the hell out of her and asked questions later. Now he almost looked amused. Maybe it was time for Damon to take her seriously . . . to show him just how bad she could be. Arching a brow arrogantly, she said, "I was looking for information."

"Information on what?"

"On where Jamie Kendrick is."

"I returned her, McKenna. I know you're lacking in intelligence, darling, but don't tell me you've forgotten."

"You returned a female. She wasn't Jamie."

He shrugged. "So? One's as good as another."

And for him that was so true. This man had no conscience, morals, or ethics. Setting up an exchange for Jamie had not only been pointless, it had been stupid. Damon Hughes did what was expedient and convenient for him. Expecting him to keep his word, act with any kind of honesty, had been incredibly naïve of them.

"Tell me where she is."

"McKenna, I like neither your tone nor the fact that you're asking questions of me."

"I don't think you get the picture, Damon. I'm not asking, I'm demanding. And guess what? I don't give a flying fuck what you like or don't like."

A fist flew toward her face; McKenna caught it with her hand and gave it a quick, hard twist. Damon grunted. Using all of his weight, he pushed her hard. McKenna landed on her butt, sprang back to her feet, and slammed her fist into his jaw.

Holding his hand against his face, he snarled, "You little bitch, you've been holding back on me."

She snorted her disgust. "Stupid fool, you have no

idea just how much. Now, either tell me where Jamie is or I'll just beat it out of you. Your choice."

Though his face went harder at her insult, he said mildly, "Did you not find the information you were looking for on my computer?"

"I found plenty of information about your drug and arms smuggling, as well as gambling and prostitution."

Damon grimaced. "My downfall, I fear, is that I keep excellent records. And I hate paper waste. The clutter appalls me, not to mention the damage to the environment."

"Yeah, you're a real humanitarian."

"Sarcasm is such an unattractive trait in you."

"Tell me where Jamie is."

"No. And since I'm the only one who knows, I guess it will have to stay a secret. But tell me, what would you do if I told you? Call the authorities, who don't even believe I'm alive? Tell them I've kidnapped a woman whose abduction everyone else believes was arranged by her ex-husband?" He shook his head. "Poor, stupid McKenna. They'd probably actually lock you up this time."

"Fine, I'll just beat it out of you." Swinging her arm back, she put everything she had into the punch as she belted him in the gut. Damon grunted. His fist swung at her again; she dodged it and came back at him with another jab. Before she could deliver it, a giant hand grabbed her from behind. Out of instinct, McKenna whirled and punched. Agony vibrated through her arm as her fist slammed into a rock-hard chest. Simon, the one who'd grabbed her from the helicopter. Close to seven feet tall and built like a tank. Not a man she could take down with just one slug.

Simon didn't even flinch. Before she could try another punch in a more vulnerable area, he spun her around to face Damon and then picked her up as if she were a doll.

"Thank you, Simon," Damon said. "I was beginning to wonder if anyone was going to come along and take care of my troublesome fiancée for me."

McKenna felt like the girl in the *King Kong* movie. Simon held her at least two feet above the floor. Making use of her dangling legs, she focused on the one area of Damon's body that would cause him the most pain, the most embarrassment. Wishing for steel-toed boots, she made do with her bare foot and kicked him deep in the balls.

The earsplitting shriek almost made up for the suffocating agony of Simon's crushing arms. Before she could deliver another kick, Simon wrapped one of his long legs around both her legs, stopping her.

Holding his hand over his crotch, Damon was bent over, gagging. Years ago this had been one of her dreams, and she had finally made it a reality. McKenna knew she would pay dearly for what she had done, but in that one brief moment she had never felt prouder.

As Damon tried to recover, McKenna allowed herself to spew the words she'd longed to say for years. "You're a pathetic piece of shit, Damon Hughes. You think I or any other woman could love someone like you? You're nothing but vermin, garbage. You—"

Damon straightened and delivered a hard, backhanded slap to McKenna's face. She ignored her throbbing jaw as fury continued to fuel her. "You think you can do anything to anybody, but you're nothing but a lowlife, a good-for-nothing piece—"

The next blow caused stars to appear. Stunned into silence, McKenna blinked rapidly, fighting to gather her wits.

Damon's face was purple with rage. Tears of pain poured from his eyes. The kick had definitely done some damage. The bastard would try to punish her more, but at least he wouldn't try raping her for a while.

Once again, McKenna used the only weapon she had left. "You're nothing but an ugly-as-sin, tiny-dicked moron."

Snarling, Damon lunged forward, wrapped his hands around her throat, and squeezed. The roaring in her ears battled with the thundering of her heart. His face blurred before her . . . she was losing consciousness. She twisted, squirmed, tried to kick, to get away. The roaring in her ears deafened Damon's words as he screamed at her. His red, furious face was the last thing she saw. . . .

With extreme effort, Damon removed his hands from McKenna's neck. She was slumped over. Unconscious or dead? Checking her pulse, he was only slightly relieved that he hadn't killed her. Pain speared through his groin and nausea clawed inside him. She deserved death, but what McKenna didn't seem to understand was that his love was forever. Just because she chose to hurt him didn't mean he stopped loving her. She had hurt him years ago and it hadn't killed his love.

But now her punishment would be more severe than he had originally planned. Before, he had been prepared to spend only a day or two on disciplining her. Now that had changed. McKenna would know weeks, perhaps months of agony. When she emerged from her punishment, there would be no defiance, no anger inside her. Even if he had to burn, beat, and fuck her to within an inch of her life, she would be a changed person. The McKenna of today would never exist again.

Still, he had already made plans, and everything would go forward. McKenna would just be a little more silent than usual. "Take her back to her room. Tie her down. I'll be there soon."

Simon threw her slender body over his shoulder as if he were carrying a feather. Not for the first time, Damon was happy to have found the ox. He might be low on brains, but he more than made up for it by his amazing strength.

Their marriage would take place tomorrow, but there would be one additional bit of entertainment to add to the festivities. He had thought to present Lucas Kane's dead, bloodied body as a wedding gift. Instead, it would be a performance of spectacular proportions. He'd rarely had an audience when he killed; tomorrow he would make an exception.

He had hired a photographer to come in after the ceremony. Damon only hoped the man wasn't too squeamish. Pictures of Lucas Kane's blood-drenched carcass would be a perfect addition to the wedding album.

twenty-one

McKenna woke slowly, painfully, aware that something was very wrong. Moving her head slightly, she moaned at the excruciating pain coming from her neck and throat. Tears sprang to her eyes as she tried to swallow. Agony! Was it strep or something worse? Her throat hadn't hurt this bad even when she had the flu. Her mind was blurred, felt dim and slow.

She moved to touch her throat and realized she couldn't. Her arms were tied to the side of the bed. Her legs were bound, too. Memory slammed into her like a sledgehammer. She'd challenged Damon, hurt his pride and his manhood; he'd almost choked her to death. And now she could barely move.

Great going, McKenna.

Lying back on the pillow, she tried to ignore the pain in her throat as she reviewed her options. As satisfying as it had been to hurt him, she knew she was lucky he hadn't killed her. Even though his insane delusions told him he loved her, he could have easily lost control. The selfishness of her act wasn't lost on her. If he had killed her, Jamie Kendrick might never be found.

McKenna didn't waste time castigating herself. It would do little good. What was done was done. She just needed to figure out how she could overcome her carelessness and get Damon to tell her where Jamie was. Now that he knew she wasn't the weakling she used to be, he would be much more wary around her. What little cover she'd had was blown. Only good thing about that was she no longer had to act like an imbecile, nor did she have to pretend to enjoy his hands and mouth on her. No matter what he did to punish her, she'd never let him touch her again without causing him extreme pain.

However, no way in hell would Damon willingly tell her where Jamie was. How could she get him to talk?

He was planning something for today, and she greatly feared she knew what it was. More than once since she'd been here, he'd mentioned marriage. What other grand celebration would he be planning besides her forced marriage to this pig she despised?

It wouldn't matter. She'd die before she said "I do." If the minister, or whatever the hell kind of person Damon brought in to do the deed, tried to marry them without her consent, she'd scream no at the top of her lungs. No one would doubt the extent of her unwillingness to marry the groom. She would never say yes to the bastard.

Brave thoughts for a girl who could barely swallow, much less move.

What was she going to do?

Lucas paced around the room, cursing his confinement. He was beginning to think that kidnappers were some of the rudest people alive. This was the second time in less than a year that he had been abducted. And both times he'd been left alone for hours at a time.

Escaping and hunting down Damon had been his goal. Unfortunately, that wasn't going to happen until someone came to let him out. The door was impenetrable. Not a regular household door, it had some kind of steel reinforcement behind it, thick and solid, almost like a vault.

Lucas concluded this room had been created for one purpose: to keep whoever was locked in it from escaping. Even the lock was impossible to pick, which pissed him off mightily since that had been one of his best skills at the agency. The only window in the room was a skylight about twenty feet above him. He was tall, but not tall enough even if he stood on the bed.

The delay infuriated him; he had no real choice except to wait. He worked hard not to think about what McKenna might be going through with the bastard. How Hughes had gotten to her again didn't matter as much as what he was doing to her. Since she'd left him less than a week ago, he could only assume the bastard had nabbed her not long after they'd said goodbye.

That was good in one way—he'd hadn't had her for long. It was bad in another, because five minutes with the perverted creep was too long. His memory was hazy because of the drug he'd been injected with, but from what he could remember she'd looked healthy. He had seen no new visible scars or bruises. However, Lucas knew the worst damage Hughes might inflict could be on the inside. Places where injuries didn't show but the pain lingered for years.

How he wished he could erase all the damage that had been done to her, but he couldn't. However, now that he'd found the bastard, the man's time on this earth was limited. Failure wasn't an option; it never had been with him. He didn't consider his attitude one of arrogance as much as one of determination. McKenna would be freed today from the devil who'd hounded her. What was in store for them after that was entirely up to her.

For so long she hadn't had a life at all. Had been living without choices. After today, she would have all the choices in the world. Lucas hoped that choice included him.

Noises outside her room told McKenna she was about to find out what Damon had planned. No matter what it was, she vowed that at some point today she would get the information she'd come for. If it was the last thing she did, Jamie Kendrick would be rescued.

The door opened, then closed. McKenna twisted her head to see a tuxedoed Damon approach the bed. Dressed for a wedding, no doubt. Damned if she'd let that happen. He'd have to kill her to marry her. She'd rather be dead than wed. She felt a small amount of amusement at the rhyme. Who knew she had a talent for grimly humorous, bad poetry?

Damon pulled up a chair beside the bed and sat down. "Good morning, my love. I know it's considered bad luck for the groom to see the bride before the wedding, but since there are some things I think we need to clear up, I chose to buck tradition." He smiled. "Once you understand, we'll pretend it never happened and we'll have the traditional wedding that I know all young girls dream of."

Curses sprang to her mouth, and McKenna shouted at him. Only nothing came out—a mere gasp of air, no words. Oh God, she couldn't speak!

Damon nodded, his smile one of supreme arrogance. "Your vocal cords are frozen. After your unattractive outburst last night, I realized that you wouldn't be able to keep your mouth shut. And let's face it, no one likes a loudmouthed bitch for a bride."

He slid a caressing finger over her neck. "While you were unconscious, you were injected with a drug that temporarily freezes your vocal cords. It'll wear off in a few hours, after the ceremony, but I must say I do like this silent side of you. I'll have to check with my medical friends to see if it's something we can use on a regular basis. As much as I love to hear your sweet voice, when you become a screaming shrew, it's not nearly as pleas-ant. Having the drug on hand will be helpful in the coming weeks until you become accustomed to married life."

The pain she endured to come up with a croak wasn't worth it. Letting her eyes speak for her, she showed him contempt, revulsion, and hatred. His widening smile told her he really didn't care what she thought.

"Here's the plan for the day. In a few minutes, Margret will arrive to help you shower and get ready." He grinned. "Be nice to her—I think she's a bit jealous that you're marrying me.

"Then a woman, along with her two young daughters, will come in to assist you with your makeup and hair. Now, I know you'll want to resist, but you need to understand something. All three are unaware of our, shall we say, relationship difficulties. If they get any kind of hint that you aren't the happy bride, I will break their necks. And darling, you know full well I can and will do that. So the choice is yours. Allow them to make you into the beautiful bride of my dreams and we'll have a wonderful day. Or you can come to me as a not-so-attractive bride and the mother will watch her daughters die, before I kill her. Your choice."

He stood. "I told them about your unfortunate attack by some thugs yesterday. They were horrified, as you might guess, and have promised to cover all of your bruises. And they understand that you can't speak. They're so sweet and sympathetic. Especially the young girls. I'd hate to have to kill them."

On his way out of the room, he stopped and turned. "We'll have a happy life together, McKenna. How soon that happens is entirely up to you." His smile grew wider. "I can't wait for you to see the preparations I've made or the special gift I brought you. This day will be memorable for both of us."

Tied up and mute, McKenna could only glare at him as he went out the door. He had her exactly where he wanted her, but not for long. There was no way in hell she would jeopardize three innocent lives. And he knew that. But once she was assured of their safety, she'd be damned if Damon didn't pay.

For so long she had wanted to see him dead. She had told Noah that she couldn't do the deed. Now she knew she could. However, Damon couldn't die until he gave her the information she needed. If Jamie was dead, her body should be returned to her family for burial. But if she was still alive, then she needed to be rescued.

She would go along with Damon until she could get him alone. And then the man would learn that her well-placed kick last night was nothing but a mere twinge compared to what she was capable of delivering.

Damon stood in the midst of beauty. He had demanded that a modern-day garden of Eden be created, and his commands had been obeyed. Flowers of every hue and variety were represented. Some were in pots, lining the walkway to the arbor; others hung from hooks attached to invisible wires and looked as though they were floating in the air. Every flowering tree available stood in the background.

The wedding planner had exceeded his expectations. When he'd called and informed her that the wedding was back on and she had even less time than before, he had expected at least a small protest. There had been a long pause and then she had agreed to his requests. Having that much power was a powerful aphrodisiac. Despite the injury McKenna had inflicted last night, Damon was more than ready for his honeymoon. He might not be able to perform as quickly as usual, but there were many things he intended to do to his bride, all of which would give him satisfaction and pleasure in some way. And he was certain one of them would resurrect his injured manhood.

Leaning down, he inhaled the floral beauty of a rare orchid. No woman could ask for a more beautiful wedding day. Not that his bride would appreciate the trouble he'd gone to, but that was all right. He was getting what he'd wanted since the moment he met her. Soon McKenna Sloan would become McKenna Hughes, and all would be as it should have been eight years before.

It was true that the McKenna from years ago had changed. The young and innocent girl from Nebraska had morphed into a spitfire. Damon found himself looking forward to the challenge of taming her. He might have eventually tired of the docile, lifeless McKenna she'd been before. This new, strong-willed McKenna fired his blood and made him pulse with a passion he had never felt before. She would be like a wild filly; he could barely wait for the breaking-in to take place.

Hearing a sound, he turned and lost his breath. The bride was a vision in white. The most beautiful bride ever, and she was his. The designer wedding dress had cost a small fortune, but Damon hadn't minded. A girl only had a special day like this once in a lifetime.

Fortunately, the dress, though sleeveless, was high-necked and hid the bruises from their little spat last night. And the bruises on her right cheek had been successfully covered. Their wedding photographs would only show a beautiful woman on her wedding day. Years later, when McKenna looked at their wedding album, she would be grateful he'd been so considerate.

Gratitude wasn't what he saw in her eyes at the moment, but that didn't matter, either. She couldn't yet speak, so that smart mouth she'd developed over the years wouldn't get her into trouble.

Her eyes glinted with hatred and her expression was one of revulsion. He had considered trying to figure out a way to freeze her face into a smile and had even gotten one of his pharmacist friends out of bed this morning to discuss the possibility. The man had advised against it; the risk of possible side effects, such as permanent nerve damage, was a bit too great.

Didn't matter. Damon knew his own smile was big enough for both of them. As she drew closer, he held out his arms in welcome. "Darling, you look beautiful."

Being his stubborn McKenna, she stopped walking, which meant he had to either lower his arms or walk with them outstretched. His smile went brighter as he lowered his arms. Once he reached her, he pulled her close and whispered, "Darling, the anticipation of our honeymoon almost overwhelms me. You will know such agony that your screams will be heard for miles. The sedative on your vocal cords will be gone by then, which means I'm going to relish every single cry of pain."

When she tried to jerk away from him, he said softly, "The minister is waiting for us. He was told you have laryngitis, so all that will be required of you is a simple nod of your head at the appropriate time. If the wedding goes without a hitch, he'll be handsomely compensated and go on his way, happy, healthy, and completely oblivious to our relationship problems. If, however, there's a glitch of any kind, his brain will be splattered at your feet. The choice is yours."

Satisfied he'd made his point, Damon led her toward the arched trellis he'd had erected just for this event. The aforementioned minister stood waiting for them. He looked mildly curious but apparently saw nothing wrong with the bride and groom having a small chat before the ceremony.

He would soon get a bit of a shock, but Damon had chosen this man with great care. He might be an ordained minister, but he had more than a few secrets

Damon would gladly expose. After the wedding festivities had passed, they would visit and he would learn what would happen if he ever revealed what he saw today.

Sad, really, that there were no guests to witness the grand event, but he hadn't wanted to risk his friends and business acquaintances seeing McKenna's reluctance. Talk of her defiance would spread and he would become a laughingstock. Other than four of his most loyal men, he had sent everyone away for the day, including his dear Margret. The poor woman was heartbroken that he was getting married, so it was a kindness that she was missing the ceremony.

Additionally, the special event he planned for after the ceremony needed to be witnessed by as few people as possible. Not because he feared retribution, but because this was an intimate gift, straight from his heart. How much more intimate could it be than to present your wife's former lover to her and then disembowel him in front of her?

Once McKenna was fully in line and tamed to his satisfaction, he'd throw a party so all his business acquaintances could meet his sweet and very obedient wife. He smiled in anticipation of how he would soon begin those lessons in obedience.

Standing at the side of the closed door, Lucas waited. It was mid-morning. He'd been in the damned room for well over twelve hours. Was it Hughes's plan to leave him here to die of dehydration and starvation? That didn't seem in keeping with the bastard's psychotic tendencies.

No. Damon Hughes would want to use Lucas as a focal point for something. His best guess was that he intended to do away with Lucas in front of McKenna. Not only would it amuse the creep, but if he had gauged

Hughes correctly, it would feed his ego to have killed one of the wealthiest men in the world. These two things were mere by-products of the real reason he'd been abducted and brought here: Hughes wanted to hurt McKenna as much as he could. By killing Lucas, Hughes would be delivering one more lesson.

For the first time since he'd come up with this idea, Lucas doubted himself. It had seemed so damn simple when he'd been at home planning the bastard's downfall. But that was when he had thought it would be a somewhat simple kill. Having McKenna anywhere close when he took the man out wasn't something he felt comfortable with. Not only because she still didn't know Lucas had the skills to do the job, but because McKenna had been exposed to too much violence already. He had wanted to get this over with and then present her with some sort of evidence that Damon Hughes could no longer hurt her.

The click of the door unlocking alerted him. Whether he was comfortable or not, it was time to do what he'd come here to do. Adrenaline surging, Lucas moved several feet away from the door, prepared to strike the moment it opened. Seconds later, Simon's large bald head peeked inside. Lucas sprang.

Simon turned just in time. He swung his big fist, catching Lucas's jaw with a glancing blow. Determination fueling him, Lucas took the punch. Whirling his body, he kicked Simon in the gut, followed immediately by a kick to the man's chin. Another whirl and kick had Simon down on the floor. Lucas leaped on top of him and pressed his forearm against the man's neck.

"What does Hughes have planned?"

His eyes saucer wide, Simon looked too stunned to speak. Lucas pressed harder till the man gurgled. Lucas eased the pressure and snarled, "Talk."

"He . . . he's having a wedding in the courtyard. I'm supposed to bring you to him."

Shit!

No time for finesse. Lucas punched Simon's jaw hard once, twice, till he lost consciousness. Grabbing plastic ties from the man's pocket, he ran out the door, slamming it behind him. Racing toward the front of the mansion, he had only one thing on his mind: Damon Hughes would die before he had the chance to become a bridegroom.

Her mouth clenched in fury, McKenna's eyes roamed the elaborate setup as Damon led her down the aisle. The creep had spared no expense. The overdone courtyard looked as though an entire florist shop had vomited. As far as the eye could see, there were flowers. The overwhelming fragrance created a sickening, cloying scent that made her want to gag.

After the humiliation of being bathed and dressed by a grim-faced Margret, she had to sit still as a woman and her two teenage daughters giggled and chatted excitedly while they styled her hair and applied makeup. How she wanted to scream at them to get out as fast as they could. Instead she had smiled and done her best to appear happy. Getting them away from Damon without any suspicions had been her priority.

There were no guests to witness the spectacle, which was a small blessing. Other than Elliott, she saw only two other men. With a weapon, she could take them out fairly easy. Since her clothes had been missing when she woke this morning, the letter opener she'd stolen was no more. Without a weapon, taking all the men out would be much harder. She assured herself it was possible.

A dark-suited older man holding a Bible and wearing a benign smile waited for them under the flowered arbor. There was no indication the minister knew that anything was amiss. His life was important to her. No innocent person would die today, but the others wouldn't be so lucky. She still wasn't sure of her strategy. Since Damon had to stay alive, she'd have to find a way to incapacitate him and then get rid of the others. How, she didn't know, but she was good at improvising.

First she'd disable Damon, then Elliott, who stood a few feet to her left. He was rather large and she might have some difficulty, but he was the closest to them and should have a gun; she'd steal it and disarm Damon's other men. Then she and Damon would have a very serious talk.

Her adrenaline surging, McKenna tensed, gearing herself up to attack.

Damon came to a sudden halt and hit his palm against his forehead. "How could I have forgotten our most honored guest?" His facetious grin told her it was all an act. "Must be wedding jitters."

Before she could react, she heard what sounded like feet shuffling toward them.

"Ah, here he comes . . . our one and only guest. My wedding gift to you, my love."

McKenna looked over her shoulder. Her heart stopped in her chest, then dropped like a ton of cement to the ground.

A tall, blond man shuffled toward them, a fierce expression on his bruised face, his hands and feet bound. Not just any man, but the man who held her heart. *Lucas!*

twenty-two

Maintaining an expression of cold impassivity, Lucas took in the scene. McKenna stood in the middle of an aisle in a wedding dress. Somehow Damon had gotten her this far. Why the hell had she gone along with this? He'd seen her in action. The woman could kick ass with the best of them. What the hell was she waiting for?

Frowning, Damon's eyes searched behind Lucas. "Where's Simon?"

Lucas shrugged.

Indecision and arrogance were strong enemies. Arrogance won. Apparently not suspecting that Simon had been incapacitated, Damon jerked his head over at another big lug standing close. "Elliott, why don't you go stand by Mr. Kane?"

The man marched toward him and took his place directly behind Lucas.

As he looked around the elaborate wedding setup, Lucas had some decisions to make. Damon's expression was once again stamped with arrogance. McKenna's face had gone from pale to sheet white, her expression horrified. Apparently this was her first knowledge that he was here.

"Looks like I'm a bit underdressed for the occasion," Lucas said.

Damon grinned. "Nonsense. We're just thrilled you could join us." The look he shot McKenna was one of sly superiority. "Aren't we, my love?"

Oddly enough, McKenna didn't speak. She gave a frantic shake of her head, her expression panicked. Even though Lucas had set this scenario up, guilt seared him. McKenna was reliving her worst nightmare: having someone she cared for die at Damon's hands. That wouldn't happen, but she didn't know that.

But why the hell didn't she say something?

Damon gripped McKenna's arm and whispered something to her. Her eyes grew even wider; she jerked away and took a step toward Lucas. Damon grabbed her again.

Lucas growled, "Let her go, Hughes."

"Let her go? She's mine. Has been from the moment I met her." Turning around, he pulled her with him to the arbor, where a man holding a Bible waited. "I think we can get started now."

The bewildered minister seemed stunned to see a tied-up man attending the wedding. His worried gaze moved from Damon to Lucas. Apparently he wasn't in on this. If not, Lucas wouldn't touch him. Everyone else, though, other than McKenna, was fair game.

"Did you hear me?" Hughes snapped. "Let's get started."

The man's eyes were round with fear. "But . . . I . . ."

"You what?" Damon asked. "You're hundreds of thousands of dollars in debt, you've fathered two children by two different women in your congregation, and you're addicted to three types of prescription drugs. That information can stay with just the few of us here or it'll be in tomorrow's newspapers. Your choice."

The minister's audible swallow was loud in the too-quiet courtyard. His hands shook so hard, the Bible he held looked as though it would jump out of his grasp. In a high and squeaky voice, he began, "Dearly beloved, we are gathered . . ."

Lucas stopped listening. It was time to act. Damon's

arm was around McKenna's shoulders. He was apparently coercing her with something, the way he had with the minister. Damned if the man would get a chance to finish the ceremony.

Since Lucas had been standing here like a whipped puppy, Elliott had backed away slightly. He had secured his own hands and ankles, so the bonds would break with one good jerk. Bending quickly, Lucas pulled the knife he'd stuck in his sock earlier.

Hearing the words "Do you take this man . . ." Lucas sprang into action. He turned and with a flick of his wrist sliced Elliott's throat. He caught the giant before he could fall, preventing a thunderous crash.

Turning back to the display in front of him, he noted two other men. Both had their eyes focused on McKenna and Hughes. Lucas crept closer, preparing to spring into action.

McKenna's heart pounded so loudly, she could barely think. Not since her parents were killed had she felt such fear. Damon had whispered an ultimatum: marry him or Lucas would die. How had he even known about Lucas? She'd never gone out in public with him. Had made sure she was never followed when she went to his home. How had this happened?

And now what could she do? If she didn't marry Damon, Lucas would die. She wasn't stupid enough to believe that Damon would let Lucas go if she complied. No, once they were married, he would kill Lucas anyway. Somehow Damon had discovered her feelings for Lucas and this was a lesson. And once again, someone she loved would die because of her.

It was too much. She couldn't let it happen again; she couldn't. Even if she had to die, no one else would suffer because of her mistakes.

Twisting slightly, arm up, McKenna slammed her

elbow into Damon's face. Screaming, he fell to the ground, clutching his busted nose. McKenna turned to go free Lucas. Only Lucas was no longer tied, no longer being held hostage. And he definitely didn't need her help. Elliott lay on the ground. And a grim-faced Lucas was headed determinedly toward Damon.

One of Damon's men leaped toward Lucas. She barely had time to comprehend the swiftness of Lucas's movements as he whirled and kicked, knocking the man backward and then leaping on top of him.

Out of the corner of her eye she saw another one of Damon's men pull his gun. McKenna pirouetted and kicked, knocking the gun from the man's hand. He swung a fist at her; she ducked, turned, and side-kicked him in the chest. He stumbled slightly and came at her again. She waited until the last second, made a half twist with her body, raised her arm, and elbowed him in the throat, following it with a hard kick to his groin. Screaming in pain, the man fell backward; she heard a satisfying crack. Hopefully that would keep him out for a while.

Seeing that the minister was cowering in a corner, she nodded at him and held her hand up as a signal that he needed to stay put.

She turned, looking around for Damon. Where was he? Where the hell—

The blast of a gun had her whirling around. Lucas had a gun and was shooting at someone. She saw a dark head peeking from around a statue. Damon! Lucas was shooting at Damon.

Oh God, Damon couldn't die yet. She made a mad dash toward Lucas, stumbling in her shoes. Dammit, she couldn't even scream at him. Stopping abruptly, McKenna pulled off her shoes and threw one at Lucas's head. It was a poor throw, landing in front of him, but at least it got his attention. He turned and saw her coming and whispered harshly, "Stay put. I'm going after Hughes."

McKenna flew at Lucas, leaping onto his shoulders. His gun went skittering across the brick tile.

Dropping her to her feet, Lucas faced her, his expression one of furious disbelief. "What the hell's wrong with you?"

Shaking her head frantically, she gestured at her throat, trying to make him understand she couldn't talk.

Before he could speak, a noise a few yards away told them Damon was on the move again. Lucas pushed her into an alcove. "Don't move."

She pulled at his shoulder and shook her head again.

"McKenna, I don't know what your problem is, but I'm not going to argue with you. Stay here." He took off toward where Damon had disappeared inside the house.

Having no choice, McKenna ran after him. She had to get to Damon before Lucas did.

Something came at her from the side, slamming her sideways against a brick column. Temporarily dazed, she looked up to see Damon glaring at her. He'd apparently gone in one door, run through the house, and come out behind them. McKenna told herself to shake off the pain. A bruised shoulder and hip were nothing compared to what he had done to her before.

Damon's bloodied nose had doubled in size; the wickedness in his eyes matched what she had seen the night he'd killed her parents. "Bitch," he snarled. "Did you think you were going to get away from me that easily?"

Taking a breath, she raised her fist and with all her strength punched him in the face. He staggered back.

"Hughes, get away from her!" Lucas shouted.

She turned; Lucas headed toward them, gun in hand. No, she had to find a way to make Damon talk. The cold, murderous expression in Lucas's eyes told her she wouldn't get a chance.

An arm wrapped around her throat. *Damon.* He stuck a pistol to her head and shouted, "Put the gun down, Kane, or she dies."

"You damage one strand of her hair and I'll tie your balls into knots."

Holding her as a shield, Damon began to back away. "She belongs to me. No one takes what's mine."

McKenna read Lucas's expression. He knew she could get away from Damon. A kick in the shin, a direct hit to his groin, a sharp elbow to his stomach—any of those could incapacitate him long enough for her to get away from him. Then Lucas could shoot him. For right now, her body as shield worked for both of them. If she could get Damon alone, she would overpower him and then tie him up. Until then, she had to stay in front of him to protect him from Lucas.

"Lucas . . ." The sound was barely above a whisper. No way in hell could he hear her.

Damon pulled her with him toward the house. McKenna didn't fight. *Get him alone. Overpower. Make him talk.*

"Dammit, McKenna!" Lucas shouted, the fury in his voice apparent. She had no choice; she had to protect Damon. Lucas wouldn't dare shoot until she moved away from Damon, and if—

Damon's grip abruptly loosened. A split second later, McKenna's ears registered the blast of a pistol.

She whirled around; Damon lay at her feet, a neat bullet hole in the middle of his forehead.

A cry built inside her she couldn't express. Her heart pounding with dread, she dropped to her knees and checked his pulse. None. Damon was dead.

"It's over, McKenna," Lucas growled above her.

Jumping to her feet, she whirled around and slapped him.

He caught her hand before she could deliver a second slap. His face a dark mask of fury, he snarled, "I don't know what the fuck your problem is, but we're getting out of here. Then you can tell me why the hell you all of sudden didn't want the man who killed your family dead."

Jerking away from him, she turned and scanned the area. She needed to search the rest of the estate, something she'd never had the chance to do before. Though almost certain Jamie wasn't here, she had to make sure. An arm wrapped around her waist as Lucas picked her up. Before she could twist away, she felt his hand on her neck and then there was nothing.

McKenna blinked rapidly. She was lying on something soft; there was movement beneath her body. Comprehension came quickly. She was in the backseat of a car. Scenes from what had happened flashed through her mind. Grief and fury quickly followed. Grief because she was no closer to finding Jamie Kendrick than she had been before, and fury because of what she had seen in Lucas.

The man was a trained assassin. There was no other explanation for the way he'd moved, the way he'd taken those men out. And the shot that killed Damon. That had been no lucky shot. She had been standing right in front of Damon. An eighth of an inch off and the bullet would have hit her. No one could have made it unless they had specialized training. How had she missed the evidence? Just who the hell was Lucas Kane?

That hurt would have to be dealt with later; she still had a mission to complete. She could not give up just because Damon was dead.

McKenna sat up and pushed her hair out of her eyes.

She was in the backseat, Lucas was in the driver's seat. She gazed around. Palm trees and massive mansions were a blur as the car sped down the highway.

Lucas shot a glance at her over his shoulder. "I see you're awake."

The quiet fury in his voice was unmistakable. *Tough shit*. She had much more reason to be angry than he did. Clearing her throat, she was relieved to actually hear a noise. Anger set aside for the time being, she whispered hoarsely, "I need a phone."

"What's wrong with your voice?"

"I need a phone."

"Sorry. Thought it best to get away as quickly as possible. Stealing a phone wasn't exactly on my agenda."

She looked around the luxurious interior. Hell, this was a Rolls-Royce. If it didn't have a phone installed somewhere, something was very wrong. Thankful that at least Damon had chosen a short wedding dress, McKenna pulled it up farther and crawled into the front seat.

She felt Lucas's eyes on her as she began pressing buttons and opening compartments.

"What are you doing?"

"There's got to be a phone somewhere." Finally she pressed the right one and a compartment opened, revealing a phone. Grabbing it, she punched in Noah's private number.

He answered on the first ring. "McCall."

"It's me. Damon's dead."

"And Jamie?"

"She wasn't there." She swallowed and added, "I didn't get a chance to look around the estate, but I think he sold her. He told me he was the only one who knew where she is. I'm sorry, Noah. I failed."

"We may have some information. Where are you?"

"I still have no idea." She glanced over at Lucas,

noticing his expression had changed from anger to wariness. Yeah, he was beginning to figure out that he'd created a major fuckup. She'd deal with that later. "Do you have any idea where we are?"

Lucas gave a quick nod. "Florida. Palm Beach. I saw a sign a few minutes ago."

She spoke into the phone. "Did you hear that?"

"Yeah. And I'm assuming that Lucas Kane got involved in all this?"

"Yes." She released a heavy sigh. "Long story. You said you may have some information?"

"Yes. Go to the Miles Hotel on Royal Avenue. I've stayed there before. Large enough to have what you need, but the staff is professional and will ensure your privacy. We don't need the press to know that Lucas Kane is in town. I'll gather a team. We'll be there tomorrow at ten."

McKenna closed the phone, and because it hurt too much to look at him, she kept her eyes on the road ahead of them as she asked, "Do you know the Miles Hotel?"

"I'll find it." After a palpable silence, he said, "So I'm assuming I just screwed up an op?"

"That's about the size of it."

"And you weren't being held captive?"

"I was, but . . ."

"But what?"

She leaned her head back against the car seat. "It's a long story."

"I've got nothing but time."

She twisted her head to look at him. "Good. Then you can tell me exactly where you learned to shoot like an assassin and move like a ninja."

"Ninja? Really?" He grinned. "Thanks."

Any other time she would have laughed. Instead she glared. "It wasn't a compliment. Who do you work for?"

"Kane Enterprises."

"Don't play games with me, Lucas."

"I'm not playing games." He drew in a controlled breath. "Look, I think we both have some things we need to tell each other, and neither of us is at our best at the moment. Let's get to the hotel and then we'll talk."

"Should we call the police?"

"I imagine the terrified minister who was hiding in the bushes when we left took care of that. He was the only one still conscious."

McKenna shrugged. He was right about that. She wished she could have at least taken Damon's laptop. Maybe Jamie's whereabouts weren't there, but there might have been other information that would be helpful. One of LCR's analysts could probably have broken the other passwords.

She couldn't think about that now. What was done was done. All she could hope was that Noah had some information that might help them. She certainly didn't expect that Lucas would have a reasonable explanation for being a trained killer. After all the things she'd told him about her life, he'd obviously left out some vital information about his own. Not only that—just how had Damon known about him in the first place?

With a long, low sigh, McKenna leaned her aching head against the pillowy seat cushion. She had a gut-wrenching feeling she was about to find out several disturbing things about the man she had thought she knew better than anyone.

Lucas kept one eye on the road and one eye on the exhausted woman beside him. As he followed the directions to the hotel given to him by the GPS computer in the car, his mind reviewed what he knew and suspected. He'd obviously screwed up an op and felt like shit for that. Now, not only did he need to figure out a way to rectify that mistake, McKenna was looking at him as if he were her enemy.

Telling her about his agency experience went against his oath. Not telling her went against his conscience and his heart. He owed her the truth. Maybe Jared had been right all along. If he had told McKenna the truth about his past, would it have changed the outcome? Somehow he doubted it.

"How did Damon know about us?" Her voice was hoarse, but he heard the pain in her words.

"There were photographs of us together. Newspapers printed them."

"And I'm assuming these photographs were taken at your estate?" she asked dully.

"In front of my estate. The first day you came to visit. Photographer must've been lying in wait for something to happen."

After a palpable, ominous silence, she said, "You could have stopped the photographs."

"Yes."

She turned to him then. The fury he could deal with; it was the betrayal and hurt that speared him. "You bastard," she whispered. "You set me up."

He glared at her. "I set Damon up, McKenna. Not you. I didn't hire the photographer, but I made use of the photographs to get to the bastard. He deserved to die for what he did to you. The kind of life you were living was no life at all."

"That wasn't your decision to make. It was mine."

"You had no decision to make. You could barely go out in public. Shit, McKenna, despite the fact that I fucked up an operation, you can't be sorry that the son of a bitch is dead."

"And that's all you can see, isn't it? You got rid of him, solved my problem. I never asked for your help."

Lucas shot her a frustrated, angry glance. "I get rid of

your worst nightmare and you're angry? Damon really screwed up your mind, didn't he?"

The instant the words were out, he wanted to call them back. She flinched, and he felt as if his heart had been pierced. After the initial show of pain, her face froze into a mask of icy indifference. It was an expression he'd never seen from her before, and it made him feel a thousand times worse. She had closed herself off. McKenna had always been so open. Even when she was keeping things from him, she'd been honest about it.

"I'm sorry, McKenna. I didn't mean that."

She turned away from him and stared out the window. *Hell and damnation.*

twenty-three

McKenna emerged from the shower and wrapped a giant towel around her. As soon as she'd walked into the hotel room, she'd stripped off the vile wedding dress and dumped it in the garbage. Then she'd stood under the hot spray of the shower and scrubbed as hard as she could. Part of it was to get the feel of Damon's filthy hands off her; another reason was to occupy her mind to keep from crying. It had been a while since she'd wanted to just curl up and sob her heart out.

She tried to tell herself that all was not lost. Apparently Noah had some good intel or he wouldn't be gathering a team and coming here for a meeting. Jamie Kendrick could still be alive and rescue could still be possible. She prayed with all her heart that it was true.

But Lucas . . . Tears filled her eyes before she could stop them. Lucas had lied to her. The most authentic, beautiful relationship she'd ever had was based on lies. Not only had he used photographs of them together to lure Damon, he was apparently some sort of assassin. Former or current, she didn't know. But no one could move the way he had, make the execution-style shot he'd made, without extensive, focused training.

She had been stupid enough to buy his earlier explanation that he had taken training because of his wealth. It had been a long time since McKenna had felt so naïve and stupid. She despised the feeling.

What other lies had he told her? He claimed that he

had lured Damon out to kill him for her. That she believed. But what about the way he'd treated her? His kisses, his lovemaking. Had those been to keep her there? Were they all part of an elaborate scheme? Had she fallen in love with a man who in his own way had been using her?

"McKenna, don't."

She turned to see Lucas standing in the doorway. "Don't what? Don't doubt everything you've ever told me? Don't doubt that every word that came from you had a secret agenda behind it?"

"What secret agenda would that be? Trying to protect you?"

"Dammit, Lucas. You're not my bodyguard. I never asked for your protection."

His jaw worked as he apparently tried to control his temper, something she hadn't even known he had. His face went hard as he spotted the bruises on her face. Then his eyes flared hot when he saw her throat. "The bastard hit you and almost choked you to death, didn't he? Is that why you can barely speak above a whisper?"

"He gave me some sort of injection . . . froze my vocal cords so I couldn't speak during the wedding." The pain Damon had inflicted was no longer significant. It was the bruising of her heart she wasn't sure she'd recover from.

He blew out an explosive curse. He was obviously furious, but dammit, his fury couldn't begin to rival her hurt. She endured his hard stare for several more seconds, returning it with one of her own.

Finally he said, "I've ordered food. You look ready to drop, and I haven't eaten in over twenty-four hours. Let's eat and then we'll talk."

Her stomach twisted at the thought of food, but she knew he was right. She hadn't eaten a real meal in almost a week, not since she'd left Lucas's home. Giving him a stiff nod, she said, "I'll be out in a minute."

With one last frustrated glance, he closed the door, allowing her privacy.

Taking advantage of the bath amenities on the counter, McKenna at last started to feel almost human again. She pulled the hotel robe from the hook and wrapped it around her body. At some point she'd have to figure out a way to get some clothes. Right now she couldn't care less. This robe was the first thing she'd worn in days that wasn't tainted by Damon. She relished the stench-free feeling.

The sound of a door being closed and low male voices told her their meal had arrived. Straightening her spine, determined to get answers and deal with whatever she had to, McKenna opened the door.

Lucas looked up as McKenna entered the room. Her anger at him was understandable and expected. He could deal with and identify with that. Even while he'd been making the plans to remove Damon from her life, he had recognized she'd be furious once she found out. Her hurt, however, was another matter. And from what he could tell, she was not only hurt because of the photographs, she was hurt that he hadn't told her about his past.

"Come eat." Luring her with food was a dirty trick, but right now he had to use all available weapons.

She sat down at the small table, and without asking her, he began to fill her plate. He took a seat across from her and then poured two cups of coffee. When she did nothing other than pick up a piece of toast and nibble on it, he realized the weapon wouldn't work this time.

He sighed. "Okay, McKenna. Let's get it out in the open. First, tell me why you were at Hughes's estate."

"I went to . . ." She cleared her throat. Her voice sounded a little stronger but was still hoarse. "He kidnapped a woman, Jamie Kendrick. I went in to rescue her."

Lucas shook his head. "Too easy. From what I know about the man, Hughes wasn't into kidnapping. Tell me the whole story."

"Jamie Kendrick has an amazing resemblance to how I used to look years ago. Damon's people abducted her, believing it was me living under another name."

"That's why you left London." His gut clenched. She had known when she left him that she'd be facing her worst nightmare. Part of him was in awe of her courage and selflessness; another part wanted to spank her ass for being so damned willing to sacrifice herself. When the hell would she start looking out for her own well-being? He ground out his words through clenched teeth. "I'm assuming you made an exchange."

"That was the plan. LCR was helping. I contacted Damon, arranged the exchange. Our plan was to get Jamie, but also capture Damon."

"So you *do* work for LCR?"

"I didn't when we first met. I do now."

"And things didn't go as planned?"

"The woman he brought wasn't Jamie. I'm not sure who she is. The men who brought her got away. A helicopter swooped down and a man hanging from a ladder was there to grab me." She shrugged as if it were no big deal. "Since I knew it wasn't Jamie that Damon had released, I had no choice but to go with him."

Lucas nodded, trying to appear undisturbed by her statement. Hard as hell to do. She could easily have been killed, yet she talked about her experience as casually as if she'd been chatting about the damned weather. He kept his tone even. "So you sacrificed yourself to rescue the girl. You could have been killed."

Again she shrugged. "I knew Damon wouldn't kill me."

"No, just rape and beat you." Lucas took a breath. He had to know. "Did he rape you?"

"No."

Relieved beyond words, he looked at the hideous bruises on her neck. The fury reemerged. "But he did hit you, choke you."

When she shrugged again, it was all he could do not to shout at her that her life was worth a hell of a lot more than she apparently thought it was. Raising his voice and giving in to his anger wouldn't solve a damn thing.

Either she was getting better at reading him or he wasn't as skilled as he used to be in hiding his thoughts, because she sighed and said, "I had to take the chance, Lucas. She never would have been taken if I—"

Leaning forward, he locked eyes with her. "Dammit, McKenna. You have got to stop blaming yourself for Damon Hughes's acts."

She looked down at her plate. "I guess that's a moot point now since he's dead."

"Is it? Or will you try to find every person Hughes ever hurt, as if you're responsible for the bastard's existence on this earth?"

She flinched again. This time Lucas refused to feel guilty. However, he did want the rest of the story. "I'm assuming you had a plan if you got taken?"

"I had a GPS device . . . a ring."

For the first time Lucas saw something different in her eyes: shame. Through clenched teeth again, he said, "He made you strip."

She nodded. "In the helicopter. He threw everything out the window; LCR couldn't track me. When we got to his estate, I hoped Jamie would be there. She wasn't. I asked him where she was. At first he denied that it hadn't been her. Then when I told him I knew it wasn't her, he just shrugged and said one girl was as good as another. And that he was the only one who knew where Jamie was."

"That's why you needed to keep him alive."

"Yes."

" 'I'm sorry' sounds trite in the aftermath, but I am."

"You're right, it does sound trite. I know you didn't intend to mess things up, but my God, Lucas, how could you have done this? Not only have you lied to me almost from the moment we met, you could have been killed."

"First of all, I haven't lied to you about anything. Yes, I kept some things from you, but I damn well didn't lie. And I might have been killed, but getting him out of your life was worth the risk."

"That wasn't your choice. I fight my own battles, my own demons. I've never asked for your help."

"Friends don't have to—"

Her eyes blazed with hurt fury. "No. Stop right there. Don't you dare use the friendship card with me. You want to talk about friendship? Let's talk about sharing everything, including the fact that you're obviously a trained assassin."

Damned if he'd apologize for that. "I swore an oath, McKenna. One I take very seriously. When I left the agency, I was never to speak of it."

"I understand all about promises, Lucas, but I also understand something you don't seem to get." She leaned forward, and the hurt he had glimpsed earlier was so much worse than what he'd thought. "I told you every single fucking thing about my entire life. Everything, Lucas. Even the parts that totally humiliated me, that tore me to pieces. I opened my soul and let you in."

"McKenna, I—" Hell, what could he say? From her perspective, she was right. From his, the two weren't even close. "The things you shared with me . . . your pain, humiliation. Those were personal, heart-wrenching things. My experience with the agency was a job. An important one, but still just a job."

"A job that defined you. Just as my experience defined me."

"Hell, no. Not in the same way."

She blew out a sigh. "You took your former experience and used it to . . ." She rubbed the side of her head as if she had a headache. "Dammit, Lucas, I feel so damned betrayed, I can't even speak my mind." Dropping the toast she'd barely nibbled at, she stood.

"Where are you going?"

"I haven't slept in almost a week." She turned and shuffled toward the bed. Seconds later she was curling up on her side, facing away from him.

Pain wrenched deep within Lucas. The expression on McKenna's face, the way she held herself . . . they tore at him. For the first time since he'd met her, she looked dispirited and defeated.

There were a lot of things Lucas wanted to say to her, wanted to do. He wanted to hold her and promise her everything would be perfect. That he would fix everything for her. He wanted to haul her into his arms and tell her she damn well should understand his perspective. He'd been trying to take care of a major problem for her. And he had solved one problem, but in the process he had screwed up a job, and another life was still on the line.

He closed his eyes. Hell, what could he say? He had fucked up, big-time. And now just what the hell was he going to do about it?

twenty-four

Warm arms surrounded her; McKenna snuggled back against the hard body behind her. She was only half awake, but her subconscious mind was aware enough to whisper a reminder of Lucas's betrayal and lies. Her heart, though bruised and aching, told her to cherish being in the arms of the man she loved, no matter the cost. McKenna shut down her mind and listened to her heart.

Turning in his arms, she breathed, "Make love to me."

The darkness cast his face in shadows, but she was able to see the tender desire in his expression. His lips, hot and wild, pressed against hers, seeking entrance. McKenna opened hers and moaned as his delicious, familiar taste filled her mouth. Only this one man had ever created this powerful, life-affirming feeling inside her. As if he was the key that unlocked every secret door she had. Every need met. Every longing answered.

He drew back, his breath feathering her face. "I know we still have things to sort out, but this here, between us . . . it's real, McKenna. *We* are real."

Unable to give him an answer, she pulled at his shoulders to bring him down for another kiss. She didn't want to talk right now. If she did, she'd start thinking. And that would bring back the hurt.

Resisting her attempts to pull him down to her, he said, "Lie back, love. Let me show you how real it is."

McKenna dropped her arms to her sides, but Lucas had other ideas. Pulling each arm from the sleeve of her robe, she thought he would let them go. Instead he held both her wrists in one hand and whispered, "Do you trust me, McKenna?"

Before today, the answer would have been a fervent yes, without even thinking. Now she hesitated. And though she couldn't see his face, she could feel the hurt she'd just dealt him. Yet she had to answer yes. Because despite everything, she did trust him. Unwisely, perhaps. But there it was.

"Thank you, sweetheart," he said softly. Then, still holding her wrists, he told her, "Wrap your hands around this post. Don't let go. Okay?"

Her heart thudding in excited anticipation, she wrapped her hands around the post at the top of the bed.

"Close your eyes."

Again McKenna complied. And then she felt soft kisses, starting at her forehead and moving over her closed eyes, her cheek, her chin. Moving as lightly as a feather, he once again used his lips as a paintbrush. Going lower, he stopped and softly kissed the savage bruises on her neck caused by Damon's hands. Then he continued on. Heat bloomed, almost as if the sun blazed down on her; her body turned into a burning mass of aroused nerves. When he stopped at her breasts and instead of kisses laved first one nipple and then the other with his hot, moist tongue, McKenna gasped and squirmed.

Leaving her breasts still aching, still wanting, he traveled down her torso. Stopping at her navel, he circled it again with his tongue, then pressed his tongue deep. An incredible erotic charge flared through her. Groaning with need, she opened her legs in invitation. The memory of how his tongue felt inside her created a hot, throbbing desire that only Lucas could ease.

His head moved lower, but much too slowly for her; the anticipation was almost more than she could bear. "Lucas, please . . ."

"I'll give you everything you ask, McKenna, I promise. But for now, let me savor you."

Instead of putting his tongue in the hot center of her need, he softly kissed the inside of her thighs and continued down her legs. At her feet, she was surprised at the rasp of his tongue on the sole of her foot and the answering erotic throb deep within her. A long, low groan emerged before she could stop it. When he picked up her other foot and did the same, McKenna was shocked to realize she was close to climax. No one had ever taken such care, concentrated so intently on every part of her body, and never would she have guessed that her feet had some sort of erogenous sensor that was directly connected to her womb. Her body arched as he laved the bottom of her foot, then took her toe inside his mouth and sucked. Lightning flashed behind her closed lids and her body undulated, searching for release that was barely a second away from exploding within her.

She was at the point of screaming when he pulled her toe from his mouth and started up her other side, once more whispering those soft, mind-stealing kisses. When he'd reached the top of her thighs again, McKenna opened her legs wide. Embarrassment disappeared; inhibitions vanished. She had to have his tongue inside her now.

"What, sweetheart? Tell me what you want."

Brutally blunt in every area of her life except intimacy up till now, McKenna didn't hesitate to voice her needs. "I need your tongue inside me, licking at me, eating me."

"With pleasure." And he followed those words with action. Her eyes still closed, she felt him move between her thighs. Cupping his hands under her knees, he lifted

her legs, pushed them up and out till she was totally exposed, and then licked her once. McKenna exploded.
Her soft cry of fulfillment didn't stop him; he thrust
into her over and over.

Unwilling to let go of the post, McKenna arched her
body again and again, meeting each tongue stroke. Tension filled her body, lights flared; she arched up once
more and came again.

She returned to earth to hear her own soft sobs of fulfillment. Lucas was once more bestowing hot kisses all
over her body.

Her hands aching to touch and hold him, she whispered, "I want to touch you, Lucas."

"In a moment, love. I promise." And then his hot
mouth was on her breast again, licking her nipple, then
her entire breast. He pulled away and blew softly on her
wet skin. McKenna cried out at the sensation. And then
he gave the other breast the same treatment.

Frustration, desire, and an urgent, aching need built
toward a crescendo inside her. Squirming, she gasped as
his marauding tongue continued a path down her body,
leading her toward a total destruction of her senses. She
was to the point of either screaming at him to take her
or throwing him to the mattress, jumping on top of him,
and burying him inside her.

"Roll over for me, McKenna."

She shook her head in desperation. "I need you inside
me."

"And you'll have me soon. Please, sweetheart?"

Everything stilled within her. A sob caught in her
throat as a stunning revelation swept through her. Lucas
had never asked her for anything. The impact of that
one word stole her breath. How stupid she had been;
how unbelievably selfish she was. He had never asked
her for anything. He had done nothing but give. And she
had taken and taken. The secretive things he'd done

were wrong and stupid, but he had done them because he cared. And what had she done for him? What had she given him?

"Sweetheart, what's wrong?"

Going against his wishes, she let go of the post and threw herself into his arms. He closed them around her and just held her to him. His hard, naked, beautiful body felt so wonderful against her . . . so right.

Between gasping sobs, she said, "I can't . . . believe how . . . stupid I've been."

"What? How have you been stupid?"

"All the things you did . . . you did them for me. I've never had anyone care for me like that."

"But I screwed everything up."

Laughter blended with her tears. "Yes, you did, but you had the best intentions. Thank you, Lucas." She pressed kisses all over his face, his chest.

"Aw, sweetheart, thank you."

She pulled him down onto the bed with her, and with all the love and gratitude in her heart, McKenna opened her legs, and let passion take over.

Lucas gritted his teeth as he entered the hot, moist channel waiting for him. He'd been close to explosion for half an hour, and he didn't know if he could hold on another second. But he wanted to make this as wonderful and memorable for McKenna as possible.

He had never been so focused on a woman's pleasure, on her arousal, on her need. Sex had always been an enjoyable pastime. With McKenna, it reached heights he hadn't known existed. Her sighs, gasps, and moans were music to his ears and fired his blood more than any erotic play he'd ever been involved in before. Pleasing McKenna meant more to him than pleasing himself ever could.

Thrusting deep inside her, he watched the play of

emotions run across her face. She had never looked more beautiful to him than she did at this moment. Leaning down, he covered her mouth with his, plunging his tongue, mating with her mouth as he moved deep within her. Her inner muscles worked at him, pulling, clenching, sucking him even deeper. He didn't want to let go but knew he had no choice. Electricity zipped up his spine, and with a long, low growl he buried himself to the hilt and exploded. McKenna climaxed seconds later, her inner muscles pulling at him again; Lucas ground his teeth as the sensation of a heated vise gripped him hard.

Breath rasping from his labored lungs, he rolled over, taking her with him. She settled into his arms, her head on his chest. For several second he just held her, absorbing her warmth, the wonderful strength of McKenna.

"Lucas?" she said softly.

"Yes?"

"Why did you do it?"

She didn't need to explain what *it* was. Denying the truth never entered his head. "Because I couldn't stand the thought of you having to face him again one day."

"But you could have stopped the photographs from being published."

"Yes, I could have."

"You didn't even try?"

Lucas released a ragged breath. "I had them delayed. Hoped that my investigators could find Hughes and I wouldn't have to use them. They came up dry. The photos seemed the best way to lure him."

"Why?"

"The bastard needed to pay for what he did to you."

"But why was it so important to you?"

"Because, dammit . . . I love you, McKenna. Haven't you figured that out yet?"

Releasing a soft sound between a sob and sigh, she

propped her arm on his chest. Leaning over him, she whispered, "Thank you, Lucas. I love you, too."

Cupping her face in his hands, he drew her down and took her mouth, thrusting his tongue in over and over again. Then, pulling back slightly, he whispered, "Forever?"

"Yes. Forever." Her smile was sweet and sexy at the same time as she settled back against his chest.

Lucas stared up at the dark ceiling of the hotel room. A desperation he'd never felt before washed over him. McKenna was special. From the beginning that had been apparent. What he hadn't expected was this incredible vulnerability he felt with her. Control had been a part of his life for so long; McKenna challenged that control. She had shared everything with him; he had known that and had accepted it, admiring and appreciating her honesty. What he hadn't expected or acknowledged was her need to know everything about him.

Yet if the positions were reversed, would he not expect to have his questions answered? McKenna was right—she had bared her soul. Could he do anything less?

He loved her; she loved him. Loving meant sharing the deepest part of yourself with someone else. Lucas had never understood that so completely until now.

He drew a breath. He was about to speak of something he'd sworn an oath never to divulge. His loyalty to the agency was strong, his love for his country undying and deep. His love and loyalty for McKenna went realms beyond.

"When I was a young man, no more than twelve, my father and I would shoot skeet. It was a mindless, fun pastime. I was excellent and even won a few awards as a teen. Yet I never expected it to be more than an enjoyable activity. While I was at university, I belonged to a shooting club. After practice one day, I was approached by two men who said they admired my skills. We went

for coffee. Had a long conversation that lasted into
the night."

She rose up on her elbow. "These men were with the
British government?"

"One of them was; the other was American."

"That's unusual, isn't it?"

He chuckled. "IDC is an unusual organization."

"IDC?"

"International Deep Cover. It's composed of men and
women from fifteen different countries."

"What is its purpose?"

"Safety, security, freedom."

"Can you tell me what you did?"

"I can tell you a few things. Much of it was research,
going deep cover occasionally."

"And I guess your shooting skills came in handy?"

He blew out a sigh. "Yes, my shooting skills were in
high demand. When the agency had a need, I was usually the one they called. Brutal dictators who thought
nothing of massacring their own people, a suicide bomber
standing in the midst of a busy marketplace filled
with women and children, tribal leaders who perverted
their beliefs to justify some sort of sadistic ethnic cleans-
ing . . . those and several more." He shrugged. "I was
damn good at it."

"And this is a government agency?"

"One agency, approved by all governments that par-
ticipate."

"So I guess the secrecy comes from the need to be deep
cover?"

"There's that, but there's also a philosophy held by
many that governments should only see to the welfare of
their own. IDC bucks that thinking by being able to
work without those restrictions."

"How long were you with them?"

"It was supposed to be a ten-year commitment. At

least, that's what I had planned. It didn't work out that way."

"Your father died?"

"Yes."

"Do you miss it?"

"Every damn day."

She rose on her elbow again. "What do you miss?"

"The knowledge that I'm making a difference, saving lives." He shrugged. "The usual things."

"And the adrenaline rush of danger?"

He smiled. Should've known McKenna would understand that mentality. "That too."

Sighing softly, she settled back into his arms. "I wish you had told me."

"Looking back, I wish I had, too."

"I'm still furious about the photographs."

"I know." He closed his eyes. Everything needed to be revealed. Even if it made her furious again, he had to tell her. "Remember the first time you came to my home?"

"Yes."

"I knew that you were hiding from someone . . . that you were frightened." He swallowed hard. Looking back on it now, it seemed so damned devious and seedy. He'd never meant it to be. "I took your fingerprints from the dishes and ran a trace on them."

She stiffened in his arms. He waited, knowing she was remembering all the things that happened after that.

"So when I told you about my family . . . you already knew."

"I knew some. Not all. And I didn't know that Hughes was still alive. The reports said he died in a fire caused by a riot at the prison."

A breath shuddered through her. "It hurts, Lucas."

"I know, love. I'm sorry. I wish I had told you before. I just wanted to get him out of your life."

"Thank you for telling me now."

His arms tightened around her. Silence followed. Wondering if she was gearing up the anger, he shifted so he could look down at her. Her eyes were closed and the shallow, even breaths told him she was deeply asleep.

Lucas dropped his head back onto the pillow and gathered her close again. Had it hit her yet that she no longer had to be afraid, no longer had to hide? For years she had been on the run. Had shut herself off from a real life and any kind of relationship. Now that she didn't have to run, would she be content to stay still?

She woke the next morning to an empty bed. Rolling over, McKenna squinted at the clock, surprised to see it was almost seven. Noah and his team would be here at ten. She needed to get some clothes before then. Going to an LCR meeting in a robe didn't exactly inspire confidence. And nothing in the world could make her retrieve that hideous wedding gown from the trash.

Wondering where Lucas had gone, she sat up and looked around. There was no sign of him. If she didn't have the delicious aches on her body and the heady fragrance of uninhibited sex on the sheets and her skin, she could almost believe he hadn't been here.

"Lucas?"

Since she had been furious with him when they'd checked in, she'd demanded a suite with two bedrooms. He'd apparently gone back to his room to shower. Grabbing the robe from the floor, McKenna shoved her arms into it and opened the door to the other room. Empty. A sinking feeling of dread filled her as she went to the bathroom across the room. He had been here not too long ago. Steam still lingered and the shower door was wet.

Turning back to her room, she worked hard not to be hurt. He had never made her any promises. He had achieved his goal of taking Damon out. Maybe he felt that since he'd done that there was no reason to linger.

No. He'd said he loved her. And you don't just make love to someone like he did to her and then walk away. You just don't. There had to be another explanation. Trust came hard for her; she'd learned some painful lessons. But she trusted Lucas. After the things he'd revealed last night, her trust had been shaken, but it was still there. Lucas would not abandon her.

She headed to the bathroom. After showering, she would work on getting some clothes delivered. She needed to be dressed for her meeting with Noah. She had a rescue mission to complete. No matter what she and Lucas faced, her job was priority one right now.

Still, the doubts lingered. Cursing her lack of faith, she turned the water to full blast and stood under the hot, hard spray. He wouldn't just leave . . . *he wouldn't.*

Lucas eased the door open, hoping he'd made it back before McKenna woke. The sound of the shower told him he hadn't. Hell, he should've gone out earlier, but with McKenna finally in his arms again, he had slept so damn deeply, he'd had a hard time waking.

Placing the packages on the table, he picked up the phone. Neither of them had eaten last night. If they were going to meet with Noah McCall about rescuing this young woman Hughes had kidnapped, they'd need all the strength they could get.

After ordering a meal big enough for a large family, Lucas turned around. McKenna stood at the door of the bathroom, once more wrapped in the hotel robe. The expression on her face caught his attention. She looked stunned. Even though she tried to cover it up with a small smile, he'd seen the vulnerability. Hell, had she thought he had just up and left her?

His heart ached because he knew that was exactly

what she'd thought. McKenna had been hurt and betrayed by so many. She was probably much more surprised when people actually treated her with kindness and kept their promises.

Figuring she was too proud to admit her fears, Lucas chose to pretend he hadn't read her thoughts. At some point she would learn that not all people were snakes. He squashed the voice that reminded him she already felt he had betrayed her. Just because he'd opened up last night didn't mean all was well between them.

"I ordered breakfast. You've got to be starving." He picked up the bags holding the clothes he'd purchased. "The shops downstairs were good enough to open early. I think these will fit."

When she didn't move, he took her hands and dropped the clothing bags into them. Seeing that she had a hold on them, he stepped back and said, "I watched the local news while I was waiting for the salesclerk to ring these up. Looks like the authorities got to Hughes's estate about half an hour after we left. The minister is telling quite the tale of how a beautiful blonde and her handsome companion kicked some bad guy's ass."

He meant for her to at least smile. Instead, she said softly, "I thought you had left."

"I know you did. I'm not like that, McKenna. I don't leave."

She shuddered out a breath and then gave him what had to be the most beautiful smile he'd ever seen. "I'll get dressed."

Turning away from him, she dropped her robe to the floor. Lucas groaned and turned away himself. They didn't have time for what his body wanted. It was going to be hard enough watching her eat without jumping her bones. Damned if he needed the extra enticement.

Thankfully, the food arrived before he could change his mind. As he set things out for them, she came back into the room, wearing the clothes he'd purchased. The slacks, blouse, and thin sweater appeared to be a perfect fit.

She gave him a small smile. "You're very good at picking out women's clothes."

"Part of my Englishman's training."

"Really?"

He chuckled. "No. I'm embarrassed to tell you, but my third—no, she was my fourth—stepmother used to take me shopping with her. I was her clothes caddy."

"That must have been boring."

Grinning, he shook his head. "Actually, no. I sat and watched beautiful women walk out of dressing rooms and preen in front of mirrors. Several of them would ask my advice. I even got a couple of dates."

Her eyes twinkling with amusement, she sat down at the table. He watched as she loaded her plate and was relieved to see that her appetite had apparently returned.

"This looks delicious." She took a large bite of her omelet and sighed. "Heaven."

Lucas swallowed a groan and filled his own plate. Dammed difficult eating with a hard-on, but he had no choice. McKenna plus food equaled extreme sexual arousal. They ate in relative silence for several minutes. Since they were both ravenous, the meal disappeared quickly, for which Lucas was thankful. Any longer and he'd be throwing McKenna back on the bed.

"Noah should be here soon." She eyed him speculatively. "Are you interested in helping out?"

"If that's not against protocol, I'd like to."

"I assisted in two rescues before LCR even knew who I was." With a small, impish smile, she added, "I'll get you in."

Unable to hold back any longer, Lucas stood and pulled her into his arms. Covering her mouth with his, he relished the taste of McKenna's lips, flavored with strawberry jam and coffee. Weaving her fingers in his hair, McKenna moved in closer, rubbing her soft mound against his erection. He grabbed her hips and fitted her at the exact spot they both needed him to be. They moaned in unison.

A knock on the door had both of them moaning again, but for a new reason. Two seconds more and he would have been inside her.

Breathing out a sigh, he whispered against her mouth, "Later."

"Definitely," she softly promised.

twenty-five

Noah's first glimpse of a seemingly healthy McKenna gave him enormous relief. Every LCR operative who knew McKenna and had heard about her abduction had been almost as concerned as he had been. Though he never rejoiced at someone's death, there were few who deserved death more than Damon Hughes. And if the intel he'd received was correct, the horror of Hughes's existence continued. Jamie Kendrick was in the midst of hell.

Though the emotional undercurrents coming from McKenna and Lucas were thick and volatile, they did their best to hide it. Not that it did much good. Even the most clueless person could see there was something going on between the two. He hoped that once Jamie was safe and secure, McKenna got a chance at the happiness she deserved. And from the glances Lucas Kane was throwing her way, the man intended to be personally involved in seeing that take place.

Noah wished them both well, but first there had to be a rescue.

After introducing Dylan and Aidan to Kane, Noah sat on the sofa. "Dylan and Aidan were on assignment yesterday. While I waited for them to return, I was able to gather even more intel on Hughes." He leaned forward as he revealed his findings. "The bastard was into almost every vile and illegal activity known to man. Though human trafficking wasn't one of them, he was known to be generous with his male employees or business acquaintances if they pleased him. Or, if he tired of a woman, he might sell her at what he considered a bargain price."

McKenna nodded. "I was only able to open one file on his laptop when I was snooping. I found a list of women's names and dollar amounts. I'm assuming he sold them."

Didn't surprise Noah one bit. "When this is over and Jamie's safe, I'll make sure the authorities go through his records. There may be many more women like Jamie."

"How did you get your information on Hughes?" Lucas asked. "My investigators came up with a multitude of his illegal activities but discovered almost nothing about the man's personal dealings."

Instead of answering, Noah looked at McKenna. "At the failed exchange, the young girl posing as Jamie . . . did you get a look at her?"

McKenna shook her head. "I saw the black hair under her wig and knew it wasn't Jamie. But everything happened so fast, I barely got a glimpse of her face."

Having seen more than his share of brutality and the aftermath, Noah nevertheless felt his gut clench as he said, "Her name is Lilly. She'd been Hughes's prisoner for almost two years. Having been with him that long, she picked up an enormous amount of information about the man." He shrugged. "Either Hughes wasn't aware she was around most of the time or didn't think she was a threat to him, because the information she gave us was incredibly detailed."

"Where is Lilly now?" McKenna asked.

"Still in the hospital." Noah ground his teeth as he explained, "When Jamie arrived at Hughes's estate, Damon believed it was you. As a reward to the man who kidnapped Jamie, he gave him Lilly for the night."

McKenna's expression was one of sad acceptance. "How is she?"

"Let's just say it was sheer desperation and guts that she was able to walk those few steps off the boat. As soon as the helicopter picked you up, she collapsed on the pier."

"Will she recover?" Lucas asked.

Noah lifted a shoulder. "Physically, yes. She should be released from the hospital within the next few days."

There was no need to explain anything more. Physical injuries could be determined and dealt with so much more easily than emotional ones. After the hell she'd been through, God only knew if that kind of mental torment could be overcome. Noah had seen it happen in others, but each person had their own strengths and breaking points.

"So what was she able to tell you?" McKenna asked.

"Damon had no real friends but did have several close business associates. One in particular seemed to get the most favors from him. Man named Stanford Reddington. Lilly told us she'd seen Reddington at Hughes's estate half a dozen times. At least three times that she knew of, Damon gave him a woman as a parting gift."

"Any idea if Reddington kept them for himself or sold them?" McKenna asked.

"Lilly isn't sure. The man's in his late forties and has one son who travels with him. Lilly wasn't able to shed any light on him other than that." Noah pulled a folder from his briefcase. "A couple of days ago, I sent out notices to several contacts to see if I could pick up anything on Reddington. Yesterday I received some interesting faxes from a source in Madrid. Apparently Reddington is a well-known and well-respected businessman there. Few know about his association with Hughes."

"How does your source know about the association?" Kane asked.

Noah shrugged. Usually averse to giving details on how and where he received his intel, this time he couldn't have explained it even if he had wanted to. Raphael hadn't told him how he had obtained the information. However, he trusted the young man and believed its accuracy.

McKenna held her hand out for the faxes. Skimming them, she said, "So she could be with Reddington in Madrid?"

"Possibly. My contact has a description of Jamie. He may be able to verify whether she's with him or not."

Kane's brow rose. "He's that close?"

Noah nodded grimly. Raphael had a strong desire to work for LCR. Partly from gratitude—LCR had rescued him a couple of years ago. The other part was the sincere desire to do something good with his life.

Noah had encouraged the young man to finish college first and promised him they'd discuss it further once he graduated. Raphael had agreed, but when Noah sent out a notice about Reddington, he'd immediately heard from Raphael with this valuable information.

Noah was a man known to use almost any means necessary to get the job done; putting Raphael at risk wasn't one of them. The kid had been through too much in his young life already. Any further assistance other than what Raphael had already provided wasn't something Noah wanted. The kid had a stubborn streak a mile long, though. Ignoring Noah's demand to step back, he had stuck his nose in even further. Noah only hoped he didn't stick it so far that they ended up needing to rescue more than just Jamie Kendrick.

"He's supposed to call within the hour. He mentioned that Reddington has a vacation place in Bustarviejo, just outside of Madrid."

McKenna looked up from the information she'd been studying. "Your source is going there?"

Who the hell knew? Noah shrugged, unable to give a definitive answer.

As Lucas listened to Noah McCall, he kept a close eye on McKenna, trying to tell himself his worry for her would do no good. The three men from LCR looked like giants next to her, yet he knew from experience she could handle herself. That didn't mean he didn't want to pick her up and carry her away from all of this. She had been through so much. Problem was, it was a useless want. She felt responsible for Jamie Kendrick's abduction and would do what she could to save her. Lucas bore a strong obligation himself. If he hadn't killed Damon, what information could they have gleaned?

Turning to McCall, he said, "I'd like to help with the rescue."

Black eyes narrowing in speculation, the head of LCR settled more comfortably against the cushions of the couch. "Help how?"

"I have some training," Lucas admitted.

"What kind of training?"

Lucas glanced at Aidan Thorne and Dylan Savage, then back to Noah. "Specialized training."

McCall shot a questioning look toward McKenna.

"He's good. He's got the moves of a trained operative and the shooting skills of a sniper."

Noah McCall continued his speculative observation. "You care to share where your training came from?"

Returning the look, Lucas answered coolly, "No." He wouldn't elaborate or offer excuses. His help would either be accepted or not.

Another long hard stare and then McCall nodded. "Fine. We could use you."

At the sound of a vibrating cellphone, everyone listened as they watched Noah answer with "What did you find out?"

Bustarviejo, Spain

Dressed in black, with a black skullcap to cover her hair, McKenna waited for further instructions from Noah. It was three-thirty in the morning. The mountain cabin, so well hidden it looked as though it was part of the forest that surrounded it, was dark and silent. They would go in under the cover of that dark silence. Soon they would get their go signal.

Noah's source had given this place as the most probable location for Jamie. McKenna still had no idea who the source was or how he knew so much. She only knew that Noah was sure enough of the intel's authenticity that he'd contacted the Spanish authorities. And whatever he had told them convinced them to join with LCR in the operation.

According to Noah, his source was inside that house, meaning there was more than one innocent. Instructions were that no one was to be hurt during the raid if it could be prevented. LCR would rescue Jamie and take her away. The authorities would handle Reddington.

The entry would be a soft one. As long as no one saw them, panicked, and started shooting, it should be fairly simple—a routine rescue. Noah, Dylan, Aidan, Lucas, and herself together should ensure enough force to subdue and defuse any danger to Jamie or anyone else.

Working with Lucas should have felt awkward, but it didn't. Not only had he proven himself more than capable, she felt a comfort with him she had never felt with anyone else. It was a degree of trust that pierced bone and went straight to her heart. She trusted Lucas on every level.

She had forgiven him for his deceit. How could she not? Yes, it had been a boneheaded thing to do, but he'd done it out of his love and concern for her. Even though it had screwed up her mission to get information on

Jamie, she couldn't be angry with him. Having him sacrifice himself, put himself in danger for her, went beyond what anyone had ever done for her. How could she resent anyone caring for her that much?

His confession that he knew about her past before she told him had stunned her, and she couldn't deny the hurt. There was manipulation there, and though he'd done it to help her, what he had done stung. But she refused to hold that against him. Lucas wasn't perfect; he was human. He'd done what he thought he needed to do because he loved her. A thrill of electrical excitement zoomed through her. *Lucas loved her!*

Having him tell her about his past government experience meant more to her than she could express. When he began to explain, she had realized how much he trusted her. Except for his wonderful lovemaking, that had been one of the most precious times of her life. Lying in his arms, having him share his past with her, meant so much.

"McKenna?"

She turned to see Lucas standing behind her. Switching off her mic, she whispered, "You need to get into place. We're going in a few minutes."

"I will. Just wanted to check and see if you were okay."

Lucas might not be official LCR personnel, but he had to know that breaking position to check on another operative wasn't exactly proper protocol. Maybe working with him wasn't that good an idea. His protective instincts might hinder his concentration.

"I'm fine. This should be a soft, easy rescue."

"Just be careful. Okay?"

Her heart melted. Even though she was used to LCR men being protective of her, they'd always treated her like their kid sister. The night was too dark to see

Lucas's expression, but there was nothing brotherly about the tone of his voice.

Her voice thick with emotion, she said softly, "We have a lot to talk about when this is over."

"That we do, sweetheart." In a voice filled with laughter, he added, "Talking and a whole lot of other things, too. Count on it."

Her heart triple-timed. "I am."

"Everyone in place and ready?" Noah's voice in her ear jerked her out of her dreams of the future.

"You need to go," she whispered to Lucas.

Pressing his fingers to her mouth briefly, he disappeared into the inky blackness as if he'd never been there.

"McKenna?" Noah said.

Switching her mic on again, she answered, "In place and ready." Dylan and Aidan answered and then she heard Lucas's crisp British voice say, "Ready, mate."

"Okay," Noah said. "We go on my say-so."

Adrenaline surging, McKenna mentally reviewed the plan. Two policemen would knock on the door and ask to speak with Reddington. While he was preoccupied with them, their source inside would open the kitchen door, which was in the back of the house. Noah and Dylan would enter, spread out, and search for Jamie. Aidan would stay outside, a lookout at the back.

McKenna and Lucas would be on either side of the house. If anyone tried to escape, they were to restrain them. As soon as Jamie was located and rescued, they would receive the news. With Jamie's safety secured, if no one was being restrained, all operatives were to retreat and meet at the end of the drive where their van was parked.

"Go," Noah said quietly.

Hidden behind a large leafy bush, she focused on the patio, her eyes zeroing in on the glassed double door. If any resident tried to escape, this would be a reasonable exit.

Noah and Dylan would be stealthily quiet as they roamed the rooms in their search for Jamie. She didn't expect to hear voices until they spotted her. Minutes that felt more like hours passed. The silhouette of a man appeared at the glass doors. McKenna held her breath. Someone trying to escape or just looking outside? Crouched low, she moved closer.

Standing on the north side of the house, Lucas tried to forget that the person on the other side was McKenna. He knew she was well trained. That knowledge didn't negate his worry. From the moment he'd met her, he had wanted to protect her. Now here he was, working an op with her.

Lucas tensed as a shadow appeared on the second-floor balcony. Light from the window revealed a man running to the railing. He hauled himself over, hung suspended for a few seconds, and then dropped to the ground below. Lucas took off after him.

In the midst of his run, Noah announced, "Dylan has secured Jamie. We're coming out the back. Everyone check in."

"All clear here," Aidan said.

"I have a target. Going after him," Lucas said.

"I have one here, too." McKenna sounded winded, as though she were running. "I'm on it."

"Aidan, assist Kane," Noah said.

Like hell! "I don't need help. Assist McKenna. I'm fine."

Thrashing through the underbrush, the barefooted, almost nude man in front of him sounded like a bull lumbering through the forest. Lucas tackled him and took him to the ground. Idiot only had on a pair of underwear.

Speaking in thickly accented English, the man bucked beneath him and muttered, "I did nothing wrong."

Wanting to get to McKenna as soon as possible, Lucas pressed his knee into the small of the man's back. Silently and with quick efficiency, he pulled the guy's arms behind him, locking them together with plastic ties. Then he did the same with the man's feet. Spotting a skinny tree a few feet away, Lucas dragged him toward it. Ignoring a new stream of vile curses, he took handcuffs from his utility belt, wrapped one on the man's wrist, and attached the other to the tree.

Leaving him to curse and proclaim his innocence to himself, Lucas took off toward McKenna's location. On the way, he reported, "Got one man tied up on the north side. I'm headed over to—" The blast of a gun on the other side of the house had him sprinting.

Lucas halted when he saw McKenna squatting behind a bush. Relief almost put him on his knees. Stooping low, he ran toward her.

"Who the hell is shooting?" Noah asked.

"Guy came out the south patio," McKenna said.

She turned when she heard Lucas behind her and whispered, "Jerk shot at me before I could even get close to him."

"Where is he?"

"He jumped off the balcony . . . ran behind that brick wall at the back."

Lucas scanned the darkness, looking for a way to sneak up on him. "I'll go a few yards back into the woods and then come at him from behind."

She gave him a look like she would argue but finally said, "Okay, I'll yell out a few insults and keep him focused on me."

"Don't keep him too focused on you, okay?"

She smiled. "Gotcha."

Lucas took off, dropping behind trees and bushes as

he made his way around the house. Out of the corner of his eye, he saw a policeman running toward McKenna. Another shot was fired; the policeman went down. His heart dropped as he watched McKenna run toward the injured man.

Needing to get the shooter's attention off McKenna, Lucas shouted: "Hey, asshole, put the gun down!" It worked—the man fired toward him. *Ping!* Wood flew from the tree Lucas stood behind. Damn, the man wasn't a half bad shot.

"Lucas, are you okay?" McKenna asked.

"Fine. Stay out of sight."

"Noah," McKenna said softly, "we have an officer down; he needs medical attention."

Noah cursed softly and then said, "Medics should be here soon. Stay with him."

"His partner's here with him. I'm going to assist Lucas."

Lucas jerked around to see that another policeman was crouched beside his fellow officer and McKenna was headed his way.

"Stay put, McKenna," Lucas whispered harshly. "Don't give the bastard another target."

Her answer was a derisive snort.

Knowing it would do no good to tell her again, he watched as she ran toward him. The clouds that had been obscuring the moon shifted, allowing him to see her better. Within feet of reaching him, he saw her expression change from determination to fear. Her eyes wide, she shouted, "Lucas, watch out!"

Lucas turned. He'd been so focused on McKenna, he hadn't seen the man step out from behind his hiding place. He had a clear shot at Lucas and was poised to fire. Lucas turned back to McKenna, knowing what she was about to do and unable to prevent it. Having only one choice, Lucas flew toward her at the very instant she leaped on him. He caught her in his arms the instant a blast of a gun rang through the air.

Arms wrapped around each other, they fell to the ground.

Lucas heard another blast farther away and a loud grunt. Apparently someone had finally taken the shooter out. Rolling off McKenna, he glared down at her, ready to deliver a stern lecture about staying put when she was told to stay put. Lying facedown on the ground, she wasn't moving.

"McKenna?" he whispered hoarsely.

Heart thudding with dread, Lucas turned her gently onto her back. Her eyes were closed, her expression one of peace, as though she were sleeping. He felt for a pulse. There . . . but dammit, not nearly as strong as it should have been.

In the darkness, her black clothing revealed nothing. Forcing the fear away, Lucas quickly ran his hands down her body, searching. Fingers touched a warm, wet spot on her right side. Breath halted in his lungs as his worst nightmare was realized. McKenna had been shot.

twenty-six

Lucas wasn't much of a praying man. He figured he'd been blessed more than most people; asking God for more seemed damned presumptuous. Now, as he stood over the bed of the woman who was his life, he uttered every reverent plea he'd ever heard, hoping this one prayer would be answered. Emotions exploded like bombs and his entire being felt as if it could disintegrate at any moment.

She had saved his life. Bloody hell, she had saved his life and had almost lost her own.

Though the bullet in her side had gone straight through, missing vital organs, and the surgeon insisted her injury wasn't life-threatening, she still hadn't opened her eyes. The doctors believed the cause of her continued unconsciousness was blood loss blended with extreme exhaustion. All vital signs were good. But when the hell would she wake up?

Not one to doubt his decisions once they were made, Lucas now questioned his every move from the moment she'd rescued him in Brazil. He shouldn't have pursued her. If he hadn't been so adamant that they meet, he wouldn't have been on this op where she thought she had to save his life.

And the entire setup with Damon. Hell, he'd screwed that up, too. Used the photos to lure Hughes when he could have easily had them destroyed. Lucas had always known he had a touch more arrogance than most people, but it had always gotten him what he wanted. This time his arrogance could have cost McKenna her life.

"How is she?"

Lucas looked over his shoulder at Dylan. Though he'd only known the man a few hours, Lucas got the idea that not much fazed him. Now, however, his eyes were dark with concern.

"Doctors said she'd wake up when she was ready. I've had four specialists in here. All of them swear it's not a coma."

"Poor kid's got to be exhausted after what she's been through." He shot a commiserating glance at Lucas. "Waiting's the worst."

"You speak as a man who's done his share."

A slow shrug and the blankness of his expression increased. A man who didn't like to talk about himself. Something he could identify with.

"How's the young woman . . . Jamie?"

A small flicker of something showed in Dylan's expression before he quickly masked it and said, "Damaged but dealing. She's in a room down the hall. You'll want to meet her."

Lucas nodded absently. McKenna was his only priority right now. "She tell you what happened?"

Another slow shrug. "Some. Said Reddington was keeping her at the cabin for his son and the kid's weekend friends. Good thing about it—" He gave a snort of disgust. "If you can call it a good thing. Hughes had beaten her so badly, she was still recovering . . . so they'd only been entertaining themselves with her for a few days."

Lucas's stomach churned. Long ago, he had stopped asking himself what turned people into conscienceless savages. Evil could not be reasoned with or understood, only fought against. "Sounds like the Reddington family had a lot in common with Damon Hughes."

A quick nod. "She talked a little about her abduction. Hughes's men took her from the laundry room in her apartment complex, knocked her out. She was gagged the whole time, so she didn't get to ask them what they wanted. Apparently her ex-husband had made some threats against her, so she just assumed he was responsible."

"I hate to think what the bastard did when she told him he'd made a mistake," Lucas said.

"She didn't tell him. He found out for himself."

"Why didn't she?"

"He disabled her vocal cords; she couldn't speak for a couple of days. By the time she could speak, she was afraid to tell him, figuring he'd kill her. Said she hoped he'd let his guard down and she could escape. Only he found out before she got a chance."

Lucas didn't have to ask how he found out. If he saw Jamie's body at all, he would have seen she didn't have the scars or brand Hughes had put on McKenna's body.

"I'm surprised he didn't kill her."

His jaw working, Dylan said, "I'm not so sure a small part of her doesn't wish he had."

There was nothing he could say to that. Wishing for death rather than going through hell was understandable, considering what the young woman had experienced. McKenna had once felt that way, had taken sleeping pills to escape. How many more times had she wished for death because of Damon Hughes? When the bastard killed her parents? When she'd watched her sister die? Every time he raped or tortured her?

Lucas didn't want to think about that. McKenna was alive, strong, and resilient. A survivor. And now, soon, she could actually have a life.

"So, physically, Jamie's going to be all right?" Lucas asked.

"Yeah. Should be well enough to go home in a few days. She's going to need some counseling, though."

Lucas looked back at McKenna. How the hell did she deal with what was probably a monthly if not weekly job for her—saving victims from unspeakable horror? In his former job, he'd dealt almost solely with bad, sorry-assed vermin who enjoyed killing others. Rarely were there victims to save.

"Samara's flying in tomorrow. Noah thought it might help both McKenna and Jamie for her to be here."

Holding McKenna's hand, Lucas couldn't help but wonder if he should be here. She had called him arrogant and stupid. He'd defended his actions, but now they haunted him. He couldn't get it out of his head: she could have died because of him.

Dylan sighed. "I doubt it'll do any good to tell you this, but blaming yourself doesn't help."

"Does anything?"

"Yeah. Making sure it never happens again." He jerked his head toward McKenna. "That's why she does what she does—why we all joined LCR. We know what can happen; it's either happened to someone we cared about or to us. Preventing it from happening to others deadens the pain."

Dylan Savage didn't look like he'd be one to share this kind of confidence with anyone. Lucas appreciated the man's insight, allowing him to see LCR in a different light than before. He might have always admired their purpose and the work they did, but he couldn't say he'd ever given thought to their need to exist outside of the work they performed. Now he understood that not only did LCR save lives and rescue victims; the organization also helped those who worked for them. As it had McKenna. Saving others had given purpose to her life and had eased her guilt.

"I know you don't want to leave her, but I'll stay here while you go meet Jamie."

"Why?"

"You'll see."

"I—"

"Room 412. Three doors down, on the right. I'll call you immediately if McKenna wakes."

Thinking it odd that Dylan was so insistent, Lucas didn't argue. Besides, he did need to meet with Jamie Kendrick. If she left the hospital before McKenna woke, he wanted to be able to assure her he'd seen the young woman in person and that she was indeed alive and as well as could be expected.

Giving McKenna one last glance, Lucas turned and went through the door and down the hall to room 412. Rubbing his neck wearily, he prepared himself to meet with a ravaged young woman. Knocking softly, he was surprised when Noah opened the door.

"Is Jamie up to having a visitor?" Lucas asked.

Surprising him even more, Noah McCall gave a broad smile and said, "She's anxious to meet you. Come in."

An odd feeling of déjà vu washed over him. Lucas walked into the room, then jerked to a halt. Speechless for the first time in his life, he could only stare at the person sitting in a chair by the window.

Consciousness returned in increments. McKenna heard a soft sigh, then the crinkle of paper, as if someone had turned the page of a book. Something told her she needed to wake up. She blinked. When light pierced her eyes, she closed them quickly.

"Hey sleepyhead, are you finally awake?"

Samara? That was odd. What was she doing here? And where was *here*?

Willing her eyes to open, she blinked again. Finally, able to squint, she saw Samara sitting in a chair beside her bed. Her bed? What was she doing in a bed? She leaned forward to sit up and hissed as pain slashed at her side.

"Don't try to move," Samara said. "I'll raise the bed so you can sit up a bit."

The electronic hum was McKenna's first awareness that she was in a hospital bed. What had happened? And then in a flash, she remembered. "Lucas!"

"He's fine."

Her eyes searched around the room. Her heart thundering, she whispered, "You're sure? Where is he?"

"Absolutely. He just stepped out to visit with the doctor again. He's convinced they're not telling him the truth about your injury. He's already consulted with all the doctors here and three others outside, two in London and one in Boston. And now he's threatening to fly his personal doctor in." She grinned. "I imagine the entire hospital staff will throw a party when they find out you finally woke."

Bewildered, she shook her head. "But why?"

"You've been unconscious for over two days. Everyone's been concerned. Lucas . . . well, let's just say he's been on a different level altogether. You scared the hell out of the man."

"And you're sure he's okay? He wasn't hurt?"

"He's fine, I promise."

"Thank God." Her eyes widened again. "Jamie . . . how is she?"

Something flickered in Samara's expression, replacing her earlier humor.

McKenna's heart jumped. "What's wrong? Is she badly hurt?"

"No, she's got some bruises. I think most of the physical damage that Hughes inflicted has gone."

"There's something else, though. What?"

"Nothing. Other than you're going to want to meet her."

Yes, she knew she should. If nothing else, she needed to apologize.

Samara huffed a sigh. "Get that look of guilt off your face."

"How can I not feel responsible?"

"Because you've done nothing wrong. You did not create Damon Hughes. You're not responsible for what he did."

Leaning her head back on her pillow, McKenna closed her eyes briefly. "I'm just not sure what I'm going say to her. I'm sorry you had the misfortune to look like me?"

Samara smiled. "I think you'll find something. You two have a lot in common."

"I guess we do. How bad is she?"

"She's going to need counseling, but she's incredibly strong. She'll get through it. She said she survived other bad stuff . . . and she would survive this, too."

Sadness filled her. Apparently Jamie hadn't had an easy life, and thanks to Damon Hughes, it had only gotten worse. He had damaged so many people. But now, thanks to Lucas, he couldn't hurt anyone else.

"I can't believe it's finally over."

"You've got a lot of thinking to do. You're free for the first time in years." Samara stood. "I need to put Lucas out of his misery and let him know you're awake. Are you ready to see him?"

Resisting the urge to let Samara tell him to come in right away, she said instead, "Do you have a hairbrush I could use?" Then, grimacing at the foul taste in her mouth, she added, "And maybe a toothbrush, too?"

Laughing, Samara went to the small bathroom and returned with a cosmetic bag and a glass of water. "Go ahead and get presentable while I'm here. The moment I step outside and tell him you're awake, I won't be able to hold him back."

McKenna hurriedly unzipped the bag, making use of the toothbrush and toothpaste. That one thing made her feel a thousand percent better. She brushed her hair quickly. Knowing no amount of brushing would get rid of bedhead, she dared a glance in the handheld mirror and decided she didn't look as bad as she could have. Maybe two days of sleep had been good for her. Though her skin was still pale, the dark shadows beneath her eyes had disappeared. She shrugged and put the mirror aside. This was the best she could do until she could take a shower.

Lifting the covers, she grimaced. A catheter tube lay against her leg. After she saw Lucas, she'd get that taken out and then she'd take a long, hot shower.

Too impatient and anxious to even consider waiting any longer, she looked up at Samara. "Tell him."

Laughing softly, Samara went to the door.

Her heart pounding with excitement, McKenna kept her anxious eyes on the entrance. She didn't have to wait long. The door swung open, but it wasn't Lucas who came through the door. A gray-haired nurse entered, followed by a dark-haired, smallish man in a white coat and a bright smile.

The doctor said, "Finally, our star patient is awake."

"Star patient?"

"Since Mr. Kane has created such a stir, you've become quite the talk of the hospital."

Having hidden a good part of her life, she wasn't comfortable with the thought of being the topic of conversation. Frowning, she looked at the closed door behind him. "Where's Lucas?"

"He'll be here in just a few moments. I wanted to make sure you're as well as you claim."

Though she didn't want to wait to see Lucas,

McKenna was relieved to have the catheter removed. Then, as she suffered through having her vital signs checked, her impatience increased. The doctor looked at her wound while asking seemingly endless questions. Her eyes remained on the door. Was Lucas really waiting outside? Or was she just being told that? Had something happened to him and they weren't telling her? Was that why the doctor was asking all these questions? To see if she could handle the shock?

Throwing the covers back, McKenna swung her legs over the bed.

"Where do you think you're going?"

"I need to see Lucas."

"He'll be here in just a few—"

"Look, I'm fine, but if Lucas doesn't get in here right now, I'm going after him."

Huffing out an exasperated breath, the doctor backed away. "You and Mr. Kane have much in common. Get back in bed and I'll get him."

McKenna willed the door to open. Yes, she knew she was being irrational, but she couldn't help herself. Until she saw Lucas and knew that he was truly okay, she could not relax.

The door swung open and there he stood. It took every bit of her willpower not to jump out of bed. Knowing it would hurt like hell was the only thing that stopped her.

He looked exhausted. There were dark shadows under his bloodshot eyes and his golden hair looked as though he'd run his fingers through it a thousand times. To McKenna, he looked beautiful.

Sitting in a chair beside the bed, he took her hand in both of his and pressed a kiss to her palm. Oddly enough, he didn't speak. She didn't know what she expected him to say, but she hadn't expected him to just stare.

"Lucas?"

Finally he released an explosive sigh. "I've gone through this scenario in my head a million times. What I would say to you when you finally woke. Now that you have, I find myself speechless."

"Why?"

"Because I want to hold you and kiss you. At the same time, I want to shout at you and threaten severe punishment if you ever put your life in jeopardy like that again."

Not the least bit intimidated, she grinned. "What kind of severe punishment are we talking about?"

A small smile shifted the grim line at his mouth. "Limiting your dessert intake, or only allowing you one serving of your favorite meal."

"Wow, that's a pretty stiff penalty."

Pressing her hand to his mouth, he whispered against her skin, "Don't ever do that to me again."

She raised a brow. "And didn't you do the same thing?"

He snorted. "I thought I was protecting you and got you shot instead."

"You didn't get me shot. The idiot was intent on shooting someone. I just happened to be the unlucky recipient."

"How are you feeling?"

"Not bad, actually. A little stiff and sore, but I feel amazingly energized."

"I'm glad." He paused for a second, then said, "I asked the doctor to examine you before I saw you."

"Why?"

"There are some things we need to discuss. I wanted to make sure he felt you were healthy enough to hear them."

Her heart dropped. "What things?"

"There's something I need to tell you, sweetheart."

Dread returned. His face held a look she'd never seen before; one she couldn't read. "What's wrong?"

"Actually, I think things are finally turning out right for you."

"What do you mean?"

"There's something you need to know about Jamie Kendrick."

"Dammit, what?"

"When she was fifteen years old, she lost her immediate family. An older relative took her in and raised her. She changed her name when she moved away."

McKenna nodded. She wasn't sure where Lucas was going with this, but it must be damned important for him to worry about her reaction.

"Her name was changed to Jamie Kendrick." He paused for a second, then asked, "Don't you want to know what Jamie's real name is?"

Still having no clue what he was trying to tell her, she shook her head in confusion. "What do you mean?"

"Sweetheart, Jamie's real name is Amy Sloan. Your sister is still alive."

twenty-seven

If she were standing, McKenna knew she would have fallen to the floor. Her entire world had just tilted sideways; she struggled to absorb Lucas's words. "What?"

"Amy is alive."

She shook her head. "But that's not possible. She died. They reported it on the news. I went to her gravesite, put flowers on it. She's buried between my mom and dad."

"She was badly injured and in the hospital for a long time. For her protection, it was reported that she died. At that time, you and Damon were both still considered criminals. They didn't know how determined Damon was to kill everyone in your family. They wanted to make sure she stayed safe. After she was released from the hospital, your Aunt Mavis, your father's sister, took her back to Louisiana to live with her."

"But her name . . . ?"

"Your aunt changed her name, even went so far as to put up a fake headstone. It was supposedly all done in an effort to protect Amy."

McKenna couldn't stop shaking her head. That wasn't possible . . . it just wasn't possible. She still had a sister? Amy was alive? And no one had told her?

"But when I came back . . . why didn't anyone tell me? I saw my aunt at the jail . . . when I was returned back to Nebraska. Why didn't she tell me?"

The sadness in Lucas's eyes gave her the answer. No one told her because they considered her a bad seed.

Even though the charges had been dropped against her, so many people still believed she was guilty. Not deserving to know that her own sister was alive. She remembered the hatred burning in her aunt's eyes when McKenna had seen her. The one and only comment she'd given her niece had been pure condemnation. "I hope they give you the death penalty."

"Your aunt died a while back, but your sister has been looking for you for years. You had disappeared so completely, she couldn't find you, but she never stopped looking."

McKenna tried to get her head wrapped around what Lucas was telling her. "But Damon was charged with her murder, too . . . wasn't he?"

"No, I had my investigator go back and look at Damon's charges. He was prosecuted for your parents' death, but there was a glaring omission surrounding your sister."

"I never asked to see anything . . . just took everyone at their word."

"Your aunt apparently had money and influence, along with an iron will. Perhaps because Amy was a minor, they left all the information out to protect her. I don't know. Amy isn't sure, either."

"But how did Damon know . . . ?"

"He didn't. She looked so much like you that when his men saw her they assumed it was you. He never figured out she was Amy."

"My God." McKenna gazed around the hospital room. In the span of seconds, her entire life, her whole outlook, had changed. A million emotions flooded her at once. She didn't know what to feel first. Taking a breath, she pushed aside anger and hurt at her aunt's cruelty to focus on the most important thing of all. Her sister was alive!

"McKenna?"

Hearing the concern in his voice, she turned back to Lucas. "She must hate me."

His eyes blazed. "Hell no, she doesn't hate you. She's able to see things much more clearly than you. She knows exactly who's responsible. Damon Hughes was the monster."

McKenna closed her eyes against the threatening tears. She knew she needed to concentrate on the miracle of Amy being alive, not the evil deeds of a madman. Taking a deep breath, she said, "I want to see her."

"I'll go get her. She's just a few doors down." He turned to leave.

"Lucas?"

He glanced over his shoulder. "Yes?"

She swallowed hard and whispered, "You're sure she doesn't hate me?"

He came back to her. Instead of answering with words, he cupped her face in his hands and put his mouth on hers. The kiss started softly and tenderly but as each of them breathed into each other, renewing their bond, passion ignited. McKenna moaned under his mouth, Lucas licked at her lips. She opened her mouth and took him deep, savoring his taste, loving his passion.

Lucas pulled away, his breathing slightly elevated. "I promise, no one hates you, sweetheart, especially your sister. Now let me go and get her before I forget where we are and that you're still recovering."

"I love you, Lucas."

Pressing a soft kiss against her forehead, he whispered, "I'm going to hold you to that." He turned and walked out before she could ask what he meant.

McKenna took a breath, preparing herself for something she never thought she'd ever be able to have. Another chance with her sister. She actually still had family. A multitude of questions sprang to her mind, but one was at the very top and wouldn't go away. How could Amy not blame her for what Damon had done to her and their parents?

Several minutes later, the door opened and a young woman walked into the room. McKenna felt as though she was looking into a mirror from eight years before. No wonder her sister had been mistaken for her. Other than some slight differences in facial features, she was the spitting image of the young McKenna Sloan. How could she not have recognized her when she saw the missing person's report?

"Amy?" Her voice was so thick with emotion, she wasn't sure her sister heard her.

McKenna's worry that her sister blamed her was immediately answered when Amy ran across the room and threw herself into her arms. Holding her tight, McKenna barely felt the stitch in her side. Nothing could spoil the joy of being able to hold her little sister in her arms.

After several minutes of shared sobbing, Amy pulled away and whispered, "I'd given up on ever seeing you again."

"And I never thought I'd get the chance. I thought you were dead."

"I almost was. I was in and out of consciousness for several days. Then they put me in a drug-induced coma. Those first few weeks are a blur. I don't remember much of what happened."

Moving over a little so her sister could sit on the bed with her, her eyes roamed over Amy's face. She was just so lovely.

McKenna cleared her throat. Things needed to be said before they went any further. "I'm so sorry for everything that's happened."

Amy snorted. "Lucas told me you'd apologize and

that's ridiculous. The dead bastard Damon Hughes is responsible, McKenna. I never blamed you for anything."
She grimaced. "I know you were treated horribly when
Damon brought you back. And I think Aunt Mavis had
a lot to do with it."

"What do you mean?"

"I was unconscious for several days after it happened.
When I woke up, Aunt Mavis had taken charge. My
memory was so spotty . . . I tried to remember everything, but I think I ended up sounding like an idiot.
When they asked me if you'd been involved in it, I denied it. I might not have remembered all the facts, but I
knew you had nothing to do with it. Somehow, I think
Aunt Mavis convinced them otherwise."

"But why?"

"Because I believe Aunt Mavis *did* blame you. And
she wanted to make sure you never saw me again. She
whisked me to Louisiana as soon as the doctors let her.
I was never questioned again."

"But when all the charges were dropped against me . . .
I can't understand why no one told me you were alive."

"I don't know the answer to that. All Aunt Mavis told
me was that Damon had died in prison and that you had
disappeared. I didn't know until I started searching for
you that you were even considered a suspect."

McKenna stared into space, remembering the day she
walked out of the jail a free woman—battered, ravaged,
and so determined to get away from everyone who
reminded her of what had happened. She'd stopped at a
small market, and using some money the public defender had given her, she purchased flowers for all three
graves. She'd taken them to the cemetery, said goodbye,
and then she'd left.

Had anyone ever tried to find her, to tell her that her
sister was still alive? She would probably never know.

"You weren't responsible, Kenna. In fact, I blamed myself for a long time."

Shocked, McKenna asked, "For what?"

"I told Mom and Dad about Damon. If I hadn't, I wonder how this would have worked out. I think part of his problem was being told he couldn't see you again."

Lucas was right. They were both taking on guilt that belonged to Damon only.

"You're not responsible, Amy."

"And neither are you."

McKenna smiled. "Samara said we had a lot in common." The smile vanished when she saw the yellow and brown bruises beneath her sister's makeup. "I am sorry for what you went through, though."

Amy's mouth trembled as she shook her head. "I can't talk about it yet. Okay?"

Understanding that better than just about anyone, McKenna swallowed another lump and said, "Just know I'm here to talk if you need to."

"Thanks. And, oh, would it be too weird to call me Jamie, not Amy? I've kind of gotten used to the name over the years."

"Jamie's a lovely name. And it suits you."

"It was one of the few things Aunt Mavis let me have a say-so in."

"What do you mean?"

Jamie's nose scrunched up into a grimace. "Remember how sour she always was?"

McKenna nodded.

"Remember Daddy's nickname for her?"

Ignoring the clutch to her heart at the mention of her father, McKenna nodded again. "Aunt Pickle."

"And she never got any less sour, believe me. But when she convinced me to change my name, I chose the name Jamie Kendrick."

Enlightenment dawned. Amy had used her entire fam-

ily's name to create her own. Their mother's name had
been Jane and their father's name had been Rick. The
"Ken" came from her sister's nickname for McKenna,
"Kenna."

McKenna smiled at her sister's cleverness. "Did she
ever figure it out?"

Jamie shrugged. "She may have but she never said.
You know Aunt Mavis wasn't one to talk much anyway."

"I'm so sorry."

Jamie huffed out a sigh. "You have to stop apologizing. What Damon did to our family was all him—not
you. Okay?"

Awed and humbled by her sister's generosity and ma-
turity, McKenna nodded.

Shifting a bit to get more comfortable, Jamie gave her
a mischievous all-girl smile. "So, tell me all about Lucas
Kane."

It was as if they'd never parted. McKenna found herself telling Jamie about how she met Lucas and how
wonderful he was. There were still things to say, secrets
to share, sorrows to overcome. That could wait till later.
For now, McKenna leaned back against her pillow,
watched her sister's beautiful face, and rejoiced in the
fact that miracles really can happen.

Hours later, Lucas stepped back into McKenna's
room. The sisters had spent several hours together until
the nurse came in and shooed Jamie back to her room to
rest. And from the looks of the sleeping McKenna, the
visit had exhausted her as well.

Lucas eased down into a chair beside the bed and
watched her sleep. He'd made some damn difficult decisions in his life, but he was about to make the most difficult one of all. Was it the right one? Yes. That didn't
make it any easier.

"Lucas?"

"Didn't mean to wake you."

Her smile was one of warm, sleepy contentment. "I'm glad you're here, but you look exhausted."

"It's been a rough few days."

She scooted over in her bed and whispered, "Hold me."

Unable to resist temptation, Lucas slipped off his shoes and slid into bed.

Wrapping his arms gently around her, he breathed in her fragrance. The tension he'd been carrying for the last few days eased, though not totally. He'd been damned terrified when she'd been shot and hadn't woken. Now that he knew she would be all right, the relief was immense, but there were still things to get through.

"Did you have a good visit with your sister?"

Her head rubbed against his chest as she nodded. "It was wonderful. She's so bright and interesting . . . funny, too. And she's absolutely beautiful."

He smiled against her hair. "That's because she looks so much like you."

"You're prejudiced."

He couldn't deny that. To him, there would never be a more beautiful person inside or out than McKenna.

"The doctors said I can leave the hospital tomorrow."

Lucas stiffened. This was the perfect time to tell her, but dammit, not yet.

"You need to take it easy for a few days."

She snuggled deeper into his arms. "I intend to."

Lucas swallowed hard as arousal surged. His body didn't care that she wasn't up to making love; it only knew what it wanted. And from the first time he'd met her until his death, he would want McKenna. That wasn't something he could change.

Kissing the top of her head, he whispered, "Go to sleep."

"Night, Lucas . . . love you."

Lucas stared up at the white ceiling of the hospital room. There would be no sleep tonight. Damned if he'd miss one moment of having McKenna in his arms. Morning would come all too soon.

McKenna hurried through her shower. She'd woken alone this morning, but with the knowledge that Lucas had stayed with her all night. She'd woken several times to the comfort of his arms around her. Each time she'd fallen back into a deep sleep, relishing an enormous sense of relief.

Last night she hadn't said anything, but she could tell something was bothering him. He wasn't the easiest person to read, but she'd gotten pretty good at it. Exhaustion could be one of his problems. Poor man looked as though he hadn't slept in weeks.

Samara had brought her some clothes yesterday, so at least she had something to wear out of the hospital. Slipping into a pair of khaki pants and a button-down pink cotton shirt, McKenna spent a few precious minutes adding color to her cheeks. Though her eyes sparkled and she had a bit more energy than she did yesterday, she still looked paler than she would have liked.

She opened the door to find Lucas setting out a breakfast tray and coffee for her.

"Good morning."

His perfect mouth moved up into a smile, but his eyes remained solemn and serious. Something was definitely bothering him.

A good strong cup of coffee was needed before she asked any questions. McKenna grabbed a cup, took a sip, decided it wasn't too hot, and gulped it down.

As she returned the empty cup to the tray, she noticed Lucas's grin. "What?"

"Were you thirsty?"

Laughing, she stood on her toes and pressed a kiss to his mouth. "No, just needed some caffeine. Good morning again."

Instead of returning the kiss, he put his hands on her shoulders and pushed her slightly away. "We need to talk."

"What's wrong?"

"I'm headed back to London today."

Her heart plummeted. A million questions and protests came to mind. All she could manage was "I see."

"Do you, love?" As he held her hand between his, his expression was as earnest as she'd ever seen it. "For the first time in years, you can finally breathe easier. Finally have a life. You no longer have to look over your shoulder to see if anyone is following you. You've lived in the shadows for so long, without choices. You said yourself that you've been on a roller coaster. Now you have an opportunity to get off that roller coaster and see what life has to offer you."

"But you—"

"Don't look like that, McKenna. I'm doing this because I love you, not because I don't."

Only able to concentrate on one thing, McKenna felt as if her heart would explode. "But you said you don't leave."

Silver-gray eyes locked with hers. "You know where home is, sweetheart. You've always known. Take some time to think. Do things you've always wanted to do. Get to know your sister again. Get to know yourself again." His mouth tender on hers, he softly repeated against her lips, "You know where home is, my love."

Speechless, unable to do anything for the mountains of tumultuous emotions bubbling inside her, she watched as Lucas walked out the door.

twenty-eight

One month later
London

McKenna stood on the steps of Lucas's home. Her heart was pounding so hard, she probably didn't even need to knock on the door for anyone to hear her. Would he still want to see her after all this time?

The second after he'd walked out of the hospital room, she'd burst into tears. A box of tissues later, she'd pulled herself together. And then she'd finally thought about what he said . . . and she had understood. At least she hoped she understood. Lucas had said she finally had choices, and he was allowing her to choose. Something she hadn't been able to do in a very long time.

The fact that he knew her so well boggled her mind and humbled her. From the beginning, Lucas had been able to see through her tough-girl persona. He knew the real McKenna, the one she hid from the rest of the world. How could that make her feel anything but incredibly special?

The heady feeling of not having to look over her shoulder and hide like a criminal was unlike anything she'd ever felt before. Freeing . . . and scary as hell. That alone was an incredible rush. But in combination with the miracle of her sister being alive, it had been almost more than she could comprehend.

Samara and Noah had left the same day as Lucas.

Noah's words as he'd hugged her goodbye told her his thinking was in line with Lucas's. He'd said, "Give yourself time to figure out what you want from life, McKenna. You'll always have a place at LCR."

Noah's words had helped what Lucas had said sink in even deeper. She had decisions, choices, options. McKenna began to feel like a kid who'd been let loose in a toy store. She wanted to experience everything all at once. Though a large part of her had wanted to rush after Lucas, she accepted that she did need some time, not only for herself, but to spend with her sister.

She and Jamie had been released from the hospital on the same day. They had gone to Paris the day after. Not only was it the city she'd spent the most time in as an adult, McKenna had never had the chance to truly explore like she'd always wanted. And since Jamie had never been to France, it thrilled her to be able to explore the city with her sister at her side.

They had played tourist together. Going to restaurants and museums McKenna had always wanted to go to but couldn't. Every public, well-known place she'd avoided before, she visited and savored the fact that she could do so without fear.

Shadows of remembered pain still darkened Jamie's eyes, but McKenna was amazed at her sister's strength. She was so determined to overcome what had happened to her. She still couldn't talk about what Damon had done to her or her experience in Spain, and as much as McKenna wanted her to share with her, she refused to push her.

Until Lucas came along, McKenna hadn't been able to talk fully about her own experiences with anyone. Jamie would come to that place in her own time. She just wanted to make sure her sister knew she would help her any way she could.

Not only had she and Jamie gorged themselves on

Paris, they spent hours upon hours getting to know each other again. When they were kids, McKenna had never fully appreciated her little sister. Having lost her and now found her again, she was determined to never take their relationship for granted.

And she had done what Lucas wanted her to do. Think about her choices. She had given a lot of thought about what she wanted out of life. The answers were numerous and varied, but there had been only one concrete absolute: she wanted to be with Lucas.

He had said she knew where home was, but that had been a month ago. Was that still true?

Jamie had returned to the States with the promise to come to London for a visit soon. She still had issues related to her ex-husband that she needed to sort out. McKenna had encouraged her to seek counseling and Jamie promised that she would consider it.

Saying goodbye to her sister at the airport had been difficult. The only thing that made it bearable was the fact that Dylan had suddenly shown up at the airport right before Jamie was to leave. He explained that he had business back in the States and had heard from Noah that Jamie was returning home today and thought he would accompany her. The interesting glint in Jamie's eyes assured McKenna that her sister didn't mind the company at all.

Having Dylan escort Jamie back home was enormously comforting, but the minute her sister disappeared from view, McKenna began to miss her. She'd only just found her again, and letting her go was extraordinarily hard. The knowledge that she would see her soon helped tremendously. She vowed to never lose her sister again.

But now it was time to face Lucas. To see if he had meant what she thought he meant. He had said he loved her and she didn't doubt his word, but that didn't still the anxiousness inside. That could only be done when she was back in his arms.

Her heart continuing its thundering boom, she raised her hand and knocked.

Conrad opened the door, his usual impassive expression in place until he recognized her. Then his face lit up as if delighted. "Miss McKenna, please come in."

She breathed slightly easier as she stepped into the foyer. At least someone was happy to see her. "Hello, Conrad. Is Lucas here?"

"No, he's at the Millington Awards. He's their man of the year, you know."

McKenna swallowed a small sob of disappointment. Of course she knew. The Millington recipient had been announced at the beginning of the year. The award was given to one individual each year for outstanding charitable works and contributions. She had noted it with no small amount of pride, pleased that Lucas was being recognized and honored for all the good things he had done. She just hadn't remembered that the ceremony was tonight. Reading papers had been something she refused to allow herself to do. Lucas had been in her heart and mind; reading about him would have only added to the aching loneliness.

Knowing Conrad was awaiting her reply, she shook her head. "I didn't realize it was tonight."

He beamed with pride. "Mr. Lucas is the youngest recipient to ever have been given the award."

McKenna smiled at the obvious pride in Conrad's words. "Do you think it would be all right if I came in and waited for him?"

"Perfectly fine. However, there's something else that would be finer . . . and that would be if you joined him."

Swallowing a laugh, she looked down at her worn duffel bag. She'd brought a few clothes with her, but nothing that nice. "I don't believe I have anything that would be appropriate."

"If I may . . . Mr. Lucas had hoped you might come before tonight. He ordered several dresses for you to choose from."

Tears sprang to her eyes before she could stop them. "He did?"

Conrad nodded and glanced at the grandfather clock against the wall. "The ceremony is probably over, but the ball will go until dawn. You could be there within the hour . . . if you like."

Could she do this? The ceremony and subsequent ball was one of the biggest events of the year. The most influential and wealthiest people in England would be there. Even the queen was known to attend. Reporters and cameras would be everywhere. After living in the shadows for so long, could she come out in such a blatant way?

Apparently seeing her hesitation, Conrad added, "I believe it would mean the world to Mr. Lucas if you joined him there."

Those words tipped the scale. Lucas had gone to the trouble of buying a dress for her to wear; he wanted her to be there. How could she not go? Standing on her toes, she kissed the kindly butler's weathered face. "I would like very much."

Blushing slightly, he turned to lead her up the stairway. "I'll show you the dresses. Hammond, the chauffeur, took Mr. Lucas in the limousine, but I'd be happy to drive you into the city."

Resisting the urge to kiss him again, McKenna settled for a grateful smile. "That would be wonderful. Thank you."

Conrad led her to the room she had used when she stayed before. He opened the closet and waved his hand at a half dozen glittering gowns. McKenna's heart leaped as she took in the beautiful array of elegant eveningwear. Then her heart almost stopped as her eyes focused on one in particular: a glittering red silk sheath with an overlay of silver sparkles. It was a gown of elegance, sophistication, and pure femininity. And one that people would most definitely notice. No blending into the background, hoping no one paid attention to her. The gown was the most beautiful thing she had ever seen.

The older man nodded his approval at her more than obvious admiration. "I believe that one was his favorite. There are shoes and . . ." He blushed again. "Um, other apparel for you to wear, too."

Feeling a bit like a princess with a fairy godfather, McKenna said, "Give me half an hour and I'll be ready."

Conrad turned to leave. "I'll bring the car around." Before he closed the door, he said, "And ma'am, welcome home."

Lucas took a long swallow of his bourbon. Why the hell had he stayed? Coming to the ceremony had been necessary. Staying for a ball when he had no desire to be here was foolish.

Stupid, really, but he had thought to attend the ball with McKenna. Her life had been full of hiding and running; he had envisioned bringing her to the event as a celebration of no longer needing that secrecy. Though inviting publicity wasn't something he liked to do, he had despised not being able to go out in public with her. Not because he wanted people speculating on their relationship or seeing photographs in the gossip columns. No, he'd wanted it because not going out in public made their liaison seem secretive, not real. Or, even worse, made it appear as if there was something to be ashamed of. Everything about them was real, and he was so damn proud of her, he wanted the world to see it, too.

But he'd left the decision in McKenna's hands. She deserved the opportunity to choose her life. So far, her choice had not included him.

Leaving her had been one of the hardest things he'd ever done. But if he had stayed, he knew he would pressure her, whether he meant to or not. Reconnecting with the sister she thought she'd lost was important. As was learning who she was without the shadow of fear she'd lived with for so long.

"Lucas, could we talk a moment?"

He turned at the familiar voice of his former employee. "Hello, Humphries. How are you?"

The older man gave him a small, grim smile. "Better than I deserve to be. I wanted to thank you. I never did before."

Before Lucas could answer, Eleanor Humphries, Stanley's wife, came to stand beside her husband. Tears glistened in her eyes. "He told me everything, Mr. Kane. We just wanted you to know how much we appreciate what you did." Her expression was one of love and understanding as she glanced at her husband of forty years. "Stanley's getting the help he needs to fight his addiction." Her eyes went back to Lucas. "But what you did was so generous."

"My father—"

Stanley shook his head. "Your father would have kicked me out on my ass, as you should have. I'm just grateful you didn't. I hope to repay you someday."

Lucas could have said no, that repayment wasn't necessary. However, he knew more than his share about pride and holding himself responsible for his mistakes. Being able to pay Kane Industries back would go a long way toward easing Stanley's conscience and help him regain the dignity he'd lost. "If you're interested, I believe we could arrange part-time work. Your skills and experience have been missed. Part of your salary could go toward repayment."

Humphries's slumped shoulders straightened; relief replaced the shame on his face. "I would like that. Thank you."

Accepting a grateful kiss from Eleanor and a handshake from Stanley, Lucas said, "Call me on Monday." Then with a nod he moved away. Having this kind of conversation in the midst of a large crowd wasn't a good idea. Only a few knew about Humphries's problems; Lucas wanted to keep it that way.

Several more people tried to get him involved in a conversation. Lucas eased his way across the ballroom. Nodding, smiling, and murmuring appropriate responses, he kept one eye out for the closest exit. Getting away from the mass of people had become a priority.

Nodding politely at the matronly woman who was in the midst of extolling her daughter's attributes, Lucas moved his head slightly, his eyes targeting an exit only a dozen yards away. Murmuring, "Excuse me, won't you?" he headed toward freedom.

His mind on getting out of there without attracting any more attention, he barely noticed the slight stir in the ballroom until he heard several awed comments, including "What a stunning-looking woman" and "Who is that vision?"

Seconds from going out the door, Lucas caught a glimpse of red out of the corner of his eye. He jerked to a stop. Turning slowly, he lost his breath. A vision indeed . . . one that appeared in his dreams nightly. Wearing his favorite of the dresses he'd purchased for her in hopeful anticipation that she would be with him tonight, McKenna was lovelier than he could have imagined.

Her hair had apparently grown quite a bit since he'd

seen her, as she was wearing it up in some sort of casual but chic style that emphasized the purity and delicate femininity of her elegant face. He'd always thought McKenna beautiful; tonight she went far beyond.

She'd been gazing around a bit cautiously, as though uncertain of her right to be there. The instant she caught sight of him, a myriad of strong emotions played out on her face. And every one of them caused his chest to tighten.

Sounds disappeared. Every person in the room ceased to exist with the exception of one. The only one that mattered. As if they were the only two people in the universe, Lucas began to move slowly toward her. He was reminded of the day she came to him in Paris and how he'd been afraid she'd disappear like the ghost she claimed to be. That same surreal feeling washed over him.

She met him in the middle of the room, her expression one of such wonder and beauty that Lucas's already tight chest constricted even more. Two feet from him, she stopped. He closed the distance between them and said huskily, "You came home."

Her smile holding every promise he could hope for, she whispered, "Yes."

Pulling her into his arms, he asked, "For how long?"

Her heart in her eyes, she whispered the word Lucas ached to hear: "Forever."

"Thank God." His eyes roamed over her; she was even more beautiful than he remembered. "You look stunning."

"So do you." Her eyes twinkled. "I've never seen you in a tuxedo before. I'm surprised you're not surrounded by a multitude of women vying for your attention."

He shook his head. "There's no other woman who could catch my attention."

The palm of her hand touched his jaw in a tender, sweet caress. "Are you well?"

"I am now."

Though more than aware that the entire room had almost stopped breathing as they watched them, Lucas didn't give a damn. Nothing could spoil this moment for him.

McKenna's trembling smile told him she was a little less confident about attracting so much attention. "We seemed to have stopped the party."

"Only because the most beautiful woman in the world has arrived."

Instead of smiling as he intended for her to, her face went solemn. "I love you so much."

Privacy suddenly became imperative. Taking her hand, he led her through the giant ballroom. Ignoring the cameras flashing and whispered speculation, Lucas took her out a door onto a side veranda. Sparkling lights glittered the walkway as he stalked to the farthest corner of the long portico.

"Where are we going?"

"As far away from the party as possible."

"We could leave."

"We will soon; this can't wait." Finally reaching the end, Lucas pulled her into his arms. Covering her mouth with his, he savored the flavor and beauty of the lips he'd missed tasting.

McKenna moaned under his hot mouth. How many nights had she lain awake, dreaming of this? Lucas's reaction to seeing her was all she could have wanted.

Lifting his mouth from hers slightly, he growled against her lips, "Never stay away from me that long again."

More than ready to give him that assurance and so much more, she whispered, "I promise."

Sealing that promise, he closed his mouth over hers

and once again, McKenna lost herself to the magic. How she had missed his kiss, his taste.

After several seconds, he loosened his arms, and asked, "How's Jamie?"

She smiled, anxious to share with him everything she'd learned about her little sister. "Amazing. She's so savvy and incredibly smart. She has a degree in elementary education but has only been able to teach for a year. The guy she married ended up being a major jerk. It only took one time for him to get abusive and she was out of there."

"She sounds like a remarkable woman. And she obviously has a lot in common with her sister."

"I can't wait for you to get to know her. She's such a wonderful person."

"Did she come with you?"

"No. I wanted her to, but she had to go home to get some stuff sorted out. We've promised to call each other every day, and she'll either come here or I'll go to the States to see her soon."

"She'll definitely have to be here for the wedding."

Her heart stopped. "Wedding?"

As if he hadn't heard her, he continued, "And when we get back from our honeymoon, maybe she'd like to come stay with us. Or live with us if she wants to."

"Honeymoon?"

"Where would you like to go?"

Her breath coming in rapid pants, McKenna pulled away to stare up at him. "You want to marry me?"

"You sound surprised."

"I just . . ." How did she tell him that she'd never in her life imagined anything so remarkably wonderful as to be married to him?

"You just what?"

"I never . . ."

"McKenna?"

There was uncertainty and vulnerability in Lucas's expression. Something she'd never thought to see in him.

Emotions clogging her throat, she swallowed hard. Tears sprang to her eyes and she didn't bother to try to stop them. Her voice thick, she whispered, "I just never thought anyone as wonderful as you could happen to me. You've given me more than I could ever dream of having."

"I want to give you the world."

She shook her head. "I don't want the world. I just want you."

"And you have me. Always."

"What about the past?"

He frowned. "What do you mean?"

"The instant people learn who I am, they'll delve into my past. Everything will come out."

"I can get the records buried, if that's what you want."

"I just don't want any of it to taint you or your family. I—"

McKenna gasped when he grabbed her shoulders and shook her slightly. "Do not even use that word. There is nothing about you I'm ashamed of or want to hide. The only reason I asked was for you. I don't give a damn what anyone says, sweetheart. But the last thing I want is for you to be hurt."

A lump developed in her throat. How had she gotten so lucky? "You're the finest man I know."

"I'm just a man totally and forever in love with the woman of his dreams. It's that simple."

"Take me home and make love to me."

"There's nothing I'd rather do, but before we leave, tell me if you want me to cover your past. The charges against you were dropped. There should be no problem in getting your record expunged."

McKenna took a breath. She'd been living in the shad-

ows for too long. The things she had endured were horrific, but if she hid them, she would still be in the shadows, still hiding. So what if people knew? The two
people she loved, Lucas and her sister, knew everything.
What did the rest of the world matter? "Don't do anything."

His smile told her he wholeheartedly approved.
"Good." Pulling her with him, they headed back inside.
"There are a couple of friends I want you to meet."

Hours later, lying in bed, wrapped in Lucas's arms,
McKenna relived the evening. He had led her back into
the ballroom without telling her what he was going to
do, nodding and smiling at several people, all the while
ignoring the cameras flashing like fireworks all around
them. Nothing had stopped him until they approached a
door with two British soldiers standing on either side of
it. Lucas had murmured something and one of the men
opened the door and they'd walked in the room.

Lucas had said he wanted her to meet a friend. She
was in the middle of the room before she realized that
friend was the Queen of England. *Flabbergasted* was the
word most descriptive of her feelings. She'd done her
best to act proper, curtsied when she thought it appropriate, and stood in wide-eyed awe as Lucas explained
that she was his fiancée.

After that, meeting anyone else had been anticlimactic. Thankfully, Lucas hadn't wanted to stay much
longer. He sought out the prime minister and his family
and did another introduction. On the way out the door,
he stopped to say hello to his friend Jared Livingston
and his wife, Lara. Then he was nudging her in the direction of the nearest exit. The second they were in the
backseat of the limo, she was back in his arms, where
she wanted to stay forever.

Bringing her back to the present, his mouth at her ear, he whispered, "What are you thinking?"

"That I could stay in your arms forever."

"And that's where I plan for you to be."

She raised up on her elbow to look down at him. Moonlight reflected on his face, revealing his beautiful smile, his eyes glittering with a deep contentment. "Can I ask you something?"

"Anything."

"If I hadn't come back, would you have just let me go?"

His expression grew serious. "I would like to say that yes, I would have, simply because if you hadn't come back to me, I knew it would have been your choice. But I would never have given up hope and I probably would have eventually come for you."

"I'm sorry I put you through that."

"You're here now. That's all that counts."

She snuggled deeper into his arms.

"I have a confession to make," Lucas said.

"What?"

"I've been in touch with Noah McCall."

She smiled against his chest. She'd talked to Noah yesterday. He hadn't told her he had talked to Lucas, but she had a feeling she knew what was coming.

"About what?"

"I told him I'd like to do some work for LCR from time to time."

"Why?"

"Because I've seen the good they do. The training I have should be used for something good."

"Think we'll be able to work together without getting each other shot?"

He held her tighter. "I'll make sure of it."

"We'll both make sure of it." She pressed a kiss against his chest. "Thank you, Lucas."

"For what?"

"For loving me."

Rolling her over onto her back, Lucas loomed above her and whispered against her lips, "Sweetheart, loving you is the easiest thing I've ever done."

With a groan, McKenna surrendered her body to the man who had stolen her heart. She'd never thought she'd find happiness. Never believed she deserved it. But now, because of Lucas, all of that had changed. Her one chance for love had turned into a lifetime of happiness.

acknowledgments

It's with enormous gratitude that I say thank you to the following:

My husband, Jim, whose love and belief in me has made all the difference in my life. And to the darling little creatures who sleep at my feet and bark excitedly at everything and nothing while I work.

My mom, sisters, and aunts for their support and encouragement.

Danny Agan for his help with guns and knives, and Kerry Holder for her assistance with all things British. Any mistakes are entirely my own.

Darah Lace, brainstormer extraordinaire, who always asks the right questions at the right time.

Kate Collins, my kind and talented editor, who had a vision for this book and made it so much better with her insight. And to all the talented and wonderful people at Ballantine who made this book possible, with special thanks to Kelli Fillingim, Beth Pearson, and Sue Warga.

Kim Whalen, my spectacular agent, for her enthusiasm and encouragement.

To the readers of the Last Chance Rescue books, thank you for making the hard work so much fun.